The Vision
of Elena Silves

The Vision
of Elena Silves

A NOVEL BY

Nicholas Shakespeare

Alfred A. Knopf   New York   1990

Copyright © 1989 by Nicholas Shakespeare

Grateful acknowledgment is made to Williamson Music Co. for permission to
reprint an excerpt from "I'll Be Seeing You" by Irving Kahal and Sammy Fain.
Copyright 1938 by Williamson Music Co. Copyright renewed.
Used by permission. All rights reserved.

This is a work of fiction, although the story of Ezequiel is based on my
research into the Shining Path guerrillas of Abimael Guzmán, which
culminated in an article for *Granta* magazine in 1988. For my account of the
1965 insurgency, I have drawn on Richard Gott's *Guerrilla Movements in
Latin America* (Nelson, 1970), and for the San Francisco massacre, on
Amnesty International's report, "'Disappearances', torture and summary
executions by government forces after the prison revolt of June 1986".
I am indebted to John Hemming for his chapter on Messianic movements
in *Amazon Frontier* (Macmillan, 1987) and to Karen Armstrong
for her guidance in religious matters.
I would also like to thank the monks of La Recoleta monastery in Arequipa
where I spent a retreat. I cannot name the priest I would like to thank most
because he lives in the dangerous thick of it all.

N.S.

Library of Congress Cataloging-in-Publication Data

Shakespeare, Nicholas, [date]
    The vision of Elena Silves — a novel/by Nicholas Shakespeare. —
1st American ed.
        p.   cm.
    ISBN 0-394-58477-5
    I. Title.
PR6069.H286V57   1990   89-77862
823'.914—dc20   CIP

In memory of Bruce Chatwin

I'll be seeing you
In all the old familiar places
That this heart of mine embraces
All day through.
In the small café,
The park across the way,
The children's carousel,
The chestnut trees, the wishing well.
I'll be seeing you
In every lovely summer's day
In everything that's light and gay
I'll always think of you that way.
I'll find you in the morning sun
And when the night is new,
I'll be looking at the moon,
But I'll be seeing you.

*(Irving Kahal and Sammy Fain 1938.
Recorded by Frank Sinatra 1961.)*

Part One

1983

Chapter 1

IT IS EARLY MORNING in Belén. The jungle is quiet. The sky over the rooftops stretches clear and colourless, except for a red clawmark where the day has pounced.

The air is so fresh you want to inhale it in deep breaths. It smells of copa de oro.

Apart from the tented shape of Sebastián under his black hood and Vásquez washing his barrow by the cathedral steps, the square is empty.

An old man emerges from the corner of Calle Raimondi. He crosses the road to where Sebastián huddles beside a pile of newspapers. Aware of his approach, Sebastián holds up a yellow bucket and rattles it. The percussion of small change is the only sound in the street.

The old man throws in a coin and takes a newspaper from the pavement. He folds it under his arm and shuffles towards the bench under the statue in the middle of the square. In one hand he carries a large canvas bag; in the other a handkerchief. He is about to wipe the surface of the bench when he notices that instead of dew it is covered in blood-red beads. Putting down his bag he reaches out for one. He holds it to the light. He finds himself looking at a dead cattle-fly, half an inch long, the same colour as the sun.

"Colihuachos," he says to himself, throwing it back among the other flies. They lie there as if a string has broken on a necklace. They cover the bench, the ground in front and the flower beds behind.

The old man brushes them off the seat with his handkerchief. He shakes the cloth, replaces it up his sleeve and sits down.

He is Don Leopoldo.

He wears no hat and his face is lined, as if he has walked into a spider's web and forgotten to wipe it away. His love of precise dates and proven facts has earned him a reputation for being a little pedantic. He knows more than is necessarily interesting about the yellow cathedral, its cartridge-shaped windows, its Swiss-made clock; about the origin of the tiles on the old Palace Hotel and about Admiral Grau, the man in whom Peru had once put all her hope, whose bronze whiskers bristle defiantly as if he is still on the deck of the *Huáscar*.

This morning, the flies on the Admiral's head and epaulettes have the appearance of laurel leaves.

Don Leopoldo looks beyond the statue to the metal house opposite, its roof stained with the sun. He can tell anyone who cares to listen – fewer and fewer nowadays – about this house, constructed by Eiffel for the Paris Exhibition of 1896, dismantled for its voyage to another continent altogether, and then transported two thousand miles upriver from Pará to be reassembled, bolt by bolt, for an absentee rubber lord.

The Club de Leones has since moved its premises to a floor above the Banco Industrial, but Don Leopoldo remembers when the members played their poker in Eiffel's folly, drinking bottles of Allsopp's Pale Ale in a hot metal room like an oven.

El Club de los Pájaros Muertos, they called it.

He gazes at Eiffel's house and the buckled pillar into which a car has crashed. It upsets him no one has repaired it. These days he finds it easy to be upset. That's what happens when you are a dead parrot with long memories. Don Leopoldo can remember a time when there was no cathedral and women walked beside the open drains holding geranium-scented handkerchiefs to their noses. He remembers the town in the days when you bought your clothes from Don Ramur – Scotch tweed, alpaca, boaters; when the ice cream you ate in the Booth supermarket came all the way from Liverpool; when the port you drank with Orestes Minero in the Café Nanay was Taylor's finest, shipped from Pinhão.

Now the river is silting up and no boats come from Europe. Now you bought your shirts off the pavement and they had crocodiles on the pockets. Now in the café they hold aerobics classes.

The cobweb tightens on Don Leopoldo's face. They don't even keep photographs of the old town, to remind people it was a town of millionaires and palaces, not of soldiers who have appropriated the

Palace Hotel and let it collapse about them. Instead of picking their noses, they should be restoring the chipped Evora azulejos. They should be repairing the fine ironwork and scrubbing the frescoed ceilings instead of straining their eyes upriver to Ecuador. Besides, who would invade Peru nowadays?

Live for today, forget about yesterday, then show your money with a fanfaronade and wait for the next boom.

As an historian, Don Leopoldo finds this recipe for life unworthy of Peruvians. But to be a Peruvian. What does that signify to the world outside? Nothing.

Don Leopoldo speaks harshly of his countrymen because he loves the land that gave them birth. As a young man he maintained the time had come for Peru to produce her popular historian. A man who could liberate the country from its cosy, obfuscating myths. A man such as Admiral Grau or Lord Cochrane who could ignite the masses like the blue touch paper on a firework. A man who could show them the path they should take by illuminating the path by which they had come.

As a young man he had wished for himself that role.

As an old man he regrets that he prepared himself for it by first writing a *History of the Colonization of Belén*.

At the end of each day since the day of that decision, he has returned to his room and added another manuscript sheet to the disorderly mound by his bed. Don Leopoldo's lucubrations pile up to several thousand pages. These are the pages which every morning, and in no particular order, he stuffs into the mouth of his green bag and carries to the bench.

Often he is influenced by what has been discussed on the bench. Sometimes his companions remind him of things he has quite forgotten. Sometimes they tell him of things he never knew. Always he tries to be on his guard with what they have said. But at night he is not entirely able to shake their voices from his head. Indeed, he sometimes has the uncomfortable impression that what he writes is a mingling of their voices.

Don Leopoldo's *History of the Colonization of Belén* has taken a decade or two more than ideally he would have wished. He convinces himself it is lacking only a final chapter (on the territorial dispute with Ecuador, with a commentary on Gregory XVI's Bull of 2 June 1843 recognizing Peru's right over the diocese of Soreto). Plus an index, of course.

He has given up hope that when complete it will immortalize his name and cause the jungle round about to break out in psalms.

His magnum opus has taken so long because Don Leopoldo finds it easy to be diverted by parallel research. Not a day passes without him making copious notes from some historical journal. By now, even Don Leopoldo considers it unlikely he will survive to embark on the project that would have swept the reader back to the time of the Incas, to a Golden Age when there were no thieves or idle men or adulterous women, when a man who ravished a virgin was buried alive.

Clearer than the outline of Don Leopoldo's thesis is the melancholy which originally informed it (and which he attributes, erroneously, to Portuguese saudade). Although he has with some pride traced his ancestry to a learned quinologist from Ceuta, he feels the blemish of his European blood. It is sad beyond the power of Don Leopoldo's expression to contemplate the arrival of the bearded men from Spain.

After the Age of Gold, the Age of Manure.

What could be expected of a country whose fortunes were built on the violet grey sap of a tree and mountain upon mountain of birdshit?

"No wonder the only people who flourish are terrucos," he murmurs to himself. The only terruco he has time for is Lord Cochrane.

At night, looking into the kerosene lamp, Don Leopoldo can hear the sound of Lord Cochrane muffling his oars on the evening of 5 November 1820. In the flame he hears him creep towards the Spanish flagship *Esmeralda* whose spars are cracks in the darkness. He hears him whisper to his men (the same number, he notes, as had taken Peru three centuries before). "One hour of courage and resolution," he is saying, "is all that is required for you to triumph." The promise stirs them. Don Leopoldo, dressed in white and pike in hand, lifts his tense face to the night where the 44-gun frigate rolls gently in the fog.

But the courageous, resolute men around him don't need an hour. Cochrane and his patriots need only fifteen minutes to board and capture Spain's impregnable flagship (guarded by 27 gunboats and 300 shore guns) and so finally slip cable on the royalists, those pig-farming illiterates who had destroyed a perfect civilization.

Had he wished it, as Don Leopoldo wishes it for him, Lord Cochrane could have been first Admiral of Peru. It is sad that no one else except Grau, sixty years after him, has seized such an opportunity for Peru to be faithful to herself.

The sadness has a cumulative effect on Don Leopoldo. More and more often as he puts on his jacket in the mornings, he wonders if he still has the strength to walk the two blocks to the square. One day the effort will be too much. Who will then wipe the dew from the bench, or the cattle-flies?

This is his favourite hour of the day, when the only voice on the bench is his own, when the square is empty and silent and he can imagine the town as it has been, before it is overcome by the noise of cars and ant-headed motorbikes and buses which, because of the drowsing heat, have no glass in their windows. His eyes water as they move over the buildings – the Bishop's palace, the cathedral, the Zumate pharmacy and Pía Zumate's small hotel on the corner of Raimondi which shares a recessed entrance, always in deep shadow, with the Café Nanay.

His eyes are lingering on the hotel when they catch a movement at a window on the top floor. Don Leopoldo swears he sees a face looking out of the half-open louvres. Before he can make it out, the face has vanished.

"So," he says aloud. "The soft-shoe artist is back."

The movement at the window has ruffled his day-dream. He unfolds his paper. He begins reading.

He has reached *El Oriente*'s leader (on the economic consequences of the current called El Niño) when a second man arrives and sits down next to him. He wears a brown alpaca cardigan and a jipijapa panama that curls at the edges like a leaf. It is made of a straw so fine it can pass through a wedding ring.

This is Don Wenceslau.

He is a thin man with bony shoulders. The creases about his crotch imitate those about his eyes. They are eyes as red as the spirit he buys from Don Vásquez's barrow.

"How many tributaries has the Amazon, Don Leopoldo?"

"Eleven thousand and eighteen."

Don Wenceslau must know each one of them. If he can paddle off on a tangent, he will. He is a story-teller, a lover of red herrings, but they are best caught before lunch when he starts on Vásquez's masato. Until midday, his hangover makes him lucid and he can tell stories even Don Leopoldo listens to with interest. The square is his theatre. As he speaks, he points at things which transform themselves into his narrative. So the yellow copa de oro bushes behind them become the Nanay, the clock in the cathedral tower becomes the moon, the bronze Admiral becomes Christ descending into the Cocha and Vásquez's barrow the house of stone discovered in the jungle, where no stone exists and where chickens nest on an alabaster staircase.

Don Wenceslau sits down heavily. He greets Don Leopoldo. He has a stomachache, he says. He holds his head.

"Never eat cebiche at night, Don Leopoldo, that's my advice." It is not the first time Don Leopoldo has heard it.

"No sign of García?"

"Not yet."

"Probably had a night of it with his whores at the Teletroca." The copa de oro bushes rustle behind them. A man breaks cover.

"Not whores, Wenceslau, princesses," he says. He sits down next to Don Wenceslau, crosses his legs and stretches an arm along the back of the bench. In his face there are the remnants of a good-looking man. The finest feature is a moustache. Its greyness matches the colour of the felt trilby cocked rakishly over his nose. From his breast pocket tumbles a bright red handkerchief.

He is Don García, the singer and a devoted Donizettian. Listening to Donizetti he is almost persuaded to be a Christian. He believes the Italian rescued music from the dissipation into which it sank after that barbarian Rossini – that Marat of melody who would set a laundry list to music – broke the unities. Sometimes, to fill a rare silence, he treats his two companions to an aria from *Lucia di Lammermoor.*

Don García is ever in search of similes to describe life as he sees it – afresh each day – in this square. His temperament gives rise to flights of operatic fancy, such as his belief – though Don Leopoldo assures him repeatedly it is out of the question – that Caruso once sang at the Alhambra in the role of Lord Henry Ashton.

Don García's eyes cannot help prancing over the road to the site of this theatre where on the night of 24 October 1927 the receptionist fell asleep with her cigarette between the pages of Ouspensky's *Tertium Organum* (and where ten years later the celluloid overheated during a showing of *The Rubber Man's Daughter*). On each occasion the place was burnt to a cinder.

Don García does not see the grassed-over stage occupied by three chickens and a derelict bus. He sees the dado mosaic floor, the spangled velvet curtains, the massive backdrops, the castles rising from landscaped gardens. He does not mind that this backdrop was used whatever the work: opera, film, or pantomime. He never minded either when a French company performed *Così fan tutte* and Don Alfonso's beard fell off; nor when in the love scene the chaise longue slid into the orchestra pit and broke the legs of a Swedish cellist (nor when the shoes of the prompter appeared under the curtain). He never minded because he is a man for whom disbelief suspends as easily as that curtain. Which is why he imagines every now and then, when the wind from the river is right, he can hear the opening notes from "Una furtiva làgrima".

Don García is also a picaflor. He likes women. He more than likes them. He adores them. He remembers, before the Alhambra burnt down a second time, when money was in pound sterling and you could get a girl for the price of the handkerchief in his pocket. He spent a lot on handkerchiefs. All men were children of Adam, he used to say then. It was the silk that made the difference.

Now the girls never look at him. But it doesn't prevent him, if a pretty one walks by, from arranging his face to look mysterious, haughty, someone of infinite possibility, when he knows in his heart that all the girl sees is a piece of flotsam on a bench. Or three old men on a bench.

They sit here in the same position every day, the singer, the drinker, the local historian. Three narrators watching over the same scene. No one can hope to cross the square without their knowledge. From the glimpses of those who pass by they concoct whole lives.

"What's this?" says Don Wenceslau, noticing for the first time the dead flies at his feet. He picks one up at the second attempt. He caresses the ruddy wings.

"They're colihuachos," says Don Leopoldo.

Don Wenceslau frowns. "And what is a colihuacho?"

Don Leopoldo tells him.

Don Wenceslau looks closer at the bloodsucking cattle-fly. He imagines its journey from the southern lakes, over the desert and the Andes to the cathedral square in the jungle.

"El Niño?"

Don Leopoldo nods. He passes *El Oriente* to him, his finger on the headlines. "And it's getting worse. The worst in memory, they say." He taps the paper again. "If you can believe it, and I'm not sure I can. Floods on the coast, crocodiles in the sea, plants never before seen springing up in the desert. Worse and worse. Like the terrorists." He pauses. "You hear they've blacked out Piura?"

"Vásquez told me."

"Calling themselves the Shining Path – then leaving everyone in darkness."

"Chimbote, Puno, Tacna," recites Don Wenceslau. "Soon it'll be every department in Peru."

"Not Soreto."

"No, not Soreto. Not yet, anyway."

"You wait," says Don García, from the other end. "I saw Lieutenant Velarde last night. He spoke as if terrucos are behind every carob tree. He said the police and the military have reached the end of their patience. He said they only need one small excuse – and boom."

"Velarde has got to catch them first," says Don Wenceslau whose distaste for men in uniform is well documented on this bench. "And

Velarde never caught anything except a fever."

"They'll catch them," says Don García. "They always catch them."

"I don't know," mutters Don Leopoldo. "There's something about these terrorists . . ." Something which made him frightened for his country.

"They caught the terruco that came from Belén," observes Don García. "They caught Gabriel Rondón Lung."

"Gabriel Rondón Lung." Don Leopoldo tries each word slowly. "The Chino."

Don García nods. "The one in prison in Lima. Remember him? The one who screwed up Velarde's promotion."

"I don't remember the terrorist," says Don Leopoldo.

Don Wenceslau obliges him. His head is clearing. "He was a tall man. But you know what they say. Tall men steal light bulbs."

"I'm well aware of his height, Wenceslau. What I meant is that I never thought he would turn out as he did."

"So good looking," agrees Don García. "Every girl in Belén – their mothers too – he could have had any of them . . ."

"But he didn't, did he?" says Don Wenceslau.

"No, he did not," Don García sighs, overwhelmed suddenly by a sense of waste. "No. He kept his Chinese eyes for Elena Colina Silves."

The name is a spell that sends the three men into silence. They think of that handsome young couple, kissing on the bench opposite, leaning over the Malecón's balustrade to watch the ships sail by, elevated by memory into the envy of Belén.

"I forget what happened to him when she was taken away," says Don Wenceslau. "Didn't he vanish too? Do you have any idea?"

Don García leans forward. His eyes are shining.

"If I had been him," he says, unable at that moment to find a suitable model in Donizetti and thinking instead of Verdi's trouba-dour, "I would have gone knocking on the doors of every convent and religious institution in Peru until I found her. And that, I imagine, is what he did."

"That's more than 1700 doors," calculates Don Leopoldo. He has never concealed his opinion that the only thing capable of being set to Don García's music is nonsense. "He didn't come back for, let me see, another fifteen years. That's 150 doors a year. Possible, I suppose," he adds in a manner suggesting he thought it wasn't.

Don Wenceslau, who would like to think that melody and speech sometimes belonged together, says: "Isn't it more probable he spent those years with Ezequiel? I read that some of those terrucos spent at least fifteen years training for their revolution."

Don Leopoldo snorts. If only his *History* had taken that time. The time it has taken has given the local historian a contempt for the quotidian. In Don Leopoldo's eyes, men were either books or newspapers. The man next to him was a newspaper. "You oughtn't to believe everything in *El Oriente*," he says.

Don Wenceslau snaps open the first page again. "'El Niño – the worst in living memory'," he reads. "'Record rainfall in Lima. Arequipa and Silar two months now without rain.' You can't imagine it, can you, sitting here?" he says, smelling the inky blooms of the copa de oro and casting his eyes to the untroubled sky. "You can't imagine, at the end of February, that somewhere they've still got El Niño."

Don Leopoldo thinks of the stream known as the Child because it comes at Christmas. He thinks of the hot-headed current crawling every seven years along the coast. He thinks of it elbowing Humboldt's cold drift with all its pescado and pejerrey into the Pacific, beyond the reach of fishermen and guano birds.

"Not even the Christ child caused so much damage," he says.

Don Wenceslau turns to Don Leopoldo. "If you ask me, that's why the terrucos have spared Belén. Our climate. They'd just go off to the Teletroca with García here and that would be that."

Don Leopoldo points to the ground. "So, explain the colihuachos."

Don Wenceslau looks at the dead flies which have tumbled from the sky's belly.

"Ah, the colihuachos. Yes, well." His eyes return to the page. They alight on a paragraph from a correspondent on the coast. "It says here that in their nets men have discovered feathered fish."

"Journalism," says Don Leopoldo.

Chapter 2

THE SIMPLEST WAY to reach Lima's Establecimiento Penal San Francisco is to take one of the crowded collectivo buses from the Inca market. A thirty-five-minute journey along a featureless highway brings you to the northern outskirts of the city. A narrow dirt road, sandwiched between several stalls of avocado pears and sometimes hard to find, leads to San Francisco's entrance.

It is a low prison made from brown brick that merges into the sandhills. During El Niño, the only way for the water to drain was down these hills. The water washed everything in its path – Gloria milk tins, husks of maize, empty bottles of battery fluid – until the detritus of the surrounding shanty-towns slopped against the prison walls and became home to the dogs and buzzards that rooted there day and night, infuriating the guards so much that the towers rang out with the shooting matches they held whenever the Governor took the puddled road into town to be straddled by his mistress.

That Tuesday morning a man joined the friends, relations and lawyers walking up the hill. He was small and square, with brilliantined hair that fell over his ears in dark coils. He walked a pace or two behind the group, looking at his feet and hopping across the rivulets.

One of the avocado women watched him leave the stall where he sheltered from the rain. She called over to a friend. She pointed at the man's receding back, bowed into a dirty leather jacket.

"Palanca," she called. Substitute.

The avocado women knew that in an hour's time when the group came down again, it would not include that man. But in a few minutes they would be passed by another, on his own, who wouldn't be looking at his feet but at the sky, who would start with fright at unexpected sounds.

Sometimes, when the avocado women saw such a man, they liked to shout.

At the main entrance to San Francisco, the man in the leather jacket separated from the others and made his way to a metal door at the side of the prison. He knocked, waited, then knocked again.

The door opened.

Someone emerged, walking in rapid steps down the hill.

He entered.

He walked through a number of green doors, each guarded by a uniformed man on a stool who rose in silence and drew back the bolt. He counted six of these men. Bolt, open, clang. Bolt, open, clang. Bolt, open, clang. Bolt, open, clang. Bolt, open, clang. The last guard wasn't sitting, but scrubbing the concrete floor with a brush. The brush had few bristles and made a scraping sound on the concrete. The concrete was dark with shit, mud and water from the feet of those passing through the sixth door. The man knew once he went through that door, he was on his own.

The only time a guard went through that door was to shoot.

Clang.

The door led into a large open compound. Despite the rain, it was crowded with prisoners. Camarada Edith had described to him the kind of prisoner – pick-pockets from the bull-ring, narco-traffickers from the Huallaga who continued to deal in cocaine paste, murderers, lunatics, innocents.

One or two wore plastic bags over their heads and shoulders. Most did not. They sat with their backs to the brown wall, drenched and glistening, like the animals rooting through the rubbish on the other side. They wore few clothes. The only life came from their eyes, pickled by cocaine or potato-skin alcohol, which licked over him as he stood by the door. He could smell the brutality. It was even stronger than the smells emanating from the soaking pyramids of excrement. These mounds rose from the mud wherever he looked.

He clenched his hands into his jacket pockets. He began walking.

"Two dormitories lead immediately off the recreation ground. You want the one on the right."

As he picked his way through the pools of water to the building, fewer people stood in his path. Those that stared before moving aside were neater dressed and cleaner. Their faces weren't dazed by pasta básica. They were forbidding in a different way.

Walking by, he felt their eyes. They were more uncomfortable than the eyes wanting to violate him by the compound's entrance. Feeling them, he forgot the smells from the drains and the flies rising and falling in a dense bush on the crapheaps and the naked man who lay across the top of one, giggling a hymn.

Suddenly his only thought was to enter the building where there was no one to look at him like that, just a long, empty, high-ceilinged corridor down which he walked towards the men who sat guarding the final door of all, the door into the dormitory.

There were three of these men. They sat on chairs behind a table, reading. The man knew they exerted more power than anyone else in the prison, except those through that door who, like them and like the men staring at him in the compound outside, awaited trial on charges under Decree 046 of "the law against terrorism".

He reached the table.

"I'm the palanca," he said.

Inside the dormitory, about forty young men in their early twenties were arranged on benches, listening to a tall, thin man who stood reading from a book. The light came from a skylight above him. Apart from his voice, the only sound was rain falling on glass.

The palanca moved towards the man in the light. "We know that a revolution is always religious," he heard him say. "The word religion has a new value and it no longer serves only to designate a ritual or a Church."

The palanca found an empty bench. He sat down and looked at the man reading, taking in the first sentence or two. He saw his clean-shaven face, his blond curly hair and the scar on his cheek which darkened when he concentrated. This was Comrade Chino of Belén, one of the first heroes of the revolution, he reminded himself. This was the man who for three years had sent out prisoners to run some of Ezequiel's most effective missions. This was the man who had bribed the guards so he, the palanca, could sit here for a week while someone blew up the electricity pylons in Jauja. Or whipped dogs through Ayacucho with grenades round their necks. Or exploded a donkey in the market at Huanta. Or worse.

Early on he'd offered his services, but while they hadn't laughed, they'd made it clear he was too old a mongrel to teach the tricks they now liked you to learn from the age of six or seven. "To become a Senderista doesn't take months," they said. "It takes many years." But they'd kept his name all the same, which was why one evening a month ago as he was unzipping himself from the overalls he'd bought when he first came to the station as a young boy, he found himself looking at a woman who introduced herself as Camarada Edith. She wanted information, she said. Information that would assist the revolution. And she wanted something else.

"We want you to take someone's place," she said. "Just for a week. We want you to be a palanca."

He thought of the man whose place he was taking, at that moment walking past the avocado women, the man who for a week was carrying his name, his double. Thinking of him, he felt uneasy about someone out there with his name. Dead pylons. Dog bombs. Donkey bombs. He could live with those. But recently he had read of other bombs. Human bombs. Mother bombs. Child bombs. Nor was it just the child bombs. It was the throat-cutting, the head-cutting, the ball-cutting. What if they caught the man who was him slitting a PIP throat, red-handed with the bastard's blood? What then? Then it wouldn't be just a week in San Francisco prison.

Under the skylight, the reader looked up from his book. His oriental eyes fell on those sitting there. "When a tree gives bad fruit, it must be cut down," he said. "We cannot build without first destroying. We cannot have a new birth without blood." He closed the book. "Long live the world revolution."

"Long live the world revolution!" shouted the men on the benches. "Death to the President of the Republic! Long live Presidente Ezequiel!"

When they dispersed, the palanca rose and walked into the light. He kept his eyes on the floor. He saw the man's bare feet. They were watermarked to their ankles in slime from the compound.

"Comrade Chino?" He sensed the man's eyes on him. "I'm the palanca."

"The one from Electro-Peru?"

"Yes."

"From Silar?"

"That's right."

He felt the man before him nod. "Sit down," he said.

They sat on a bench. "The emergency pylons – you've brought details?"

The palanca slapped his leather jacket. "The plans are here." He produced an envelope and handed it over. Without a word, the man placed it between the pages of the book in his lap. Then he said, "What's going on? For two months, all we've heard is rain."

So the palanca told him. He told him about the drought in Silar and Arequipa, where the cattle savannahs had gone without water for nine weeks. He told him about Piura, where the air was usually dry as a cracker. (It had rained night and day for two months, flooding the cotton crops and rotting the cherrywood bed in the house where Admiral Grau had first seen the light of day in June 1834.) He told him about Chimbote, where smell had always meant money and where the harbour's florists stank of pulverized meal from the fish factories. (It was now common to see doorways spilling over with people who had fainted in the odourless air.)

He told him of things he had heard in the electricity station and read about in newspapers. How, germinated by El Niño's strange interaction of water and air, plants were growing along the river banks no botanist had ever seen. How scallops floated on the waves as if boiled in the water. How a burst river had carried a crocodile out to sea where it bobbed for an afternoon among a school of distempered seals.

"In their nets," he said, "men have discovered feathered fish."

And the more he talked without being interrupted, the more confident the palanca became until he found himself able to look into the face of his listener.

"What do they say about us?" said the man eventually.

"They show pictures of Ezequiel with a Devil's tail. They say he drinks the blood of those he executes. They say no one knows where he is. Sometimes they say he's dead."

"No," said the man, turning to the poster on the wall behind him.

The same poster was pasted on the walls of the compound and along the corridor to the dormitory. It showed the handsome face of Ezequiel holding a flag and smiling as he pointed to the sun. The New Dawn. The Dawn which would greet them after the revolution.

"No. He's not dead."

The palanca cleared his throat. "Comrade Chino, I have two messages from Camarada Edith."

The man looked round.

"Well?" he asked.

"One she passes on from Lieutenant Velarde. Something he was overheard saying in a club. She says you might be amused to hear it."

"What does Lieutenant Velarde have to say?"

"He says if you show your face in Belén again, he'll skin it."

"Velarde couldn't skin a carapama. What's the other?"

"She says you've been here three years and not once have you had a palanca. She said she could arrange one for you. She mentioned the name Julio."

Anguish flickered in the blond man's eyes. "How many times does she have to be told I don't want a palanca."

"She knew you'd say that but she said the committee needs to speak to you. There are things you need to be told face to face. She said Ezequiel would wish it."

"Ezequiel would wish it," the man repeated. "Tell me, do you think Ezequiel's wish is a wish, or is it an order?"

The palanca was silent. He was remembering the face of the woman who had come to the electricity station. He was remembering the fear he had felt when she talked, except when she mentioned the name of Comrade Chino.

"Tell me."

"I think it's a wish," the palanca said, and then quickly, "she asked me to tell you they're very pleased with you. She said 'Tell him he's doing a good job'."

"And I'll continue to do a good job – but from here."

"She wants to see you," the palanca repeated.

"No." Comrade Chino shook his head. "It's far too risky."

For a reason he couldn't explain, the palanca found it hard to equate his previous image of Comrade Chino, the revolutionary hero, with the person in front of him. At the electricity station he dealt in every variety of current and short circuit. He prided himself on his ability to detect the same energies at work in people. He looked into the petroleum-coloured eyes of the man on the bench. They didn't conceal passion, he thought. What they concealed was hurt.

Later, the palanca followed the others into the compound. In the rain men were queuing for soup. The liquid was the same colour as the mud they stood in, boiled from the bones of no animal the palanca had ever tasted. It left a flavour in his mouth he couldn't get rid of. Leaving half of it undrunk, he sought out Comrade Chino. He found him lying under a blanket on the floor, reading the same book. He saw the title. *Seven Interpretive Essays on Peruvian Reality* by José Carlos Mariátegui. He sat down beside him. Comrade Chino looked briefly from the pages. The rain fell on the skylight, still the only sound in the dormitory.

The palanca thought again of the man who was him. What was he doing now, this minute? He wouldn't have begun to blow up his pylons, or chase his dogs. He would be releasing other energies. He would be chasing women. He bet he was a one for the women. Whatever this mission, he would have a woman somewhere along the road.

"Don't you miss them here?" The question was cruel. It reflected the taste in his mouth. He felt superior in asking it. It was the only time he had felt superior all day and he felt like this because he knew how much they missed women in San Francisco. They missed them so much that new inmates were taken off and violated by every madman, killer and narco in sight. It wasn't the food or the guards that turned you into dog and buzzard meat. It was cancer of the culo.

"You get used to it," said Comrade Chino.

The palanca inspected the naked pin-ups – torn from *Gente!* – on the wall above his head, beneath a poster of Ezequiel.

"Ever been in love, Comrade Chino?" he asked. He thought of that terrifying woman, Camarada Edith. He thought again of the way she looked when she delivered her message. It wasn't the way you looked when you wanted to discuss Mariátegui.

Comrade Chino put down his book. He stared ahead.

"Yes," he said. "I've been in love."

"What happened?"

"She went away."

"Another man?"

Comrade Chino looked at him. A scar swam into his face, the shadow of a fish on the sand.

"Something like that."

"Where is she now?"

"I don't know."

"Where's she from?"

"The jungle."

"Ah, the jungle," said the palanca, as if that explained everything. He had heard about the jungle, where men were turned into blow-torches and fucked dolphins.

That was where he would go if he was his double, not back to the goat-toothed mountains of Silar.

Chapter 3

ON A MAP, Silar was not far from Arequipa. Yet to arrive there by road meant a two-and-a-half-day journey over three mountain ranges, descending into a bowl fringed on its lower slopes with eucalyptus. Only a dirt track connected the town on the other side with the villages and farmsteads that rose to Sumbay, Crucero Alto and eventually Cabaña.

In completing the journey from Arequipa, the traveller crossed the provincial border into the district of Soreto. The boundary line had been pencilled in Madrid towards the end of the eighteenth century with a geometric caprice that bore no relation to the geography it defined. On noticing he had drawn a shape which at that moment reminded him of a cousin's schnauzer, the cartographer had added a long curved tail.

Silar lay at its end like a flea.

Those two lines drawn one breezy afternoon on a mahogany desk in the Old World committed Silar to Soreto – the capital of which, Belén, lay 1500 miles to the north. In reality the town had never felt itself anything other than Arequipeño.

Like Arequipa, Silar was famous for its convent, its volcano and the houses of the stone whose name it took. These houses – from the high pass they could still give the appearance of a white city – were greyer and shabbier than in the days when, to the chagrin of Arequipeños, at least two Spanish viceroys (and following Independence, a number of criollo generals) repaired there for the summer.

But, partly because of its convent, partly because of its situation off the beaten track, Silar remained an attractive town, prouder than most of its past and keen to maintain, without effort, a reputation for honesty, good schools and hospitality within reason.

That year, however, when the rain-bearing winds refused to cross the Andes, the resources of Silar's population were stretched to their limit.

It took a fortnight for the river to narrow to a slow-moving chocolate thread. One day, the town woke to find it dried completely. The onion fields it had watered turned from green to yellow to a cracked expanse of red soil which the wind blew off in dust devils. Half of the Mayor's cattle turned over in their pastures and died in masks of lime-coloured froth.

Along the river, his mango trees dropped fruit which gave a rattle when kicked. Not even his dogs, their tongues black and swollen, risked panting in the shade beneath in case they were set upon by buzzards drifting down from the mountains like open bibles.

The largest of these mountains was a volcano known as Nakaq. No one in Silar could escape the sight of its red peak. It loomed over every wall. It rose at the end of every street. Wherever you looked it was there. Normally ichu grass covered the slope which dominated the convent, disguising the letters scratched into its surface. El Niño had exposed these letters which now spelled enormously, Presidente Ezequiel.

El Niño, the Child, because it comes at Christmas, had now lasted twelve weeks and four days.

The convent was arranged around a large cloister built from the volcanic rock. The walls of the cloister were tiled, the tiles patterned with blue lilies that glared in the afternoon sun. Their workmanship suggested a European hand. They contrasted with the crude frescoes over the cell doors where the Virgin and Child had been painted in vegetable dyes and rabbit's blood.

A paved cross divided the courtyard into four squares of grass, bordered with the stalks of dead geraniums. A large chicha jar lay on its side in one corner. From another corner grew a stringy cypress which might have been dipped in dust.

In the centre of the courtyard was a goldfish pool, also built of sillar. Two dolphins balanced on a pair of livid green snouts. Their tails supported a sea-shell out of which poked a water pipe. The pipe was dry. El Niño had turned the pool beneath into a grimy pond which had to be skimmed every morning.

It was late afternoon. Inside the cloister, a door opened. A shadow emerged hesitantly into the light. It was the figure of a nun. She took one step up into the cloister, then another, before raising her hand to the sun. Her other hand picked at the habit where some wax had dried. She waited, getting used to the light, the dust, the breathless heat.

The woman's face had the complexion and pallor of the cloister's grey rock. It was without life, except for two piercing blue eyes. They made you realize how beautiful she must have been – possibly still might be under her nun's habit. They were as blue and incandescent as the sky.

She sniffed. Despite the dust there was something in the air. As she stood, trying to work out what it was, a hummingbird swooped past and hovered against the tiled wall. She watched it dash its beak into the glaze. In the drought it had mistaken the tiles for flowers.

She lowered her head and began walking. She kept her eyes on the flagstones. They were covered in the same fine powder that coated the grass, the roof, the surface of the goldfish pool. Her sandals echoed in the cloister, their prints making a rosary in the dust. They did not elaborate the rosary of someone at peace. The nun had completed three circuits of the cloister when she heard a bell. Two shapes moved along the side of the arcade that lay in shadow, then disappeared down the corridor leading to the infirmary. The one who held the bell, the Mother Superior, she recognized immediately. Her surprise in recognizing the other as a man was momentary. In looking up from the flagstones, her eyes were drawn to the mountain which rose above the chapel roof. She saw the words on its slope as she always saw the words, words which gave her the impression of belonging to the volcano – like the wisps which appeared from its cone.

The drought had multiplied these wisps.

They were the reason she stood transfixed.

Nakaq was erupting.

But as she stared, she saw that the clouds bunching the summit were motionless. Suddenly, she realized they weren't clouds of smoke at all, but of the rain she had smelt on the air.

*

A man scrambled up the sandy slopes from the river. He slipped back twice in his excitement, fell over once and when he reached the road held his sides as he ran.

"Water," he gasped to those who turned, wondering why a man was exerting himself in this heat. "Water," he repeated. A blood-red trickle of water was advancing towards Silar along the river bed.

Twenty minutes later, the four members of the town's band assembled by the river. The guitarist had chicken feathers in his hair. The drummer still wore his key-cutter's apron. Here, to the beat of the drum that bore their name, the Banda Flor Andina began playing.

Father Palacio had followed the Mother Superior through the cloister. She walked a few steps before him, ringing the bell as if she was shaking a bottle to stir its sediment. The bell announced the host in his hands, contained in a silver pyx. When he stepped down from the cloister, into the cell, the contents rattled.

The cell was cool and dark. An old woman lay on a bed under an alcove. She wore a white calico nightshirt buttoned to her throat and a cap on her head. The skin hung from her cheeks like the veil draped untidily over a prie-dieu by the door. Noticing the veil, the Mother Superior removed and folded it.

"Sister, sister," she said, squeezing the black cloth in her hands.

Hearing the quiet reprimand, the woman on the bed opened her eyes.

"I'll leave you, Father," said the Mother Superior. "I'll be outside."

Father Palacio placed his pyx on the floor and drew up a chair. He looked ahead, over the shape of the woman's legs under the blanket, into the aperture. It was designed for protection against tremors. He wondered how well it would resist an earthquake.

"Not long now, Father," said the woman faintly. "El Niño's dried me out."

"Sister, sister," said Father Palacio.

"Drier than the chapel roof."

"I've come to hear your confession."

"Bless me, Father, for I have sinned," came the voice from the bed. Father Palacio closed his eyes. At the end of her confession, she paused. Father Palacio recognized the pause. Usually it meant there was something else.

"There's something else."

Father Palacio turned at an angle to the straw mattress. He waited. The words came out in a rush, each memorized and rehearsed so much that it might have been divorced from its meaning, and Father Palacio had to lean forward and concentrate on what was being said.

The confession related to an incident that had taken place before she left Belén. It involved a young fisherman.

"He was a lovely talker, Father, such a lovely talker." He had told stories in the dark she could remember even now. He had talked her, fifty years before, into spending a night with him in a hotel bedroom.

"I gave myself."

Father Palacio nodded. He was experienced enough to know the length of shadows cast by old sins.

"And you know something, Father," came the voice.

Father Palacio tightened his eyes.

"It was wonderful."

She is dying, he reminded himself, she is dying. She has been shut up in these alcoved walls, like a widow bird. He must relieve her fluttering spirit of unnecessary freight. He opened his eyes. He drew the chair nearer the bed.

"When you made your first confession," he said carefully, closing his eyes again, "you didn't commit a sacrilege?"

"No, no, no, Father. I was sorry. I did have a firm purpose of amendment."

"But?"

"But as the years went by I kept remembering that night with Wenceslau, and the more I remembered the more I felt I had never truly repented. Not truly."

"You should know by now that feelings don't count," said the priest. "One does not have to feel sorry for one's sins. One does not necessarily have to feel that one loves God."

"That's just it," came the voice. "How can I say that I love God if I don't feel I do? What I did was a mortal sin, but, Father" – the voice was a low moan – "I cannot wish it undone."

Father Palacio remained silent.

"I see," he said.

"But, Father, doesn't this make a mockery of my life as a bride of Christ? If here, now, at the last moment, I can't feel sorry. Doesn't that mean my whole life has been a lie? Doesn't it mean I'm destined for hellfire?"

In his mind, Father Palacio saw the old woman lying on the bed as a young novice. He saw her on her knees, day after day, week after week, year after year. He saw her as someone who had not received the consolation she sought, yet all that time she had stayed there, chaste, kneeling, not giving up, despite never having felt the love of God, despite not having seen visions.

He thought of the hotel bedroom in the jungle.

"No," said Father Palacio, "you're not destined for hellfire."

He heard the release caused by his words. He felt the body before him stir under the blanket. From the bed came the voice again. It spoke with strength.

"I want to know, Father, is there love in Heaven?"

Father Palacio opened his eyes. "In Heaven there is neither marriage nor giving in marriage. We'll all be like the Angels of God. Now make the act of contrition."

She began. "My God, I am very sorry that I have sinned against Thee and by the help of Thy grace I will not sin again."

As she spoke, Father Palacio made a sign of the cross and muttered the words of absolution. He reached for the box containing the host. He picked out the round wafer in preparation for the communion.

"Go in peace," he said. "And sin no more."

Father Palacio had sailed from Spain twenty-three years before, when his hair was black and his eyes sparkled like his teeth. He had read Valverde and Zárate on the Conquest, been dismayed by all of the excesses and half expected to find cannibals among his flock.

Instead, the only voracious quality he found was apathy.

He had come with a fistful of good intentions and watched them one by one slip through his fingers. But he had kept his hair, five of his teeth and a smile that raised his eyebrows. Occasionally he thought of Burgos, his domineering sister and his parents' house, but not often.

At the age of seventeen he had entrusted himself to God, who exercising a modicum of infinite wisdom had sent him to Silar and, on this bright afternoon in March, to the convent of Santa Clara.

Father Palacio found the Mother Superior waiting for him outside. She made no mention of the dying sister. He saw no reason to speak of her.

"Father, one more thing," she said, playing with the veil in her hand. "The chapel roof." She explained as they walked.

In the drought, the polilla worm had fattened and flourished. Burrowing into the wood, the tiny bugs had scratched out trails which caught the sun like particles in a sandglass. They had gnawed at four exuberant frames of the Cuzqueño school hanging in the novice room; they had chewed away parts of Saint George's shield on a canvas attributed to Zurbarán; and then, in El Niño's final days, they had set about the chapel's bamboo roof and the leather straps binding its cane.

There were now signs – from the noises that issued whenever Sister Inés pulled the dessus de doublette – that the French organ had become affected.

"I'm no handy-man," said Father Palacio after inspecting the holes and recommending the first thing to enter his head, "but I suggest kerosene." He promised, however, to make enquiries with a neighbour, a journalist who owned a hardware store.

The sun was sinking as they walked across the courtyard. "Father, another thing," said the Mother Superior, pausing by the goldfish pool. "Is it true that you keep a full tank in your car . . . because of the volcano?"

Father Palacio raised his eyebrows without smiling.

"Is that what they say?"

"I wanted to know."

"I do," he said. "But not because of the volcano." It was a habit acquired in the European war when there was rationing. He had not shaken it off. Once or twice he had occasion to be grateful for it. His parish was a large one. There were few pumps between Silar and Crucero Alto and they were usually sucked dry by an army looking for terrorists.

"It's not Nakaq I'm worried about. The whole country is erupting."

"I heard about Chimbote," said the Mother Superior.

Two days before, the telephone exchange in Chimbote had been destroyed by an explosive attached to a chicken.

Thinking about the incident, she giggled.

Father Palacio had not expected this reaction. He stared at the cast-iron coil of dolphins, the lichen-covered spout, the slime on the water of the goldfish pool.

"There's something wrong with those fish," he said.

In the river, the water had become thicker and redder, coloured by the soil from Nakaq. It bloodied the stones and the dogs and the children who rolled in the mud, laughing.

The sounds drew people to the river. Some began dancing, pointing as they danced to the ash clouds suspended above Nakaq which now drifted perceptibly towards Silar, willed on – so it seemed – by the music.

The mountains had swallowed the sun and the band played to the light of candles, made from pig fat, which flashed on the trumpet's dented silver and the gold fangs in the cymbalist's mouth.

He sang a jubilant high-pitched song. Its words could be attributed to the festivals of Corpus Christi, their delivery to the bucket of chicha which had been carried down to the dancers. "It has the power to give twins," the chicha woman told them.

Its power could be seen that evening in the men who made up Flor Andina: the full-throated cymbalist, the guitarist whose hand strummed his catgut at a gallop, the drummer whose instrument rested on a plastic beer crate and the trumpeter whose plaster – covering a hole in the brass – had become stickier and stickier till in a fury he tore it off to give his trumpet a voice of its own.

No one remembered when the music changed, but it must have been after the trumpeter produced a set of quena pipes from his poncho. He jerked his mouth over the reed tubes, as if to clean them.

"'Ojos azules', 'Ojos azules'," shouted the chicha woman. "'Blue eyes', 'Blue eyes'."

The trumpeter turned to the others.

"'Ojos azules'?"

The drum rolled. The cymbalist answered with a clash. The guitarist tightened his strings.

"'Ojos azules', then."

The lights went on in the cloister. The two figures by the pool gave a start. Their conversation had insulated them to the darkness and to the noise from the river which they now heard for the first time.

They stood in the gloom, listening. As they listened, their attention was drawn to the woman still walking through the bright arcade.

"See her, Father?"

"Yes," he said.

"What would you say to the name Elena Silves?"

"No," he said. "Not seriously."

"Indeed."

Father Palacio pushed his spectacles up his nose and looked. In that moment something happened. The nun stopped abruptly. She turned towards the courtyard. She was listening to the music. Illuminated in the overhead light, her face was set in a rictus of agony.

The priest had never seen an expression like it. He moved forward. As he did so, the nun clasped her hands together.

"No, no, not that," she begged. Then louder and louder, "Don't! Please, Lord . . . Please, please, don't!" until in a voice that scattered a confetti of pigeons from the bell tower, she screamed "Gabriel! Gabriel! Gabriel!"

The woman collapsed as Father Palacio reached the cloister. He lifted her by the shoulders. "Take her feet," he told the Mother Superior. Together they carried the nun to a cell. The Mother

Superior went in search of water. Left alone, the priest looked at the unconscious face. Apprised of the identity of Elena Silves, he was surprised by the absence of a sign that any special blessing had been bestowed. While he was contemplating this, he heard through the open door a sound that came from the bowels of the earth, as if the mountains were clapping. It was a sound repeated in the sky as the heavens opened and the rain fell crashing into the cloister.

Muffled by the sound of rain, Father Palacio heard an explosion. Then the lights went out.

On the following Saturday, *El Oriente* carried an item on its centre page under the heading NUN ESCAPES SANTA CLARA.

"There was confusion yesterday over an unconfirmed report that Sister Colina, a nun at the convent of Santa Clara, used the blackout to escape her grounds. Madre Ana de los Ángeles, the Mother Superior, was this morning unavailable for comment. The convent, founded in 1695, is home to 21 nuns of the contemplative order of the Carmelites."

The paragraph was signed in small bold caps, A. W., and followed the report of bomb attacks on power stations in Mollendo, Arequipa and Silar. In an action blacking out these cities, "subversive delinquents" had blown up three Electro-Peru plants and eleven emergency pylons.

Both items were subsidiary to the main news of the week – the rain which had fallen non-stop for thirty-six hours, pitting the cracked fields and terraces and filling the town with the smell of onions.

Chapter 4

THE SUN has turned yellow. It has risen above the roof of the iron house and hangs there like a small ball, not impossibly hot, nor impossibly bright, but a round host that has chased away the breeze which gusted into the square, scattering the red cattle-flies from the shoulders of Admiral Grau and away from the ground beneath the bench.

And still no one has passed the three old men.

Don Leopoldo stirs. He raises a hand to his throat. He scratches its bark.

"The soft-shoe artist is back," he says.

The others lift their eyes to the window on the fourth floor of the Hotel Liberty. It opens into a rectangle of deep shadow where nothing moves. The three men gaze into the shadow.

"A long time isn't it?" asks Don Wenceslau after a while.

"Two years?" suggests Don García.

"Three," says Don Leopoldo.

"What brings him back?"

"Her," says Don García who believes the face they are searching for in the purple darkness is a woman's.

"Her then."

"Perhaps the colihuachos brought her," says Don García.

"La Palometa will be pleased."

Don Wenceslau's remark causes Don García to take up the paper he has been reading. He riffles through it studiously.

"Have we won the lottery?"

"Not yet," says Don Leopoldo.

"Who's the cheat this time?"

"A woman from Iquitos," Don Leopoldo tells him. "A lavandera. She's going to buy a flat in Miami."

"A flat in Miami," says Don Wenceslau. He thinks of how many bottles of masato that would purchase. He shows the whites of his eyes just trying to envisage the quantity. He cannot.

Next to him Don Leopoldo busily converts the property into life-subscriptions to historical quarterlies and shelves of rare books smelling of red Morocco.

Much as Don García would like to give rein to his fantasies, he cannot clear his mind of the person mentioned by Don Wenceslau. As he thinks of her, his eyes catch sight of a small shape flitting down the steps of the Bishop's palace. It carries a suitcase which is placed in the bonnet of a white Volkswagen beetle.

"Bishop Barrantes," says Don García, against the chortle of the car's ignition. "Where's he off to in such a hurry?"

"Must be the airport," thinks Don Wenceslau. "It wouldn't be the zoo."

"I've never seen him look so worried."

"Perhaps someone's told the Archbishop how Barrantes pays for those crosses of his."

The car starts. It accelerates out of the square.

"How does he pay for those crosses?" asks Don García.

"La Palometa told me. She hasn't told you?" says Don Wenceslau, teasing.

"Sometimes, Wenceslau . . ." But Don García doesn't finish. He returns to his paper. "I wonder what's on at the Bolognesi," he mutters.

The question goes unanswered. They all know the answer. They remember the rubber boom when Belén had three cinemas – including the country's very first. They remember the films – such films! – that came direct from Europe. Hardly any films come to Belén now. Don García has lost count of the times he has seen the scratched print of *The Rubber Man's Daughter*.

He finds the advertisement for the Cinema Bolognesi.

"*The Rubber Man's Daughter*," he reads out. "'The happiest and the saddest love story ever told'." He looks up from the page. "Perhaps I'll go tonight."

The thought of the film prolongs their silence. For a minute they forget the afternoons and evenings spent interpreting a soundtrack that, for a different length of time on each occasion, is out of step with the picture. Don Leopoldo even forgets his reservations about the film's historical accuracy. The three of them indulge in another fantasy. They are thinking of Luis Sintra, the hero who wins his girl. They are imagining themselves in his role. The square is an empty stage. There is no one on it to challenge them, except Admiral Grau.

While each man on the bench has enjoyed his own many or infrequent passions, each remembers only the one. For Don Wenceslau it resides in the round face of a pious girl, the youngest daughter of a sugar-boiler, in whose mellifluous arms he spent one night – his first and last – in a room on the third floor of the Hotel Liberty.

For Don García, the picaflor, the man who believes bed is the poor man's opera, it is the face of the hotel's owner, La Palometa, a face he sees every day and in which he does not make out the lines – more than the hennaed hairs on her head – nor the strands of darker hair advancing from her chin and along her lips, but the girl he first set eyes on in the Salón de Belleza, who for more than seventy years has turned up her nose at his advances.

Neither suspects Don Leopoldo of a special love. If he has women, they must be like the demure ladies of Trujillo, knitting their flag for Admiral Grau. Not that they think he has women. They suspect he has only ever taken his shadow to bed.

But he who is silent does not say nothing. Like most men in Belén, Don Leopoldo dreams of someone. The widow of a Portuguese accountant who, crossing the square with an armful of books (and a mad look in her eye that suggested to the seventeen-year-old Leopoldo, as he sat on the bench with a volume of *Os Lusíadas*, that she was intent on throwing them into the river) saw something in his own expression which made her pause and allow a different person into her face, a kind woman with sad, grey eyes who had once tried to teach the children of Funchal history and wondered if he, who balanced Portugal's greatest saga on his knee, would care to relieve her of these volumes.

The seven books she gave him included Espinosa's *People's Dictionary* and *A History of Peru in the Guano Age* by A.J. Duffield. Together with the story she began telling him on that bench, they had fired Don Leopoldo in his chosen profession. They had made him feel his existence was more than that of a swift passing through shadows.

Even today, seventy years on, Don Leopoldo doesn't know what it was that compelled a middle-aged lady to tell a complete stranger half her age the story of her life. He would like to think it was something to do with him, but he suspects otherwise. He suspects she would eventually have told this story – a story she couldn't tell her two children but which she had to tell or her heart would burst through her black dress – to anyone sitting there.

He suspects she would have told it to the grass.

Timing, supposes Don Leopoldo. That was the secret. Nothing else.

"The happiest and the saddest love story ever told," repeats Don Wenceslau. He nods to himself, thinking of the night of his life in the hotel room. "That's the truth. You pay for your happiness. Every moment of it."

Don García agrees. "One of the little things life keeps to herself. Like the fact we can't choose who we love."

"Do you know what the secret of love is?" asks Don Wenceslau.

"Yes," says Don García who thinks he does.

"It's not sex."

"No," says Don García doubtfully.

"It's laughter."

The two of them ponder this. Then Don Leopoldo says: "There's more to life than love, you know."

Don García thinks for another moment.

"No there isn't," he says. "Except music."

"Look!"

The cry is Don Wenceslau's. He is nodding at a woman walking briskly past them towards the river. She has her head in a plain scarf. She walks with her eyes fixed to the ground.

"But that face. I know that face," says Don Wenceslau who has raised his panama. Squinting at the receding figure – the first person of the day to walk by – Don Wenceslau claps his knee.

"It's Elena Silves! The one who saw Our Lady!"

Don García removes his trilby.

"I do believe he's right. Quick, quick, Don Leopoldo, look!"

"But what brings her back?" Don Wenceslau continues. "I thought she was in a convent somewhere in the mountains."

"Fancy." Carefully, Don García screws his hat back on his head. "It must be twenty years at least."

"Eighteen," Don Leopoldo corrects him.

"There must be a problem," says Don Wenceslau.

Don Leopoldo produces a peanut and cracks the shell.

"Without problems there would be no history."

The three men, the pedant, the red herring, the romantic, sit in silence watching the woman until she vanishes down Calle Putumayo. Her appearance has stirred the forgotten years like Pía Zumate tossing her hand through a bowl of dried flowers or Don Leopoldo pressing his nose to the tweed jacket – neatly folded but too small to wear – at the back of his drawer.

"The most beautiful girl in Belén," says Don García eventually. He remembers her black hair and the blue dress that always made him want to run his hands up and down it. He remembers her face, so white it could have been wrought in chalcedony; a face that melted his heart when it smiled "Good morning, Don García. And how are things with Pía Zumate?"

He remembers her eyes.

Those eyes. Where did they come from? There was nothing like those eyes in the entire Amazon basin. Compared with those eyes, Pía Zumate's were raw eggs. They must have come from Europe.

"Her mother was very lovely too," he says. "I never knew the grandmother. Didn't she have something to do with Eiffel?"

"I remember her grandmother," says Don Wenceslau. "Poor little thing. Her husband died in the jungle and she spent the rest of her life in tears."

But Don Leopoldo is not listening. He is thinking of his *History of the Colonization of Belén*. His mind is rummaging through the bag at his feet, searching through a chaos of paper and discord of voices. In his head he is trying to locate the pages his insubordinate pen has written he doesn't know how many years before on the family of the woman who has passed them, the woman called Elena Silves.

Chapter 5

A la Señora Manuela Colina Silves 1884–1943
Estimada y distinguida Amiga mía:
  In writing this chronicle of Belén I have experienced
something of what it means to be a beggar on a throne of
gold (as the historian said of our country). I dedicate it to you
in memory of our great friendship and in gratitude to the
person who opened my eyes so long ago and by her rare and
generous gifts transformed me from a frog beneath a
coconut shell, believing no other world to exist, into something altogether princelier – a student in the noble discipline
of history.
Believe me to be,
My dear Manuela,
Your faithful friend and servant,
quien besa sus manos,
Leopoldo.

P.S. At first glance, you might naturally feel that Chapter
Five – pertaining expressly to the history of your family –
should be transposed with Chapter One. Some readers,
regarding it as superfluous to the story, might even argue it
should be purposely omitted. We who know its truths know
otherwise.
Hasta cada rata.

The Silves family, one of the oldest and most distinguished in Belén,
did not, as is commonly supposed, settle immediately in the city but
in Rapoto, a town on the Curaclo River, two hundred miles east of
the provincial capital.

It was on this spot in the August of 1539 that Manco Inca, fleeing from Gonzalo Pizarro, discovered a basket floating towards the Ayaju waterfall. He waded through the reeds and mud and pushed it ashore. Inside, under a finely woven blanket, he found the body of a woman.

She had been dead for three days. Her tongue had been wrenched out, her skin perforated with arrows and her dark legs burnt to two shining stumps.

She had been beautiful once, before her rape, her torture and her sordid death. This Manco knew because he had married her.

The tears he wept for Cura Ocllo, the legend went, formed the thundering river which came to be known as the Curaclo. By the time of Alonso Silves's arrival from Portugal, its thundering days were over and it was a brackish trickle which fed the larger Putumayo.

Elena's grandfather Alonso Silves was a late arrival in the black gold rush. He looked like a pig and sucked his upper lip into his mouth when talking. "God gave me these," he joked of his buckteeth, "because he didn't want me perfect." It was his only joke. When he tried to be charming to children they cried.

As a child he had dreamed of the strange balls which Columbus had discovered bouncing between the Hawaiians. To the nine-year-old boy, those malleable globes – made of no substance Columbus had seen – were proof that the New World was not a cartographer's joke. One day he would experience it for himself.

It was not enough to finger the waterproof suit once owned by King Carlos which lay in a rumpled black puddle in Coimbra's Museo de Colares. Nor, on the one occasion the curator allowed him, to rub out with the museum's single piece of dry gum a sonnet he had composed in honour of Queen Augusta. Nor even, on the afternoon of his eighteenth birthday, to catch a glimpse of someone directly descended from the man who had done most to promote the milk-giving wood known as the jevea cau-chu.

Francisco D'Oliveira's great-grandson stood on a corner, hailing a woman with a cane. Alonso rushed after him. He wished to convey his admiration for what Francisco had achieved. By the time he reached the corner, his only link with the inventor of the rubber candle (and the bag to hold the urine of incontinents) had vanished in Coimbra's thin afternoon air.

In 1893 Alonso matriculated in mathematics at Coimbra University. He was photographed in a studio against a painted backcloth showing the university library. The expression he wore above his dark robe and rabbit collar was one of someone painfully aware that the real library had been completed from wealth amassed in the New World, not in the Old.

On graduating, Alonso became an accountant, a profession he pursued diligently until at the age of thirty-seven he succumbed to his rubber fever. His "illness" had been exacerbated by the exile of King Manuel and his mother, Queen Augusta, to Twickenham. A staunch royalist who had wept at the assassination of King Carlos, Alonso had no appetite for what life might hold in the new republic.

In the first week of July 1911 he sold his red-tiled house, placed a bunch of comparatively fresh japonica on his parents' grave and for the sum of £18. 12s. 6d. purchased a one-way passage to Manaus on the Booth liner *Ambrose*.

He arrived in Lisbon to find the *Ambrose* delayed a day. He walked to the Moorish fort. He looked out over the straw-coloured Tagus and in the evening he ate a plate of clams and pork in the dining room of the Hotel Borges. In the morning, he took a valedictory stroll through the city. Near the mausoleum to Portugal's kings, he passed a church. On the spur of the moment, he decided to enter, to pray for good fortune in the Amazon – by which he meant the same good fortune being made by ordinary Brazilians, men who could not even write their names.

On entering A Imaculada Conceição, Alonso was surprised to find himself looking down at a large heap of paintings and crucifixes. A caretaker explained the church had been deconsecrated the day before. The objects at Alonso's feet were destined for the market at Sintra.

Alonso was held by one object in particular. Stealing behind him through the Manueline door, the sun struck a painting, slightly larger than life, of the Annunciation. The sight of the Archangel delivering his message to the Virgin had a profound effect on the accountant.

"This is for sale, then?" said Alonso, unembarrassed.

"Of course."

Disregarding the status of the church, Alonso fell on his knees and offered the prayer he had intended all along. That afternoon he boarded the *Ambrose* with a small crucifix made out of Goanese ivory and the painting of the Annunciation—the work, the caretaker assured him, of one of Fra Angelico's pupils.

On the second day Alonso fell in with a couple from Oporto. The husband was a sanitary engineer who had assisted Eiffel on the Douro bridge. He was celebrating retirement with an excursion down the Amazon, accompanied by a severe wife who had a long querulous nose and lips like a dried leaf. When the three of them disembarked at Funchal they were joined on the cobbled wharf by the engineer's daughter.

Her name was Manuela and she was travelling second class by way of punishment. The engineer had always disapproved of his daughter's profession. He believed that in giving a woman an education you were handing a knife to a monkey. The havoc that might be wrought by a female teacher was beyond imagining.

Manuela was twenty-seven and unmarried, but her single status cannot have owed anything to her looks. The young woman Alonso saw on the poop deck must have been as pretty as a duchess. He introduced himself. He learnt she had spent the last four years teaching the infants of Funchal to make angels out of paper doilies. Over the next week he discovered she reserved her deepest passion for the saga of those Portuguese sailors, soldiers and missionaries who had discovered, conquered and converted the world – and then in a blink lost it.

One day he knocked on the door of her cabin and she showed him a suitcase of books. These included an account of Prince Henry's capture of Ceuta, a life of Camões and a popular history of King Sebastián containing evidence that he hadn't died at Alcazarquivir but survived to become, among thirteen other incarnations, a pie-seller in Padua and an intimate of Prester John.

"Sometimes I have dreams he will come again," she said of her sixteenth-century king.

Below deck Alonso told her of his own half-formed dreams. She listened, and by the time the pilot boarded to steer the *Ambrose* into Pará, Alonso had announced their engagement.

Alonso and Manuela were married in Manaus in St John's Church near the floating dock. He bought her a ring from Roberto and Pelosi in Municipal Street and a blue velvet gown with golden loops made in Rue de la Paix. As their wedding gift, Manuela's parents donated a phonograph with a big horn, supplemented by five fado laments, including "Disse-te adeus e morri" (I said farewell and died) and three records of arias from *Lucia di Lammermoor*, with Amelita Galli-Curci as Lucia.

The arias were purchased in the foyer of the opera house where they had taken a box to watch Donizetti's opera performed by Giulia Ragi's Operetta Company. This was not the unqualified success it might have been, due to the indisposition of half the cast, nine of whom had died of yellow fever.

Alonso was deaf to the engineer's complaint that they did this sort of thing much better in Europe. It was his first night at the opera. He watched Lucia's passive role. He heard the celestial wedding hymns before the altar. He felt the earth move in the mad scene when Lucia imagined Edgardo had been restored to her.

That night Alonso sat on the large bed of a room overlooking the river. He stretched out a hand to his wife of twelve hours. "Fur le nozze a lei," he crooned unmelodically through his buckteeth.

The Silveses' honeymoon was marred by Alonso's discovery that he could not afford to be a rubber baron. Nothing had prepared him for the price of land, nor, indeed, the cost of everything else. The hotel bill was four times that of the Borges in Lisbon. He refused to contemplate the expense of Manuela's blue gown.

How deep was his pocket, asked the land agent in Marshal Deodoro street, a Maltese Jew. Alonso thought of the money he had saved and doubled it. The man laughed. He raised his feet to the desk. He advised him to go to Belén.

"Belén?"

"On the border with Peru. Land's cheaper there. You might be lucky. After all it's a lucky name." Seeing Alonso's puzzled expression, he explained.

"Bethlehem. You don't speak Spanish?"

Alonso said he did, of course he did, but it was not something he boasted about.

"You'll be all right then."

Alonso didn't tell the man that whereas in Portuguese he sounded like a poet, in Spanish he sounded like a waiter.

Sucking his lip, he bid farewell to his relieved parents in law – they had decided that Manaus was far enough from Oporto – and pressed on with his bride to the self-styled Pearl of the Peruvian Amazon, a thousand miles upriver.

On the boat, Manuela struggled with an account written five years before by an English evangelist. Belén, she read, lay 2300 miles inland on the northwest boundary of Peru in the heart of the montaña. It was the home of earth's most daring adventurers who cared for neither man nor God and regarded death with strange indifference. "No place on earth is more godforsaken than Belén," Manuela repeated contentedly, not fully understanding.

"Happy, dear?" her husband asked as the boat approached the city.

"Very," she replied, her hand a swan's neck against his mouth.

In the evangelist's day, Belén was producing enough rubber annually to tyre a quarter of a million motor cars. Now, in the autumn of 1911, it exuded a panic palpable even to Alonso. In the space of their journey from Manaus, the price of black gold had fallen from 12s. per pound to 9s.

Alonso reasoned to himself that with demand so low, what better time to invest. Given its constituent material, the trade could only bounce back. He was not to know he had heard the last soprano sing at the Manaus opera house and purchased from the final stock of Madame Bonneterre's dresses.

To the young Silveses, as they stepped off the *Ambrose*'s gang-plank, through the cotton bales and into the humid morning, the Amazon valley promised to be the Ophir of Solomon.

They never noticed the man in the grey linen suit, green and white striped tie and badly fitting mauve spats who stood watching them disembark.

That afternoon, at a café on the Plaza de Armas, Alonso entered into conversation with a man in badly fitting mauve spats. He had gelatinous hair and spoke in mellow Castilian tones. He was known locally as El Gordo – for the width of his stories not his waist.

He wanted to leave Belén fast.

What precipitated Orestes Minero's departure was the wind he had received of a report compiled by the British Government into the activities of the Peruvian Amazon Company. Minero was a director of the company, recently floated on the London Stock Exchange. The report described him as "a man of whom no good can be said". It was one of several phrases to which he would take exception. He was after all, not least by dint of his education, a man who had much in common with the compiler of the report, Roger Casement. He had even greeted Casement on his arrival in Belén with the words "How do ye do, sir, I'm an Englishman too."

"Indeed," had been Casement's reply. "How so?"

Three years at Margate College was the reason – the result of his father's posting as a clerk in the Peruvian Embassy. His experiences in a minor English public school had left their mark. Among the atrocities catalogued by Casement and levelled at Minero's door were crimes against the Indian rubber-gatherers "of so horrible a nature that no exaggeration is possible."

At Minero's station on the Yagua, guests reported how dogs would appear at their beds with an arm or a leg between their teeth. On one occasion, peering into a basket of what he thought was fruit, an American traveller unwrapped twenty severed heads and a sackful of ears. "Beasts of the jungle," explained Minero.

"Blow," he once ordered a Bora Indian whose wife had caught his eye, placing a rifle to the man's face. The Indian obeyed. Minero pulled the trigger. The wife became his concubine – one of several – and when, "in the gratification of his animal propensities", he acquired a foul disease, it was her he blamed. In his report, Casement suppressed the account of how she was placed in the stocks and a burning firebrand inserted between her legs. He had chronicled 2,000 similar crimes. He felt he could spare what delicacies of feeling remained to the Edwardian public.

For his part, Minero would rail against what he interpreted as a diabolical defamation. Casement was nothing more than a megalomaniac with a desire for notoriety. Where in his report did it mention the British treatment of Indians in Durban and Ireland? Nowhere was it drawn to the attention of the Anti-Slavery and Aborigines Protection Society that people were dropping dead of hunger in the lanes of Kent.

But all this was in the future. For the moment, Minero's need was to leave the scene as rapidly as possible.

Without informing his fellow directors he despatched his wife to a villa near Mérida, where, with the proceeds of a dishonest sale, he would join her.

Orestes Minero's conversation with Alonso in the Café Nanay resulted in the purchase that week of 430 hectares of "prime plantation" on the left bank of the Putumayo, 270 kilometres from Belén. Sold on behalf of the Peruvian Amazon Company, the Delicias estate was bordered on the east by land belonging to Orestes Minero himself, on the west by the Rio Yagua and on the north and south by open country.

Alonso was pleased to note that the contract was signed in accordance with articles 73 and 79 of the regulations pertaining to "terrenos de montaña".

The ceremony took place in a dingy office off the Plaza Clavero. Drawing up the trouser on his left leg, and unwrapping a bandage from his calf, Alonso released from its folds the gold sovereigns which had become an increasing worry.

"It's three days down stream," El Gordo informed the Portuguese accountant. "Two if you're lucky." Twirling a bunch of keys on a gold chain, he led Alonso back to the map on the wall. The map showed his estate in the shape of a large T.

"It's like paradise."

Alonso was in high spirits after his purchase. He returned to the Palace Hotel to find his wife arguing with the manager. The argument concerned the work of Fra Angelico's pupil.

"He says it's too big for that door."

"Look, señor."

Alonso looked. It was indeed too big for the door. There and then he decided to present the Annunciation to the recently completed cathedral in the Plaza de Armas.

"I'm not sure I liked it anyway," he lied.

Alonso left Manuela in Belén where she was diverted by the discovery of a building by her father's mentor, Eiffel, and houses along the front glazed with the blue and white tiles of Portugal.

Three days later he reached his plantation at Delicias. Instead of paradise, he found a roofless hut in an overgrown clearing. On all sides the jungle reared, its silence broken only by the patter of great drops falling from the trees.

"Green hell," said the boatman. Alonso did not reply. He stared at the unbroken wall of green, his mouth convulsing and threatening to swallow his nose.

It was not what he had expected, but Alonso was no man for jeremiads. For over a year he made a go of it, believing his fortune lay in growing the smooth-barked jevea trees in lines that imitated the plantations of Ceylon and Assam where production already outstripped the Amazon. What Alonso failed to realize was the impossibility of doing the same in a rainforest of parasites. The grey jevea only survived by scattering its seeds. Planted in a line, row on row, it lay exposed to any predator that came along.

He was lamenting the sorry state of his trees when a man climbed up from the river, accompanied by four Indians carrying Winchester .44s. The man introduced himself as an employee of the Peruvian Amazon Company. He wished to know what Señor Silves was doing on company property. Alonso explained the contract he had signed with Orestes Minero twelve months back.

"Minero is nothing but a thief," swore the man. Not only had Minero sold at a reasonable premium, he had done so with a property of which not a single leaf on a single tree belonged to him.

"You are trespassing," the man said. "You have two days to leave."

Alonso knew it was useless to protest. Although Casement's Blue

Book had made everyone consonant with the methods employed by the "civilizing" company, its publication had not effected changes in company policy. Three months before a Colombian grower at Nueva España had been chained to a tree while his wife was dragged onto the porch and raped in front of him.

Alonso could not contemplate the same fate for Manuela, whose body was racked by malaria, whose eyes became glutinous in the sun.

Clenched with shame at his easy deception by Minero, Alonso made for the town of Rapoto, five days upriver.

It was a small settlement of wooden houses. In the middle of the square was a green bust of Admiral Grau. On the edge, a factory. At night the factory's refuse was humped on the roofs and picked clean by vultures. It was forbidden to shoot the vultures. They were about the only thing protected by law.

"This is the back of beyond," whispered Manuela.

"No," said Alonso. "It's further."

They settled in a two-storey house overlooking the square. At night Alonso would sit drinking brandy beneath his ivory crucifix and dreaming of Portugal and the gold library at Coimbra, where he realized he had been so happy.

Despite some muttering of legal action, he did not refer again to his 430 hectares of prime plantation. He reverted, instead, to his old profession. By the light of a kerosene lamp, he kept the accounts of local merchants and innumerate caucheros. Rubber from this area was only subject to the Peruvian Export Duty of 2d. per pound. The duty in Brazil was over 4s. per pound. Many saw the benefit of trading or appearing to trade from the region. Word of Alonso's meticulous, professional eye spread slowly up the Curaclo. Within two years he was clacking the pearly red beads of his abacus over ledger books from plantations half way to Manaus.

He wasn't rich but his stomach for wealth had contracted. He could live more or less as he wanted. Once a year he gave a large picnic in a clearing on the Curaclo to which he invited the factory's manager, Father Felipe, the police chief and two or three of his clients.

Once the Portuguese Vice-Consul attended and spilled wine over his clean white jacket in a patch the shape of Portugal.

Manuela, as beautiful as ever, slipped fraily into the shadows with her lives of Portugal's heroes. She said "Good afternoon" to visitors but considered it indelicate to carry on a conversation. Parsimony required that she wait at table on her husband and his guests. Her own meal she ate with the children afterwards. She had borne two. A daughter, Consuelo, and a year later, in Alonso's fortieth year, a son. He was christened Henriques in memory of Alonso's professor and Portugal's greatest navigator.

A month after Henriques' birth, Manuela was squeezing avocados in the market when Father Felipe touched her arm and told her Europe was at war.

The only person in Rapoto to be affected by this news was Alonso. He felt a middle-aged man now, with a turkey flap of skin about his neck. More than ever he felt a stranger in a strange land. Due to a border dispute between Colombia and Peru, the town he had ended up in, along with its surrounding forest, had since become res nullius. An area the size of Portugal was suddenly ungoverned by any power – not even by the Peruvian Amazon Company.

Yet at home Alonso's own civilization was disintegrating.

In March 1916, Portugal entered the war on the side of Great Britain. That autumn, compounding his sense of apocalypse, Alonso heard of an eight-year-old shepherdess who had been throwing stones down a hill near Fátima when she was visited by the Angel of Peace. A later report described how the Virgin herself had appeared above a small bush, making the sound of a horse-fly in an empty water-pot. The Virgin's repeated warnings of "annihilating nations" affected Alonso in an unexpected way.

One night, in 1917, Alonso listened to Father Felipe's account of bread riots in Lisbon. When the priest had departed, he folded his glasses, lowered the wick of his kerosene lamp and closed his books.

"Botofe bo le iwa. Rubber is death," he announced mysteriously. "But I'm damned if I can't do something with that plantation."

Next morning, while the sun was still peaching the sky, he headed upstream in his best trilby and a long canoe containing his phonograph, five fados and the arias from *Lucia di Lammermoor*.

*

One of Henriques' first memories was of entering his parents' room to see his mother in a lush blue gown the colour of lapis lazuli. In one hand she held the Goanese crucifix. In the other the matriculation photograph of her husband at which she mumbled incoherently. On her head she wore his hat.

Almost a year after Alonso's disappearance, an embarrassed Indian had been spotted using the trilby as a loincloth, having scooped it off an island in the Curaclo.

Henriques never saw his mother wear coloured clothes again. From cockcrow to sunset, she dressed in black and fidgeted with a rosary made from the beads of Alonso's abacus. People resting from the noon sun on Father Felipe's thick pews knew her as the bicho triste – the sad dung beetle.

Considering his profession, it was surprising how few arrangements Alonso had left for his family. There was no insurance policy and nothing but a few sovereigns in the Banco de Crédito in Belén.

With Consuelo and Henriques, Manuela moved into a two-bedroom house on the outskirts of town. After a month she was forced to seek employment. For 190 soles a week she worked at the local factory which supplied hypochondriacs and beauticians in Europe with medicinal teas, restoratives and oil from palm tree kernels – oil, it was sworn, which would make hair regrow on an old door mat.

Each day after feeding her chickens, she walked the eight hundred yards to the shed where the oil was canned. Here she slipped into a pair of white overalls several sizes too large and sat on a stool with a drumstick. With this she tapped the tins on the conveyor belt to hear if they were full. It was, the manager argued reasonably, an undemanding job which was why they could only pay her 190 soles. Nevertheless, given the temperament of his German machines, it was a job that had to be done.

One day, after eight years, a can of hair oil resounded empty. Manuela abandoned her stool, her drumsticks and her overalls and on reaching home told her teenage daughter she could never return to the factory. Consuelo climbed from her hammock and from then on attended her mother in everything. She washed her clothes, she prepared her meals, she read her the account of King Sebastián's expedition in 1578 to subdue the Saracen. Manuela's only response was to sit blankly kneading her rosary.

Sometimes Consuelo would stumble on her watching meteors from the slope opposite and making strange prophecies. Once she caught her heaving stones into a pattern with bleeding nails. After she had finished, Consuelo led her gently home. Later when she went outside to break a chicken's neck, she saw a line of great uneven letters on the hillside spelling CRISTO VIENE.

Henriques was sixteen when he decided to find out about his father. A river steamer arrived in Rapoto and he overheard its captain mention Delicias to his Indian mate. Henriques was on deck before the boat had nudged the jetty. The captain looked at the thin, tallow-skinned boy and nodded at the Indian. Without a word, he disappeared below. The Indian, who wore rouge and reeked of cane spirit, agreed to take Henriques for the price of 100 soles if he also collected fuel.

Close to, Henriques noticed that one of his eyes was green, the other brown. The rouge disguised the fissures left by verruga fever.

The *Libertad* pushed its way north through air that was black with gnats and heavy with leafmould. Every few hours Henriques leapt ashore to gather wood for the cooking stove. At night, the captain gave him a slab of dried fish and pinched him with a friendly leer between the legs.

All next day they steamed through the tannic waters.

Late the following afternoon, they reached a settlement consisting of several small houses, a larger building which leant against a derelict watchtower and a church with a roof made of flattened kerosene cans.

"Tonight Dos de Mayo," snorted the captain. "Tomorrow, Delicias." They were the only words Henriques heard him speak.

Dos de Mayo was a garrison town. It contained four soldiers who possessed a single uniform between them. Pigs, dogs and chickens ran freely through the rooms.

The captain, his mate and Henriques ate with the soldiers. Afterwards the captain opened a bottle of rum. Towards midnight, one of the soldiers, the one with the uniform, shouted "Let's dance!" Voices and hands were raised in accord. Chairs were scraped to the walls. From behind a Chinese screen rose the sound of a scratched phonograph.

As the *Libertad*'s captain began a grotesque mince with his mate, Henriques realized the wail was familiar. He made his way through the dancers. Behind the screen, he found his body reflected in the horn of his parents' wedding present. From the dark hole in the brass spewed the maddening, wrenching, out-of-time notes of Alonso's favourite fado, "Disse-te adeus e morri".

Of the three records containing highlights from *Lucia di Lammermoor* there was no sign.

The corporal in uniform repented that the padre was the one who really knew the story. But the padre had gone. How terrible that the padre had gone. What he, the corporal, remembered of the story that the padre told him was this: Many years ago, ten perhaps, a man – an unprepossessing fellow, not a jungle type, although he was heading into it – asked the padre if he would look after the phonograph and the collection of warped disks. He would be back later to collect them. That's fine, the padre said. But when he didn't come, the padre gave them to the garrison. It was not the padre's kind of music. And the man, what happened to the man? Who knows? What happens to any man in the jungle? He may have struck lucky and got out, to Paris, Salamanca, Rome. But then, he may not. In his time in this district, he, the corporal, had found, he could count it on his hand, a man eaten by a puma at San Ramón, at Suche a man eaten by the Boras, at Delicias a man eaten by the fishes. And what happened to their bodies? Their bodies?

The padre put their bodies in the cemetery, of course.

When everyone was asleep, Henriques took a lamp and walked to the cemetery. He held the light over the wooden crosses until he came to one that told of an unknown man, found drowned near Delicias.

He put down the lamp and began digging with his machete. Near the surface, he unearthed a large sack. Inside was a piece of cloth and several skeletal remains. Henriques turned over the skull. Seeing the teeth, he had no doubt it belonged to his father.

Alonso's second resting place was a far corner in the cemetery of San Francisco church, beside an adobe wall. Henriques led the mourners. Once or twice on the path to the grave, he slowed down, putting distance between the pall bearers and those who followed. Unable to afford a coffin with a satin lining, he did not want his mother to hear at every step the rattle of her husband's bones.

The arrival in Rapoto of Alonso's remains restored Manuela to calm. She made several visits to the church in which it was observed she not only greeted Father Felipe but remembered the catechism. At home a name came and stayed on her lips.

"Mamá," Henriques said at last, "who is this El Gordo?"

Piecing together the stammered fragments, he learnt for the first time of the fatal transaction which had destroyed his father. Holding his mother's mottled hand, he made a vow.

Orestes Minero had sailed for Europe twenty-three years before. He never thought to return. He was leaving Belén not a moment too soon and with it the sobriquet by which he was known. Several months would pass before his baptismal name rolled easily from his tongue. By then he had met the mole-like financiers with whom he was to invest Alonso's money; men who were to make him into a wealthy, even respectable figure in the clearing houses of Milan, Zurich and Madrid.

He exchanged his spats for English brogues and his grey suit for Donegal tweed, but a bunch of keys still rustled from his hip. As his conscience cleared, so did his past. He founded a scholarship in his name at the University of Mérida and endowed an orphanage in Tordesillas. It was a gesture of gratitude, he explained ruffling the head of his son, Miguel, for his own upbringing at a similar institution in Belén.

Nor was Belén deaf to such activities. In 1934, with the support of both the Departmental Assembly and the Chamber of Commerce, the Mayor extended a warm invitation and the hope that Orestes Minero would accept the honour of Huésped Ilustre de la Ciudad.

In September of that year, Orestes Minero consented.

In December of that year, Henriques arrived in Belén to look for him.

It was fortunate for Henriques that on arriving in Belén he chose to stay at the pension owned and run by Madame Zumate and her three daughters. This large, rollicking woman hailed from Armenia but had forgotten her mother language as she had forgotten the names of her lovers. She had a tongue like a hornet and a heart of gold. It went out to the young man. Yes, she knew El Gordo. She had once spent a night with him. She remembered how he had folded his clothes, down to his socks, on the chair. She remembered his cold white hairless legs which made her toes curl and when she saw his beaming photo in the paper she shook her merry head.

"Por Dios," she said. "So the rat's become a cat."

In those twenty-three years, Orestes Minero had not given a second thought to the bucktoothed Portuguese accountant and the trans-action upon which rested his fortune, his reputation and the freedom of his city.

It was a city he had left as an inconspicuous chancer. It was a city to which he returned, with his wife and child, as a modest hero. It was a city, he mused benignly while strolling jacket in hand along Calle Próspero and tipping his hat to the notary Miguel Lache who thought he recognized the face, that he must endow with some enduring monument.

He was thinking along the lines of a bronze statue when he saw the sign of the Hotel Liberty. He wondered if that old whore Zumate remembered him. As he crossed the street to find out, Orestes Minero felt a sudden blow to his right buttock. Spinning clumsily he caught sight of his precious keys spilling to the pavement; then the young man from whose hand peeked the dull tip of a machete.

Orestes Minero never walked in a straight line again. The injury to his hip – Henriques had hacked through the slack flesh to just below the pancreas – ensured that to move forward he would have to sway sideways from one leg to another like one of the square's pigeons. Henriques, he knew, would have struck again had he not in a flash and after all these years seen the father in the son and, falling to the ground, blabbered Alonso's name as the blood puddled about his knees.

Later, in the house in Calle Putumayo where he remained till his death, Orestes Minero returned Alonso's sum, with twenty-three years interest. Henriques would take no more. As his father might have wished, he had squared an account. The sum would keep his mother in comfort and restore some lustre to the family name.

With the money, Henriques bought a large house two streets away from Minero on the corner of Calle Raimondi. Here he installed Manuela and his sister. Then he made for the jungle, to find the trail his father lost.

It was the end of the rainy season and the river still high when Henriques reached Delicias. For a month he cut down the forest. For a month it crept back so quickly that when he left his stick in the ground it grew into a tree. Then it let him be.

Twice he was attacked by a herd of wild pigs, once by a small puma. He learnt to rub his wounds with tobacco juice and live off leaf-cutting ants and dye his face with berries to keep the flies away.

He was not like other caucheros, half-caste rubber men stranded by the slump, who in a single week of riotous living spent the income of a year. He passed their settlements on the way to his distant tributary. They lived in rickety huts near the river, shooting cat-fish from their porches and digging crab ticks from their skin.

Invariably they bore the title Colonel. But their Indian workers knew them by the Bora for Armadillo. Because they only looked back – to the time of the rubber boom. All that remained of the boom were mounds of rusty machinery and a handful of whittled mistresses who wore Aquascutum stockings and drank tepid champagne out of gourds.

Henriques rarely left Delicias. When he did it was to sail with a laden boat for Belén.

He was at his mother's side when she died.

(Manuela's last years had been her happiest. In Belén she had made stimulating new friends with whom she could freely discuss the subjects that had animated her as a young woman. It was even rumoured she might have given her heart to one of them, which was why she died with a smile on her face.

Another interpretation had it that, smelling the creosotic fumes on Henriques' shirt, she was imagining herself again among the smoked hams of her grandmother's store in Oporto.)

He was at his sister's side when she married Diego Guzmán, the Mayor's youngest son. He gave the couple the deeds to the house in Belén and a short, solemn toast. Then before the dancing began he returned to the jungle. "He needs Delicias," Consuelo explained to the groom. "He is making something out of nothing."

Henriques was indeed making something out of nothing. The price of rubber rose again, not to the giddy heights of the boom, but to a level which earned a profit. This he supplemented by growing small-grained Carolina rice and importing cattle. His Indians had never seen cows before. On the day the animals arrived, they painted their faces with red urucum and leapt into the trees.

If Henriques was unusual in the money he was making from the jungle, he was unique for the esteem in which he was held by those who worked for him.

He in his turn understood their melancholy. It was the melancholy of a race that knew it was dying. He nodded when his mayordomo told how he came from a tribe descended from strange birds and how his wife had been created by the God Wako from tobacco smoke. He never put himself in the way of Antipa and Teberos when they asked for a few days leave, though he was well aware of their destination and the Colombian planter they would kill. The man had mutilated three of their cousins. Henriques knew they would eat his tongue for wisdom, his heart for courage and for fertility make their women chew his genitals.

He also shared their resignation. He ascribed theirs to an ability to count to infinity; his to the knowledge he was never made for the jungle. It was a resignation that came upon him at night when he sat still as a bird, listening to the notes that welled from flutes of human bone. These forlorn notes invoked the tree spirits.

They reminded Henriques of his father's fados.

Henriques was thirty-one when he left the jungle. One day he visited Señora Lache's cake-shop in Belén to queue for a rich purple pudding – a luxury he allowed himself after unloading his latex. He reached the counter and was told the last mazamorra morada had gone. Downcast, he made for the door where he met Colina Chorrera. She had heard his question. She had seen the expression on his face. She didn't want the cake, she told him. It was a cousin's birthday. Any cake would do.

They spent the rest of the morning picking at the purple pudding on a bench in the square. That afternoon he attended the birthday party. Ten days later, days which he spent in Belén, he knelt formally on her parents' parquet floor and asked her to marry him. He was sorry to be so forward, he said, but in his family a short courtship was a tradition.

On returning to Delicias, Henriques summoned his Indians and handed each a purse of gold. He told them he was leaving. They assembled on the river bank and wailed as he left, all except Tabaros, the human-flute-player, who took his hand and told him it was good. He had spilled chicha to the spirits and read his fortune in the coca leaves.

Everything was good for Señor Henriques and his beautiful wife-to-be. He did not mention he had foreseen death by water.

Colina Chorrera was the daughter of an unassuming but well-to-do merchant who had ten mills to his Spanish name, including the factory in Rapoto. She was a tall, proud girl with short auburn hair and a chin so round that as a child old men would chuck it and say one day she'd grow up to break hearts. She never did. Like Manuela

Silves, she was more interested in books than boys and though she spoke without a blush to the young men of Belén, it was clear from her mocking laughter what she thought of them.

She was twenty-five when she looked into Henriques' eyes and found there something commensurate with the men created by her authors. Whereas Henriques' mother had been devoted to history, the world as it had been, Colina's passion was for the world as it might be. She smelt of novels. Under her guidance, Henriques developed a taste for Benito Pérez Galdós, Kipling and Hardy (whose work he consumed in bed with a milk punch). Under his instruction, Colina discovered a life outside her parents' library.

Once in the early days after the scissor ants had eaten her best frock, he joked about her lack of worldly ways. Her hands dropped to her hip and her round chin flashed out. "Silves," she said, rolling her dark brows. "And you thought I was a virgin when I married you." Henriques squinted thoughtfully. "No, I didn't," he said. In reply Colina hoisted her red dress above her head and let it drop. They twisted and plunged in the cotton shadows until the sweat on their backs caught the moon.

When they married, Consuelo had offered them back the house in Raimondi. Henriques declined. With his young wife, he went to live near Rapoto. As a wedding gift, Colina's father had given Henriques charge of his canning plant. He needed a reliable manager, one who could adapt to the wind from wherever it blew. The Second World War had ended the demand for restoratives and medicinal teas. Now Europeans wanted barbasco for their insecticides, essence of rosewood for their perfumes, and the liver oil of stingrays for bronchitis. Only the market for the palm tree kernel remained unchanged.

The young Silveses lived comfortably in a roomy house which Colina filled with heliotrope. In January 1948, during the second year of their marriage, she conceived. The baby was a girl with eyes the colour of her grandmother's dress and a mop of dark hair like a door mat.

In one of the last services to be conducted by Father Felipe, she was christened Elena Colina Silves.

Part Two

1986

Chapter 6

THREE YEARS HAD PASSED since the disappearance of Elena Silves and her sighting by the old men in the square.

Shortly before nine in the morning, an hour and a half later than scheduled, the boat from Requena pulled into its berth below the Malecón. Among the last to step from the *Victoria Regia*'s plank was a tall, thin man in his late thirties.

He carried a briefcase, tied with a length of rope through its handle, and was dressed in a brown suit – the jacket more faded than the trousers (suggesting they had not been worn together, and the trousers, which were flared, hardly at all). It was a suit cut to a pattern out of fashion.

The man joined the single file of passengers ascending the steep bank. When he reached the top he turned left along the Malecón until he came into the cathedral square. Hearing the rattle of small change in Sebastián's bucket, he stopped. He looked down at the dark triangular shape of Sebastián beside his newspapers. A brown wrist, like a turtle neck, was the only flesh visible under the black hood. It responded to his presence with another shake of the yellow bucket. The man seemed about to say something, but decided against it. He added several coins, picked up a paper and walked on.

He was making for the Café Nanay when a woman pushed open its glass door and walked straight into him. She apologized, and he apologized in return. As the woman brushed herself down, she could not help noticing he was a good-looking man – one of those blond Indian mulattos which in Brazil they called mameluco. His fair hair – slightly fairer than the moustache he stroked – fell in curls about his collar. His narrow eyes were green and steady. Had he looked in better health he would have been a most attractive man.

"I'm late," she said and hurried out across the square.

He entered the café.

The Nanay was a single room crowded with tables, beer crates and a jukebox. In its day it had been a favourite meeting place for the city's business community who discussed their whisky shipments from Leticia over tall glasses of café con leche. Like most of the objects under discussion, the coffee they drank had usually been winked through the customs.

Behind the jukebox was a staircase. The man had never seen anyone climb it. He imagined the steps led to a room where larger deals were hatched and sealed by those trafficking in everything from cocaine to assassination.

On this day, the café was empty. He ordered a coffee and a sandwich from the boy behind the counter, then sat down at a table overlooking the square.

It was 9.05 by his watch. Though the boat had been late, another 25 minutes remained before his appointment with the Bishop.

The boy walked over with his sandwich and coffee. He thanked him. He looked into the boy's face but he didn't recognize it. He hadn't recognized the face of the woman either. In fact, he wondered just whose face he would recognize in Belén.

After six years he wondered who would recognize him.

Pía Zumate, perhaps. Capitán Velarde. But the policeman wouldn't be on his guard, not now. And Sebastián, to whom he had nearly spoken. Otherwise, he couldn't think of anyone – except Edith.

He swallowed a mouthful of coffee and looked out of the window. In the centre of the square, he saw three old men on a bench. The face of the one on the left was lost under a newspaper. The paper gently rose and fell in time with the old man's breathing. The headline could be read from the table. BRUTAL REVENGE KILLING, it ran. VIOLENCE REACHES SORETO.

He unfolded his copy of *El Oriente*. The headline described the murder of four villagers in Cabaña, a village to the far south of Soreto. The villagers had been accused of co-operating with the armed forces. The executioners had been led by a woman.

"In an unusual departure from their traditional policy of silence, the Shining Path has accepted responsibility for the murders. The action was in retaliation for the massacre of 257 prisoners last week at Lima's San Francisco prison."

In a brief statement Capitán Velarde, Belén's new Deputy Chief of Police, promised his men would not rest until the delinquent murderers had been brought to justice.

The rest of the page was devoted to the prison massacre in Lima of the week before. A spokesman for the military insisted that San Francisco's governor himself had invited the armed forces to quell the mutiny. A novice in the shanty-town above said the gunfire had continued through the night like the popping of grilled maize. A spokesman for the government confirmed that all survivors had been moved to the penitentiary of San Eduardo in the suburb of Monterrico.

There was a blurred photograph of the bombed-out dormitory and beneath, a list of those presumed dead. The man's expression changed only once, when he saw the fifth name on the list.

It was his own.

Gabriel finished his coffee. He rose, took the glass to the counter and asked for another. He checked his pockets for money. There was enough to get through the morning. After that, he would have to rely on Edith.

While the boy reheated the milk, Gabriel made his way to the jukebox in the shadows under the staircase. He looked down through the curved glass dome, searching for a particular record. When he found it, he inserted a coin. There was the sound of crackling, then music.

He returned to his table where he sat, leaning on his briefcase, listening.

Hipólito used to sit here, pounding the table with a purple fist so that the sugar bounced out of its bowl and the coffee had to be mopped up with a tut-tut by Elena. He hadn't thought of Hipólito for a long time. Nor Elena.

Without her he wouldn't be here.

Two weeks, that's all, since Elena's reappearance in the pages of a three-year-old copy of *El Oriente*. The newspaper had been used to wrap a book requested by Gabriel (a banned biography of Mariátegui). Even then, the chances of him seeing the item were slight had he not torn out the centre spread to clean his feet and found himself immobilized by A.W.'s brief account of Sister Colina's escape from the convent of Santa Clara.

Immediately, he did something he had never done in six years. He arranged a palanca. The palanca was his childhood friend and comrade, and the man who had sent the book, Julio Ángel Medina.

Gabriel's face hardened at the memory of Julio as they passed in the guardroom corridor. The corridor was rancid with detergent. Someone had shot away the overhead bulb.

"Thanks, Julio." They touched hands in the dark.

"You know I'd do anything for you, Gabriel."

"You understand, don't you?"

"Yes."

"The chances are hopeless, but I've got to find out."

"Gabriel, I understand."

It was too much for Oliveira, the guard, who didn't want to hear why Chino was taking a palanca all of a sudden and was beginning to regret, despite the wad of notes in his pocket, that he hadn't pressed for an extra packet of Hamilton Lights. He pushed Gabriel in the back, towards the door in the wall.

"Two weeks, Chino. That's all you've got. Then your friend here gets his balls chewed off."

Twenty-four hours later Gabriel was in Arequipa, having slept the night on the bus. In a shop window he saw the moustache he was growing to match the portrait in his documents. He spent the next night on a bench at the station. At six in the morning, he boarded the bus to Silar. Raindrops appeared on the windscreen as it headed out, late, over the Bolognesi bridge.

The road which lifted across the plateau like a rifle barrel began to coil and twist once they reached the first pass, but the rain still gave it the sheen of gun-metal. In the afternoon the bus stopped by a roadside stall selling fruit and bread. The driver advised any passenger who hadn't done so to stock up. This was the last food they'd see for twelve hours. Gabriel bought a loaf of stale bread and six oranges. The stall had been erected where the tarmac ran out.

Because of the weather, the journey to Silar took longer than two and a half days. Gabriel spent most of the time staring blankly through the window from a seat in the back. Once he asked the mother of a little girl when they would get to Silar. She sat against the other window reading a photo-story and chain-smoking. Her daughter's eyes rolled open and looked up at him.

"Further on, after La Falda. I'll tell you." She brushed some ash off her jeans and returned to the story. The girl closed her eyes.

He reread the paper he had bought in Arequipa. On this day in 1610, he learnt, Philip III established the Inquisition in Cartagena. On the same date in 1925, Mao Tse Tung made his historic return to Hunan. It was the actress Cyd Charisse's birthday.

He dozed until the bus entered a town, the first they had come to. The woman seemed prepared for his questioning glance. She smiled and shook her head.

"La Falda," called the driver, looking up into a juddering mirror. "La Falda, La Falda," he repeated.

No one got in or out and the bus lurched off.

They came to Silar in mid-afternoon. He felt the little girl tug at his arm. "Silar," she whispered. In the corner her mother slept. Gabriel was leaving when a soldier pushed past him.

"All out! Come on, all out! And your luggage."

They filed into the Guardia Civil station. No one seemed concerned, except the driver. He looked at the soldiers going through his bus, shaking his head.

Gabriel waited behind a fat man in a cloth cap. As they queued to present documents and open their cases, an officer appeared. He walked down the line. He had brown eyes that never blinked and a mouth he kept shut until he came to Gabriel.

"Name?"

"Julio Ángel Medina."

"Documents."

His eyes remained on Gabriel as he flicked through the forged pages.

"Destination?"

"Here. Silar."

"Ever been to Cabaña, Señor Medina?"

He looked intently at Gabriel.

"Cabaña?"

"That's right. Cabaña."

"No."

"Ever heard of it?"

"No."

"What's a pituco from Lima doing in these parts?"

"I'm writing a story for *Caretas*," Gabriel replied as if his presence in the sierra was a triumph of duty over disdain. "About nuns."

The officer decided to smile. His sister was a nun, God alone knew why. With the Bethlemites. Unhealthy lot. Did he know them? They all had boils on their chins and man's hands and thick glasses. He was sorry for this delay, but. . .

"Capitán, Capitán," interrupted a soldier from behind the low table. He had been searching the mother's bags and now held up her documents.

"No, later dear," she was telling her daughter, nervously lighting a cigarette. She still had rings of sleep round her eyes.

"Momentito," snapped the captain, returning Gabriel's identity card.

Eventually, they were allowed back into the bus, all except the mother and her girl.

No one spoke as they drove into the centre of Silar. No one looked at each other, not even the driver at the mirror. The absence of the two passengers was like the removal of a tongue. When the bus stopped in the Calle Tristan, it disgorged people who wished to go their own way.

Gabriel walked down the street until he found a green Dodge taxi.

"Santa Clara."

The taxi reached the convent in under five minutes. He leant over the seat, counting out change, but his attention was so drawn to the building on the other side of the road that an exasperated driver had to pick the coins from his palm.

For a moment Gabriel stood on the pavement, coming to terms with the place which might have contained Elena for the last twenty years, whose white walls stretched either side of an open gate, thirty feet high, for a block. He crossed the road.

"No es turístico," said a woman selling biscuits at the entrance. Further along a man with a wire brush was scraping away the large red letters which had been sprayed on the wall. VIVA PRESIDENTE EZEQUIEL!

The same name remained indelible on the side of the mountain at the end of the street.

"Please. Can't I look inside?"

The woman hesitated, then wheeled her stand a foot or two along the pavement, allowing room to slip by.

The patio lay in shadow. There was a padlocked door on the right and, beneath a concrete sign with the word Silencio, a wooden tournière. A schoolgirl sat on a bench against the wall, her legs up, reading a book. Her mother, on the bench beside her, delivered a scolding, painting a finger nail as she did so. Neither paid attention to Gabriel.

He revolved the tournière. As it span, he bent to look at the space between the frame and the wall. He revolved it several times, then returned to the entrance where he bought a biscuit in the shape of a star.

Gabriel still had its dry, salty taste in his mouth an hour later when he entered the offices of *El Matutino* in Calle Molgar. The building, sandwiched between a tour company and a bookshop offering mimeograph services, was one of the few two-storeyed houses in Silar. A number of brass plaques encrusting the entrance announced that the ground floor was rented out to a lawyer, a doctor and an oculist.

"I'm looking for someone who might work here," he told the receptionist. "I don't have the name. Just the initials."

The woman smiled when she saw them. "That'll be Arturo."

It was a bad time for Arturo Walker, *El Oriente*'s stringer in Silar. His grey cardigan and once chubby face bore this in their shapelessness. The family business – a chain of three hardware stores – was one step away from the receiver's after an imprudent investment on the Arequipa bourse. His wife, he suspected, following the discovery of four prophylactics in the pocket of her smartest jacket, was conducting an affair with the branch manager of the Banco de Crédito. And his boss had taken off to Argentina on a skiing holiday.

Normally, his boss's absence would have been welcome. When not fulfilling his commitment as *El Oriente*'s correspondent in Silar, Arturo acted as features editor on the local paper, a position he much preferred given the distance and the antipathy (at least on Silar's part) existing between the two cities. Though *El Matutino*'s circulation was tiny compared with Belén's *El Oriente*, Arturo enjoyed greater scope in writing about what interested him. Especially when his editor was away.

For the past two days, however, he had realized his duties this week would consist not in writing anything himself, but in reworking agency copy from Lima.

Most of this concerned the San Francisco massacre.

Even Arturo Walker had to admit it was a story which took precedence over his appreciation of Simón Bolívar's death in exile. That article, provisionally subtitled "Take our bags to the boat, they don't like us anymore", would once again have to wait.

It was at times like these that Arturo Walker – a second-generation Peruvian and the grandson of a Macclesfield carpenter – wished he was not Peruvian at all. But a visit to the British Consulate in Arequipa had confirmed what he feared, that he was stuck with the land of Henry Walker's adoption, rattling like a can on his tail.

He was therefore impatient with the man who walked into his office that afternoon and demanded to know about a dead and irritating story. Had he not announced himself as a journalist from *Caretas*, Arturo Walker would have sent him packing. Not that he seemed particularly well informed. The fellow didn't have a clue about the story which Arturo had just spent a day putting to bed.

"What massacre?"

"You, a journalist, and you haven't heard? Jesus."

Arturo filled him in as he burrowed through the filing cabinet. "According to the government it's all a terrible mistake. Last night the president was televised live in the ruins of the dormitory. You should have heard his voice. 'Either all the culprits go, or I go.' At the moment everything is pure speculation. The culprits, the reason for the mutiny, the names and number of the dead. Ah, here we are."

He produced a sheet of paper from a green folder. Shutting the cabinet with his knee, he held the page at arm's length. For a moment, he did not see the small cutting glued to its centre and underneath the pencilled date, 3 March 1983. Instead he saw the demonic shapes of his three hardware stores, a wife who didn't love him, a brother in Miami who could afford a boat.

Gabriel took the page from him. His face was pale. "That's all?"

"That's all."

"You wrote this?"

"If you can call it writing," shrugged Arturo, who, if he hadn't become an average journalist, was not above believing that his attention to detail and observation of character would have made him a good novelist.

"Why didn't you follow it up?"

A woman entered carrying an electric typewriter. She deposited it on the table. "It works, señor. Only the fuse."

Arturo thanked her, glad of the distraction. "I can't remember," he replied, pressing his fingers on letters that refused to tap. "This happened three years ago, for God's sake."

The explanation remained a long time in the air. Gabriel said nothing. Arturo bit his lip. If the window wasn't shuttered he'd have looked out of it, like his boss had done. More vividly than he cared, he remembered the meaningless shuffle of papers on the desk, the muttered phrases – "highest authority", "know how you feel", "for her own good" – until with a hand on wood came the exasperated shout, "All right, so it's Bishop Barrantes who's made us spike it." That was the turning point, Arturo saw now. He should have stuck his neck out or got out. Gone to the capital, worked for a decent paper where they didn't bend to pressure from corrupt clergymen fifteen hundred miles away in the jungle. A paper like *Caretas*.

"Anyway, how did you find that?" He smacked the page held by Gabriel.

"It's on file."

"They file our stuff in Lima?"

"The most interesting."

Arturo tapped thoughtfully at the obstinate key board. He couldn't conceal his pride.

"I don't suppose there's any harm telling you." With a resounding click and spring of machinery, his index finger found a button that responded to its probing.

"I was with Father Palacio when the Mother Superior rang to say one of her nuns was missing."

Gabriel found Father Palacio over the river, behind the mass table in the Recoleta church.

The congregation was a nun, an Indian girl with a pony tail like a garlic string and a businessman who remained standing for most of the service. "Patrem omnipotentem factorem coeli et terrae visibilium," they chanted as the sun spread its honey on the vault through an onyx window. "Omnium et invisibilium et in unum Dominum."

In his prayers the priest mentioned the dead men in San Francisco. He prayed for their souls and for the souls of those responsible. Gabriel remained seated throughout, his eyes fixed on the communion table and the Virgin towering above him in a haze of blue neon. Then, when the wafer had become Christ and the church had emptied, he walked to the rail.

"Wait for me there," said Father Palacio.

They sat at a table in the communal dining room in a modern building behind the church. On the oilskin cloth a Coca-Cola bottle sprouted four artificial roses. A framed poster of Dali's crucifixion hung on the unpainted wall. Apart from a black piano with a scatter of *Études progressives* on its lid, the room was bare and smelled of cooked guinea-pig from the night before.

Out of his vestments Father Palacio wore a white, tieless shirt, buttoned at the neck.

"Who told you?"

Gabriel told him.

"Of course, of course." Walker had been there. He had found a can of something for the woodworm from his hardware store in Calle Barranco.

"Are you a friend of his wife's?"

"No."

A finger fretted at Father Palacio's lower lip.

"You've been to the convent?"

"This morning. They wouldn't let me in. It was like knocking on a battleship, Father."

"It is," concurred Father Palacio, "highly unusual for a man to be allowed inside."

He filled two mugs from a saucepan, and stirred in spoonfuls of coffee powder which formed lumps in the hot milk.

"Oh dear, this always happens. Do you mind?"

Squashing the blobs in his mug, Father Palacio described the afternoon on which he had been summoned by Madre Ana to hear the general confession of a dying nun, and the moments leading up to the collapse of the sister he discovered was Elena Silves.

"We covered her with a blanket and I went home. Naturally, I was worried, but I made it clear to the Mother Superior she should ring me if she needed to. I cannot say I expected a call. The sisters have their own medic."

He placed his mug on the table and raised his eyes, over the man's shoulder, to the window. It overlooked a small yard containing Father Palicio's pride and joy, a thin puya raimondii which flowered only once every hundred years. He had yet to see its white bud, though he had watered it religiously for twenty of them.

"But she did ring you."

"The following morning. And she was extremely distressed. Sister Colina . . . Elena Silves had been discovered missing."

"Go on."

"To begin with it was feared she had come to and panicked on finding herself in the dark."

He recalled his own return through the blackout, the police whistles, the radios instructing people to cross at street corners, the disembodied flashes of torchlight. He remembered just before he reached home how he stumbled into a couple by a wall. The woman had her hand inside the man's trousers. Seeing the priest, she withdrew it, laughing, burying her face in the man's neck. In that laugh, Father Palacio was confident he recognized Arturo Walker's wife.

"A search was ordered. Finally, when Madre Ana was at her wit's end, the under-prioress came upon a parcel in the laundry room containing Sister Colina's habit. This led to a suspicion something quite different might have happened. The search resumed and at midday they found the rope from the telegraph pole bordering the kitchen yard."

"What did you do?"

"There wasn't much I could do. It was more a matter for Bishop Barrantes in Belén."

"Whom you rang?"

"Whom I rang, and in whose hands it was insisted I leave things."

"And . . .?"

Father Palacio met his eye.

"That was the last I heard."

"She never came back?"

"No," said Father Palacio quietly. "No, she never came back."

"So where is she now?"

"I don't know. If anyone knows anything it's the Bishop – or rather the former Bishop. He was retired last year in circumstances still not entirely clear."

"What's he like?"

"Eucario Barrantes?" The priest contemplated the question.

"There are certain men of God," he said, "who believe the Catholic who is not a revolutionary is living in mortal sin. Eucario Barrantes is not such a man."

"Where do I find him?"

Father Palacio gave an address and the telephone number of a priory in Belén.

"Tell him you want to see his crosses," he added kindly. "He is proud of his collection and might be well disposed to those who share his pride."

"Brrrr," said Gabriel, bringing his elbow down to cause a tremble among the plastic petals. He rose to his feet. His eyes skidded over the bare walls, out into the yard and back into the room.

"I'm sorry."

He lifted his jacket from the back of the chair and picked up his briefcase.

"Sorry," he repeated.

He stopped by the door. He noticed the piano and the scores on its lid, and spread his fingers. He lowered them evenly onto the keys.

"A tuning's long overdue," Father Palacio admitted, responding to the distended chord. "Like that band."

"The band?"

"The band by the river."

"Why," Gabriel asked over his shoulder. "What were they playing?"

"To tell the truth, I'm not very keen on music – that's Father Mariano's piano. But I have a feeling they began with an Ave Maria. Pretty soon after they were onto 'Flor de la cantina' and 'Ojos azules'."

"'Ojos azules'?"

"You know the song. One heard it all the time in the sixties. In fact," said Father Palacio. He tapped his lips. "I remember now. That's what they were playing when she fainted."

In the Café Nanay, the record had come to an end. Gabriel looked at his watch. Another ten minutes. He drained his glass. He drew back his chair from the table. Barrantes was his last hope. After Barrantes, the tarmac ran out.

He rose, inserting another coin in the jukebox. Once more came the sound of crackling as the song he had been listening to began again.

> "Ojos azules no llores,
>   No llores ni tengas amores,
>   Llorarás cuando me vaya,
>   Cuando remedio no haya."

Chapter 7

THERE IS NO BREEZE. In the heat, the gardener pauses under a copa de oro bush. He wipes his forehead, then returns to picking up the yellow leaves flecking the sparse grass.

The square smells of fresh-ground contraband coffee from the Café Nanay. A girl walks into the day from the café's dark recess, holding an ice-cream, and hurries back to work. A dog watches the vanilla dripping from her fingers. It ambles from under a bench and licks the melting drops.

The sound of Sebastián's bucket is joined at the far end of the square by the rattle of a shoe-shine box. The boy rattling the box is hidden by the epaulettes of Admiral Grau. The sun glints on the brave sailor's brow.

Don Wenceslau sighs. In an hour he has hardly seen anyone he knows. He recognizes their faces, not their names. Who has he seen? He spreads a leafy hand to count them.

He has seen Vásquez, with whom he always stops to talk first thing before coming to the bench. He likes to inspect the masato bottles on his barrow, to see there are enough.

And Sebastián, of course. He flattens out a second finger. He squints at the pavement opposite, by the old Club of Dead Parrots, where Sebastián sits in a pyramid of black, holding up his bucket whenever he hears footsteps.

Few know what the face looks like beneath that hood. Don Wenceslau remembers Don Leopoldo thinking he knew. "La Verruga," said Don Leopoldo. "Augustus Zárate referred to it first in 1543 and I believe it is mentioned by Cosme Bueno in *Descripciones Geográficas*." He then repeated in detail Dr Lache's description of the morbid growths, the black swellings, the bleeding warts that characterized the primary stages of the disease.

But Don García disagrees. He does not believe Sebastián suffers from verruga. He believes his disease can only be cured by a dust made from fire-flies.

"He has la uta."

"And what does la uta do?"

"It eats away the face until it is just a hole surrounded by teeth."

Don Wenceslau has never liked to imagine Sebastián's face after that. Instead, he thinks of another face that has passed by them that morning, its nose pointing firmly at the sky – until it notices Don Wenceslau.

"Good morning, Don Wenceslau, and how are you, it's a long time since you entertained us with your amusing stories. . ."

It was the warmth in La Palometa's greeting that caused the man now snoring gently next to him to cover his face with *El Oriente*. But Don García has no grounds for jealousy.

Pía Zumate is called Palometa after a fish with a red fin, because of the henna she still applies to her grey hair in the hope that one day news will come of the Booth liner *Ambrose*'s return to the river, and with it the officer who promised his heart fifty years before, over something he called a pink gin.

Don Wenceslau shivers at the thought of her permanent smile that gives an oval frame to teeth the colour of palm hearts. He has never seen a woman smile like that. It is a smile that has bewitched Don García since he saw it on her young face, seventy years ago, behind the counter of the Salón de Belleza in Juan Próspero, the drug and beauty store now owned by her youngest sister, Dominica.

"She lives in hope," Don García likes to explain. It must be years since anyone has softened her breasts with their touch. Over these years Don García has asked both his companions for their opinion of La Palometa. According to his stomachache Don Wenceslau would reply: "Don García, you know me, you know what I feel, women and melons are hard to know." Or, if after lunch: "There's no such thing as an ugly sweetheart." Or, once, in an unguarded moment: "Why is it as women get older, they look more like men?"

Don García has stopped asking Don Leopoldo, since the time Don Leopoldo replied by saying: "One thing I would say about women. . ."

They had both turned at that, even Don Wenceslau. He never

thought Don Leopoldo believed in anything – except silence and history.

"And. . . what is that?" Don García had asked.

Don Wenceslau cannot help laughing to himself at the memory of Don García's face as Don Leopoldo pronounced.

"A woman with a beard," he had said slowly, "salute at a distance."

Don Wenceslau looks at his hand open with three fingers. Who else has passed this morning? No one, not unless he counts the face at the hotel window. He can't really include a face he doesn't know, though he has grown used to its furtive appearances, one moment pressed to the shutters, the next, away like a hummingbird.

But all this is forgotten as Don Wenceslau sees a shoe-shine boy curl round the base of Admiral Grau. With a whistle, he summons him.

The boy settles at his feet. He opens his box and produces a number of perforated sheets, detaching three of them. Don Wenceslau leans back and extracts a number of coins from his trouser pockets. He counts them out.

"My turn," he tells the boy, with a wink, dropping the money into the box. He folds the three sheets and inserts them in the mouth of the bag at Don Leopoldo's feet.

There are days when it seems the only thing which keeps them going is the prospect of a win on the lottery, but Don Wenceslau wonders what would happen if they did draw the prize and had to turn out that bag to find the tickets. What magnificent wastes would they find among Don Leopoldo's papers, what years of hope, what secrets?

"Now," he says to the boy. "My shoes."

Don Wenceslau always feels important as he lifts his feet onto the wooden stilt, which is why, every day, he indulges in the operation twice. This morning, because of his stomach, he feels in special need of attention.

"No," he says firmly. "That's red and you know it is. I want brown."

He is proud of his shoes. He bought them in a sale from Mr Cazes, the departing British Consul, in 1921. They have leather soles which don't make his feet sweat and long thick laces. Barely decipherable on the place where his heels wriggle are the words Ducker & Son, 12 The Turl, Oxford. For some reason, the boy always tries to polish his Duckers – or Doocares, as Don Wenceslau pronounces them – with a polish the colour of cherry.

"Why do you do that?" he asks in his dyspeptic way.

The boy grins without answering, and scrapes his denim cloth along the scuffed caps. Rouged and browned and blackened from polish, his hands are those of an artist. He taps a sole to indicate he is ready for Don Wenceslau's other foot. Perhaps cherry is cheaper, thinks Don Wenceslau, or brown is in short supply, but the boy never has any trouble in producing the brown tin. It is one of those inexplicable things.

Like the figure in La Palometa's hotel, above the room where he spent the night of his life, where now a sheet hangs out to dry so white he can almost smell it.

He looks at the newspaper sulking beside him. He imagines Don García's eyes closed beneath it, the dreams cavorting under their lids. He looks at Don Leopoldo, who has a fleck of shaving cream in his ear.

"What do you think?" he asks them both.

Don Leopoldo has his eyes shut in the sun. In the lobster glow, he is remembering the shave given him first thing that morning by his barber, and the hair oil applied to his balding head. His face still tingles with the closeness of the blade, sharpened on a strap under the mirror. Don Leopoldo never likes to look at himself in the glass. As his face is squeezed and powdered and sprayed with cold cologne, his eyes fix instead on the deposits of dust on the bumpy wall or the jar of water where the barber dips his comb. That morning his mind had been on a most interesting article he had happened on in the Buenos Aires *Revista*. The article, by Dr López, an historian from Montevideo, argued that the Quechua language was of Pelasgic origin and that the Incas were of Greek descent. A footnote referred to a polemic in another periodical which tendered the thesis that the Incas might have been paper-makers to the

Roman Empire. . .

Aroused by Don Wenceslau, he shakes his head.

"What do I think about what?" he asks with irritation.

"About our friend on the fourth floor."

"Have you seen him?"

"I wanted to know what you thought."

"You know perfectly well what I think."

"You haven't changed your mind?"

Don Leopoldo rubs his eyes as if the soft flesh were dough. No, he has not. In six years, there has been nothing to alter his suspicion that the face belongs to one of the cocaine traffickers who speed the river in gleaming launches.

"I still think he's an Irish peer," says Don Wenceslau, who believes all evils emanated from the land which had given birth to Roger Casement, the insatiable pederast who had blackened the name of Belén.

"That's even more ludicrous than Don García's suggestion," says Don Leopoldo.

At the mention of this name, the newspaper moves. Don García emerges from under the headlines. He seems in a better mood.

"Talking about my Argentine?"

For Don García, the picaflor, there is no other explanation for the soft-shoe shuffle which keeps Pía Zumate awake on the floor below and the American songs which repeat themselves over and over and over again at all times of the day and night, than that their owner is a dancer in exile, an exponent of the Boca's most incautious tangos, a woman locked away by whoever it is that settles the monthly bill and who is only waiting for the appropriate moment to throw open her shutters and let down her coffee-dark hair for Don García to climb.

Don Leopoldo has never made any secret of the fact he considers this interpretation incurably frivolous.

So it is that for want of anything more to say on the subject, the three of them are looking in the direction of the hotel when a light flashes in the entrance lobby as the door of the Café Nanay catches the sun. A man emerges and stands in the brightness of the day. He inspects his watch and makes off down Calle Juan Próspero.

"I am dreaming," says Don Wenceslau. "Tell me I'm dreaming. Surely the bastards. . . "

Don García's reaction is a frightened whisper. "It's not possible. He's a dead man. I've just seen his name in the paper."

Don Leopoldo prefers to believe the evidence of his watery eyes. "Dios," he says, shaking his head.

A noise blares from Juan Próspero. A car drives into the square. "The happiest and the saddest love story ever told. . . " says the loudspeaker on its roof. The square is assailed by information about the day's film at the Cinema Bolognesi. "*The Rubber Man's Daughter*, starring Luis Sintra. . . " The car drives twice round the square and off down Calle Raimondi before anyone speaks again.

It is Don Wenceslau who breaks the silence. He stretches out his feet to inspect their twinkling caps. He wriggles them to catch the sun.

"He must have come back to find her," he says.

Chapter 8

AT 9.30 A.M. Gabriel entered the Franciscan priory in Juan Próspero, four doors down from the Salón de Belleza. It was a small house with ornately grilled windows and a facade of modern tiles. The tiles in the hall were older. They dated back to the rubber boom, when the building belonged to a company manufacturing water-tube boilers.

The hall was in darkness. Gabriel made out the shape of a woman behind the reception desk. She was applying lipstick in the dark. When she saw Gabriel she jumped, put down her compact and touched a switch on the wall. In the light, Gabriel saw clearly the woman's tight white trousers, the overgenerous lips and the bruises on her face where someone may have beaten her. He thought he recognized the woman. He did. They had collided outside the Café Nanay.

"Have you an appointment?"

"Yes. I rang three days ago from Lima."

"Lima?"

"I spoke to someone again yesterday."

"Was it you who rang from Requena?"

"That's right."

She examined the appointments book on her desk. The book was empty except for a name entered in large blue letters.

"Julio Ángel Medina," she reminded herself. "From *Caretas*." She looked up. "You've come to interview His Lordship about his crosses."

"His Lordship?" said Gabriel. "I thought he had retired."

"Yes, but he likes to keep up appearances."

That morning Eucario Barrantes had woken in a great damp patch.

His incontinence had worsened since his enforced retirement and the appointment of a new Bishop to Belén the year before. In his disappointment he consoled himself by accepting most of the invitations he received, from receptions at the Club de Leones to Rotarian dinners at the Hotel Liberty.

In company, with a drink or two, he could forget. Alone in his bed he could not.

It was a disappointment that had taken seed many years before with the vision of Elena Silves; a disappointment fed by his decision to listen to that grison Don Miguel.

It was Don Miguel who had seen the gold at the end of this rainbow.

Poor Bishop. To be struggling through such a no-man's-land.

"A no-man's-land? What're you on about Don Miguel?"

At the bar in the Club de Leones, Don Miguel repeated his phrase, adding a sad smile.

A no-man's-land between the Church's decision on whether to turn the site into an official shrine, and the Church's ability to recoup something from the pilgrims visiting the site.

"There must be thousands, no?" said Don Miguel, urging him to think about it. It was well known the Bishop was in two minds. He should continue to indulge this doubt. The sooner he decided against Elena Silves, the less money Don Miguel could guarantee the offertory.

"And you ought to believe her, Bishop. After all," said Don Miguel, "look at me. I'm the living proof."

The Bishop had looked at him and thought about it. In fact he had thought about nothing else for weeks. The thought of Don Miguel's bribe occupied him as he poured the wine at Mass, it occupied him as he drank it at midday, it occupied him as he passed it from his tormented body in the evening. It was on his mind when he asked Elena's aunt for the umpteenth time about her father's ivory cross from Goa. Nor did it budge a fraction when she told him, Yes, she would sell it, it had brought no luck, and then named a price so ludicrous he was left with no option but to agree that Don Miguel was indeed a living proof and the sooner a diocesan commission was appointed to investigate the vision of Elena Silves the better.

But Bishop Barrantes only knew the fullest flower of his disappointment after Elena Silves' escape from the convent of Santa Clara.

His failure to discover her whereabouts had been greeted in Lima and in Rome with a monstrous frown. They were already tired and suspicious of Barrantes. They were aware it had taken seven years to authenticate the apparition at Fátima. But after eighteen years of prevarication, they smelled a jungle rat. Elena Silves' escape offered the chance to locate it.

The Papal Nuncio was ordered to conduct a discreet investigation. In a despatch to the Curia in Rome, also circulated to the Cardinal Archbishop in Lima, he summarized the results.

Of the twelve members appointed by Barrantes, only seven had found time to discharge their duties. In eighteen years, these members had submitted thirty-seven pages. The Nuncio's gravest charge concerned the Bishop's obsessive devotion to the cross. There was no way, he wrote, that Bishop Barrantes' celebrated collection of crucifixes could have been financed from the stipend due to an Apostolic Vicariate.

Bishop Barrantes was never to know the exact reason for his premature retirement. Not knowing it, he misattributed it, and misattributing it, he felt a certain biliousness towards the world at large and the person he believed responsible.

His reception of Gabriel that morning was tempered by the expectation that a favourable profile in the weekly journal *Caretas* – not a periodical he regularly saw, but one whose influence he didn't deny – would give as much pleasure to his former parishioners as it would discomfort certain quarters in Lima. It was a matter for regret, he saw now, that his attitude towards the press had been one of supercilious avoidance.

The receptionist knocked twice on a door in the hall. When there was no answer, she stood aside for Gabriel to pass.

"Wait in here."

The room was unlit and decorated with the less memorable gifts donated to the Bishop in the course of his episcopal duties.

A bowl from officers serving with the Customs and Excise in Belén, por su valiosa colaboración; a corner cabinet of coins and medals; a silver-plated beer mat from the municipality of Piura, his first diocese, etched with a message of eterno agradecimiento por sus bendiciones, and, on a table in the middle of the black marble floor, a plate with the words Coca-Cola, donated by Belén's small but prosperous Chinese community and containing a cigarette stub.

Gabriel was looking at a framed photograph of the Pope when the Bishop entered. He walked like a parrot with clipped wings, with a stooping back.

When he shook hands, the gesture was more a clasp than a greeting.

When he spoke his breath smelled slightly of mint.

"Did you see His Holiness in Lima?"

Gabriel shook his head. "I was on another assignment."

"A wonderful occasion," said the Bishop, settling into a wooden chair from which his feet hardly touched the ground. "He insisted on flying to Peru despite the threats on his life. A truly impressive person. Now," he said rubbing his hands, "what can I do for you, young man?"

Gabriel opened a notebook. His editor had sent him to find a colour story. Something to interest Caretas's readers. They had been gorged on terrorists. Someone in Lima had mentioned the Bishop's collection of crosses.

"It sounded ideal."

From the depths of his chair, the Bishop swelled visibly. "Quite right too. You Limeños only notice us when the food is spoiling in your freezer. At least these terrorists are forcing people to realize we exist. . . but perhaps you'd better not write that." On reflection, he did not wish the readers of Caretas, still less the members of the Club de Leones, to think they were dealing with a liberation theologian.

"Not that there will be many terrorists left after that business in San Francisco, eh?" The Bishop laughed. "What do you think about that? I suppose you're one of those pressing for an enquiry. If you ask me, it was a massacre waiting to happen."

"I take it your collection is photogenic?"

"Does a fish swim? It's a collection without parallel. Come."

The bishop slipped from his chair and ferreted in his back pocket for a bunch of keys. The first door he unlocked opened into a dining room. On the wall, suspended from a nail through the trigger guard, was an old-fashioned rifle. It stretched at an angle beneath the skull of a small deer.

"My greatest sin," explained the Bishop enthusiastically.

"Once a year Capitán Velarde invites me to shoot with him in the Putumayo. Once a year only, because I'm so bad."

He unlocked the door into the next room and pressed a bank of switches.

"There," he said. "My inner sanctum."

The grey interior was a forest of crucifixes. On all sides, Christ twisted in metal, wooden and ivory agony.

"What did I tell you? A collection without parallel."

He picked up an effigy and blew gently on Christ's head. A nebula of dust rose from the yellow thorns.

"Sixteenth-century elephant's tusk from Goa. Commissioned for the King of Portugal's private chapel." Gently, he handed it over.

For the best part of an hour, the Bishop rotated about the room.

"That's Izearda with a Z," he would say, urging Gabriel to make another entry in his notebook.

Or, "That was a gift from the Marquis of Leiria, a wonderful man, but you had better not put that. The family might not. . . "

Or, "Thieves have only once broken in. All they stole were a pair of my slippers and an eiderdown."

As he scribbled these things down, Gabriel became aware of other items in the room. Behind one crucifixion, an onyx ashtray in the shape of a revolver; behind another, a miniature electric fan with green blades; behind another a ceramic vessel from the Chimu dynasty. When he looked at the walls, he also discovered unlikely objects among the pendulant rosaries; a calendar with a bare-breasted girl, a plastic parrot on a wire perch ("It makes no mess," joked the Bishop) and, in brass surrounds, a number of photographs revealing the Bishop as a younger man. In each he was found to be standing beside someone famous or embracing someone famous until, in a prominent portrait on its own, he appeared to have reached that state himself.

"Come," said the Bishop when they had moved full circle, "I want to show you something very special." He arrived before a large safe.

There was another catechism of keys and the cast-iron door swung open. The Bishop began piling its contents into his arms. When he turned about, he was holding about thirty flat green boxes. These he kept in position with his chin.

"The other room."

Reinstalled in his chair, the Bishop began opening the lids, removing the tissue paper and scooping up the objects that lay in the cotton wool bed. Each was a small cross; each he held up to the light and fondled before passing over. Black pearl, glass, ruby, gold, emerald from Lisbon, Murano, Salamanca, Trujillo. Thirty-five to a box – the boxes specially made in Seville, but he had run out of them – over seventy boxes, almost three thousand crosses and thirty years in amassing. The statistics sent their speaker into ecstasy.

He removed another lid. "Ah," he said, "my favourite. My absolute favourite. Late sixteenth century, commissioned by the Viceroy for his second wife. A silver and ruby Lord of Miracles."

Gabriel held the minute cross in his hand. "Beautiful," he agreed. "Exquisite."

He raised it to the light. "Your Lordship, do you believe in miracles?"

"Oh, yes." The Bishop's eyes seized on another example of Spanish craftsmanship.

"What about visions?"

The Bishop deposited the last of his boxes on the marble floor and sank his head back in the chair. He looked at Gabriel, scratching the hairy back of a hand.

"You're referring to this man in Chile everyone's talking about. All I can say is I've heard the cassettes – they're in my office if you want to hear them. I must confess, I'm not yet convinced."

"Not him especially. In general."

The Bishop caressed one of the chins that concealed the white rectangle of his calling. "I believe they are possible. But the Church has to be very prudent." He formed a circle with his thumb and index finger through which he pretended to peer.

"There must be checking and double checking and doctors' reports before one can trouble Rome."

"What about Elena Silves?" said Gabriel.

The Bishop coughed. His hand wriggled into a pocket from which he produced a handkerchief. He blew a dry nose.

"In the case of Elena Silves, I would say, yes, up to a point the Church was satisfied. My own opinion is that the phenomena, though curious, were not very impressive." His face arranged itself according to his notion of a worldly grin. "Perhaps we have been spoiled by television and Hollywood. The Holy Mother is going to have to advance a little if she wishes to make a competitive appearance in today's world. But the case of Elena Silves was an exceptional case. It can be of no interest to a sophisticated Limeño.

"Now, let me tell you more about myself. My upbringing in Piura. My modest achievements in Belén. My monograph on Jean Gerson which, incidentally, the Spanish publishers intend for next year. And we must discuss arrangements for a photographer. When do you think your article will appear?"

Gabriel looked at the Christ in his palm.

"I'll be honest. I had intended originally to write about Elena Silves."

The Bishop frowned.

"Elena Silves?"

"I want to talk to her."

"But. . . that's impossible. She's in a closed order. She has been for almost twenty years."

"I know. I've been there."

"You've been there? Where?"

"Santa Clara."

"And?"

"They wouldn't let me in."

"Out of the question. Besides," said the Bishop quickly, "from what I hear, they're all extremely ugly. A handsome chap like you would have them abandoning their vocation before you could peel a grape."

Gabriel smiled weakly. When he smiled his scar became another laugh line.

"She was Sister Colina, wasn't she? She was the nun who escaped."

"Why are you so interested? Why? The whole structure of our society is collapsing and what are you doing? Chasing nuns."

"Elena Silves is my cousin."

There was a silence. The Bishop was goitrous. He tried rising from his chair. He waved at the box lids. "You mean, this. . . all this was an excuse."

"No," said Gabriel. "I'm here to write a feature on you. But since I was here, I had to ask. You're the only person who can tell me where she is. The family has not heard a word. They don't even know if she returned to Santa Clara."

The Bishop calmed himself.

"No, she's not at Santa Clara."

"Where is she?"

"I have no idea. The matter has been out of my control for some time. In the interim I have heard nothing, I have read nothing. I can't help you."

Gabriel knocked his forehead in frustration. "Don't you think it odd that a woman who was twice blessed with a vision of the Virgin Mary, to the apparent satisfaction of the Church, should suddenly vanish after eighteen years and that no one is the slightest bit interested – least of all the Church?"

"Young man," said the Bishop, weighing his words as coldly as a money-lender, "you misrepresent something you know nothing about. Whether or not the Church is satisfied, it is concerned about your cousin. Exceedingly so. But the matter, as I said, is out of my hands."

He began replacing the lids. "If you wish to pursue your investigation, I suggest you make contact either with the Cardinal Archbishop – or the chief of the Policía de Investigaciones."

"For God's sake, why the PIP?"

"This is speculative, certainly not for publication in *Caretas*," said the Bishop. He relieved Gabriel of his cross. "It is thought that your cousin escaped to look for somebody."

"Who?"

The Bishop returned a sheet of tissue paper to the box in his lap. When the lid did not fit, he removed the paper and screwed it angrily into a ball.

"His photograph was discovered among her belongings. Someone she was involved with before the appearance of Our Holy Mother."

"But why the police?" Gabriel repeated, with less conviction. The Bishop put down his box and inspected his ringed fingers – the fingers he would lick when Gabriel had gone, that would search through five issues of his secretary's *Caretas* for the by-line of Julio Ángel Medina; the fingers he would jab at the intercom and tap on the blotter while he waited for the call to go through to Capitán Velarde, the city's new Deputy Chief of Police; the fingers that now formed a gothic vault as he gave his answer to Gabriel.

"It transpires she may have escaped Santa Clara to look for a well-known terrorist."

Chapter 9

"WHAT I HAVE TO TELL YOU about Gabriel's grandfather is not first hand. There is no one alive who met his grandfather. I discovered the following from his father, the mechanic, a courteous man who used to service my motorbike in the days when I could ride one. He seemed pleased at my calculation that the Lungs were almost definitely the fourth Chinese family to settle in Belén.

"In 1872 Achin Man Lung came from Hiempen to work on the railroads. In a contract celebrated at Macao, the twenty-one-year-old coolie placed himself at the orders of the American industrialist, Henry Meiggs. For a term of eight years, he pledged to serve as agricultural labourer, gardener, shepherd, house servant and general workman.

"The following week he boarded the *Lady Charlotte*.

"We may judge from Felix Cipriano C. Zegarra's perfectly serviceable work, *La Condición Jurídica de los Extranjeros en el Perú* (Santiago, 1872) that the journey to Peru was a terrible one. Over seven hundred coolies had joined the *Lady Charlotte* at Macao. Only two hundred and ninety-two of them survived.

"According to the English captain – a metal-hearted sailor who boasted that everything he knew about the sea could be learnt on the Mersey estuary – Johnny Chinaman was not a particularly sturdy race.

"At Callao, the harbour for Lima, the captain ordered his decks to be scrubbed with lime chloride and the vomit to be washed from the survivors. When they were clean, he gave them each a pair of wide calico trousers, a trunk the size of a tea chest and a cane hat.

"'Models of health and sound of limb,' was how the Mersey sailor described his cargo, his mouth widened by a passion for cigars and curses.

"Achin Man Lung did not live up to the advertisement. Dysentery had scooped him away. His eyes were lifeless tadpoles, his mouth a trembling slit. Meiggs' representative squeezed his biceps and spun him like a top.

"'$350, no more.'

"Achin worked on the Meiggs railroad, then on the coast at Pabellón de Pica. He lived in a cave – its rafters made from the ribs of whales – and cleared four tons of guano every day in a tin barrow with a loose wheel. When scurvy made him useless, he was sold to a hacienda at Upaca where his galled ankles prevented him from joining a mutiny. At the age of thirty, because of his experience on the Lima to Jauja railway, he was recruited by the Peruvian Amazon Company. They were planning a narrow-gauge track from their warehouse to the river bank. They wanted cheap, experienced labour.

"It came no cheaper than Achin Man Lung.

"His papers were examined and returned to him by the interpreter. There was one problem. They had an Achin.

"'Call him Pancrasio,' said the agent. He looked out of the window at the line of Chinese coiling like a pony tail around the outhouse.

"'We've got a Pancrasio,' said the interpreter.

"'What about Pedro?'

"'No, sir.'

"'Then call him Pedro. No, wait, I've a better idea.' The agent walked to a shelf. He removed from it a large book. It was Radcliffe Crocker's *Diseases of the Skin – their description, pathology, diagnosis and treatment*.

"'Let's call him Prurigo.'

"So Prurigo Man Lung – those in the queue after him bore names like Tylosis, Tonsurans and Unguentum – was entered into the company ledger. Age 30. Stature – medium. Colour – yellowy white. Forehead – high. Eyes – small. Mouth – wide. Particular marks – a finger missing from his right hand, run over by a guano barrow.

"Prurigo who had been Achin settled by the Moronacocha lake on the outskirts of Belén where he married a loquacious Bora Indian and dropped dead one day without a whisper. The fire had died within him when he walked onto the *Lady Charlotte*, but it reignited in his children and in their children who kept his contract in his tea chest and vowed never to be so subservient . . ."

In his thirty-nine years, Gabriel Rondón Lung had only been subservient to one man. The man whose handsome face looked out from posters on the walls of houses and churches and town halls of every town in the land.

The man who called himself Presidente Ezequiel.

One could no more hope to live without the presence of Ezequiel than one might hope to eat one's food without swallowing dust, or sleep in the jungle without scratching for fleas or look up to the red, volcanic slopes of Nakaq without seeing his name.

The man was everywhere.

Gabriel left the priory and walked down Juan Próspero towards the contraband market. He walked slowly, his briefcase knocking against his legs. His interview with Barrantes had left him in a state of despair. After two weeks, the knowledge of Elena's disappearance was something he couldn't absorb, something unbearable. All of a sudden he wanted sleep. He screwed his eyes tight and opened them again. No. He mustn't. He looked at his watch. 11.35. He had an assignation. To keep himself awake, he changed his pace.

Like a cauchero mistress, Belén still clung to her shawl of tiled palaces and broken-toothed colonnades. They lay in tatters under a clear sky. The rubber days were over, but she continued to deck herself in the proceeds of the jungle. After rubber, oil; after oil, cocaine.

"Whatever applies to other parts of the country," he had told Hipólito, who only half listened as he gave another spin to the balding tennis ball on his finger, "doesn't apply here. Belén is an island in the jungle. People are happy with their lot. There's no need for revolution. There is no desire for it."

"We must try all the same," Hipólito said.

"Why?"

"Because, like you, I cannot stomach the fact that I am a middleman in my own country. Because I believe something can be done about it." He threw up the ball and caught it. "It's not going to be easy, that's all. Catch."

When Gabriel reached Sargento Lores he turned left into the crowded stalls. Under the blue plastic canopies, he saw the commodities he had known as a child. They came from the far corners of the world. Coffee from Brazil, creamery butter from Dublin, aftershave from Paris, gin from London.

Gin from London . . . Hadn't this been the spot where he had met Elena's aunt, her basket clinking with green bottles? Here on this very corner, probably by this same stall, he had asked her the question which he had been asking himself every minute for the last two weeks, the question that had lain dormant for twenty-one years.

"Where's Elena?"

The memory of it engulfed him as strongly as the crowd. No, he thought. His assignation would have to wait. He needed first to sleep.

It was an hour since Barrantes' call.

Capitán Velarde, Belén's newly appointed Deputy Chief of Police, looked at the telephone on his desk. The mouthpiece in his old machine had broken and this grey replacement, smelling of chicken flesh and the colour of putty, was all the exchange could offer. At least it didn't smell of mint, he thought, thinking of Barrantes' breath.

That morning the former Bishop had expended a lot of it telling Velarde about a man who clearly wasn't who he claimed to be.

"Who did he claim to be?"

"A journalist from *Caretas*. Julio Ángel Medina. But my secretary's rung their office and they've nobody with that name. The point is, this man's in town looking for Elena Silves."

"Elena Silves?"

"He says he's her cousin. I only realized afterwards she never had a cousin. The thought crossed my mind it might be Gabriel Lung but, of course, he's dead."

"So far as we know," said Velarde, who, as soon as he heard the name, felt a nasty contraction in his throat as if he had just bitten deep into a hot pepper.

But that first name. Julio Ángel Medina. That was also a name which meant something.

"By the way, Capitán, since I've got you, what about Elena Silves? Any leads?"

"Father Barrantes," said Velarde deliberately, "Elena Silves is the least of my worries. Recalcitrant nuns are your problem, not mine. At present I have a massacre on my hands."

But, an hour later, Capitán Velarde was opening a slim file on Julio Ángel Medina, dated 1965, which linked him with the names of Gabriel Rondón Lung, Edith Pusanga, Bonifacio Medina and a dead man called Hipólito Mercedes. Once more Velarde looked at his phone. "Emergencia 05" he noticed in the centre of the dial. Who the fuck does a policeman dial in emergency?

Take your pick, he thought. The army, the navy, the air force. Or perhaps if it was refinement you were after, army intelligence, navy intelligence, air force intelligence. It didn't much matter. They were all piss poor and none of them talked to the others anyway.

Then again, he could dial his own crack regiment, the Sinchis, those bastards who came in from Satipo with knives in their boots and coke up their nose and thought they were God, except they shitted on God too most of them. They were as bad as Sendero. And Sendero were bad. Bad, bad, bad, he said rapping the desk with his Ray-Bans.

He must buy a new pair next time he went to Lima. The fucking things were too small. They fell off whenever he lost his temper.

An electric fan swivelled on the floor by his feet, ruffling his trouser legs. He would have liked another day to nail Barrantes' reporter. Nail him so the shithead sang like Aunt Angelica's canaries and he could hold his head up in the Club de Leones and say See you mother fuckers, you can't get the better of the Guardia Civil – not a good Guardia Civil.

He would have liked an extra day because it was that terruco friend of Hipólito Mercedes who had fucked up his promotion six years ago. But what if "the man from *Caretas*" was one of those responsible for the murder at Cabaña? If that was the case, then professional pride didn't come into it. It didn't matter who caught him, so long as he was caught and after what the village storekeeper told him, the sooner the better.

Cabaña. He'd never heard of Cabaña till the previous day. He'd had to take off his sunglasses and peer at the map until he gave up and told the storekeeper to point it out, which he did with a trembling finger that covered the whole of a village he'd never heard of because, of course, it was over a thousand miles south of Belén. That was one of the troubles with the jungle. It went on forever.

"But, Señor Capitán . . . it's in the desert." The storekeeper had hardly been able to get his words out standing there by the desk, his hands bunching the hat he held against his crotch as he begged for protection.

He smelled of cane spirit and fear. They had been after him as well, señor, but he had been above the village when they came. He had been unloading cement bags into the schoolhouse.

It was his wife who saw everything, saw them order everyone into the square, saw them line up four men under the goalpost, the alcalde, the postmaster, the magistrate and his cousin who kept the keys to the graveyard.

"And me, señor, then they asked for me."

But they couldn't find him and his wife said nothing, just watched with clattering teeth as they read out something about the People's War and Mao and Mariátegui and jerked their heads back like chickens.

It was a woman who slit their throats so the blood spurted into the bucket she held up to their necks. She was old for one of them, about forty, señor, and she daubed the walls of the church and the door of the school with their blood.

LONG LIVE PRESIDENTE EZEQUIEL AND THE NEW DEMOCRACY! she wrote. This I saw with my own eyes, señor, he had said pointing to two bloodshot orbs that couldn't stay still for a second. And I saw the bodies, he stammered. They were lying on the priest's floor in a dark purple pool like the dye used by the women for wool. They looked twisted and wrong. Then he saw why.

The feet and the heads of the four men had been hacked off and crudely sewn back on.

"The wrong way, señor," came the storekeeper's whisper.

The phrase had haunted Capitán Velarde ever since. As a policeman, he could be next in line. He had found himself looking over the desk at the man's feet poking from rubber tyre sandals and speculating what difference it would make. You could watch yourself shitting, he supposed, but girls would be a problem.

"Corporal," he ordered. "Take this man to your grandmother. Give him the usual allowance – and I mean him, not you, or whoever you spent it on at Señora Zumate's. Yes, I know about last time. But we're going to need him again."

Eighteen hours after he had dismissed the storekeeper, promising him three months' protection, Capitán Velarde's mind was still stained with an image. He saw the dead men, all four of them – their heads like that so they couldn't see their murderers, their feet so they couldn't follow.

No, he couldn't afford to fuck up this time. He lifted his phone. Bracing himself against the smell, he spoke into the mouthpiece.

"Get me head office in Lima. No. I don't care if it takes an hour."

Chapter 10

IT WAS NIGHT when Gabriel emerged along the street known as Venecia. He had slept in a derelict hut on the rice flats. He had slept for eight hours. Now he walked quickly.

The stale light of a lamp stretched his shadow across the mud path and up against the wooden houses. The street was deserted but for a dog that howled like a cock. A television set cast coloured shadows on a clinkered ceiling. In the distance a boat droned. Two kilometres from the cathedral square of Belén, this was a district of fishermen and smugglers and the river's most foetid smells.

Short of the waterfront he turned right and after a hundred yards came to a narrow passage leading to the river. Its entrance was lit by a paraffin lamp. Along one side was a counter lined with bottles. Gabriel knew them to contain aphrodisiacs for men about to enjoy the canoieras – girls who plied the water in flat-bottomed canoes. A man leant against the counter. He was telling the serving-woman that his name was Babilonia. He worked as a cleaner in the Hotel Liberty. He was waiting for the rain to stop.

"It has stopped," said the shrivelled woman retrieving his glass. Her husband who brewed the chuchuasi to raise Babilonia's dead lay on a hammock, snoring.

Gabriel walked to the water's edge. He whistled. From across the river came a cry, then nothing. He heard the sound of splashing. Presently a ferryman emerged from the dark, kneeling at the front of his canoe.

They slid into the night. Gabriel heard the lap of couples making love on either side as they crossed the river.

"Busy tonight?" he asked.

"Busy enough," said the other without turning. His shirt was undone. His knees poked from rolled-up trousers. He dipped his heart-shaped paddle in the water. "But now everyone goes to the Teletroca."

"The Teletroca?"

"Señora Zumate's place near the airport. Only the old ones stay."

"Old chickens make better soup," said Gabriel. The man gave an appreciative cackle and lay his paddle flat.

From where they landed, it was a five-minute walk to the house on San José. The front door was locked. A wire of light shone through a shutter. Gabriel ignored the door. He continued to a fence of corrugated iron. Locating the place where two sheets met, he prised them apart. He stepped into a small courtyard overlooked by an open window.

"Edith," he called softly. He tapped the shutters. Silence. Nothing moved in the room. The floor creaked. It creaked again. A figure edged into the light.

"Hello, Edith," he said, stepping from behind the shutter. The woman looked at him, the gun in her hands pointing straight at his chest. Despite heavy make-up, her face was blank, like the space on a wall where a portrait had hung. She moved forward one step, then another until the pistol pressed against Gabriel's temple. She pushed it into his forehead so that he was forced to move back.

"Gabriel?" Her hands began shaking. She rested the gun on the sill.

"Gabriel?" she said again. "Thank God." And she reached out to embrace him, holding his head tight and kissing and kissing the spot where she had made a cold red circle.

"You've grown a moustache. Different colour, but it suits you," she said, the life returning to her face.

Gabriel looked at her. The features had set in furrows, but it was the face of a still attractive woman.

She sat beside him on a wooden bench in the front room. She squeezed his hand. "I thought you were dead," she went on. "When I heard, I went out for a long walk. I found myself kneeling in church and praying. I was almost glad you were dead. It meant I didn't have to hope."

"Edith," said Gabriel.

"No, don't," she let out. "I know why you're here. It's not because of me." She raised a hand. "Don't even pretend. It's because of her, isn't it? Isn't it?"

"Edith, later," said Gabriel. "What about you? What have you been doing?"

"You caught me doing my washing." She wiped her eyes, attempting to laugh. "Then I heard the chickens and I thought one of those PIP bastards had come for me."

"An operation?"

"Back yesterday."

"Where?"

"Don't let's talk about it." She put a hand to his moustache. "But how dare you survive. How dare you?"

"I went back, Edith. I got into San Eduardo. That's where they've moved the survivors. I saw Rolando."

"I want you to tell me," she said, running her thumb over and over and over the bristles. "Everything. But first I'll get some coffee. You could do with it, couldn't you?"

She squeezed his hand. He returned the pressure. When she returned with the coffee, she found his hand again.

"Now tell me," she said.

So blowing into his cup, Gabriel told how, on his return from Silar, he had visited San Eduardo.

Like San Francisco, the prison had its market women in the road below. He bought a sack of avocados from them. The guards weren't interested in the sack. They just wanted to put a rubber stamp on his forearm.

"New security measures."

Gabriel sat in a booth. On the other side a man drew up a chair.

"Are you mad?" came the hiss through the mesh.

"Hello, Rolando."

"But they think you're dead."

"Then it makes things easier."

Rolando looked down at the formica table. His hands started fluttering. He dug his fingers in his arms to stop them. He was trembling badly.

"Rolando."

"It was terrible," he whispered. "They've all gone, Chino. Fanor, Gregorio, Flores, Néstor. . ." He produced a cigarette from his trousers. The trousers were pulled up to the knee. They revealed a network of moon-coloured blisters on his calves.

He tore off the filter and lit the cigarette.

"Start from the beginning."

"You'd gone when we had the order. It came from Ezequiel himself."

"From Ezequiel?" Gabriel leant forward.

"Néstor took it. He told us the President was hosting an International Socialist Conference. Four hundred journalists had come from all over the world. A perfect time to act." Two trails of smoke descended from his nostrils. He tried to laugh, but he coughed.

"The signal came at daybreak. We gathered in the dormitory. Néstor had fixed guns. On the stroke of six we shouted that a prisoner was ill. Oliveira was the guard. He suspected nothing. He was in the corridor at the time. He walked towards us whistling. Remember how he whistled? When he opened the dormitory door we dragged him inside. It was easy as breathing.

"The Governor turned up. He took away our list of demands. He was furious. He said he might be able to do something about the garbage dumps. He might even be able to help over the food allowance. But did we think anyone would listen to our other requests? He marched off locking the door into the yard.

"We waited all morning. Then on the radio we heard the government had gone into emergency meeting. A statement was read out. It said the President couldn't tolerate the conversion of prisons into a territory beyond the state. It also mentioned a Peace Commission was talking to us. It was the first we knew of it. We'd seen no Peace Commission. We'd seen nothing for eight hours. And why? Because when the Governor locked the outer door, we couldn't hear a thing. Apparently some arsehole was blowing himself blue through a megaphone, calling on us to surrender. It was all on Channel 7. Our failure to respond was taken to be a refusal. In fact, it was because we couldn't fucking well hear. I suppose we would have surrendered by mid-afternoon. By then it was too late. They'd called in the army."

The man threw his stub to the floor. He twisted a heel and lit another cigarette. He didn't remove the filter.

"We heard the helicopter bringing the General. That was at five. Then half an hour later they fired a bazooka at the outer door. It didn't make much of an impact. Some of us took shelter in the small bathroom. Oliveira was shitting himself, telling us it was all over, the military had taken the prison. The next explosion made a hole in the wall. That's when Néstor decided to surrender. He walked over to the figures who were crawling through. There were four or five of them. They wore black uniforms and ski masks round their eyes.

"He said something to them. They shot him in the stomach. More followed behind. They grabbed anyone they could and forced them through the hole. We were pushed into the patio and made to lie down with our hands on our heads. The General was strutting round with a megaphone. I heard him shouting 'Anyone who looks round will be shot.' I heard people say 'Douse them with petrol.' Someone else mentioned an order that none of us should remain alive. Someone else said 'Just do it, eliminate them.' They began to yank us by the hair, demanding our names.

"Your palanca, Julio, was next to me. He shouted he was a journalist. He always wrote good things about the police in the newspapers. He was taken away. Then it was my turn.

"They dragged me to the baths behind the dormitory. They made me strip naked. When they'd got five of us, they took us out and they shot us. I was hit four times, twice in the shoulder, twice in the feet.

"They dug a trench. They threw me in it with the others. They must have dynamited the second floor some time after that. I was buried for two days. I crawled out of the rubble on Friday. By then none of the dormitory was standing. They had blown it all up, the whole bloody thing," he said.

"They wrapped me in a blanket and took me to the hospital. I was told my life had been religiously spared. 'Not even your relatives think you are alive,' they said."

He snorted. Gabriel continued to say nothing. The room became loud with the sound of whispers from other booths. In one a woman giggled. Hearing her, Rolando clawed the mesh.

"Christ, I could do with a woman."

A bell rang. The guard by the door straightened his cap.

Time was up, he shouted. He advanced along the booths, banging each with his rifle butt.

"Come on, you cholos, out, out, out," he said, shaking Gabriel's shoulder.

"What about your woman. Did you find her?" But Gabriel couldn't bring himself to tell Edith that.

"Bastards," said Edith.

"I took him some paltas."

"Fucking, fucking bastards."

"Rolando said Ezequiel was having an emergency meeting. He said you would know the details."

Her face revolved until it stared into his.

"So here I am. Where's the meeting?" he asked.

In a sudden gesture, she took both his hands in hers. He held her to him and shook.

"To bed," she said, removing the cup from his hand. "We can discuss what needs to be discussed in the morning."

They went into another room. It had a couch, a chair and a large cupboard. A number of photographs were pinned to the side of the cupboard. Gabriel looked at them as he unbuttoned his shirt. "Is that me? I don't believe it." A younger man leant at an angle against a bar with a raised glass. It was the bar of the Café Nanay.

"When did you take that?"

Edith turned out the light in the passage. She fetched a glass of water which she put on the floor by the bed. "Don't you remember? No, I suppose you don't," she said, raising her shirt over her head. She wore nothing beneath. "Just before you went to prison."

Gabriel kicked his shoes to the floor. He took off his trousers. Edith stood waiting for him. She heard him remove his underpants, then his watch which made a hard sound on the chair. She knew when he approached he would turn her away from him. She felt his searching hardness against her back like a blind man's hand. She thought, "He doesn't want to see my face." She bent forward onto the creaking couch. She reached back between her thin legs to help him. She heard the slap of flesh accelerating against flesh until the moment he came.

"You're the only one, Edith," he whispered above her.

"Apart from Elena," she choked.

"Apart from Elena."

Gabriel woke early. He lay looking at his younger self on the wardrobe. He heard Edith wake beside him. He felt her hand spider down his stomach. When he asked about Ezequiel, she released him from her grip.

"How is he?"

"The same."

"Where is he?"

"I can't tell you. Not yet. But safe."

"Satipo?"

"Gabriel."

"Piura?"

"Gabriel, don't."

"So now the orders come from you?"

"You've been away."

She withdrew her hand and turned her back to him.

He chose his words carefully. "It's up to you to decide whether I attend the meeting?"

"If you like."

"Don't then."

Eventually she said, "You know what that means."

Gabriel slipped from the bed.

"It's a risk I have to take."

"It's against our code, Gabriel." She spoke to the wall. "To put a personal matter before duty. It's against everything we've been fighting for."

Gabriel pulled on his trousers.

"This concerns something that happened before either of us knew about codes. And you know it. I have to find her, Edith."

She turned over. She lay on her back, her hands held to her mouth, the tips of three fingers between her teeth. She bit hard on the painted nails.

"Don't you feel anything, Gabriel? Anything at all? How many have we lost? Two hundred? Three hundred? People you've lived with night and day for seven years, some you've been working with since we went to Ayacucho. But you're not thirsting for vengeance. Vengeance is the last thing on your mind. Your mind is full of a girl you last saw more than twenty years ago."

"Vengeance is a dish that can be eaten cold, Edith."

"But how can you not feel anything, at this moment of all moments?"

"What did you feel when they arrested me at Requena?"

"Gabriel, no... no..." She twisted, looking up at him from the bed. She couldn't see his face. A muscle prodded the inside of his back.

"Where were you and Bonifacio? Where were my dear comrades who had sworn to defend each other to the death?"

Edith didn't speak. She saw the *Victoria Regia* make its approach to the jetty. She saw the line of policemen, blowing on their hands because the morning was cold. She saw the panic erupt on Bonifacio's face, his flight to the engine room, his arm round the boy's neck, the boy's eyes, the boy's finger pointing at the hole smelling of grease and sawdust and rotting bark where they kept the fuel. She heard the sounds above as the *Victoria Regia* berthed. She realized it was too late to return on deck and protect Gabriel, who sat beneath a blanket nursing his torn cheek, frightened and suffocated.

"No, Edith," said Gabriel. "I don't want to betray the revolution. I just want to forget it for a while."

He walked into the other room. Through the window came the sound of men and women loading their market stalls. He opened the shutter a fraction. He saw black fish and cabbages and the hairless heads of howler monkeys. Across the street a woman swatted flies off a row of chicken parts. Another rolled cigarettes, pasting the papers with yucca gum.

On the tin roof opposite, a vulture arranged a black shawl of feathers, then heaved into the air. The river glared beyond. It flowed into a grey horizon, a frayed green belt of trees.

My home town, thought Gabriel.

When they tortured him, he'd erased it from his mind. In the bath, with the hood on his head, he had drowned his memories. When they came to use the electric wire – Verónica, they called it – he was a man who had never been to Belén.

Not that, strung upside down, he was unaware of Verónica's touch on his gums, his nipples, his foreskin, of cigarette jabs up and down his stomach, of lights shone into his face by men with tender voices and eyes bright with cocaine. But he occupied the torn skin of a man ignorant of anything that could help them.

"In Argentina," said the officer in charge, "we would have thrown him from a plane."

In Peru, they had sent him to San Francisco prison, to join his comrades.

Once you've been tortured, you're always tortured. That's what he'd heard. His suppression of himself had lasted until the moment he read Arturo Walker's article. Now, back in Belén, he wanted only to remember. Only by remembering would he piece together the man who had loved Elena.

He found an open bottle of Inca Kola on a shelf beside the basin. He swilled a mouthful round his dry tongue. The sickly green liquid was flat but out of habit he burped. Stretching his arms, he walked about the room until he came to a shelf of books. He recognized several as his own.

He passed a finger over the spines. To his father's annoyance, his handsome face had been buried in these pages all day. "One deed creates more propaganda than a thousand leaflets," the mechanic used to bark, twisting Gabriel's ear with a paraffined hand. "Now off those steps. I need two bottles of beer from Don Tonsurans."

By the time he was twelve he had read Schiller, Conrad and Bakunin. He knew *Los Tiranos* by heart, and Fanon's *Wretched of the Earth*. He believed he understood what Buonarroti meant when he said no means are criminal which are employed to obtain a sacred end.

He was fifteen before he came upon the blue and white covers of José Carlos Mariátegui, the founder of Peru's Communist Party. He removed the volume from the shelf. These seven essays on Peruvian Reality – written in the 1920s – had affected him most of all. Mariátegui's belligerent vision of a socialist future, dependant on the Indian, was a vision that matched his own. He looked at the confident scribbles of his adolescent pen. He reread the message they underlined.

Colonial rule was a cruel irrelevance. What mattered was restoring the empire that existed before the Conquest; a classless empire invoked by Mariátegui as Tawantinsuyo, the land of the four winds, in which the earth goddess Pacha Mama would be her golden self again.

"The strength of revolutionaries does not lie in their philosophy," wrote Mariátegui in one double-ringed passage. "It is in their faith, their passion, their will. Theirs is a religious, mystical and spiritual strength." And at the age of fifteen Gabriel had felt imbued with it. What Mariátegui had preached from his sofa, he, Gabriel Rondón Lung, would one day put into practice.

At fifteen he had been unaware of Marx's dictum that men about to make a revolution pretend they are restoring a vanished past. Would he have acted differently, he wondered? He replaced the book. He couldn't answer. Things had not turned out as he had foreseen. Certainly not as Hipólito had foreseen.

"Do you still think of Hipólito?" he asked the woman washing her face in the basin.

She glanced at him. The water dripped from her cheeks. It formed a patch on her shirt. "Stupid question."

"Well?"

"Sometimes," she said through the towel. "I try not to. It doesn't help anything."

"Would we be reading his poems today?"

"I don't know. Who cares about writers? I'm going out to get some food. You shouldn't be seen in the street."

The door slammed.

"Hipólito," he said aloud, invoking his friend, the impetuous revolutionary. He saw his morose chubby face, the face of a mediocre poet worried that South American literature was flowering rather well without him. He saw the large animated features which might have suited a character in a cartoon, but in the flesh looked ugly.

He looked down the street to the river where his friend had died. Where that tug is, he thought. That was near enough the spot where he had gone under, his head cracked like a coconut by

Don Miguel's third shot.

How many years? Twenty? Twenty-one? They were off to join the guerrilla leader Federico Fuente. Five students from San Agustín College, who would sail down to Requena and cross into the valleys. Five teenagers who would take power, inspire the masses and destroy the bourgeois regime.

The tug disappeared upriver. Watching its wake rub against each bank, Gabriel forced himself back. If he was to reconstitute himself, he would have to confront that day in May which had determined his future. His future and Elena's.

The boat had been late, which was why the five of them had booked into a hotel. After signing their names and professions – Hipólito put "astronaut" – they had walked to a bar in Plaza Clavero. That was when the police arrived. It wasn't the astronaut which had alerted them. It was Don Miguel, strutting past with his tart, in his embroidered lace shirt with its little silver ends screwed to the collar and a face that would have silenced a howler monkey.

He must have heard something in the customs house. He was still working the river then. He didn't yet have his mayoral ambitions. He didn't need them. For the right sum, you could smuggle anything past Don Miguel. The contents of the contraband market. The hold of a Booth liner. Even the boat. But you couldn't rock Don Miguel's cosy number. And that's what they would have done by sailing to join Fuente, and Don Miguel knew it. He knew the guns and the gelignite and the detonating fuse they carried in their canvas sacks had all passed under his Roman nose and he knew the police would find that out.

So before they did, he told them.

Hipólito had laughed when Corporal Velarde asked for his documents. "I'm the man in the moon," he replied, putting down his glass and running outside. Gabriel followed, shouting for the others to scatter.

The two of them had dashed to the river, into the canoe of an old woman who sold porridge and stewed turtle from two large tins in the stern. The canoe possessed only one paddle. Hipólito had steered them into the river by the time the police arrived on the waterfront. There were civilians among them, encouraged by Don

Miguel's rumours of a terrorist group armed to the teeth with machine-guns. They all had shot-guns, except Don Miguel who had a long hunting rifle which he started to fire. With his first shot he knocked the paddle from Hipólito's hand. Round and round the canoe had spun, dizzying the two on board so they had fallen to the bottom in a wet heap, washed by the warm liquid from the punctured tins.

"Stop shooting," Hipólito had cried, standing up and waving his arms. "Stop, stop, stop," he had cried, struggling to shake his T-shirt like a white flag. A bullet reddened his stomach and he toppled out of Gabriel's reach into the river, clinging with his fingers to the side. "Man in . . ." he whispered. That was before the shot from the shore which exploded his skull.

Gabriel threw himself over the other side. He swam deep, with a full breath, and pulled himself under until his lungs tore at him to come up for the air which he finally drew in with huge gulps in the shadow of a boat.

He could see it now from the window. The floating church of the Seventh Day Adventists.

"Hipólito." Once more he walked to the shelf. Edith must have it. Sure enough, among the books he had loosened, he found the slim volume printed on Hipólito's press.

The Indignant Savage: Poems by Hipólito Mercedes.

He turned the flyleaf. The very first poem he came to was "The Amazon Dolphin", dedicated to G.R.L. and E.C.S.

"It's a sort of love poem. Inspired by Aragón – but you can sing it to the tune of 'Ojos azules'."

Chapter 11

"NO ONE KNOWS where the problem lies. Everything was planned by an English engineer, an amateur plumber called Horney. In laying out his unique system of pipes, he made only one oversight.

"He forgot to leave a blueprint. . ."

To Don Wenceslau and Don García, staring out of the Café Nanay at the waterlogged square, it seems they have heard Don Leopoldo give the same explanation on every wet day there has ever been.

This was a day in January 1965, during one of the intense but intermittent downpours which made Belén heavy with jungle smells and because of a fault in the drainage system turned its roads into sudden rivers – and its squares into lakes.

On this day Gabriel and Hipólito stood in the entrance to the university canteen.

It was Hipólito who first alerted Gabriel to the girl from the house on Calle Raimondi. The two boys were in their last year at San Agustín College, in the next street. At Hipólito's request they had attended a pedestrian lecture by a member of the city's fledgling Communist Party. Neither wished to comment on it.

"It's stopped," said Hipólito. "Let's go."

He set off, expecting Gabriel to follow.

"There's a girl I want you to meet."

Gabriel came after on tip-toe, his trousers raised so they wouldn't get wet, his shoes getting damper and damper.

"Her eyes are bluer than. . . the cobalt sky," rhapsodized the poet. "God knows what she's doing working for Don Miguel."

The offices of Eden Expeditions were housed on the ground floor of Orestes Minero's old house in Calle Putumayo. On his death – he lived to be seventy-six, surviving his gouty wife by ten years – Orestes' son Miguel had inherited the building. He moved upstairs and converted the ground floor billiard room into a tourist company. Through Eden Expeditions he hoped to open up the jungle to elderly Americans and Europeans.

Hipólito led the way into the downstairs room. There was a map of the country on the right-hand wall, below it a row of empty chairs. The room was divided by a frosted-glass panel and dominated by a desk. Gabriel's view of the girl behind this desk was obscured by a large, furious woman in a taffeta dress. In late middle age Ruth Etty had come from the Welsh hills to see if life was any better in the town where her late and only brother had spent twenty years working as resident manager for the Booth Lines. It wasn't. There was no water in her hotel, despite the fact it faced a river which every day poured more water into the Atlantic than the eight great rivers of Asia. There were no seats to Lima for another two days. And this girl hardly spoke English. How Clarence had lasted so long, she didn't know.

"Tell your elusive boss I've got to see him tomorrow. Tell him... tell him I'm a friend of the ambassador," she said before steaming out like one of her brother's boats.

Catching sight of Hipólito, the girl behind the desk had laughed.

"I didn't understand a word. Did you?" She stood to allow him to kiss her cheek.

"Elena," said the poet. "My greatest friend, Gabriel Rondón Lung. Gabriel, la señorita Elena Colina Silves."

What were his first thoughts? She was young – about seventeen. She wore her black hair in a loose pony tail. She had large blue eyes without any trace of coquetry and a finely angled nose. She was dressed in a pair of olive shorts, which he remembered thinking had been ironed wrong because they had two pleats. Something about her, though he couldn't put his finger on it, suggested a girl with a mind of her own. The one surprising thing was that Hipólito had never mentioned Elena Silves was white.

But then perhaps he had and he hadn't listened.

"Gabriel Rondón Lung." She spoke his name aloud. Pronounced in her mouth, each syllable a separate note, he became important.

"I can't stay long," she said, walking with them to the Café Nanay. She explained that Don Miguel had employed her because she could read English. He wanted a Spanish guide-book translated by the end of the month. He said there was nothing in English for the whole department. She was finding it an effort. She laughed. "You saw how well I did then." And lifting her face to Gabriel's and running a hand slowly down her arm: "Did anyone ever tell you you looked like Luis Sintra?"

"Why does she live with her aunt in that large green house on the corner of Raimondi? I'll tell you why," Don Leopoldo says. "She's an orphan. Her parents drowned in a freak storm near Rapoto when she was six."

(Henriques was taking his sick wife to Belén. In his impatience, he set off in a narrow launch belonging to the factory instead of waiting for the larger river boat. The wind had blown against the current. Colina never noticed the water tumbling hungrily over the stern, or Henriques reaching out for her, or the river cover them.)

"She also has a very fine voice," says Don García. "Quite a lot of men come to church to hear it, I tell you. That half-witted poet, he's always there on Tuesday evenings, two rows in front of me, his tongue hanging out like a water dog."

But it was plain to everyone that Elena didn't reciprocate Hipólito's feelings. He seemed not to mind. She was an excuse for him to take the lid off his pen and write verses in honour of her hair, her mouth, her lips, her eyes.

Whether she read these outpourings, Gabriel never knew. Those Gabriel read were banal and derivative. They included the poem dedicated to him and to Elena, written after Hipólito discovered what was going on.

But in a way, Hipólito had promoted that too. "The guide-book Elena's doing for Don Miguel. You wouldn't have a look, would you?"

Gabriel's knowledge of English was well-known. He had taught himself since he was fifteen. The texts he wished to read were banned in Spanish and available only in American editions smuggled from Leticia.

One evening he offered his services.

"Hipólito's put you up to it, hasn't he?"

"No, he hasn't."

She handed over her exercise book.

"I don't believe you. Look, you're blushing."

Gabriel took it to read on the Malecón. He sat on the balustrade, kicking his feet between its teeth. At his back a steep bank crumbled into a tongue of vivid green rice fields. According to Hipólito, they were the colour of a poisonous snake that had shed its skin.

"Belén," he read, "still retains the charms of the past which have prevailed throughout the last two centuries, constituting a most valuable cultural patrimony."

There followed a brief resumé of the town's history to the present day. "The Peruvian Amazon now lives in the apogee of tourist possibilities. New urbanizations are emerging in almost all the surrounding suburbs, making Belén a city of sudden contrasts and beautiful combinations. Yet Peru's tropical gateway city and door to the mysterious Amazon still pulses with the raw energy of a frontier outpost. The jungle here is a benevolent wilderness. The many Indian tribes of the Amazon are perfectly adapted to their environment, successfully leading their lives long before 'civilization' came. . ."

The last pages dealt with the town's ancient buildings. These included the cathedral, completed in 1911, with its famous Annunciation. "This painting, believed to be the monstrance of one of Fra Angelico's pupils, is of appalling beauty. But it must be protected from the greed of mankind and the action of time."

Gabriel told Elena he would work on the text. "It's pretty bad, isn't it?" she said in a hushed voice. Gabriel agreed. With her thumb she indicated that the shape through the frosted glass was Don Miguel.

"You can't have something of appalling beauty," Gabriel said, not lowering his voice.

"Can't you?" She seemed disappointed.

Later, walking her home, Gabriel said, "The plea for that painting. Was it your idea?"

"A bit. The original didn't mention what an awful state it's in. Have you seen it? It's really beautiful."

When Gabriel didn't reply – he hadn't seen it – she added it was

also a matter of loyalty. The painting had been donated by her
grandfather.

"Poor deluded man," she said, then told him about Alonso, the
bucktoothed accountant from Coimbra – which was when Gabriel
warmed to her.

Outside Edith's house, someone knocked.

"Edith!"

The voice was a man's. He rattled the front door. When nothing
happened, he moved to the window. He gave a loud whistle.

Gabriel waited against the wall until the man walked away. He
waited a few minutes more. From where he stood, he noticed a
paraffin stove under the basin. He filled a kettle with water and lit
the blackened gauze.

Sitting at the table, he reopened Hipólito's book. He found the
poem again. He read it unseeing. He knew it by heart. Instead of the
images on the page, he began to remember the boy and the girl who
inspired them.

One day he took her to the zoo at Quistacocha. The zoo lay ten
miles west of the city along a red track which petered out into the
trees. The track was the only road that led from Belén. Rich young
men, like Don Miguel's son, used it to race the cars they imported
from Brazil.

On the bus, Elena told Gabriel how Don Miguel had shown his
translation to an American priest. The priest had approved it.

"Your translation," said Gabriel.

"No, yours. I had nothing to do with it."

"Why do you work for him?"

It was well known that her father had been instrumental in
bringing down the Minero family. But some parts of the jungle
cover tracks quicker than others. Perhaps Don Miguel had a
superstition about the power of Henriques. Perhaps he couldn't find
anyone else. To Elena the matter was simple.

"To qualify as a guide with the Escuela Nacional de Turismo, I need a diploma. And he needs me."

"A crook like that?"

"He's ill."

"Every pig has its Martinmas," said Gabriel. "He's the most corrupt man in Belén. He stinks from the head down."

"He's got cancer of the pancreas, Gabriel. Dr Lache has found a tumour the size of a fist."

Gabriel decided to talk about the diploma.

"What else do you need to know?"

"Everything," she sighed. "Hotel prices, the times of boats and flights, what films are on, where to rent motorbikes and cars, the best discos. . ."

"Which are the best discos?"

"The Surcusal in Próspero. The Dalmacia in Nauta."

"Let's go tonight," said Gabriel, trying to recover some ground. She shook her head. "I can't. Not tonight."

"Why not?"

"I'm doing something else."

Gabriel was too proud to ask what. Instead he said, "You enjoy learning this?"

"Of course – and Gabriel, don't sulk." She quoted: "'Tourism has had the biggest economic and social impact on our century'."

"Where does it say that?"

"Here, in my guide-book." From her bag she produced a thin pamphlet. She showed Gabriel the sentence. It was underlined in yellow crayon on a page headed "What is tourism?"

Gabriel read the answer.

"It's free.

"It creates work.

"It makes one understand the true history and geography of our marvellous land.

"It is important for men and women to be able to change their lives and abandon their traditional place of work."

The aspirations of the Peruvian tourist board were similar to those of Mariátegui, thought Gabriel. He returned the book.

"Face it, Gabriel, you're an out-of-touch intellectual. Come on, move, we're here."

Quistacocha was named after a legend that a local Indian tribe had seen Christ descending into the lake, or cocha. Other legends were painted on a wall leading down to the lake. Yacuruna, the green-skinned river god which never closed its eyes and lived under water with those it had captured. Sachamama, the mother of the mountains, an enormous yellow serpent with little ears. The Tunchi or devil, which took the shape of a man and on dark nights announced its presence with the whisper: "Fin. . . fin. . . fin."

The waters of Sachachorro.

Gabriel pointed. "You know their story?"

"Once you've drunk them you never leave Belén," replied Elena. "They rise below that Benedictine hostel in town, beside the large rubbish tip."

"You'll pass," he replied.

"What about this?" she said of a painting half-hidden by leaves. She brushed them back to show a silhouetted river boat. Its lights blazed, its funnel trailed a wreath of grey smoke, its paddles propelled it forward into the inky dusk.

"The phantom river boat," they both read. "On the night of the full moon, this mysterious shape can be seen sailing down river while its passengers indulge in orgies and bacchanals."

"Where do we board?" asked Gabriel, but Elena was serious.

"My father believed it. He told my aunt he once travelled as a passenger on something similar. One of the men had different coloured eyes."

Gabriel thought better than to contradict her. "Perhaps it was the Tunchi?"

They walked until they came to a fork in the path. One side led down to the warm lagoon – part of a paiche breeding project – and a stretch of sand where two people were punching a volleyball. The other led into the trees.

Elena reached for Gabriel's hand. She pulled him over a rickety bridge to a raised cage. It lay in a clearing in the subaqueous light of the forest. Around the cage, the shadows cast a broken net which caught the sun, diffracting it into a shoal of fishes.

"Look," she pointed. "Isn't he wonderful?"

A jaguar lay panting on its side across the length of the new cage.

Its eyes were shut. Its heart beat rapidly under a white chest. Every now and then an ear twitched against the flies. They flew up from the chicken claws and the dried slugs of faeces on the floor.

As Gabriel took in the creature, he noticed a couple seated on a bench under the trees. From where he stood they also seemed framed by the cage. The jaguar heard the giggles of the girl as the man tried to kiss her. It opened its round black eyes. The giggles grew louder. The jaguar licked its paws. It rubbed its neck against the mesh. It grabbed its own legs for something to play with.

The dress slipped further from the shoulder.

The animal closed its eyes. It screwed up its face as if it were weeping.

The scene affected Gabriel. He felt like the jaguar, a creature condemned to live imprisoned within his own habitat. Yet looking at the bench, he felt a different stirring.

"Turn round," said Elena. "I want to take a photograph. And, Gabriel," she said, stamping her feet, "smile."

He tried a smile. He heard the camera click. "No, stay there." She wound on and clicked again. "Just making sure."

"Now you." Gabriel reached for the camera.

But she backed away, refusing. She hated being photographed – and they had an argument which resulted, finally, in Elena allowing herself to be taken standing stiffly against the cage with her eyes closed, like the jaguar.

It was on a bench in the cathedral square that he began telling Elena of his admiration for Castro and of how it was possible for a handful of people to cause a whole system to come crashing down with a single push.

"Would you want that?" she asked.

He hesitated before answering.

"I don't know."

What he did know made him rise every morning with a hard knot in his stomach as bitter as a lime. The bitterness related to his father.

Gabriel's father was a man who had spoken with fire in his eyes about love and women, but he had never been in love except with

Gabriel's mother, and probably only after she had died.

Gabriel never knew his mother, who came from a family of fishermen from a village near Leticia. She had died in giving birth to him. But ten years after her death he suddenly realized that people had been whispering all along how his parents' relationship was really one between brother and sister.

Nor, though they shared a house, did he know much about the woman his father married a year before his own death. All Gabriel knew was her unhappiness. Each morning he saw her rocking in the shadows, adjusting the red velvet cushion at her back and worrying a mole on her cheek as she remembered every injustice that had ever happened to her in more detail than Funes the Memorious.

She never responded beyond a curt nod of her small head and a stretching of her legs, when Gabriel urged her to cheer up for God's sake, everybody loses their husband some time or other. She understood that, but what she could not understand was how fate could deal the mechanic she had married so late in life a hand that matched his father's, the Chinese coolie from Hiempen.

Prurigo's trunk lay by her chair covered in cream muslin and supporting an out-of-focus portrait, framed in tin, of his lean face – as well as an oval photograph of Gabriel's father on a motorbike (outside the garage from where he returned every night with hands as black as saw blades).

She continued to curse the day on which Gabriel's father had set off to give Don Miguel once and for all a piece of his proud mind.

"That's it, that's it, that's it," he said on receiving the compulsory purchase order which Don Miguel had served on him in order to make the garage, his life's work, a showroom for, he could hardly bring himself to say it, outboard engines. Who knows how many blind eyes must have been turned for Don Miguel to win the concession. Gabriel's father couldn't have counted if he had a 100 fingers. But he knew it was not right, and that's what he went to tell Don Miguel in his wedding tie and jacket, leaving his motorbike in its usual place under the open window.

They found his body next day in the lake at Moronacocha, his head bump bump bumping against a Petro-Peru container, his face mother of pearl in the oil, his lungs full of mud, cold spit and grape-skins. Corporal Velarde could offer no solution, but that he had slipped and hit his head.

Don Miguel said this unfortunate incident had taken place before the intended meeting. The last time he had set eyes on the mechanic was a fortnight before when he was adjusting a piston to his son's Chevrolet. He had yet to receive a bill, but nothing would please him more than to forward an amount he could be confident would cover it.

To the young Gabriel immersed in Mariátegui, the death of his father was a blow that put into painful relief all the things he had read about in his small back room where each night he heard his step-mother tossing and turning and waking in her raving sleep with a curse for each man, woman and child she had ever known or was likely to meet.

"There doesn't seem to be a peaceful way for this country," he told Elena. No amount of legal reform was going to change the system. Three per cent of the population owned eighty-three per cent of the land. In Puno, there was one doctor for 98,000 people. About fifty per cent of all children were dying before the age of five – and it was getting worse.

"But when you Spanish arrived we had one of the most sophisticated empires on earth."

"My family came from Portugal," she reproached him. "Yours from China. And these statistics are as absurd as. . . as saying that the human body is seventy-five per cent water, or whatever they tell us at school."

"You know what I mean."

"What about Hipólito? Does he agree?"

"Hipólito's a poet."

He was not going to tell her about Hipólito. Hipólito wanted the revolution to begin tomorrow. Hipólito quoted Che Guevara in time with his tennis ball. "It is not always necessary (thud) to wait until all conditions for revolution exist (thud), the revolutionary foco can create them (thud)." Their arguments rang out in the shed by the river where Hipólito had installed a press. Arguments about the need for real organization, about the necessity to have the masses on their side, about the inevitability of violence. Arguments familiar to every student revolutionary from Vienna and Paris to Guatemala City. Arguments that raged as Hipólito ran off his poems and Gabriel stacked them in neat piles ready for distribution to the editors who would consider Hipólito Mercedes' unsolicited offering but he must understand that journalism was a hard and unrewarding profession and they could give no firm date as to when publication might be.

"Is he a good poet?" Elena asked.

"That's not the point."

"What is the point?"

"The point is how can we sit here knowing that after four hundred years of colonial rule, the lot of the average Peruvian hasn't improved one bit? He has no rights. He has only obligations. If I make a complaint, it's regarded by Don Miguel as insubordination. If I organize a petition, it's looked on as a rebellion. And you know why the average Peruvian has no rights?" he asked. "I'll tell you why. Because he's illiterate. And he's illiterate because he speaks Quechua. Yet there's not a single school in the whole land which can teach him to read and write in his native tongue. Don't you think that's disgusting? Don't you think that's really disgusting?"

"Do you speak Quechua?" Elena asked innocently. Then spotting Hipólito on the corner of Próspero she jumped up and waved.

"My saviour," she greeted the poet. "Just in time to stop my indoctrination. Now will you both walk me to my aunt's. I forgot to tell you, she's taking me to Lima. You won't be seeing me for a fortnight. When I return, I promise, promise to visit you both in prison."

"Gabriel, what have you been saying?" said Hipólito later.

"Nothing, nothing."

"And it was you who told me to be so careful."

Chapter 12

GABRIEL HAD KNOWN ELENA for three months when she flew to Lima with her aunt Consuelo. In the week that followed he experienced a violent change in his feelings towards her. One day he woke knowing something had happened. He rose from his bed and realized what it was. He was in love.

The day was no different from any other except he felt out of breath at not being with her and the sore shape of his heart in his chest. That night he couldn't sleep. He imagined the warm skin of her back beneath her shirt. Her blue eyes. Her laugh.

He found the glass of water she had left when collecting the final pages of the translation. He kept it by his bed, sipping it in small doses as if he was drinking part of her. He smelt the velvet cushion on the rocking chair where she had sat. All he smelt was worn fibre and the cheap scent of his step-mother.

"I've fallen in love with the gringa in Raimondi," he told his step-mother helplessly. In five years he had never confessed anything to her.

"What do I do?"

"Fly to Patagonia," she grunted. "I've never seen such a six-foot death wish."

Gabriel missed her so much, that on the fourth day he took the photograph of Elena with her eyes closed to the Salón de Belleza and had Dominica Zumate make thirty copies in different shapes and sizes.

"You must care for her a lot," she said. She knew rather too many women who would appreciate such attention from a good-looking boy like Gabriel.

"I do."

He pinned the photographs to his bedroom wall so that before he went to sleep and after he woke and whenever he looked up from his books he might see Elena in close up, or standing by the jaguar's cage, or with the couple kissing in the background.

But still he missed her.

As the week went on, he went from one pitch of emotion to another. When she comes back, he thought, I must not see her or speak to her. His step-mother was right. What can she see in me? She is white, from a European family. I am a Chinese cholo. We are different animals. I must not expose myself any more. I must put a tourniquet on my feelings.

But he could no more stem his feelings than he could stop the flow of the river he saw every day from the Malecón. In his thoughts Elena became a gazelle – a borrowed image, he realized, never having seen such a creature except in books. A shivering, beautiful animal who might, if he was lucky, edge towards his outstretched hand. But who would leap to the high ground at any sudden move he made, and turn her gaze to another view.

To consult Hipólito was out of the question. Gabriel turned instead to a fellow student at San Agustín. His name was Julio Ángel Medina.

"So what do I do, Julio, what do I do? I'm going out of my head."

"Love is a four-letter word," said Julio. "But it's a good one. Just be cool."

"I am being cool," he screamed.

"Then all I can suggest is manteca de bufeo," said Julio. "Dolphin lard. Rub it on your balls, and you have any woman you want."

"But I don't necessarily want her like that. I want her to feel the same for me."

"It can have that effect too."

"I don't believe you. But if I did, where would I get some?"

"There's a brujo at the end of the Maniti. My brother Bonifacio has directions." Julio smiled. "If it works, let me know."

At first Gabriel resisted the idea of heading upriver to a tributary where the waters turned black from the decomposed forest. Nor had he any desire to take refuge in a witchdoctor's lotion. A week later he stepped ashore at a community of five thatched dwellings called Nuevo Triunfo.

A tin roof balanced over the brujo's hut like a saucepan lid. The mud floor was beaten to a shiny blackness. A table stood in one corner, stacked with perfume bottles containing coloured ointments. There was also a Bible, an astrological almanac and a selection of the *Reader's Digest* from 1957. A calendar pinned to the wall behind showed the motor yacht *Skorpios* among the icebergs of the San Rafael lagoon, Chile.

"Come here," said the brujo. He was an old man with eyes like pockets of cane spirit and the skin of a prune. One of his trouser legs was sewn up at the knee. In Gabriel's honour he had brilliantined his hair and changed into a pair of green trousers.

"Yes, come here," he said. He indicated the floor where he sat, and lit a large home-rolled cigarette.

A fire burned beside him. The empty spit was supported by a black tapir skull and a charred sewing machine.

Gabriel sat.

"Well?"

Gabriel explained.

The brujo smiled.

"What is the reason for living if not the love of a woman. Do you have pictures?"

"Not with me."

"Pity. It's better with pictures." With pictures he could go into the grass outside and when the sun came up he could bury the picture of Gabriel. When the sun set he could bury the picture of Gabriel's woman with some earth, some bones and some leaves wrapped in red thread.

"Then never more will your two souls separate, till death. And you will keep on singing, singing, singing."

"I haven't any pictures."

"I know another spell."

With that he advanced on Gabriel and puffed a gust of smoke down his front. "Nana nee," he began in a high-pitched whine, rubbing the stump of his knee against Gabriel's back.

"Egan nee nee nee nee," he chanted, invoking the spirits of the white ant crawling over Gabriel's leg and requesting that Elena be drawn to him likewise.

"Then I start sucking on your stomach, this side of your neck, your feet. Then you lie down and you promise to diet and you promise to diet well and you promise not to eat chicken or pig. Yes, sir, because the Lord is helping us. The powerful Father whose power is the highest. Sir Jesus Christ who will make her feel love every hour and feel that way all day long. Nee nee nee nee, du!du!du!du!" he continued, puffing deeply on the cigarette, which had gone out, and blowing into his cupped hands. With a final moan it was over.

"What about manteca de bufeo?" said Gabriel.

"As well?"

"Just in case."

"All right," sighed the brujo. "I'll give you manteca." He rose and hobbled to a table. He produced a Nescafé tin from among the bottles.

"Here," he said. "You'd better take the lot."

"What happens when you use it?"

"The person you desire will love you and never leave you. Apply it sparingly."

On the stove the water came to the boil. Gabriel found a tin mug. He stirred himself some coffee, thinking of the Nescafé tin which had caused him such embarrassment.

He had not applied its greasy white contents sparingly enough on the afternoon Elena returned from Lima. He had made a date with her at the Café Nanay. It was her suggestion. He would have preferred another rendezvous. The café was a regular haunt of Don Miguel's which was the reason Gabriel avoided it. He had an abiding vision of Elena's boss sitting at the same table every morning, wiping the crumbs from his mouth with two thick fingers as he heard out X or Y. Invariably, Don Miguel produced a handkerchief from his pocket to complete the job. After dabbing his forehead, he would stretch back, straighten his shirt over a large stomach and, the business done, lean forward to tell a joke, smiling that unfinished smile of his in the knowledge that once again he had concluded the better deal.

That evening, Gabriel's first emotion was of relief that Don

Miguel was nowhere to be seen; his second reaction was surprise on finding Hipólito with Elena.

Gabriel moved to join them. Gingerly, he positioned himself on the other side of Elena.

"Nice jeans," said Hipólito. "New?"

"Why else do you think I'm walking like this?"

"I was just telling her what a stranger you've been. No one's seen you for days. Not even in the library. Where've you got to?"

"Out and about," said Gabriel evasively, and to Elena who narrowed her eyes as she drew on a cigarette, "my step-mother wanted something taken to a cousin upriver. How was Lima?"

She wrinkled her nose. "Horrible – as usual. My aunt spent the whole time dragging me round Miraflores. The shop she wanted was no longer there."

She tapped out a list on her fingers. "She complained about the rubbish, about my job, about the kind of people she imagines I'm consorting with . . ."

Across the table, it was Hipólito's nose that wrinkled.

"What's that smell?"

"What smell?" asked Gabriel.

"I don't know, something funny."

Gabriel moved closer to Elena. On what grounds did her aunt disapprove of these imagined consorts?

"Don Miguel must have said something. Though how he's heard about you two, I don't know."

"He has his fingers," said Gabriel.

"Sacramento, I know what it is," said Hipólito. He leant forward – and dropping his voice, he told them.

"That boy behind us," he hissed, jabbing with his thumb. "That's who's got it on. Don Miguel's son, Mario."

The boy became aware he was the subject of their conversation. He glowered at Hipólito and smiled at Elena.

Elena's face glowed conspiratorially. She encouraged Hipólito to give more details. He needed little encouragement. With large eyes, he told them he had smelled it once before, in a brujo's hut on the Maniti. It was made from the bufeo, the Amazon dolphin, a pink-bellied fish with growths on its stomach like a woman's breasts and a passion for men.

"The fishermen believe that at night they turn into white people. They rise from their city under the water and go to the discos. You, for example," he held Gabriel by the arm. "You can be taken by one into the water. You are young and handsome. You meet this beautiful girl. Toot, toot, boom, boom, she takes you away. You are never seen again."

"Don't be silly, Hipólito."

"The brujos make love to the bufeos. It makes them stronger. They have to do it in pairs, though. The dolphin holds on so strongly, the brujo becomes paralysed with pleasure. Lesser mortals make an ointment from its genitals. Rubbed onto their own," he concluded, "it makes women squirm with an uncontrollable desire."

"No," said Elena.

"Hipólito, you're having us on," said Gabriel.

"Do you know something," Hipólito went on.

"What?"

"I can still smell it."

Unable to contain herself, Elena burst into laughter. She buried her head on Gabriel's shoulder.

"Gabriel?" Hipólito raised an eyebrow.

Elena lifted her lips to his ear. "Sweetheart," she whispered, "it's coming through your jeans."

That was the moment. The moment it finally came home to Hipólito what his friend was feeling. The moment Elena understood what she felt for Gabriel. A moment of supreme embarrassment which only ended when a blushing Gabriel rose from the table and walked to the jukebox.

"What've you put on now?" asked Elena, still laughing.

"My favourite song," said Gabriel.

"What's it called?"

He placed his hand on the back of her neck and sat down.

"'Ojos azules'."

Suddenly she bent forward and kissed him in full view of Hipólito and the rest of the café. So that whenever he played it he would remember her.

Chapter 13

EARLY ONE MORNING in March 1965 Hipólito came to his house. Gabriel was reading a copy of Max Nomad's *Aspects of Revolt*. He heard Hipólito in the front room.

"Morning, Señora Lung. And how is my favourite widow?"

"Tired, Señor Mercedes, tired."

The fly curtain burst apart and Hipólito's energetic face appeared, dividing the bead strands.

"We're going to Lima," he said. A friend at the telegraph office had alerted him to a meeting to be addressed by Federico Fuente, a founder member of the Movement of the Revolutionary Left.

In the end four of them had taken the Faucett flight to Lima. They included Julio, and at Julio's request, his older brother Bonifacio, a man built like a bull who worked part-time at the plywood factory. The address they sought was a house near the gold museum, somewhere in the mist which crawled with the feet of an insect over the face and covered the capital for half the year. A group of men and women sat in three neat semi-circles in front of an empty fireplace. Two men stood like fighting cocks on either side of the grate, arguing.

Gabriel's attention was drawn to the man who had been talking as they entered. Gabriel could make out nothing he was saying, though there was something charismatic about the way he moved his body, his hands, his face. It was the face of an Inca. Dark, deepset eyes. A high forehead from which the hair rose in black flames. A mouth fluent with defiance.

There was frustration in the room as the four men made their shy advance. No one wished to interrupt the argument, but the new arrivals had to be introduced. The other man by the fireplace inspected them through thick glasses, his Adam's apple pecking at his throat. He thrust out a hand.

"Federico Fuente."

One by one they shook it.

"This is Rolando," he said introducing them to those who stood up. "Néstor, Laura, Emilio . . ." and so on, round the room, until they arrived at the man who stood in silence next to him. He scratched his elbow compulsively. Despite the heat he wore a jacket. Fuente uttered his name, introducing him as a philosophy professor from Ayacucho. The man smiled, showing a mouth of perfect teeth.

The four of them found places to sit. The argument resumed. It was Fuente who began. His grey fanatic's face seemed invigorated by the new element in the audience. His subject was Castro. For an hour he spoke of the Cuban example. Fidel's revolution showed that it was possible to make a genuine revolution. That it was possible to nationalize the big companies created by the monster of the north. That it was possible to make people the owners of their own houses and the land they tilled. That it was possible to recover a sense of national independence and pride. Fidel had showed all this was possible and that it could be made a possibility elsewhere if only arms were given to the people and the people were made aware that the revolution was a historical fact which nothing and nobody could stop and which had to begin now, this moment.

At the end of Fuente's speech, the man from Ayacucho spoke.

"Fidel Castro is a chorus girl," he said.

The room was silent. A stick of dynamite had been rolled into it instead of a quiet sentence of six words. Fuente sat down stunned.

The mandarin from Ayacucho, his hands thrust into the opposite sleeves of his jacket, continued talking. In an even voice he announced he was not against the armed struggle, but that it would be far bloodier, far more violent, far more demanding of sacrifice than anyone had envisaged. That above and beyond all things it had to be an indigenous revolution which accepted nothing, not so much as a single peso, nor a single pistol nor a single bullet from outside. That each of them must be more prepared, much more prepared. That they must first learn the language of the people they hoped to liberate. That the time was not right.

"How many of you speak Quechua?"

Not a hand went up.

"If we act now we throw away everything," he said and sat down.

Gabriel was impressed. As the meeting split into three or four groups, he looked about for Hipólito. He saw his friend holding forth to some older students, next to a lamp which had been caramelized by its bulb. There was a gleam in his eye, a strut in his voice. Gabriel heard him boast about the amount of popular support which existed in Belén, the need to act, the press he owned, his poetry. . .

He moved outside onto the terrace. Fuente was having to be restrained from implementing several angry threats, each prefaced by the words "fucking provincial". Gabriel looked about for the provincial. He returned to the room. Someone told him he had left.

"Wasn't he marvellous?" said Hipólito on the plane. They were playing bingo.

"Yes."

"Fuente, I mean. Not that tiresome man from Ayacucho."

"Bingo!" shouted a woman in front. She fanned her face with a book of horoscopes. Over the intercom it was announced she had won a free flight.

Eight days later, Hipólito received a pamphlet from Lima outlining MIR's policy. It was signed by Fuente with a green swirl and contained best wishes to "our valued brothers in Belén" together with a suggestion that herein might be found the right road.

Hipólito interpreted it as a sign of alert. He became more irritable. He threw his tennis ball harder and harder against his press; against the tiled front of the Booth supermarket in Sargento Lores, against the pavements, against the doors of parked cars, against the wall of Eden Expeditions.

Thud. Thud. Thud.

The noise was always there in the background. Gabriel remembered it loudest during the early days of his romance with Elena.

The news that Gabriel, the mechanic's son, was courting Elena Silves, Señora Guzmán's beautiful niece, had taken that part of the town which cared about such things by a brief storm.

Pía Zumate – La Palometa – didn't believe it until she saw them with her own eyes embracing in the cathedral square like a pair of . . .

exactly – lovebirds. At that moment the scene filled her with unbearable nostalgia for her own youth, or rather, she realized abruptly, with what she might have made of it had not her eyes been blinded by a cinder from a Booth Line funnel called Harry.

Like many others Pía Zumate had always suspected Gabriel's celebrated indifference to girls indicated another taste – a predilection shared by the only other man Pía Zumate had loved. A man she refused to name, not even to herself, but whose advances had terminated after she apprehended him in a scuffle and grabbing of sheets with a tawny rivereño from Nauta.

For a long time she would continue to see Gabriel and Elena as she saw them then, her memory casting its muslin net over the bench to protect their image from the nuisances of the real world.

As she continued her path to Dr Lache's surgery, with a marked spring in her step that made Don García shake his head in a rapture of longing, and say "Qué hermosa!", Pía Zumate felt that if God only exerted himself it was perfectly possible for all to be right with the world.

Why the hell didn't he do it more often?

Gabriel had never been one to hold his wounded finger to the world. But on the day after the episode in the Café Nanay, he told Elena something he had not told any girl. Something he had never been able to feel, despite dreaming of it.

They were sitting on the same ivory-coloured bench where Gabriel had expounded his political theories.

"I love you," he heard himself croak.

Her response was to place a finger on his lips.

"Words come easily to you."

Gabriel remembered a line from one of his friend's sadder efforts. "The gap between the nuzzle and the kiss is the gap between the thunder and the rain." He was thinking of this line and the possible truth it contained when he felt Elena brush his hurt face with her lips, and his lips with hers. Then just as Hipólito's gap had closed, the bell of the yellow cathedral sounded across the square.

Elena pulled away. She looked around. With regret written in her eyes, she said she had to go.

"It's the *Messiah* next week," she explained. "No, you needn't come. I can imagine your position on religion."

"What about tonight?" he asked. He held her hand as she stood up. "What about going to the Dalmacia?"

She looked down at him. Her smile conveyed the expression she had to do something she wasn't particularly keen to do. "I'm sorry, Gabriel. I've planned something else."

He didn't ask what. He was at that stage in love when you do not ask to know more than you are told.

She tapped his nose and walked off without looking back.

"Did you pray for me?" he asked next day.

"Only a little. You don't want to get more conceited."

"Who else?"

"Oh, about thirty or forty others. My aunt, Hipólito, of course, Don Miguel . . ."

"Don Miguel?"

"Yes, I pray for him a lot. Dr Lache says there's little hope."

"Six weeks at most," Dr Lache had apparently told Don Miguel, after finding secondary nodules in his nutmegged liver. At first he hoped it might have been biliary cholic or an impacted gallstone. But the large globulous swelling in Don Miguel's ribs was now the size of a child's head.

Elena finally introduced Gabriel to her aunt.

"She needs cheering up. It's the tenth anniversary of my parents' death. Also, she says it's time she met you."

Gabriel knew the green house well. He walked past it every day on his way to San Agustín. One side, on Calle Raimondi, was shadowed by a palm tree whose leaves grew against the tin roof and curled back upon themselves. The other side, on Arana, had three doors that were never opened. Señora Guzmán was always shooing figures from the steps where they sat eating aguaje fruit. Once a week, she swept the dried peel away with a furious glance which the fruit seller ignored as she had ignored it every Saturday for fifteen years while she scraped the orange flesh with a knife that still lacked a handle, and a smile that said Consuelo could complain till she burst like a melon.

Gabriel knocked on the door at the appointed time. He wore a linen jacket and a sober tie fastened in a tight knot. He was led upstairs to a room filled with books and flowers.

Consuelo was on her second pink gin. Her eyes were bright; her face puffy, causing its white hairs to prick out against the chinchilla shawl on her shoulders.

"I'm draped in black, but perfectly all right," she reassured him. She offered a hand. In her other hand she held a glass rimmed with purple lipstick.

"I thought we'd eat here, in what used to be my husband's study. Elena's still changing, so we can have a word."

She mixed Gabriel a drink, dropping an ice-cube on the floor.

"Don't worry, I'll pick it up later. I hope this tastes all right. I got worried they'd watered the gin. In fact it was the tonic."

They talked, or rather, she did.

"I suppose you're a communist. Young people like you always adore anything left wing. I don't mind. But middle-class people like myself – not millionaires, but middle-class – who have a certain standard of living, we ought to leave. This is no country for our children. I think I will leave now my husband's dead."

She was interrupted by the telephone.

"Hello. Bishop Barrantes? How nice to hear you. Yes. You'll have to shout. Who've I got with me? No. Gabriel Lung. The mechanic's son. Elena's friend. You know, the old garage behind the Cinema Bolognesi." She looked at Gabriel. "I suppose he could be called good-looking."

As she spoke a man in a dirty white jacket entered. She held up her glass. He filled it. Two ice-cubes separated with a loud crack.

"En silencio," she hissed, and gestured at the melting cube on the floor.

"Yes, Bishop. Of course I will give you first refusal." Her brown eyes muddied and strayed to an ivory cross on the wall. It hung above a frame containing the matriculation portrait of Alonso Silves in his rabbit-edged gown. "What? This line's terrible. Yes, yes. If I do decide to sell it – no, I'm not saying I won't – you shall be

"I'm going home."

"No, wait."

He came after her, enveloped in his silence. When he bent to kiss her goodnight she clung to him.

"Is your aunt in?" he asked. He rested his chin on her head. He looked up at the dark windows rising from the single wooden balcony.

"No, she's in Lima."

"And I can't spend the night?" He rocked her back and forth.

"No, Gabriel, not yet. When I'm ready. I promise you, when I'm ready."

"When will that be?"

She was prevented from speaking by a movement in one of the locked doorways. A shape slouched towards them. It stepped into the damask glare of the street light, shaking a black, grease-stained head. With a moan, it stretched a talon towards Elena.

"Get along with you," snapped Gabriel, consigning the figure to the night.

Then, reassuringly to Elena, his face pressed against a cold earring, "Only a beggar."

By accepting back the book of his favourite essays, Gabriel was making a tacit agreement to keep that part of his life separate from hers. Whenever he saw her, once or twice a week, he avoided all mention of politics. He never talked about Hipólito's impatience, nor of his growing impatience with Hipólito.

Nor, when the moment came, did he tell her of the man from Lima.

It was a Thursday night. Gabriel had walked down to Hipólito's shed on the river, built from the planks of an old river boat and now used to store machines awaiting repair – coffee percolators, outboard engines, television sets, sewing machines, goods imported by the very boat which had been metamorphosed to house them.

Here, under a green tarpaulin, Hipólito kept the small press he had acquired when El Oriente modernized its offices. Hipólito had originally seen the press (made in Hamburg, according to a metal label on its back, in 1925 – "the same year as Borges' *Luna de enfrente*") as a means of publishing his poetry. In Lima, he had boasted about it to Fuente's followers. He was disappointed, then flattered that the interest they registered had nothing to do with his verse.

The shed was empty. Gabriel was on the point of leaving when he heard a strange tapping. He turned. There was a man leaning in the doorway, drumming a biro against the frame. He had a stringy moustache, short hair swept back from a lined forehead and the tense air of someone more accustomed to the boardroom of a provincial bank than a riverside hut with a dirty concrete floor. "Hipólito Mercedes?"

At that moment Hipólito appeared behind him, drinking a bottle of Inca Kola. "Our friends in Lima sent me," said the man, loosening his tie. His name was Gasco. He had just come from a meeting at Fuente's headquarters on the Urubamba. He had been charged with setting up a foco in Belén – as well as the country around Piura. He hardly knew the jungle, but Fuente had said not to worry, they had a strong body of sympathizers in the city. He sincerely hoped so, he told Hipólito, because things had to start happening like yesterday. Heaving himself onto an empty oil drum, Gasco reached into his jacket pocket.

"I think this is what you've been waiting for."

Hipólito spread out the folded pages. He began reading. Gabriel looked over his shoulder. In small, neat handwriting was declared Fuente's revolutionary proclamation. Armed with both the necessary weapons and the knowledge that they had correctly gauged the people's feelings, MIR called for the immediate dissolution of Congress, a general amnesty for political prisoners, the handing over of large estates to the workers and "the recovery of full national sovereignty".

"At last," said Hipólito. "At last." He glanced at Gasco on his perch.

"Well?"

Gasco nodded at the press. "I want you to print it," he said. "I want you to distribute it as widely as you can. And then, at the given time," he said, slipping onto the floor and rubbing his hands on his trousers, "I want you to go into action."

"But what does he mean by action?" said Gabriel after Gasco left. He was exasperated. "Action against what? Doesn't he know there's only four of us? What are we meant to do? Toss firecrackers at the Mayor?"

"He's promised all the weapons we need in good time," explained Hipólito. "And we'll be told what to do. The point is that the right conditions will be created once everything gets under way. Once we've printed this, once people know what's happening, we'll be joined by many more. You'll see."

Gabriel thought back to the room in Lima and the professor from Ayacucho, who had left Gabriel in no doubt of his desire – expressed quietly and ruthlessly – for what all of them wanted in that room. Yet he had been so sure of himself in advising caution.

What Fuente was proposing seemed absurd.

"No, Hipólito. You don't eat chicken when the meat's still red. Nor do you start a revolution because that's how you happen to feel."

"You're wrong," said Hipólito. He laughed.

"I'm not."

"Does that mean you won't help me print this?"

"Yes."

So it was Hipólito alone who hauled the tarpaulin off the press. He cleaned the italic fount and with surprising speed set the text so that it resembled an introduction to an epic poem rather than a revolutionary proclamation. He ran off four thousand copies and spent a day wandering the town like a seed-sower leaving them in empty class-rooms and in bus stops, on benches and doorsteps and in the hall of the Club de Leones.

As Hipólito predicted, several promised their support immediately; once it was noted how unhurried the authorities had been in removing the posters, a number of others joined them. Lacking any instruction, Hipólito told them to prepare themselves. But the strain was showing. The tread on his tennis ball disappeared altogether. It was now a shiny, bald globe that he bounced off everything in sight, including on one occasion the windscreen of Don Miguel's Chevrolet which braked angrily at the corner of Putumayo and remained there, menacingly still, its doors about to burst open, before gliding off down the Malecón.

"Coward," said Hipólito, retrieving his weapon from the road, then hurling it back towards Edith.

"Here, catch."

She watched the ball roll away without unfolding her arms and only by running hard did Hipólito prevent it from bouncing into the river.

Edith Pusanga was Indian and proud of the fact she had no Spanish blood. She was prouder still of her descent from a Chanca chieftain who wore stolen spurs like sea-urchins and separated from the Incas because he considered them too lenient on Pizarro's brother, Gonzalo. On a captured horse – at first he thought the animal and its original rider one and the same beast – he had led his tribe to a peak near Tarapoto where he founded a city of handsome men whose only blemish was an addiction to human flesh.

Hipólito used to joke that Edith had inherited his tastes.

Gabriel never made such jokes with her, which might have been why she confided in him.

"You're more patient, Gabriel. It runs deeper with you." They were collecting drinks from the counter of a bar which had opened two blocks away from the Café Nanay. At a table by the door, Hipólito was pretending to read Elena's palm. "You're going to be discreetly unfaithful tonight," they heard him saying.

"You're stronger, too," Edith went on. "I feel with him it's only half serious. It's a pose. Something to take his mind off other things."

"Like what?" asked Gabriel.

"Like his poetry. Like the fact he can't write a single line without one feeling embarrassed for him."

"Edith!" He looked into two heavily made-up eyes. "From you of all people."

"You know it's true."

"Because he doesn't write his poems for you?"

"No, he doesn't," she answered. "But that's not the issue. He knows he's a terrible poet, but he drowns the knowledge of this in playing dangerous games. Look at him. What do you really think he feels for the plight of the Indian deep down? Beyond some romantic notion, very little. He's just a sentimental hangover from the poets of the Twenties. A café revolutionary. Could you honestly entrust him with a gun? It would go off in his jacket, if it didn't fall through the hole in his pocket first."

"Are we that different?"

"Yes, we are. What's more we know it. We're in this for real."

"Then why do you stay with him?" Gabriel asked. He gathered up three glasses, leaving the fourth on the counter.

"Because I'm fond of him." She reached for the thin flaring stem. She took a sip. "And sorry for him."

"That's how he gets all his women," said Gabriel. "They fall for him because they think no one else will."

He began moving to the table, but she held him back.

"And you. Why do you think women fall for you?"

"Do they? I don't think they do."

"She does."

"The exception."

"But she doesn't sleep with you."

"Is that a question?"

She turned her kohled eyes on Elena.

"She's not one of us at all."

In the second week of June, news reached Hipólito that Fuente had attacked the Santa Rosa mine in Andamarca and removed a large amount of dynamite.

"It's just a matter of time," Hipólito promised. "Gasco should be in touch any day now."

But he wasn't. Not that it seemed to matter. At last something was happening. A bridge was blown up on the Maraniyoc and another at Comas. Three haciendas were sacked. A police detachment was ambushed and a sergeant killed.

Nor did it really matter that around the city the military began acting as if there was something in the air more urgent than the threat from Ecuador. It proved they weren't dealing with a handful of horse thieves, as the government was branding Fuente's men.

Then, towards the end of June, Hipólito received a roneoed letter from Fuente. He was taking advantage of a halt in his march, he said. He was writing things "as they came into mind". There was a lot to say. Events had not only justified initial expectations, but progressed further than could have been hoped.

The support given by the peasants had been enormous. Even after a disastrous ambush when a comrade, since reduced to the ranks, had let off his rifle prematurely. It had been an extremely valuable experience. For three days they had fallen back, and learned from their mistakes. Measures were under way to restore contact with the masses.

"It doesn't inspire confidence," said Gabriel. He passed it over to Edith.

Hipólito ran a hand through his hair. "We've got to do something soon. We've got to. Where is that fucking Gasco. It's all slipping like water through our fingers."

"Wait, Hipólito," said Edith. "Give him a chance."

"Gabriel?" Hipólito challenged him.

Gabriel retrieved the pages from Edith's lap.

"I think he's had it," he said.

Hipólito snatched the letter from him. He was furious. "Observe, observe, observe. That's all you ever do. You never act, ever. Well, I'm an actor," he snapped, unconscious of any irony.

And the vigil went on.

One afternoon Gabriel called at Señora Guzmán's house in Raimondi. It was a hot day, hotter than usual, and the few people about kept to the cooling tar of the shadows.

Consuelo's side door lay in full sunlight. The heat made it painful to the touch. Gabriel knocked hard once, then less hard a second time and waited.

He was taking Elena to a film at the Bolognesi. He hadn't seen her for ten days and for all of that time, as for all of the times when they hadn't seen each other or spoken, she had been a shade in his mind.

For ten days he had imagined the evening ahead; the short walk to the decrepit cinema near his father's old garage; the two hours spent watching Luis Sintra's famous love story, daring to press the hand he held in his lap when one of the scratched scenes seemed an apt commentary on their own situation; and afterwards, the frustrating walk back through the warm night to her aunt's house, into which he would have to condense the thousand things he had stored up to say.

"She hasn't come home," said Consuelo, walking onto the balcony. Gabriel took two steps back and looked up. She had her father's crucifix in her hand. She was rubbing it with a cloth. "Try the office."

He walked to Eden Expeditions where he found Elena behind her desk, typing.

"We're late," he said.

She apologized. But Don Miguel had detained her with a last-minute booking. She'd come in early tomorrow to complete the forms.

"It's the least I can do. You may not like him, but he's dying, Gabriel."

"How long has he got?"

"Dr Lache says a matter of days."

They made their way to the cinema. As they walked, a helicopter flew overhead and deafened the square with its chatter.

"Wait." She reached for him. "It's saying something."

Gabriel stood, shielding his eyes. Above the engine noise, he heard the rasp of a loudspeaker. The machine descended and a flock of leaflets tumbled from its belly. A group of schoolchildren scattered to retrieve them. Gabriel snatched one from the air. His lips enacted a silent curse.

"Gabriel, what are they saying?"

But as the helicopter lowered itself closer to the square, dipping the trees and sending an old man's straw hat into the road, no interpreter was needed.

Armed agents were abroad. They were in the pay of foreign governments. Their aim was to subvert the nation. Anything suspicious must be reported. Anyone concealing weapons or spies would be punished. For those attacking the established order, the penalty was death.

"Come on, or we'll miss the film."

"No." She pulled away. "Don't patronize me. I don't mind if we miss it. What's going on, Gabriel?"

"What do you mean?"

"You know perfectly well what I mean. Look at me. Tell me you don't know."

"I don't."

"Then why is everyone forbidding me to see you?"

"Who is . . . ?"

"My aunt . . . "

"I thought she liked me!"

"Don Miguel."

"Screw Don Miguel," cried Gabriel. "Why is he so bloody important all of a sudden?"

"He isn't, but he's the reason I was late. He told me seven soldiers have just been tortured to death at Yahuarina. He said he never wanted to see you in the office again. Or Hipólito."

Gabriel's face tightened.

"So do you want to end it?" he asked. Somewhere in his mind the soft cold nose of a gazelle was drawing back. He felt its tense body preparing to leap.

"I don't know," said Elena. "What do you want? All I know is that I can't go on like this. I've never felt so lonely. It's as if you're afraid of talking to me."

Gabriel put a hand on hers.

"No, Gabriel, you can't deny it."

"You're always busy in the evenings. You're always doing something."

"So, you suspect someone else," she flashed, putting her hands on her hips and throwing up her chin and looking suddenly like the photograph in Consuelo's house of her mother, Colina.

"I don't know what to suspect."

"Well, you're right. There is another man."

"Elena . . . "

"And not only one. Twenty, thirty maybe." She laughed bitterly.

"Boys with no legs, children who can't speak, men who can't eat or walk or smile."

A man walking by quickened his step.

"Where do you imagine Sebastián goes at night? Have you ever thought, you who are so busy changing the lot of the poor? Have you ever stopped to ask yourself what kind of roof he has over his head, or hundreds like him? Have you ever stopped to think what his head actually looks like? No," she said calming herself. "Of course, you haven't. He's just another abstraction. Well." She drew breath. "I know what his face looks like. I know what sounds he makes when you feed him. And I know where he sleeps. It's where I go to at night. I go with the Belgian sisters. There are four of them. They look after the handicapped children who have been thrown into the street like chicken bones. No clothes. No food. No love.

"Last week we ran out of rice to feed them. I told one boy with cerebral palsy there was nothing to eat. He smiled and said 'Don't worry, Elena, we'll pray.' That's all he said. And I thought . . . pray to whom, I thought. You can't live on prayer. It's not something you can eat, not something you can drink. I felt more confused and useless in that moment than I've ever felt. And I'm not much help. I don't suppose I'm any help at all. But I'm learning. And I feel at least it's better to do something – anything, however small, even if it's only washing someone's hands or heating a bowl of soup – than to talk about it."

She looked up.

"But it's not Sebastián I'm worried about right now. It's us," she said. "I try not to think of your politics, of what you might be getting up when you can't see me. I try to suppress these thoughts, but I can't. I've never loved anyone before, but never for a moment did I imagine love could mean this."

They arrived too late for the film. The foyer was deserted. Elena leant against the locked ticket booth, creasing the posters tacked to its red chintz surface which showed the black and white hero of *The Rubber Man's Daughter*.

Gabriel looked at the girl he loved, who would not let him love her as he wanted. He looked at the posters behind, of Luis Sintra, the native of Coimbra who left Portugal to make his fortune in the jevea forests of the New World; the legendary cauchero, the man of mathematical genius who could paralyse ladies with his smile, but who had only ever smiled at one of them, the Rubber Man's daughter.

He looked again at Elena. An eyelash had lodged on her cheek. He wanted to wipe it away. Involuntarily, like a sneeze, he reached out his hand. She flinched. "No, I'll do it. Just tell me where." Taking one of her fingers he brushed it back and forth across her face.

"There."

"All clear?"

"Let's go to the Dalmacia," he said suddenly. "Let's go dancing."

She looked into his eyes, through the thickets where his mind was stumbling.

"All right," she said. "Let's do that."

They went that night. Elena wore her grandmother's blue dress and they danced and danced until the afternoon was forgotten and Gabriel could finally put his arms around her without feeling they embraced a tense girl who might turn her back on him at any second.

"You're appallingly beautiful," he said, affected by the music and the lights. She kissed his ear. "That's like a corny line from the movie we missed."

He felt the texture of her dress.

"Can we make love tonight?"

The words tumbled out before he knew it. They were dry and pleading. His fingers went on kneading the blue small of her back.

"Not now," she said, detaching herself. "But soon."

Soon. The promise sustained him when, at the beginning of August, the air force bombed Pucuta and captured three guerrilla bases in the mountains nearby.

All this absurdity would soon be over, he thought. He wouldn't have to make a choice between Elena and Hipólito. Soon Hipólito's revolution would be buried for good in some remote southern valley and he could devote himself to winning round both Hipólito and

Elena to the revolution he believed in.

His hopes grew when a US Marine Corps adviser in a combat jacket was spotted on the cold slopes leading up to the Mesa Pelada plateau. There in the ichu grass, it was thought that Fuente's men might have regrouped.

Then came unconfirmed reports that napalm had been used against them, that one of Fuente's own men had betrayed him when he made a break for Amaybamba, that the guerrilla leader had been sat on a crate of dynamite and blown sky high.

"I'm not waiting for Gasco," said Hipólito on hearing the news. He slammed his ball against the shed door and walked out.

Next morning, positioned between advertisements for car-hire and bedding, a notice in *El Oriente* called for all those who supported the heroic actions of Comrade Fuente to assemble at the Café Nanay at four o'clock.

"You're mad," raged Gabriel. "You're out of your fucking skull. You might as well pack up now. It was lunatic of you to announce the revolution before it happened. But to invite everyone to turn out in broad daylight as if you were throwing a tea-party . . . "

But Hipólito was radiant. He seized Gabriel by both arms. Didn't Gabriel remember what Fuente had said about the Peruvian peasant? How he was slow to make up his mind, but how when he finally reached a decision he was unmoveable? That was one of the reasons this revolution had taken so long. But that's why when it happened, it was going to be the most effective revolution in the whole history of the world.

"And we've got to make it happen right this minute, before it's too late."

"All right," said Gabriel grimly. "Since you've forced the issue. But we'll skip thé-dansant." He would round up those he could. They might be able to count on eight, ten at most. Then there was the problem of weapons.

"Come," said Hipólito. He left the shed. Gabriel followed him. They walked round the back to an allotment where a neighbour kept manioc and chickens and the rusting carcass of a Toyota pick-up. Hipólito lifted the seat. In the cavity below, badly wrapped in pages of *Caretas*, were ten rifles.

"Arrived last week," explained Hipólito, "from a contact of Edith's in Leticia."

Gabriel stood with his back to the pick-up. He looked at the pale afternoon sky. "Look," he pointed. "A full moon."

Hipólito followed his gaze. "The man in the moon," he said. "He's smiling on us."

"You can't seriously think that looks like a face?"

"Yes," said Hipólito. "I do." His eyes dropped to the ball in his palm. He drew back his arm and threw it with all the strength he had in him.

They watched the ball rise above the roof tops and the buzzards, above the finger-shaped clouds, above the nail-coloured moon, until it disappeared in a flash of sun.

They only heard the nearby thud as it fell on Vásquez's roof where the barrowman's wife had spread two paiche skins to dry, and the subsequent plop as it bounced among the tiny, faded boilersuits which Vásquez had never suffered to be washed until that morning, and the brown meadow butterflies which Francisco, his son, attracted with a paste of mashed banana and urine, and the north end of the market where he sold them in camphored matchboxes, and the frail stands on the steps down to the Plaza Clavero which supported buckets of writhing black carapama, like prehistoric toys, and kerosene for termites, and bootleg cassettes, and perfume with names like Royal Wynsor and Happened Love and Wild Leather, and bottle after bottle of thick creamy lotions for chicken pox and eternal love which Don Emilio recommended only after you had exhausted the powers of the ayahuasca which he sold, whistling like a Tunchi, with a promise that if you crushed its roots and boiled it for seven hours and drank it warm, you would live for a thousand years without ever feeling sickness, somewhere in this teeming, noisy world in the middle of the jungle, Hipólito's ball bounced out of sight forever.

Inspecting his bare hands, Hipólito spoke.

"I'm prepared to go it alone, Gabriel."

Gabriel had pledged his support believing there was still time to persuade Hipólito that his scheme was ludicrous. As Gabriel understood it, this involved boarding the evening packet to Requena and striking overland to join Fuente's last known redoubt in a valley near Manzamari.

In the hut he searched for a piece of paper. The only piece to hand was one of Hipólito's proclamations. Turning it over, he scribbled a note to Elena. He wrote that he would be gone a week, or perhaps two, he didn't know how long exactly. She might hear things but she must not believe them: he would be back. He loved her very, very much, he wrote. She had no idea how much. After entrusting Pía Zumate to deliver his letter – a matter of the heart, he explained, knowing her history of delicate lusts – he went down to the river.

They had assembled on the bank above the Requena wharf. There had been five of them, Bonifacio materializing at the last moment in a floppy denim hat.

"The boat's late," said Edith. She raised her sunglasses and squinted at Gabriel with the sun setting behind him. "Could be later this evening, could be tomorrow."

Gabriel glanced at the pile of canvas bags. "We can't stand here. Let's find a hotel."

Julio agreed. It was risky to be seen in town. He had just come from the cathedral square. The police had blocked off the entrance to the Café Nanay. Its owner would love him for that, said Hipólito, smiling. No one said anything. All of them had misgivings about his advertisement in *El Oriente*.

They carried their bags to a pension two streets behind the waterfront. Hipólito disappeared upstairs to the caballeros. They agreed to meet him at a bar on the Plaza Clavero. Edith left to buy some cigarettes. Julio's request for something to smoke had revealed the five of them had neither cigarettes nor matches.

"How would we have set off the bombs?" one of them joked later in the bar. The others tried to laugh, but their laughs were dry and without humour. The truth was, they were scared stiff. Gabriel saw his moment to stop them. He cleared his throat to speak.

That was when Hipólito began telling him about the dreams he'd been having in which no one talked to him.

That was when Don Miguel walked by with his tart and realized that the guns he'd let through customs with such a magisterial nod could not possibly be destined as hunting rifles for the Club de Leones. Those rifles, he realized, catching sight of Gabriel and Hipólito and the black bundle at their feet which contained them, might tumble something out of the trees but it wouldn't be a turkey cock.

Chapter 15

FROM EDITH'S WINDOW Gabriel could see the floating church where he resurfaced.

He had taken two deep gulps and dived again, following the contours of the hull until he was certain it shielded him from the opposite shore. Then he came up for air.

He coughed as he took in a mouthful of water. His feet found the bottom, but to stand there would have meant sinking in mud. He used his hands to propel him to the bank. One of his espadrilles was missing and his arm was bleeding from where he had torn himself against the hull. But he heard no more shots. When his breathing was steadier, he rose.

A police launch throttled into sight. It sent up large waves that rocked the floating church. Across the river, the crowd were pointing at something in the water. They were pointing at Hipólito, thought Gabriel with a lurch as blood and water dripped from him onto the oily mud.

He made for Hipólito's shed, where Elena found him two hours later. He lay in a heap against the wall, squeezing his arm to stop the blood.

"Oh, my darling," she said. She rocked him in her arms. "My poor, poor darling."

When Pía Zumate delivered the letter, she had rushed immediately to the cathedral and begun a fervent prayer. In the middle of it she heard gunfire. She opened her eyes and found herself looking at her grandfather's Annunciation. As she stared at the Virgin and the Archangel, she realized with horror that she knew the reason for the shots. She had run to the river. All along the waterfront people were talking about how a dangerous terrorist had been killed while escaping. Another terrorist was thought to have drowned, swallowed by Yacuruna, the angry river god.

"I thought it was you they had shot. They hauled this body onto the deck of the police boat. They tried to hide it from us but I saw Hipólito's shirt. I was so relieved. Isn't that terrible?"

She spoke through her tears, as if to herself. "But I knew you would be with Hipólito and I prayed and I prayed that you were still alive, that you hadn't drowned or been shot as well. And I waited while they searched the river and found nothing. Then I decided if you were alive there was only one place you would go and I climbed up here, and sure enough I found you," she said, looking at Gabriel's head in her lap and bending to kiss his muddy forehead. "In this horrible place."

"Come, it's not that bad," said Gabriel. He sat up, grimacing.

"Who knows about it?"

"Only a few."

"Is it safe for tonight?"

"Think of somewhere safer."

"I'm going to get you some dry clothes and medicine."

She left and it began raining. No one would look for him in this weather, thought Gabriel, listening to the sting of water on the roof.

Elena returned after dark. She poked her aunt's umbrella through the door. "It's me," she said. She carried a plastic bag. It contained sandwiches, a bottle of iodine, a clean shirt and a pair of jeans. The jeans were too tight around the waist.

"You must leave first thing in the morning," she said. "You were on holiday in Leticia. When you come back you can say you had nothing to do with this afternoon."

Gabriel laughed. "No one's going to believe that."

"But what have you done?" she asked. She dabbed iodine on his wounded arm. "Nothing," she went on. "Precisely nothing. Which I dare say is a major problem for a firebrand revolutionary, but which also means they can't accuse you of anything."

"They'll find something. I was a friend of Hipólito's. That's enough."

At his name, Elena knelt back on her heels. She bit her lip. "I'm so sorry about Hipólito," she said. She stared at the bare floor. "I know what he meant . . . " she added helplessly, and then unable to find the words, her chin dimpled like choppy water and she was about to cry again.

"I know what you and he . . . " but in a sudden movement Gabriel reached out and stopped her mouth with his own. He clung to her, losing himself in the kiss, until, relaxing, she responded and the two of them slowly leant back on the floor.

"Now," said Gabriel.

She made no reply. Then she said, "Let me get rid of this."

She sat up. He saw she was still holding the bottle and the ball of cotton wool. Caressing her arm, he waited for her to screw the top back on.

She looked at him. Her blue eyes had never been brighter. He smiled. He bent to take the cotton wool and the bottle from her hand.

When he raised his eyes, she was still looking up.

But no longer at him.

Chapter 16

A NOISE interrupted Gabriel's reverie. Edith was in the room. She was saying something.

"What?"

"I said the police are everywhere."

"Is that unusual?"

"Very." She placed her basket on the table.

"No one saw you yesterday?"

"No."

"Not even Bonifacio?"

"Bonifacio?"

"He found me in the market just now. He said he'd tried the door."

"No," said Gabriel. "He didn't see me."

"It's better he doesn't know you're here."

"Why?"

"I don't know. It could be dangerous." She began emptying her basket. "He blames you for his brother's death," she went on. "He told me they'd found Julio's body. In an unmarked grave near the beach at San Bartolo."

Gabriel remained silent. Edith continued tonelessly. "He's just come back from Lima. He flew down to confirm Julio's identity and give him a Christian burial. He had to steal the body. He told me he was lucky to find it at all. Some of the bodies had been given false names. The military are still denying everything."

She unpacked a jar of coffee on the table, from one of the contraband stalls in Sargento Lores which had mushroomed under Don Miguel. Then a bottle of nail varnish remover from Dominica Zumate's pharmacy.

"Bonifacio now looks after the explosives."

"Edith . . . "

"He's a bastard," she said filling the kettle, raising her voice above the water. Her hands were shaking.

"Edith . . ."

"All right," she let out, through closed teeth, before spinning round to face him. "We'll talk about Elena. What is it you want to know?"

"Only if she's been here."

Edith sat down. She avoided Gabriel's eyes.

"Yes, she came. About three years ago."

"What did she want?"

"You," said Edith. "She wanted you."

"What did you tell her?"

"I told her where you were. I told her I didn't know when you would be released, if ever. She appeared to understand. She's not stupid."

"Did she know about Don Miguel?"

"Yes. She didn't say much about it, only that she'd heard."

"What else did you talk about?"

Edith pulled her face around and looked at him. "It's all right. I didn't tell her everything."

"I didn't mean that. Did you find out where she was going?"

"She didn't say. I'm not sure she knew herself. She wanted to see me before deciding. I think I was her main chance of finding you. I had the feeling she didn't expect much to come from it."

"And that was three years ago?"

"Yes."

"When three years ago?"

"I can't remember. Sometime during the Niño."

"And you haven't seen her since?"

"No, Gabriel, I haven't seen her since, not since she walked out that door."

Gabriel stood. He picked up her purse from the table. He extracted some notes.

"Gabriel. . . "

"I'm only going to the church."

Edith swallowed. "This meeting with Ezequiel. If you go looking for her, I don't think I can recommend you attend."

Gabriel reached the door. "I know," he said, opening it.

*

Gabriel walked purposefully through the market for three blocks and turned left down a wide tarmac street towards the river. This was Santa María. It led directly to where Hipólito's shed had been.

Nothing remained of the building. In its place and dominating the area, rose a large basilica with a jelly-mould dome and two grey towers the colour of thunder. To the left, was a modern convent. To the right, stood the abandoned foundation of what was to have been the Bishop's new palace.

Gabriel approached the gate. A woman sat on a rug selling prickly pears and lottery tickets. On the bars behind hung the religious effigies celebrating the appearance of the Mother of God at Belén. Key rings, medallions, statuettes, and ashtrays with the figure of the Virgin Mary and a girl kneeling rapturously at her feet, unrecognizable as Elena.

In the months after the visions, 26,000 cases of holy medals and rosaries had been shipped upriver to Belén – not to mention the candles, the postcards, the bars of commemorative chocolate.

Gabriel entered the basilica. The church was empty. The only sound was the tape-recorded chant of a choir. It came from a loudspeaker on a pillar near the altar. On a ledge beneath was an angel with a lace mantilla and a bent tin wing. Its enamelled gaze was fixed on the silver altarpiece.

A girl with red hair appeared behind Gabriel. She dipped her finger in a shell-shaped bowl. The bowl was empty. The girl crossed herself and advanced along the left aisle to a cabinet containing the Virgin. She touched the glass. She lit a candle. She began praying.

Gabriel looked about him. He found it hard to imagine that somewhere under this golden dome was the patch of land where the press had stood. The arches, the cedarwood pews, the mosaic letters which rimmed the dome spelling La Inmaculada had extinguished all traces of the dirty wooden shed.

He came across Elena's favourite painting in a small apse by the altar. A framed notice explained that the Silves Annunciation had been bequeathed to Santa María at Elena's request. An earlier inscription gave the provenance of the painting, believed to be the work of Fra Angelico's favourite pupil and donated to the municipality of Belén by Alonso Mario Silves, 30 September 1911.

It was the first time Gabriel had seen the painting.

Alonso's Annunciation had been heavily restored. The Archangel delivered his message beneath a thick layer of varnish. His long wings quivered, two yellow axes embedded in his back below a waterfall of golden curls. He stretched forward. A mysterious wind wrapped his scarlet robe. One hand, holding a lily staff, pointed at the Virgin. The other at the sky. His eyes were focused on the importance of what he was saying. "Hail, thou that art highly favoured, the Lord is with thee. Blessed art thou among women." The words curved over a number of small holes where the polilla worm had fed. They reached the Virgin at the level of her halo.

She looked up from her book. She saw the Archangel. She crossed her arms against her crimson chest. Her instinct was to recoil, but what he was saying drew her to him.

Under the varnish, her listening face was phosphorescent.

Gabriel retreated to the altar. He forced his eyes to the crucifix. He thought of the time when Bonifacio had defecated on the lace cloth and inserted a number of consecrated hosts into the pat – "like one of mother's cakes." And the time before that when, a week after the basilica's official opening, he had doused the altarpiece with petrol.

"O Gabriel, it burned beautifully," he heard him saying, this man now arranging a Christian burial for his brother, Gabriel's palanca. "I was transfixed. Can you believe it? I stood watching, feeling totally at peace with myself."

Only in thinking of the flames could Gabriel easily look at the altar. And as he looked his mind cleared and the basilica dissolved and he was back in Hipólito's shed on that rainy night twenty-one years before.

"A voice was speaking to me, calmly and distinctly. I thought it was your voice. I said to myself, what's going on, what's Gabriel up to? Then I saw this light. It was more brilliant than the sun – yet the extraordinary thing was I could look into it. I also wanted to look into it because I began to see the silhouette of someone opening their arms. I saw this person as I see you, but all of a sudden I felt so insignificant I didn't notice the details. Even now I find it impossible to describe. All I know is that my heart was on fire."

And what had he seen, kneeling in a pair of jeans too small for him, a ball of cotton wool in his hand?

He had seen Elena's face as she stood and walked to the door, then out into the rain. He had watched her advance step by step through the manioc patch until she fell to her knees a few yards from the Toyota pick-up. He had looked as she tilted her face to the full moon, all the while nodding and moving her lips. And following her eyes, he had seen the candle-end of moon begin to tremble until it appeared to spin on its axis.

It was the rain, he thought – though later he was certain no water had fallen on either of them.

It could be explained by his state of shock.

But seeing Elena kneeling on the ground, he remembered thinking she had never been so beautiful.

It was a different person who stumbled to her feet. "Oh, Gabriel," she whispered.

He led her back inside. "What have you seen?"

She looked at him as if he were out of his mind.

"But didn't you see?"

"Who was it?"

"Didn't you hear?"

"Was it the Virgin?"

"A priest," she said. "I must see a priest."

Gabriel covered their heads with the green tarpaulin. He took her over the river. She refused to believe he had seen nothing except a trembling moon. Had he not seen the face, composed of a light as white as the river at Rapoto where the kingfishers plunge into the fall? Had he not seen the curls of hair which fell like gold lace onto clothes made of no colour she had ever known? Had he not heard the words, words which she was asked to repeat and remember and which reiterated that God existed, that there was but one God, one truth, and that the people must no longer try to advance without God, as if man were his own creator?

"They were not empty words like we use."

"Of course not, Elena," said Gabriel soothingly. "Of course not."

"I must return the same time tomorrow."

"You will, you will."

The rain had stopped by the time they reached the cathedral square. Gabriel removed the tarpaulin from their shoulders. He folded it while she waited. Then they continued across the square to the Bishop's palace.

He paid no attention to the three men on the bench.

"She told me to return at the same time tomorrow."

Gabriel was only half listening. He was ringing the Bishop's bell. At the same time he was trying to zip up his trousers. Before he could do so, the door opened and it was not the Bishop, but a strange man, a gringo, who told them in heavily accented Spanish that the Bishop was away in Lima and that he was just staying a few nights before. . . He was about to say before joining his mission in Delicias, but at that moment he saw the girl and decided they had better come inside.

Chapter 17

FATHER PAUL MABY was a Franciscan who had been in the jungle five years. He came from a village fifty miles south of Tulsa built of clean, fresh-painted houses and surrounded by fields of furry wheat that seemed to go on forever. A mile outside the village was a well. The most popular form of suicide in the area was to throw oneself down it.

Paul was the youngest of three brothers who had loved the same girl. For the rest of his adolescent life his dreams would draw on the memory of the twelve-year-old who stared down into the darkness where David and Martin had vanished without a sound, having expected him to keep his word and follow.

Paul Maby's hands were gripping the bricks to propel him from the rim when a mortar bee flew under his nose and he toppled backwards into a lavender bush.

Its scent reminded him of the girl he loved – the daughter of a psychotherapist from Maine. Paul had begged for some miracle which would make her love him. But smelling the lavender, he was possessed by his first certain knowledge of the difference between good and evil; also by the idea – which would never leave him – that life itself was the miracle.

Paul Maby had not broken his word since. At the age of twenty-six, he had left home to escape his father and because he heard a bishop at the seminary give a talk on Peru and ask for volunteers. His had been the first hand to go up.

"A vision, you say?" He looked at Gabriel. After five years in the jungle he knew when a man ceased to be responsible for his actions. "You'd best leave her with me."

Dazed by Hipólito's death, by his own escape and now by this, Gabriel was in no state to look after Elena. He placed an arm on her shoulder, his tired lips on her cheeks and left with a promise to see her next morning.

An hour before midnight the Bishop's door opened. The two figures of Elena and the American priest hurried down the steps and into the Bishop's car. The white Volkswagen beetle coughed three times before making a circuit of the square. When it reached Raimondi it turned left. A hundred yards on, it halted outside Señora Guzmán's house.

At five minutes to nine the next morning, Corporal Velarde could be seen knocking at the door with a loud, steady rap. In his pocket, inside a polythene bag in case of rain, he carried a warrant for the arrest of Edith Pusanga, Julio Ángel Medina, Julio's brother Bonifacio, and Gabriel Rondón Lung.

Velarde was a little irritated by the impatience with which Don Miguel, the person responsible for the warrants, had treated him. He knew Don Miguel was gravely ill, but that meant he should be taking things easy instead of looking over the corporal's shoulder as if he didn't trust him to wear his trousers on his legs instead of over his head.

Twice in the night Don Miguel had called at the station.

"Nothing at all, señor. As I said, we're looking."

Velarde had removed his new Ray-Bans for Don Miguel. He wouldn't do that for many people. After all, what happens when men with sunglasses remove them? Their eyes look raw and tender at having to confront what they see.

But Don Miguel was different. Velarde's eyes had nothing to hide from Don Miguel.

Perhaps the corporal should not have worn his glasses on that day when his captain was sick and it became his job to check the boats come in from Ecuador. Perhaps then he would have seen what he wasn't meant to.

"How much do you earn a month, Corporal?"

Velarde had told him, adding a few pesos because he suspected what was coming. Don Miguel wouldn't be asking that question if the next thing he was going to say was How's the wife and baby? Not with Velarde standing awkwardly beside him on his deck, having routinely opened one of Don Miguel's cupboards and finding there such a big bag of powder.

It would take some purchase to whiten the money Don Miguel would make from that.

"Three hundred soles, Señor Minero."

Velarde saw him reach inside his jacket. Mother of God, was he reaching in there for a gun?

"Here's thirty years' salary."

You had to have a reason to turn down such an offer. At the time Velarde couldn't think of one, though now he could think of lots of them, despite his Ray-Bans and his neat little house by the airport, and the gold ring on his finger and the gold in his mouth, and his car, which had been dented by some round object on the very day it was delivered from Brazil, and his daughter, who was going to be a handful he could see just by the way she walked across a room, and his wife whom she took after, who only loved him because he bought her alpaca jerseys from Arequipa and who insisted on wearing them when she showed her love, which was three nights a month before her flower-time, and which she liked to wear because they made her sweat in the torrents she had seen in films but which made him come out in a rash as if he had been bitten by several brigades of red ants. Yes, now he could think of reasons, but on that boat his mind had been a blank, and from that moment Don Miguel had his screws in him. Though why he should be showing interest in a teenage revolutionary who couldn't revolve a door defeated reason.

Señora Guzmán stood before him. Velarde removed his peaked cap and explained to Elena's aunt the nature of his visit.

"If you insist, Corporal. But be gentle, she's rather confused."

I bet she is, he thought, stumbling against a step he hadn't seen and then against the lion claw of a chair which finally persuaded him to remove his sunglasses and fold them with a snap into his shirt pocket.

He bet her sweet ass she was.

What was her story? Velarde asked Elena, who sat holding her hands on a sofa, with her legs crossed. His tapir eyes flicked over her black hair. Where was she last night? Where was Gabriel Rondón Lung?

But it wasn't going to be that kind of interview, he realized. Oh, no. As Elena told him what she had seen the night before, it became obvious even to Corporal Velarde that whatever she was describing lay outside the authority of Belén's police force.

Gabriel stood before the altar and shivered. He sought the cloister.

The arcades contained the original allotment; the land where the car had been and the row of manioc bushes where Elena had knelt. Two of these bushes remained, grown from shoots of the original plant. They were protected by a waist-high circular wall. Around the wall, a number of flowers sprouted top-heavily from shoe-polish tins. An open drain gurgled in the corner.

But here on the following afternoon some ten thousand people had assembled to witness the Virgin's return.

They took to the oozy paths leading up to the shed, trampling over the chicken field. People used to seeing their auguries in cloud formations and the entrails of birds; people with incurable scabs, ulcers, and varicose veins; men, women and children seeking some sign that in these dangerous times of shootings and angry helicopters, the forces of the supernatural were on their side. By bicycle and boat they came. On the tops of lorries from the Nanay, on motorbikes from Quistacocha, on the ferry which Don Miguel, forgetful of his interest in Gabriel, had chartered to bring them from as far upriver as Jiron. There they stood in the manioc, warming their soup over candles, blowing their whistles and waiting.

Ten thousand of them, said *El Oriente*.

At seven o'clock there was a stir. "Make way for the girl who's seen Our Lady," came the shout. Then Elena appeared, followed by Father Maby, Consuelo and Corporal Velarde.

Gabriel stood with four others on the roof of the Toyota. From where he stood he could see her face. She was wearing a thin necklace – a present from him – made of paiche scales. Her hair was arranged in a tidy plait.

She seemed relaxed. When the American priest said something, she laughed with her whole body.

A rug was produced for her to kneel on and there was a hush. Her hands joined in prayer. Her face looked up, alert.

"It was a clear night," said the report in *El Oriente* next morning. "The stars were salt across the sky. The moon had swum free of the trees."

From the shed's roof came a bright flash. "Our Lady, Our Lady," a woman shouted, but it was only the newspaper's photographer.

All eyes were on Elena, kneeling there. She stiffened. Suddenly her head jerked back to catch sight of something above her. At the same time a light spread through her face.

The crowd murmured.

"Look, look, the moon," someone cried. Everywhere people fell to their knees in the mud. To *El Oriente*'s correspondent, the light glowing on their backs seemed "as if it were shining down through a church window, altering everything and everyone."

A yard behind Elena, Corporal Velarde made a sign of the cross. He brought a man forward to the rug. The man produced a stethoscope from a leather bag. He pressed it clumsily against Elena's chest. He gestured for a candle to be brought which he raised and lowered before Elena's eyes. Holding it beneath her chin, he lifted the flame to the skin. Finally, after fumbling with his spectacles, he applied a needle to her arm.

All this while, Elena looked at the sky.

According to *El Oriente*, she smiled 36 times, gave 23 nods and moved her lips on no fewer than 17 occasions. The electro-encephalogram performed by Dr Lache confirmed that she was neither dreaming nor in a state of epilepsy. Her pulse was faster at 79 than the average 60. Her eyes blinked less than was normal and the pupils were dilated. Otherwise she was suffering from no sort of tension. Having examined her afterwards in his surgery, Dr Lache was obliged to declare Elena Silves to be of sound mental and physical health. He could offer little explanation as to why she failed to react when a needle was pricked in her arm – though he agreed to meet the costs of laundering the bloodstain he had caused on her shirt.

As for why her chin showed no signs of burning though he had placed a candle against it for 15 seconds, he preferred not to speculate.

"It was as if for that particular period," Dr Lache later told the elder of his two wives as he removed his spectacles for bed, "she didn't exist in our world. Either in space or in time."

"What did the Virgin say?" asked his wife, an agoraphobe who could only walk between Dr Lache's house and the supermarket on the corner of Nauta – and so remained ignorant of the separate ménage he kept in the next street.

"She said she would return again one final time tomorrow."

Then, rubbing his eyes, he went to sleep with a corner of his sheet in his mouth and his mind fixed firmly on the things of this world, such as who would pay for his evening's work.

The municipality – for surely it was something that involved the whole town. Or perhaps, that man who had telephoned him in the first place, the American priest. Or perhaps, when he returned, the Bishop.

Chapter 18

IT IS MIDDAY by the Swiss clock on the cathedral tower. The bell has rung and the square is full of schoolgirls gossiping on benches with their socks about their ankles. A baby balances on a flower bed that burns with the pink waxy flames of torch ginger. A blind woman walks by, guided by her daughter and son-in-law. The heat makes rippling shadows on the pavement. The air is inflammable with exhaust fumes. Don Wenceslau's false teeth shine in the sun, washed by the first of the masato he has drunk from Vásquez's barrow. Already his pupils are dilating.

"Why is it," he asks, "everything tastes better out of someone else's glass?"

Don García chews on a chicken leg. His hungry eyes appraise the tourists walking by. Two girls have already prompted a spurt of concupiscence. This he tries to satisfy by eating.

With his mouth full, so his words are not quite clear, he says, "One of those things, Don Wenceslau. Ask Don Leopoldo. He'll know."

Don Leopoldo shifts. He has been dreaming of the Amazons who attacked Orellana's expedition – women who lived alone, with hair that touched the ground. He has been thinking of the arrow quivering in the magnificent buttock of Fray Gaspar Carvajal. Disturbed by the conversation on the bench, he clears his head. He opens his eyes. He sees his fustian friend, Wenceslau. Ah, well, he thinks, he who sleeps in a pond wakes up a frog.

"I want to tell you what happened on that day," Don Wenceslau is saying.

Don Leopoldo sighs. There are few experiences more tedious than to be told of something he has himself actually witnessed. Most especially by Don Wenceslau. But listening to him has become a ritual, like putting out your hand to say hello, goodbye. It confirms Don Leopoldo's conviction there are only so many stories to be told, only so many characters, and these repeat themselves.

"We must have gone about this time of day. I was with you, Don Leopoldo, remember? We had crossed the river together. We wanted to be there early. You were telling me how sceptical you were. You had read an article about the Virgin's last appearance in Lithuania. You remembered her promise that she would next be seen in Egypt. You didn't believe any of it. Your friends at the Club de Leones had said Boy, are you going to have fun."

Don Wenceslau chortles. "It was you who saw it first.

"You said Look! Wenceslau, look at the sun.

"I said you shouldn't look at the sun, Don Leopoldo, it's bad for your eyes. After all, your eyes are your profession. And we aren't in Egypt. Nevertheless, I looked . . . and there it was, not hurting me in the least, but coming towards me, in, out, in, out. Then you arrived, García."

Don García nods sombrely. He assaults another piece of the chicken beside him, wrapped in the pages of *El Oriente* like a greasy flower.

"Never look at the sun, you repeated. But I wasn't listening. I said Look, for God's sake. And slowly, very slowly you looked. Heavens, you gasped, wait a minute, what's it doing? What's happening up there? And very soon all three of us were saying Look, it's coming towards us and going back and stopping. All three of us were seeing the same thing.

"But you know something, it was as if the sun was looking at us and not the other way round. As if it was talking to us in a funny sort of way, in a ridiculous sort of way. Don't you remember, Leopoldo?"

"Yes, yes, Wenceslau. I remember."

"You even hoped it might cure your haemorrhoids."

Don Leopoldo splutters. "Nonsense, Wenceslau. Never."

"Anyway, the whole point of the story . . . "

And all of a sudden, Don Wenceslau runs out of steam. He has forgotten what he was going to say. It is the fault of the man next to him. He is a patriarch, Don Leopoldo. A dampener of conversation. A misery boots. Never happier than when staring into that bag at his feet. In Don Wenceslau's marinated eyes, Don Leopoldo's bag has the messy shape of their country. He squints at the long neck contracted at the mouth. He tries to think of something pertinent with which to conclude his story. Nothing comes to mind. He looks at Don García eating.

"I used to like that part of the bird," he says cheerfully. "Until I realized it was its arse."

Chapter 19

THE BISHOP hadn't liked it. Not one little bit. He had heard the news in Lima while conducting negotiations with the departing Italian ambassador over a Sienese cross.

"Seen this?" said the wiry plenipotentiary. He came from Sapri and took scant care in concealing his desire to return there.

"The eyes of the world are on Belén," read the Bishop in amazement. It had always been his belief that few and far between were those who had heard of his city in the jungle. Now apparently the whole world would know.

To the powers that be, he thought, drumming his chubby fingers on the aeroplane's armrest, and trying to distract himself with a game of in-flight bingo, it would look very bad indeed.

Eucario Barrantes was, as one of his numerous critics put it in special reference to his glibness, the kind of man who had no trouble writing amusing entries in visitors' books. It was often said of him, and not always behind his stooping back, that he was a man on the make. His grandmother had said it. His mother had said it. His fellow seminarians at Ocopa had said it. They had said it at various times in Lima, in Arequipa but most often of all in Piura where to make his mark he had held a mass for the glorious hero of the Pacific War, brandishing, so he imagined, Admiral Grau's black and gold sword. (Actually, the sword had been donated by a group of Peruvian women in Europe long after news reached them of the tragic fate of the glorious iron-clad *Huáscar*.)

None of this worried Barrantes, a small, slight man with a lacklustre face and brightly polished shoes. What worried him was the possibility that the Cardinal Archbishop of Lima might be saying it.

Since his appointment as Bishop to Belén eighteen months previously, Barrantes had made a conscious effort to swim with the tide. Increasingly he was finding the exercise a strain. Though he bore the coveted title of Bishop, Barrantes found himself the primate of a diocese answerable not to Lima but to Rome. Due to the paucity of missions in the region, Belén was ranked as an Apostolic Vicariate rather than a fully-fledged Bishopric. It was a distinction Barrantes could not help feeling keenly.

After a prelature, an Apostolic Vicariate struck him as the lowest form of life. It suggested the local Church was not mature enough, at least not in the pastoral sense. It also meant the Church was serviced by foreign personnel.

People like Father Paul Maby, he thought, poking a finger through a number on his bingo card which corresponded at last with that announced on the intercom.

For eighteen months Bishop Barrantes had felt caught between the demands imposed on him by the Curia and his ambitions to rise in the hierarchy nearer home. Keeping both masters sweet would have been a difficult task at the best of times. This was not such a time.

The Vatican's second Ecumenical Council was drawing to a close and Barrantes had a nasty feeling that in general the tide was turning. Vagabond lily he may be, but some of the modifications proposed by the Vatican struck him – and, he suspected, his Cardinal Archbishop – as unappetizingly modern. Nevertheless, in accordance with Rome's instructions he had steeled himself to show a face of the Church that was of and with this world. A face, he reminded himself, that believed in a community of equals.

Stepping down onto the tarmac, it was a face of unconcealed irritation that he showed the American priest who had come to meet him. Only momentarily, when a reporter approached his diminutive presence at the baggage check, did the expression arrange itself more beatifically.

The Church had not pronounced itself, he smiled. Nor must it be too quick to label whatever was happening in Belén as superstition.

Not until he had sat in the front of the car did he address a word to the American. Then looking pointedly at him, he opened his minted mouth.

"Now," he said. "Tell me about this apparition on the manioc bush."

*

In his last year at the seminary, Eucario Barrantes had submitted a dissertation on Jean Gerson, the fifteenth-century rector of Paris University. It was a modest piece of scholarship, remembered by the invigilator for its curious mixture of pedantry and prurience.

Barrantes had obviously relished his investigation into the rector's pronouncements on lesbianism. Also into the surprising absence from Gerson's canon of what seemed to Barrantes a pertinent commentary on the mores of his contemporaries – and a key interrogatory for the medieval confessional: namely, the priest's demand to young women as to whether they had marinaded a small fish by placing it between the labia minora and then delivered it in a dish as a means of bewitching their sweethearts.

In a footnote, Barrantes speculated that the fish was probably a sardine. The invigilator was inclined to suggest red herring.

Barrantes' dissertation was only marginally preoccupied with deviancy. Its main thrust concerned Gerson's manual relating to cases of fraudulent sanctity, especially among women.

On the aeroplane, Barrantes repeated to himself a fragment of the rector's Latin. According to Gerson, the visions and sayings of women were "to be held suspect unless carefully examined, and much more fully than men's." The reason? "Because they are easily seduced." Before he even knew of Gabriel Rondón Lung, Bishop Barrantes had decided that the visions of Elena Silves were suspect and suspect for this very reason.

The problem remained, what to do?

The truth was that, listening to Father Maby's patient testimony in the front of his Volkswagen beetle, Eucario Barrantes felt undecided and, contrary to the impression he might give the outer world, he had never thrived on indecision.

He was anxious to be seen implementing whatever the Holy Synod desired, but what it desired for devotees of the Virgin Mary was, in his opinion, opaque. Next to Papal Infallibility, Mariolatry was the greatest barrier to Christian reunion. Barrantes had followed closely the events in Rome, but remained in several minds as to whether the barrier had been removed, fortified or simply left untouched.

The Virgin had been subjected to possibly the Vatican's closest debate ever. Should her doctrine be contained in the schema on the Church or be granted a separate chapter? The propaganda was intense. Bishops from the Ukraine and India stood on the steps of St Peter's and forced leaflets on those who entered. There were stories of an unseemly collaboration between advocates for the separate chapter and the Vatican Press Office. It was rumoured that a pontiff from Madagascar had thrown a clumsy punch at the Bishop of Toledo after the latter had argued that Mary was a most exalted co-operatrix with Christ.

Barrantes did not know exactly what he should admit to thinking on this issue. But as one who combined a legalistic frame of mind with a reverence for the scriptures, he did know that there was nothing in the Bible to justify Mary's extra dignity and status. She was mentioned a few times in the New Testament with something approaching casualness. Even Christ had shown signs of impatience.

"Woman what have I to do with thee?" Wasn't that what he had asked at Canaan? And was there any indication that he was aware of the few miracles with which she had been credited? For the Immaculate Conception and the Assumption, Barrantes argued to himself, there was no biblical basis whatever. They were inventions of the clerisy. Inventions as doubtful as the special shrines and prayers and effigies which proliferated everywhere and exalted the Mother above the Son. They couldn't even decide whether she was buried in Ephesus or Jerusalem.

According to the report in *L'Osservatore Romano* there was an audible gasp when the votes were cast and it was decided by a majority of 1114 to 1074 against the granting of a special treatise.

In his jungle, Barrantes rejoiced. Since the days of his seminary he had always been suspicious of Tradition as a source of revelation. He had also been secretly disgusted when in the 1950s the Assumption became the one doctrine to be decreed as an article of faith since the definition of Papal Infallibility. The new biblical enthusiasm of Vatican II suggested that the cult of Mary would now be contained. At the end of the Third Session, however, the Pope announced his decision to confer on her the title of Mother of the Church. Not only that, but he encouraged a rosary and a daily prayer. Then, by way of achieving a total volte-face, he sent a Golden Rose to her shrine at Fátima.

Where that left Eucario Barrantes, Eucario Barrantes was unclear. Where it left him now that the Virgin had apparently blessed his own parish was a matter of graver doubt.

"You say you saw the moon move, then next day the sun," he said, gritting his teeth as the car bounced with a clang in its bowels over a large pothole Father Maby had seen too late. "And that there's another vision planned for this evening?"

"Right."

The Bishop looked at him. Father Maby's presence in Belén was beginning to be as welcome as a dog at Mass.

"You were correct to insist on the presence of a doctor," he said. "We have had so many impostors. All the same, it's not exactly stunning, is it, what Our Lady said to her? Less charitably, one would call it trite."

The man beside him tooted at a bicyclist and shrugged.

"Playing Devil's advocate, doesn't she come to each of us on our own terms?"

The Bishop snorted. He was not a man who cared for such advocates. "One could argue that. One could also argue that Our Lady should make her identity and intentions a little bit clearer. Why is it that she always appears to young girls in the back of beyond who hardly have a clue what's happening to them?"

"Nazareth was the back of beyond," replied the American. "And I won't pretend I'm not confused. I spend my life meeting drunken messiahs in the jungle who may well be the Second Coming but who wouldn't know the Lord's Prayer from a hamburger stall. I'm also familiar with all that Fátima and Lourdes guff. But when you meet Elena Silves you'll realize this isn't a case of some little shepherdess on the hill with her lambs. For a start she comes from a good family."

"I know about her family. I know her aunt. I know the girl. I see her every week in the choirstall. What I want to know is what's going on in her mind?"

The American said, "I would say two things. One, she's as honest as a blush. Two, she's just extraordinarily happy."

"Wasn't there some specific message," the Bishop went on. "A secret only the Pope can see. A heavenly sniff of roses. A magic spring. Didn't she ask for a medal to be struck or a chapel to be built. Were there no angels with pretty fluttering wings?"

"No," replied Father Maby. "No angels."

"Why does the Virgin always look like some Murillo archetype instead of a girl in first-century Galilee? Why, if she appears today, doesn't she wear a . . ." He looked at passing houses to see how young women in his parish dressed. Failing to find them, his eyes veered to the car roof.

"Why doesn't she wear . . . a bikini?"

"Bishop . . ."

"Sorry, but I'm angry. I would almost have preferred a weeping icon." He remembered with a twitch the occasion when his maid returned from Cuzco bearing a piece of wool wrapped in red tissue and wet with the tears of a saint.

"Could it be narcotics?" he asked optimistically. "Or lack of food?"

Too late, Father Maby braked before another hole in the ground. He apologized. "I'm not used to these gears."

"Could it be an optical illusion?" the Bishop pressed on through the grinding of machinery. "I've often stared at a bright object in a dark background and thought I'd seen things."

The man at the wheel said something.

"What was that?" asked the Bishop.

"Devil's advocate again. I was thinking of the moment our whole faith rested on the appearance of the risen Christ. Before that I was thinking of the light the shepherds saw in the sky."

"Oh," said Barrantes. The Volkswagen was turning into the square when he spoke again. "Satan himself is transformed into an angel of light," he quoted. His driver raised an eyebrow.

"Saint Paul," the Bishop explained, opening the door. "Your namesake."

*

The Bishop went to see Elena Silves that afternoon. Two policemen leant against a car outside Señora Guzmán's house. They had been posted there following the cable he sent from Lima urging the Mayor to provide protection for the girl. They raised their hands in a salute.

"Why, it's the Bishop," Consuelo chuckled on opening the door. He didn't know if she was enjoying herself – or intoxicated. She led him to a room upstairs.

"One minute a revolution. Next minute a revelation. I can't keep up. She's in there." And she tottered off leaving Barrantes to find Elena with a smile on her face that reminded him with a heavy heart of that woman who ran the Hotel Liberty.

"So," he said, crossing himself and kissing her for good measure on the crown of her head. "Tell me all. She who does not speak is not heard by God."

A grim expression came to his face as she spoke, although, as she talked, he couldn't help noticing Alonso's ivory cross poking tantalizingly between her hands. He replaced his tongue inside his mouth. "What did this figure say?"

"Return to prayer," said Elena. Nothing was more important. The face then disappeared like a blown candle.

"Nothing can replace the sacrament and holy prayer," he agreed. "Not even an apparition." But he felt uncomfortable as he walked back across the square to his house. What was the Church to do with someone whose line to Christ appeared more direct than its own? How was one to bridge the gulf between a trainee tourist guide who had spoken to the Mother of God, and an official representative who had not. Mindful of the bishop who had been deprived of his authority after the apparition at Beauraing in 1933, he voiced his doubts to Father Maby.

As he did so, he began to wish there was someone else he could confide in. The American obviously believed the finger of God was here. It made him suspect. In fact Barrantes was beginning to believe the whole thing was a hoax put up by the Franciscans. If he hadn't been in Lima none of this might have happened. He could have talked the girl out of it, he could have suppressed the news.

"There are thousands of Peruvians who want to believe in

something like this. Our country has never been in more need of mothering, but that doesn't mean she saw what she claims to have seen."

"I don't want to believe it," said the American. "My whole training is against believing it. As I said before, in the jungle I've witnessed lots of so-called visionaries. Like you, I take the Church's position that all visions are false unless they can be proved true."

"Well, then."

"On this occasion I'm convinced, absolutely dead convinced that she is seeing something – whether this something is inside her or whether it exists. She could not lie. If I was to say to her, Say this, she would say But that's wrong, Father."

"Why didn't anyone else see it then? Why didn't you?"

"I didn't see the face of the Virgin Mary," said Father Maby. "But in Elena Silves' face I saw the reflection of something like it."

"I return to what this apparition is meant to have said. It seems so banal. It seems entirely without logic."

"This is a mystery which has leap-frogged over logic. After all," said the American, "we know what happens when men have recourse to argument. They argue."

From the expression on the Bishop's face he saw he had struck a chord. "At least," said the Bishop, "what was uttered is free of theological error. We can be thankful for that. And the crowds are gathering in a spirit of prayer, some who can't have experienced the sacrament for twenty years. But why has Our Lady chosen to come to Belén? Why here, of all places?"

"Because she found faith?"

The Bishop looked at him in genuine astonishment. "My dear fellow, if that is the case she must have got lost. Belén, as you must have noticed by now, is no halt on the path of simple virtue." No. Something was not right. He felt it in his bone marrow. What he needed was time, he thought, unlocking the door to his study.

Normally he would have paused, taking pleasure in the crosses displayed on the wall – a modest collection of fifteen crucifixes purchased with rather too much of his stipend. On this occasion he made directly for the bookcase by the window. He couldn't remember whether he still possessed the Latin document. He hadn't seen it since he wrote his dissertation. But there it was, between a rare copy of Miguel Alberto's *Stimuli Divini Amoris* and a first edition of Sarah Grand's *Babs the Impossible*.

He sat at his desk. In a long and carefully worded telegram to the appropriate authorities in Rome and Lima he outlined the circumstances and gave assurances that he was proceeding with extreme caution in full accordance with the *Norms of the Sacred Congregation for the Doctrine of the Faith About How to Proceed in Judging Alleged Apparitions and Revelations*.

Later that afternoon, the Bishop visited Belén. He insisted to Father Maby on going alone and in disguise. He wore a shapeless macintosh with its collar turned up around his plump cheeks. He looked like one of Velarde's plain-clothes men, thought Don Miguel recognizing him instantly and careful not to charge the full fare across the water.

Even at half the cost, the Bishop judged the price of Don Miguel's ticket exorbitant. Don Miguel may have resembled a death mask, but he had no business to be making money out of this. He must be raking it in, the Bishop reckoned crossly as the crowd pressed him further along the ferry's deck. He had never quite approved of the man. Nor had he felt the appropriate sympathy on hearing the news of his illness. The fact that Elena Silves worked for him made the whole thing worse, he thought, rubbing off the damp rust which the rail had left on his palm and taking a sharp breath as a woman trod on his foot.

He joined the procession up the bank. A white ribbon was strung out along a number of posts. Behind it, some workmen were constructing a concrete path. Further up, a man was selling white loaves on a table. At the summit, a notice warned pilgrims against looking at the sun. The day before, if one believed *El Oriente*, fifty people had to receive medical attention for eye-injuries.

The field was strewn with fish heads and piles of rice and the boiled-out skulls of goats. It smelled of urine. Near the shed, an area of land had been fenced in. It was guarded by a policeman, who prevented anyone leaving more of the tokens which festooned the manioc leaves.

Standing on tip-toe, the Bishop could merely catch glimpses of this shrine. Dozens of people ringed the fence, men and women in bare feet or in fine leather shoes, who stared at the manioc plant with the same look on their faces, hoping it might cure them of incurable ulcers and Pott's disease and lumps in their chests the size of coconuts.

They listened to a loud-hailered voice read from Saint Matthew's Gospel. "But immediately, after the tribulation of those days, the sun shall be darkened, and the moon shall not give her light and the stars shall fall from heaven and the powers of the heavens will be shaken; and then shall appear the sign of the Son of Man in Heaven: and then shall all the tribes of the earth mourn . . . "

At five o'clock Elena appeared once more on the arm of Father Maby. They were protected by three policemen. As they walked through the crowd, the voice on the loud-hailer began leading them in the rosary. Immediately, the crowd knelt to reveal an embarrassed policeman, the parcel of land on which Elena had seen her vision and, at the back, the figure of Bishop Barrantes.

Barrantes arranged his macintosh and reluctantly joined them in the mud, feeling nothing except acute irritability and a dull ache in the region of his bladder.

When after an hour the Virgin failed to appear, Barrantes experienced a wave of relief. After two hours this approached something very near ecstasy. He returned home on winged feet to find the telephone ringing in his hall. It was Corporal Velarde. He was calling to inform the Bishop of the guard he had posted at his request outside Señora Guzmán's house, and to tell him that he was increasing it by a further two officers. Not only for Elena's own peace and quiet. But also to prevent Gabriel Rondón Lung from attempting to reach her.

"Gabriel Rondón Lung?" said the Bishop.

Velarde explained. He had in his hand a letter. He rustled Hipólito's leaflet into the mouthpiece. It had come into his possession by the prompt action of Señora Guzmán. (Having promised to keep secret the incident of Gabriel's letter, Pía Zumate had finally unburdened herself. It was one thing to protect a terrorist in love. It was another to continue doing so when the Holy Mother was implicated. Velarde had used her testimony to wrest the letter from Elena's aunt.)

It was written from the terrorist to Elena Silves.

"It is," said Velarde, rereading it and experiencing a momentary pang of regret that the days had passed when he and Señora Velarde felt such passions, "a love letter."

That did it, thought the Bishop. He was exultant. Gerson was right. These visions were nothing more than a dammed-up libido. What had des Brosses said on seeing Bernini's Saint Teresa? "If this is divine love, I know what it is." Hadn't Barrantes known this all along? He was pouring himself a libation of whisky when the telephone rang again. It was the American. He was speaking above the noise of a bar in Plaza Clavero.

He didn't quite know how to put it. Something extraordinary had happened. It concerned Don Miguel who had begged Elena for help in curing his cancer. Elena had touched him as she left the site. Her employer had visited Dr Lache's surgery directly.

"And what is Dr Lache's diagnosis?"

"The cancer has been arrested."

"How does he know?"

"Apparently this Don Miguel had a lump in his side the size of a new-born baby."

"And?"

"Well, it's disappeared."

"This is something," the baffled doctor was at that moment telling an excited press corps, "which upsets all our acquired notions of pancreatic pathology."

"Bishop, you still there?"

"Yes . . . yes, I'm here."

"It's being talked of as a miracle."

The town was in turmoil. In the bars and cafés, in the brothels, the

churches and the post office, in the market stalls and on the benches
of every square there was talk of nothing else. Don Miguel's rescue
from certain death was truly a miracle which only the intercession
of the Mother of God could have effected.

Hipólito's death and the escape of his fellow terrorists, which two
days before had occupied *El Oriente*'s front page, might never have
been.

Instead there were phone calls from Buenos Aires and Madagascar and Quito and from a peculiar denomination of Italian mendi-
cants near Cortona. There were planes scheduled to arrive at the
town's small airstrip from Miami and Bogotá. There were even
rumours that the Pope's favourite theologian, Urs Von Balthasar,
had caught a flight from Zurich.

At eleven o'clock next morning, in a state of abject depression,
the Bishop took his telephone off the hook and went to replenish his
supply of Amplex from Dominica Zumate's pharmacy. Hidden
behind the stacks he overheard two girls wondering if the Virgin
looked like Martha, reckoned the most beautiful blonde in Iquitos,
or Vásquez's daughter, a sultry brunette called Alejandra.

Plainly, he thought, reaching through a mound of Peter Pan bras
for his Amplex, it didn't matter a damn that the visions had ceased.
The important thing was to remove their cause from public
scrutiny. Too big a candle could burn down his whole church.

An hour and a half later, at twenty past twelve, Elena Silves left
her aunt's house for an unknown destination, clasping a small
overnight case.

At two-thirty *El Oriente*'s correspondent revealed her whereabouts in the care of some Canadian friars near the Nanay.

At five o'clock the situation repeated itself when a journalist from
Oiga! managed to enter the Bethlemite shrine in Moronacocha
through a lavatory window.

With the arrival of Faucett's afternoon flight from Lima
containing 119 more journalists and two television crews, Bishop
Barrantes realized his task was hopeless. He was left with but one
option. This he exercised that evening. Wearing his macintosh –
though it was not raining – and leaving Father Maby in charge of
the house, he walked through the streets until he reached the

Benedictine hostel by the waters of Sachachorro.

The smell from the rubbish dump was such that he had to hold his nose while rooting for his mints — in which slightly ridiculous position the Benedictine father found him. He told Barrantes, as he led him to Elena's room, that the indefatigable reporter Alejandro Berlaguer of *Caretas* had called once and, not at all satisfied with his answer, had promised to return.

Barrantes remained standing as he informed Elena of his cogitations about her future. She was to enter a convent. It was to be far away from Belén while remaining in the department of Soreto. It was to be a closed order.

"You understand I can only suggest you stay there as a postulant. The decision to enter the religious life has to be made freely and it can only be made by you alone."

The Bishop continued. "Once you have decided, you must on no account tell anyone where you come from. You must not tell anyone who you are. You must not say a single word about what has happened here. You will have a completely new name. Only one person in Silar will know your true identity. The Mother Superior."

His voice softened as he concluded. "This is the price, my dear, for being blessed with a vision from God."

"When do I leave," asked Elena.

"Tomorrow morning. Tonight you stay with me in the Bishop's palace."

Chapter 20

FOR THREE DAYS Gabriel had heard nothing but whispers. How Elena had transformed Don Miguel into a man thirty years younger with the complexion of a grapefruit pith. How Don Miguel was set to make $700 a day from his company's tour of the site. How the Sacred Congregation for the Doctrine of the Faith was already deliberating on whether to nominate Elena for the sainthood.

The wilder the whisper the more frantic Gabriel became. He was a wanted man. He had nowhere to hide except the warehouse on the Nanay where he had spent three sleepless nights under a boiler. He had no idea how to reach Edith or Julio or Bonifacio. Far worse – and the occasion for his sleeplessness – was the fact he couldn't see Elena. The police outside her house made it an idiotic risk to shout up at her window and Consuelo Guzmán had followed Barrantes' example and cut off the telephone.

He bumped into Consuelo by chance. It was the morning after the Bishop had removed Elena from the Benedictine hostel, when the stories were so extravagant that *El Oriente* was consigning one in every three to the spike.

Consuelo was walking through the contraband market with a basket clinking of gin. At first she appeared not to recognize him. She withdrew her arm as if he was a bag-snatcher.

When he mentioned Elena, begging to know where she was, she relaxed. But she was distressed. They had taken her away. She didn't know where. Some religious institution. They hadn't told her the name of the latest one. They said it was to protect her. But Elena didn't need protection. She was happier than she'd ever been. If anyone needed assistance it was Consuelo. Her husband would have known what to do. She was too old to suffer these traumas on her own.

And why was Gabriel asking after her? Wasn't it true he had a price on his head? So that ugly corporal said, forcing her to go looking like a spy in Elena's bag.

"I ought to leave," she said, suddenly forgetting Gabriel, his letter and her niece, and thinking for no reason at all of her very first memory, a picnic given by her father at which the Portuguese Vice-Consul had lifted her high into a cloudless sky with the words "So you're Consuelo."

"I will," she said, her eyes descending to find Gabriel instead of a man in a white uniform. "I will go to Portugal."

Gabriel watched her disappear into the crowd. Nearby someone turned up a radio which had been playing American music on a stand selling Patum Peperium. There was a news flash.

" . . . We have just received this statement from the Bishop's office. 'The public is understandably anxious for the Church to say something about the events in Belén where Elena Silves claims to have seen the Virgin. Advised by the Holy See against reaching any hasty conclusions, we cannot for the time being attribute a supernatural character to these events. Only time will tell if the Church can deliver a judgement of heavenly origin. Meanwhile all might make private pilgrimages to the site for the purpose of devotion, worship and conversion. Official pilgrimages led by the Bishop are not permissible. Signed; Eucario Barrantes, Bisho of Belén, 13 August 1965'."

A fanfare followed. The announcer spoke again. "As for Elena Silves, who today leaves the care of Bishop Barrantes for a safe sanctuary, it doesn't need me to say that she departs her native city with its fullest blessings, with its sincerest hope that she will return . . ."

Those who wished to see Belén's most beautiful daughter one last time were advised to make their way with all haste to the cathedral square where news had been circulating of Elena Silves' imminent departure for the airport.

It took Gabriel seven minutes to reach the square. He ran through the narrow stalls of Sargento Lores overturning a table of cream crackers from Dublin. He ran headlong down Juan Próspero into the traffic of cars and motorcycles and motorcycle taxis which swerved and hooted at the sight of him advancing towards them in the middle of the road with arms and legs pumping, his shirt-tail behind him and his face a picture of agony.

He ran into the back of the large crowd which had gathered around the entrance to the Bishop's house and he only stopped running when having elbowed Sebastián out of his path, then Pía Zumate, then Don Tonsurans and finally Dr Lache, he no longer had the breath nor the strength to push his way through to the front.

He stood on tip-toe, panting, looking over the backs of men and women jammed tighter than pilchards.

He saw three rows ahead of him the Bishop's white Volkswagen, protected from the crowd by twelve policemen with machine-guns. He saw Father Maby run down the steps and slide awkwardly across the passenger seat to a position behind the wheel. He looked at the door from where the priest had just run. He saw it open and three people descend to the car — Corporal Velarde, Bishop Barrantes and Elena. He saw Elena. He saw the shape of his gazelle on the high ground. And he screamed.

"Elena! Elena!"

Hearing his heart-rending cry, the crowd fell silent.

"Elena!" he screamed again. With a superhuman effort he thrust himself forward to the car. He pressed his head against the window at the back where Elena was sitting. He screamed again, pounding the glass with his hand. She turned her face away. When she turned her face away, he tried to open the handle. He was about to punch the window when Father Maby engaged the gears, released his foot from the clutch and accelerated forward in a jerk that threw Gabriel back into the arms of the police.

The crowd followed the car. Forgetting Gabriel, they surged after it, singing and waving and touching the white bonnet. Not until he had driven unsteadily for two blocks did Father Maby lose them.

Only the three men on the bench saw what happened to Gabriel.

"Is he dead?" asked the youngest policeman.

"Who cares," said another. He kicked the face at his feet with such force that the whole body rolled off the pavement and into the gutter. He could promise one thing, though. Not even that bigamist Dr Lache would be able to tell if this face belonged to a Juan or a Juanita.

Chapter 21

GABRIEL EMERGED FROM Santa María and stood in the sun. The bell sounded above him. It was one o'clock. He needed a drink. He entered a cebichería on the corner. He ordered a beer and sat at a table overlooking the sandflats.

The sandflats had grown since his last visit, built from the soil of the crumbling river banks. Everything had grown. The number of houses on the rice fields. The price of kerosene chalked on the board.

"OK," said the customs officer at the next table. "You pay a hundred only. But next time it'll be more. Tell Mario that."

The cost of bribes.

Gabriel's beer arrived. He poured it, feeling the chill against his fingers. As he drank he heard laughter. A man at the bar was telling a story. The man turned, responding raucously to his own joke. He turned in Gabriel's direction. When he saw him his smile froze.

"Che, Gabriel," he said, pointing a finger. He walked over to Gabriel's table.

"It *is* you."

A grin returned to the lager-flecked lips. "Aren't you meant to be dead?"

"Not yet, Bonifacio. Not yet," said Gabriel, making rings on the table with the damp bottom of his beer bottle.

"But weren't you in the dormitory?" The man drew up a chair and sat down on it the wrong way round with his dirty fingers on the rim.

At the bar, the other men turned their backs.

"I'm sorry about your brother, Bonifacio. He was a good compañero."

"Weren't you?" hissed the man.

"I had a palanca with him."

Bonifacio hiccuped. "Yes. With my brother. With my fucking

brother. I supposed you knew what was going to happen." There was menace in his voice. His mouth was a fresh scar. He was drunk.

Gabriel poured the rest of his bottle. When the beer foamed up he placed a finger on its head and took a swallow.

"Why don't you pretend we're coming into Requena," he said, "and piss off."

"Why are you here?"

"None of your business," answered Gabriel. He rose to his feet. He put on his jacket and left an inti note on the table.

"I'll make it my business," shouted Bonifacio. The words hung in the beery air. At the bar, the men's backs were a row of trees braced in the wind. Gabriel stopped. Standing there, looking at his feet, he seemed about to swing around.

Bonifacio stabbed a finger at Gabriel's face. "It's that gringa whore, isn't it?"

But before he could put the question mark in place, Bonifacio lay on the floor like an upturned bicho, the rim of the chair back at his throat and Gabriel's body pressing down on him between the metal legs.

"You just listen," said Gabriel, holding Bonifacio's hair and slapping his head against the ground once, twice, three times.

"Did you hear what I said? I said I was sorry. You think I don't know what I owe Julio? You think I would forget?"

He leant harder on the chair.

"No, Bonifacio, I haven't forgotten. But if you want that tongue to taste beer again, don't let it mention Elena Silves."

That night Gabriel lay smoking on Edith's couch. She had not seen him with a cigarette before. He had said nothing all afternoon.

Looking down at his etiolated body puckered with scars, she was reminded of a tormented Christ in the cathedral. She scratched her leg. It was the only sound in the room, like a rat in the skirting.

The cigarette glowed and dulled. He coughed and rubbed the stub out on a plate. She couldn't tell whether he coughed out of illness, or because he wasn't used to tobacco.

She took a deep breath and looked down at the floor where their clothes lay. She knew what she was about to say contained an end to everything between them.

"They say she went to see Father Maby."

There was no reaction in the figure beside her. She turned her head. She saw his stomach lit by a spear of moonlight from the shutters. It trembled with his heartbeat.

"Who says?" he asked at length.

"I heard it from Pía Zumate."

"Where is Father Maby?"

"He's still at Delicias."

Chapter 22

I'M GOING TO TELL YOU something you'll find fascinating. . ."

Don Wenceslau is proposing to tell his story of the Amazon dolphin, the bufeo. The others have heard it before, but they let him talk. After lunch there is never any stopping him.

They can smell his breath, a raw-liver breath of food that has rotted between the few dark dominoes in his mouth and the masato which has swallowed his pupils. When the masato is the stronger smell it is better to listen.

Beneath his trilby Don García closes his eyes. At intervals he gives an appreciative nod. But his mind is not on Don Wenceslau. His mind is on women. The problem isn't getting them, he convinces himself. It's getting rid of them. That's why he likes the Teletroca . . .

Don Leopoldo gazes glumly at the shells by his feet and flicks them with a finger into a rough circle. He raises his eyes to the Admiral. He reads the words on his plinth. The words are compressed together. Some of their letters are missing, like Don Wenceslau's slurred speech.

8OCTOBER187

FOLLOWHISEXAMPL

SOL HOP

Don Leopoldo looks at the green epaulettes, parroting the bunches of iron grapes which hang from the windows of the Palace Hotel. He looks at the Admiral's face. He looks into his bronze eyes. Through them he sees the mist lifting from the sea off Antofagasta on that historic day of 8 October 1879.

On one side lies the ocean. On the other, the bare, scarped cliffs of a grey cordillera. Admiral Grau peers at the morning coast through the turret of his iron-clad *Huáscar*, the 1130-ton "Lion of the Pacific". On this boat and on its companion, the *Unión*, rest the hopes not only of the fair women of Trujillo (who have embroidered the ensign now visible through the mist), but of his whole country.

He rotates the hand-worked turret. Off the point of Angamos, at the extreme tip of Mejillones bay, he sees three pipe-cleaners of smoke. He swivels the turret. On the north-west horizon, three more!

Six ships to two, but for champions of Peruvian liberty, for Grau, and for his predecessor Lord Cochrane after whom, irony of ironies, one of the Chilean funnels is named, these are everyday odds.

He signals the *Unión*'s captain. He instructs him to make his escape. If both ships are destroyed, the country will have no navy. With infinite regret, Captain García y García – the author of a volume of sailing instructions for this stretch of coast – turns about.

"Full steam," orders Grau, the sole hope of Peru.

"Fire!"

The fourth salvo from the 40-pound Whitworth guns passes through the *Cochrane*'s galley. There are hidden cheers. They are smothered by the sound of a shell starting the bolts and breaking an iron beam in the *Huáscar*'s turret.

Escape is impossible. Grau decides to ram. The *Huáscar* advances on the *Cochrane*, shooting wildly.

300 yards.

100 yards.

50 yards.

The *Cochrane* replies.

The only fragment to remain of Admiral Grau who has given his lasting inheritance to Peru and earned his deathless fame is an inch and a half of knee-bone.

Don Leopoldo has not seen it, but he can picture the relic on its red velvet cushion in Callao's Merchant Marine College.

"It was Good Friday," Don Wenceslau is saying. "We were coming from the Puruha river. There was this young woman washing clothes on the bank. We had gone thirty metres past her when we heard shouts and screams. We looked round. She wasn't there any more, only the clothes she'd been washing. We looked everywhere. Nothing. They had taken her. The bufeos had taken her. We told the witchdoctor. He said she was under the water, alive there somewhere and living with the dolphin who had stolen her.

'Always carry a cross,' he said, 'and nothing like that will happen to you.'"

Don Wenceslau's fingers mount to the crucifix at his throat. He looks at his two companions. "That's what I did and nothing has happened."

Don Leopoldo waits to see if the story is over. Satisfied, he rubs the earth from his fingers and leans back.

Don Wenceslau drags a sleeve across his bluish lips and burps. "Don Leopoldo," he asks softly, "do you believe in the Amazon dolphin?"

"No," says Don Leopoldo.

"No?"

"You know I don't."

Don Wenceslau sighs heavily. "What about you, Don García? What do you think?"

Don García's expression implies he is not quite sure what to think. His concentration has been drawn to a girl on the bench opposite. She reminds him of a woman who used to cross her legs behind his back. His mind returns to his own bench. The bufeo. Don García knows the gallons of water which Don Leopoldo pours on this creature of myth, but he remains an agnostic. He too has heard strange stories; how the bufeo lives at the bottom of the river near big cities; how it enters town at night in the shape of a white man or woman with different coloured eyes; how you can tell a bufeo by its deformed feet and four-fingered hands and the blow-hole under its sombrero.

Perhaps Don Wenceslau is such a creature. He has the requisite bulging eyes and the smell of swamp moss and when he stands up he is slightly bow-legged.

Don García crosses himself so Don Wenceslau doesn't see.

What else has he heard? He has heard of fishermen who fuck dolphins. As a young man he met one. They were very clean animals, the man said. Not greasy, and much tighter than women. When you fucked them, they moved their tails.

"Imagine every ecstasy you ever had, Senõr García. Multiply it by whatever age you are. That's the ecstasy you feel when they move their tails."

Don García attempts a crude algebra and decides to think of something else. Such as the woman his father knew who had given birth to a child that was half Christian, half bufeo. The wind of the river, she told her husband. It was a sorry sight, apparently. When they burnt it a voice cried out with the mother's name.

But why a Christian? That is what puzzles Don García. "Why do bufeos always appear as white strangers?"

Don Leopoldo replies in that lecturing manner he adopts when he believes he knows about a subject. "Because our continent has always been dominated by white strangers. Think of Pizarro, think of the missionaries, think of the Spanish, the Portuguese, the British, the Dutch who have inflicted themselves on us. That's what the bufeo represents. It's a symbol."

"A symbol," Don Wenceslau repeats. "Like this cross."

"Like your cross, like that church, like that car, like everything that has been transplanted on us."

"Like communism," says Don García who is keen to demonstrate his grasp of Don Leopoldo's polemic.

"Like communism."

It is all too much for Don Wenceslau and not in the least what he expected when he began his story. The masato has fortified his hazy belief that whatever has been said he is right.

"Fucking communists," he mutters. "Fucking terrucos." He thinks back to what Vásquez told him barely an hour before, shaking his newspaper with a rage that rattled the barrow. What type of man is it that can send a child scampering into Lima's Crillón Hotel to explode into a hundred thousand pieces. Not a day goes by without some incident like this. He thinks of the recent mutilations at Cabaña. He thinks of the town now buzzing like a jostled termite's nest with strange soldiers from Lima and helicopters that whisk his hat away. His poor country. Overrun by the communists, by the military, by the police.

"I doubt if they'll blow up the Liberty," says Don Leopoldo, unable to resist following Don Wenceslau's line of thought.

Don Wenceslau suppresses another belch. "Pity," he says. "They might take a few tourists with them."

"What about my beautiful Argentine?" says Don García in tones of mock anguish. "Pía tells me her music is quite out of hand. The guests have been complaining. There are cracks in the ceiling where she dances . . . "

"But Pía never speaks to you," observes Don Wenceslau.

"All right, all right," he replies. "She told Capitán Velarde who told me. Satisfied? What's more Velarde told me her name." Don García looks as if he is about to cry.

"Yes?" say Don Wenceslau and Don Leopoldo together.

"She's a man."

"Called?"

"A gringo called Riddle. A writer."

"As I thought," says Don Wenceslau. "An Irishman."

Don Leopoldo is unruffled. "I wonder if he's anything to do with the Major Riddle credited with discovering the electric eel."

"Whoever he is, Pía tells Velarde he's got appalling taste in music."

"Why tell Velarde anything?" asks Don Wenceslau. "I thought she hated him. Even more than she hates you."

"They're checking out the hotels. Not just the benches," says Don García, glad to get his own back. He doesn't know the reason, but whatever it is they have left him alone. His trilby he supposes. They could tell he was an artist. Even brutes like that.

"Louts," says Don Wenceslau with emotion, reminded of the incident which had sent him in a fury to Don Vásquez's barrow.

"Asking for my documents. Who does Velarde think we are. Agents from Ecuador. You'd make a fine agent, Leopoldo," he says. He prods the man beside him. "I suppose he thought you had a bomb in your bag."

"How's the great work?" Velarde had said, inspecting Don Leopoldo's identity card, faded like a patch of old cotton, and the photograph of the young historian before he blundered into the cobwebs.

"Coming along, coming along," Don Leopoldo had muttered, peevish and embarrassed.

Bad enough to humiliate his companion like that, but to Don Wenceslau far worse was the way they had upset his own ritual. Just as he was stretching the toes in his Duckers in anticipation of his afternoon shine, just as he had summoned the boy and just as he was counting the change in his pocket with two coins extra for the tip, one of the policemen thrust out his boot and ordered him to clean it then and there.

He recognized the man. He was one of the bastards who had messed up Gabriel Lung all those years ago.

That was it! Don Wenceslau realizes. What an utter fool he's been. They must've found out about the Chino.

"They must've found out about the Chino," he says. "That he's not dead after all."

Part Three

1986

Chapter 23

THEY HAD WALKED all morning from the tributary where the boat dropped them, Gabriel and a boy from Dos de Mayo called Alan. For 200 intis, Alan had agreed to guide Gabriel through the jungle to Delicias. He knew a short cut that would halve the journey there by boat. "Coming back," Alan promised, slanting his hand through the air, "you glide."

He had a black dog, who criss-crossed the path in pursuit of butterflies, and a glass eye where his brother's machete had struck him while cutting cane.

After an hour Gabriel heard a wild turkey flap its way up a tree. Then some red paraqueets flew over, screaming. The rest was jungle static and the slash of Alan's machete.

Cobwebs marked Gabriel's face, thorns tore at his clothes, creepers tripped him. It was a long time since he had been in the jungle. Sliding on rotten logs and damp paths, he was breathless in its mosaic light.

After five hours they emerged from the jungle into a river bed with flat stones and a rut of brownish water. Even the dog was tired.

"Let's sit," gasped Gabriel. He fanned his face with a leaf. He had not expected this exhaustion. But his strength had been sapped from him. His torture, his illness, his years in San Francisco prison had scored him like a rubber tapper's knife.

"One more hour," said Alan. He patted the dog and pointed through the thin trees fringing the river bed.

Gabriel sat on a rock catching his breath. He followed Alan's hand to where the clouds dropped jaguar spots on the mountains. He relived the last time he had been in the jungle, fleeing through it with a price on his head, Edith at his side and his face a feast for every insect in miles.

*

He heard himself moaning. Someone was trying to open his eyes. He saw a dark shape blocking the sky. The moans were Sebastián's.

His step-mother stopped her rocking when she saw them in the doorway. She rose from her chair. She thanked Sebastián in an unbroken voice and led Gabriel through the coloured plastic strands to his room. She sat him on his bed while she fetched a bowl of water. She said nothing until she had washed his bleeding face and groin.

Then she said: "You can't stay here, son. Not unless you want to find yourself in the Moronacocha."

With that she left Gabriel on his bed, to buy some antiseptic cream. Gabriel knew she was leaving him to decide. He wondered why he felt no pain. He looked up.

Everywhere he saw his photographs of Elena and her face before it broke into a smile.

When his step-mother returned from Dominica Zumate, she found Gabriel standing calmly in the middle of a million fragments. He was staring at the wall above his bed. In the blank space from which Elena's images had been obliterated, he was picturing the face of the man from Ayacucho.

He found Edith in a house owned by her cousin. She sat in an empty room. Her hands were looped around her knees. She was staring at nothing. Above her a grey parrot fidgeted in a cramped cage. It pecked unblinking at an empty water tray.

"We're going to Ayacucho."

She looked vacantly at him. Tears had blotted her make-up into an oily smear below her cheeks. He held out his hand.

They reached Ayacucho in three weeks. They caught the boat to Requena after hiding for five days in a scatter of huts on the Maniti. (He wouldn't be able to find it now. Probably it was no longer there. The Indians had a habit of moving on once the thin jungle earth had given up on them.)

From Requena they took another boat to Pucallpa and then a lorry through the mountains. Gabriel sat with Edith on the truck's floor. Through the back they saw donkeys loaded with roof tiles and cattle dragging ropes along the road. As the lorry passed them, girls held out their hands for money.

At one village they were joined by an Indian band heading for the ice festival at San Juan. There were six of them, presided over by a squeaky-voiced Lord of Misrule. They wore silk scarves on their backs, patterned with a woman on horseback in a black hat.

The band played the same tune again and again. Their falsetto leader kept them awake by hurling orange peel at those who threatened sleep.

On the second day the tarmac ended. Gabriel looked out at the bleakest landscape he had ever seen. Mountains without vegetation. An implacable sky. A sun that could blister the stones.

As they climbed between a high pass of shaled sand, dust rose between the boards, covering their clothes and faces. They tasted its chalkiness, they felt its weight on their eyelashes, they sneezed it into their sleeves. By the time the lorry reached Trapala, they were statues of grey flesh.

"The man downstairs says it's one more day," said Edith. She was washing her mask away in their hotel room. Gabriel caught her eyes in the mirror. He had never seen Edith without make-up. Her face was revealed for the first time, the face of a Chanca Indian.

"Two at the most." She bared her teeth.

Gabriel spoke. "Come here," he said.

She turned. She walked to where he lay on the bed. He pulled her to him. She did not resist.

Afterwards he felt a tugging. He raised his face from the ticklish darkness of her hair, spread out on the pillow. The movement released her head. Her face came into focus. She was looking at the ceiling.

"What are you thinking about?"

She told him.

"I loved him more than I thought," she said.

"That's why we're going to Ayacucho. To see he didn't die for nothing."

"What about Elena?"

"I must never think of her."

Already Gabriel was burying her memory with the dry, colourless earth of his revolution. Instead of the seraphic glow in the sky, he was thinking of the crowd glimpsed from the Toyota roof, the sudden convergence of men and women that nothing on earth could have stopped.

The first thing Gabriel noticed about Ayacucho was its light. It struck everything with the same force – the lizard tiles, the thirty-three churches, the equestrian statue of General Sucre raising his tasselled sword to the hills.

Gabriel also noticed how thin the air was. Just to walk up the slope of the colonial square made him dizzy and exhausted.

"Your professor" – as Edith called him – had returned only recently from a trip to China. They arrived in Ayacucho in time to hear him lecture on it. His talk was given in a large room on the first floor of the faculty of education. The room was full of undergraduates and professors. Even the sharp-nosed Dean of the University in a lace bow-tie was there. Because of the low voltage, it was easy for Gabriel and Edith to pass themselves off as students. It was a time, the students used to say, when you almost needed a match to find a light.

The professor arrived punctually at six. He was accompanied by his wife, a dark-browed woman who sat next to the Dean smoothing her black and white check skirt.

There was a hush as he made his way to the platform. He produced a bundle of papers from his case. He began arranging them on the table.

He was simply dressed, in a long-sleeved shirt. An orange cravat was tucked into its open collar, hiding his neck. He had the same gleaming hair, dark eyes and white teeth of the man who had stood by an empty fireplace in Lima. But there was something severe about his face. His defiant mouth was now a hawk about to plunge.

He raised his head. "Close the door, please."

The lecture lasted an hour. It was devoted to his seven-month sojourn in the People's Republic of China and the state of that country since the Sino–Soviet split.

He began by describing several field trips made in the company of a colleague from the university – a bearded man who sat nodding in the front row. There were no slides, but every so often he produced a chalk and grated some words on the blackboard. Gabriel remembered two phrases: a quote from Mao—"without intellectuals there is no revolution" — and the derivation of the word religion — "from religare = to bind up".

For the first time since childhood Gabriel became aware of the country Achin Man Lung had left a century before.

"That's why I let you in," said Ezequiel, with a gaze that made him feel like a beetle caught between a beak. "Your Chinese blood."

The lecture concluded with the observation that China had a great deal in common with Peru.

There was a tremendous silence in the room. Then he began speaking again, this time without notes. Unlike China, Peru was a land which had not come to terms with its last 400 years. It was a place, not a country. A no-man's-land which was aware of its boundaries only through the boundaries of others. It had no pride in its sovereignty, no fairness in its government, no future in its present condition. It was a land which refused to see its own reality – that it was a land of Indians.

But he believed the secrets of the Inca empire were not lost. He believed it was possible to restore a sense of national identity. He believed it was possible to do this by overturning the entire system.

Only a violent revolution on the Chinese model would enable this to be achieved.

"Only a violent revolution," said the professor scratching his elbow, "will give us back our identity and pride."

Later, Gabriel and Edith found a bare-bulb room in the Hostelería Santa Rosa. They registered in false names, then returned to the Plaza de Armas where they sat with dangling legs in an arcade overlooking the square. Gabriel followed General Sucre's sword-thrust to the mountains. Their folded slopes were faces without features, but they reminded him of his father who had died without seeing a mountain, who believed that mountains were where the earth had shrugged when the wind changed.

On the other side of the sierra was fought the famous battle of Ayacucho. Gabriel watched the tiger-eye sun roll over the peaks. He found himself able to look at it without blinking, and as he looked it became Hipólito's ball, coming to rest at the site of the battle which had finally liberated the continent from Spain, when, outnumbered two to one, the patriot forces comprising William Miller's hussars, and men who had fought at Borodino, and a division of sightless soldiers, snow-blinded in the Andes, followed General Antonio José de Sucre on his horse, a massive charger with bollocks larger than avocado pears from whose nostrils snorted trumpets of mist as it paced the heights called Condorcunca – worthy of the condor – and, spurred on by the flash of the General's sword, put the silver-headed royalists to flight in such a way that when the Spanish Viceroy Canterac rode down to surrender, he could only say to the English general who offered him tea, it all appeared a dream.

General Miller, he said, again and again and again, as the wick lowered on the sky, and also three centuries of Spanish rule, ésto parece sueño.

Chapter 24

ON THE RIVER BED, Gabriel threw away the leaf. He rose to his feet. "One hour more," Alan repeated.

At three they reached Delicias. They came out of the trees into a grass bank that rolled up towards the village. In the river a group of naked children stopped their splashing and watched them. Over the ridge came the thump of drums.

"They're preparing the pot for you," joked Alan.

The drums grew louder as they climbed the bank, followed by the children. Gabriel traced the noise to its source in a clearing bordered by stilted huts. Three Indians sat outside one hut on the rungs of a ladder. They wore grass skirts and green feathered head-dresses. One man beat an upturned plastic bucket. Another piped a flute carved from a section of hose-piping. Another shook a pair of rattles.

"They caught so much yesterday," Father Maby explained, "they don't have to work for two days. They've been drinking masato all morning. That's how it is in the jungle. You live for today."

When the Indians saw Gabriel, they stumbled groggily down the steps. The one with the bucket made a V-sign against his lips for a cigarette. Gabriel gave him his packet.

"Stay here," said Alan. "I'll find the Father."

Gabriel took his place on the bottom rung. The three Indians converged on him, puffing their cigarettes. The man with the hose-pipe flute crowned him with his parrot head-dress. The others touched his cheeks and forehead with their fingers. It was a while before Gabriel realized they were painting him in yellow patterns like their own.

When Alan returned, he covered his mouth with his hand and whooped. The Indians yelled along with him, not quite understanding. The dog barked.

"The Father?" Gabriel asked.

"He's ill," said Alan, his glass eye on Gabriel's yellow cheeks, his other on the musicians who had resumed their playing. "But he wants to see you."

"Do I remember her?" The words were non-committal. From his hammock Father Maby took in Gabriel with eyes rusty from malaria. The priest's face was gaunt, tapering into several chins which the disease had left untouched.

"Yes," he said decisively, slipping from the hammock. His feet searched for sandals on the floor. He shuffled to the quivering fridge. He took out a can of Pilsen. As an afterthought, he produced a second.

"What the hell. If my liver's going to be ruined, I'd prefer to do it with booze, not pills."

He opened the door with a foot. With the beer cans he gestured at a table overlooking the spongy forest along the Yagua.

"Of course, I remember her. More to the point, I remember you."

It was twenty-six years since Paul Maby first walked up from the hard, ribbed sandbanks of the river below. He liked to think the mission he founded inside Henriques Silves' old rubber station was one of the Church's more worthwhile achievements in a region known – if known at all – as The Devil's Paradise.

Since making the journey from Tulsa he had not cared to leave Delicias. Disaster had usually struck the moment he had done so. Or controversy.

Even today, reminded of the incident by his pale, unspeaking visitor – a man he long had wanted to meet – Father Maby did not know whether the Church had forgiven him for the stand he took over Elena Silves' vision. He did not care either.

"A vision. You say she's seen a vision?"

Confronted that night by the two figures on Bishop Barrantes' doorstep, his first thought was to send for Dr Lache. So often in the jungle he came upon trances induced by an overdose of ayahuasca, the root of the dead. But in the dark, Gabriel's excited explanation of an apparition that had evidently passed over his head seemed more consistent with Messianism than hallucinogens.

"Let's get this straight. You're telling me the Virgin has just appeared to this girl. In a shed across the river?"

Father Maby had allowed himself an inward groan. He still hadn't forgotten the end of the world, as prophesied by Melquíades Góngora, a lathe-operator from Chorrera.

How long before had that episode taken place? No more than a year, but the details were fresh in his mind. It had been a Wednesday – he remembered this: after all, what if the man had been right? – when Góngora appeared on the river with news of his return from Heaven.

God, said Góngora – who seemed to be suffering from a catalepsy of the jaw – had entrusted him with the following message. Only those living on the Yagua river and who followed his teaching – which so far as Father Maby understood it required disciples to dance in figures of eight to the words "Elbu, elbu" in emulation of Góngora's affliction – would be spared the apocalypse intended for that night.

To be certain of deliverance, they should give Góngora their pigs and chickens. The more generously they gave, the surer they were to escape burning, the quicker they would ascend to Heaven. In Heaven, said Góngora reasonably, there was no need for pigs or chickens.

Góngora's message reassured a frightened crowd, amongst whom Father Maby recognized several of his own flock.

Three figures stood out. A wizened woman, and two elderly men who hummed in loud voices – voices fuelled by cachaza from an Allsopp's Pale Ale bottle – a familiar but maddeningly elusive tune.

This group were distinguished by their sounds. They were also distinguished by their dress. Each of the men had on a lady's crimson blouse. The woman wore a pair of trousers on her head, fastened by a band of egret feathers.

Almost at the same time that he realized this drunken trinity were none other than the Holy Ghost, Saint Joseph and Saint Mary, Father Maby deciphered in their wailing an aria from *Lucia di*

Lammermoor.

He had gone to bed early and been pleased to wake with the world and his credibility intact. But when, all those months later, Father Maby switched on the light in the Bishop's porch and saw the girl standing beside Gabriel, he knew he was witnessing a different phenomenon.

For one thing, Elena Silves wasn't suffering from catalepsy.

For another, she had obviously seen something.

He swallowed a mouthful of beer, half waiting for a belch that never came. He would let Gabriel do the talking – at least to start with.

He looked at the man sitting beside him on the bench, who gazed unseeing into the blue distance where the forest ended and the cerrado scrublands began their climb into mountains not even Father Maby had visited.

His unexpected guest did not look well. The only colour in his cheeks belonged to a patch of yellow paint. His hair was thin, his lips dry and the corners of his mouth pulled down as if hooked by some unseen fisherman. Father Maby was no psychiatrist, but he would say it was a very delicate filament which lit the heart of this man.

Gabriel scratched at a scar on his arm. In the chlorotic eyes of the priest, it had the shape of a chicken claw.

"Where is she, Father?"

"No idea. She left a week ago. Without a word. The children are still waiting for her. I haven't the courage to tell them –" There was hurt in his voice.

"Where was she going?"

"I told you, no idea."

"How long was she here?"

"Three years. More or less from the time she left Santa Clara. She had become more vital to the community than I am. They loved her . . . " His voice disappeared.

Gabriel clawed his hands together, until the knuckles whitened.

"Tell me, Father, what she was like? What did she say? Anything.

Anything at all. Please. You may not understand . . . "

"Oh, I understand," said the American priest. "I understand a great deal."

"You may think I have no right –"

"Bullshit. Everyone has the right to stew in their own juice. But we could do with another beer."

Father Maby was fond of illustrating the difficulty of his calling with a free translation of a local Indian saying. The idiom "putting up with Christ", he explained to the few clergymen who made it to Delicias, could be roughly translated as "dealing with an idiot". It was not until Elena Silves appeared from the carob trees and walked across his lawn, that he fully understood the phrase.

After eighteen years in the convent, her eyes held to the ground, avoiding contact with anything around her.

"Look at me!" he would shout. "Not there. At me."

But when he learnt what she had done, he knew there was no going back. If she was to survive in the world she had stumbled into, the sooner she looked it smack in the face, the better.

She spent much of the first fortnight asleep. Once or twice he caught her awake at six in the morning, staring from the verandah into the vast, uninhabited dawn. The first time, she tried to break the silence. It was the hour of prime, her first canonical prayers.

"I . . . I can't seem to say them."

Father Maby took her back inside. He told her if that was the case then she needn't say them. She needn't say anything.

"But when you do, when you're ready, I want you to promise me two things. The first is you won't ever lie to me."

"And?"

"So is the second."

It was a month before she was ready to speak. In that time she attended mass regularly. She seemed to need the ritual, rather than the message it contained. She had suspended her faith, put it on ice, along with the beer in Father Maby's fridge. But she couldn't forget its ceremony. It had spoken to her at a deep level for a long time. It still comforted her in moments of terror. And in those first months there were many such moments. Terror, after years of conditioning, that her life was not legislated for in all its details. Terror at the huge expanse of space that confronted her. Terror at a jungle which was so unlike the Silar desert in its seething fertility that a monotheistic belief seemed impossible.

On the day she was ready to speak, she had been treating a sore on a child's leg. She said: "Silly, isn't it? I've had to leave the convent to do one of the things I entered it for."

"Which is?"

"Live for others, I suppose. Which is what I had begun to do in Belén."

Soon she was spending most of her day visiting the sick and deformed, those whom the community traditionally placed at arm's length. She never interfered with their customs – Father Maby insisted on that – but she would sit with the witchdoctor sipping his masato so that she came to appreciate them.

She only intervened once, when the witchdoctor ordered the burial alive of a young girl suffering from leukaemia. She rose to her feet. Standing there, she acknowledged her promise never to poke her nose into the tribe's affairs.

"But the killing of an innocent is against every custom I know."

If the family would allow it, she would care for the child. In the end she got her way and the girl moved into the house. She died a year after, but she was given a Christian burial – Elena had made him baptize her – and practically the whole tribe, including the witchdoctor, attended the service.

Little by little, Father Maby learnt of her life at Santa Clara. When she caught him boiling a toothbrush – one of the few things to survive intact the journey from Tulsa was his love of cleanliness – she joked how he reminded her of the Mother Superior. Only in this respect, she added quickly.

"What was she like otherwise?"

"Oh, I think she hated me for having had a vision. She hoped I'd show signs of pride. She was ready for those. She was like a cow who couldn't jump over the smallest fence. After a while that's what I must have been to her – a small, insurmountable fence."

"Why?" He removed his saucepan from the boil.

"I suppose in the early days I knew what I thought. None of the others knew until the Vatican told them. They existed in a pleasant, irresponsible limbo, drifting down a half-lit corridor to a door that ended in God. But I felt proudly I had already seen inside. I felt that what I had seen was an answer to all the prayers I used to offer for those maimed, broken bodies. I believed what I had seen was a truth I could not forget once the door shut again. And it was not a truth that made it easy for me to pass my days making rice pictures of Saint Teresa.

"Of course, this took years to come out. To begin with, I was more preoccupied getting rid of my feelings in order to accept God's love. And I so nearly made it. So nearly. In fact when I finally changed my name and put on my bridal dress I really did think I could admit no lover but Himself. Deep down I honestly was the bride of Him whom the angels serve and at whose beauty the sun and moon stand amazed."

In front of her, Father Maby walked to the mesh door. He threw the steaming contents of his saucepan onto the grass.

"I couldn't have been more wrong," said Elena.

Another day, after he had said Mass in the small church, she stayed behind. She ran her hands over the communion table – the varnished trunk of a lupuna tree he had rescued from the river. Suddenly she said: "God's love should be enough for anybody. But I was lonely, unutterably, shudderingly lonely. Stupid things, like no one remembering my birthday. No cinema, no radio, no books, no poetry."

She laughed. "Not even a travel brochure to pit my wits against. Just myself, this lifeless, mediocre vessel – and God. Of course, I'd been well prepared for temptation. From the very first day it was drummed into me what a vile time Saint Bernadette had suffered in her convent. Not a week went by without me taking solace in our holy mother Teresa. And she spoke so eloquently. It was all there, the extreme desolation that comes after ecstasy, the absence I sometimes felt of God, of even a sense of him.

"And I took the greatest solace of all in her idea that once you reached this desolation, once you had your heart and soul consumed by it, you were really beginning to know God. It wasn't till I'd been in Santa Clara ten years that I began to think of the love that no amount of apostolic love can replace.

"A man's love.

"And I remembered the love of the man I had loved, and before I knew it I was remembering his face, his particular way of laughing and scowling and dressing, and when I caught myself doing this I forced myself, seriously forced myself so that sometimes I had to bite the inside of my cheeks, to think of him as just muscle and bone.

"How can you contemplate betraying God, I would say, for something that's three quarters water? Something that wouldn't even fill a shallow bath. At the end I was even praying to God for help, but by then He must have seen it was too late. He had looked down on the lowliness of His handmaiden and found her wanting."

She turned to Father Maby. Her blue eyes were glistening.

"Do you know what finally did it? A song. A simple pop song. I can't even remember the words. They sang it the day the rain came, ending the drought. I think they were drunk. Hearing it, I suddenly thought: Here am I who have been blessed with a vision from God, who has been chosen by Him, who knows she has stood in the presence of something infinitely greater than herself, here am I – and yet can I say to myself or to anyone else that it has actually been a blessing."

She was crying now.

"And I couldn't. I just couldn't . . . At that moment it was as if I had been inflicted with the knowledge of God, not blessed with it. At that moment I felt the knowledge of God was nothing more and nothing less than a plague."

She wiped her cheek. "And to crown it all, I find I've given up God for a man who has taken away the only life I've breathed into anyone."

Father Maby handed her the paper tissue with which he had wiped the chalice.

"If anyone deserved that, it was Don Miguel," he said.

"Don't be stupid," she laughed – one of those laughs that can only be made when crying.

"Then do you regret it?" Father Maby was aware as he said it, of how stupid the question sounded, but at that moment, by the altar, beside this woman, he could not think of anything else. He wanted also to know the answer.

"No," she replied, letting out a breath that seemed to come from the earth. "I don't. Not at all. You see, by that time I'd also discovered something else."

"There is a time for penance," Father Maby told Gabriel, "and a time for partridge. Let's eat. If you want to kill a friar give him lunch late and no siesta."

A large Indian woman with no teeth brought a dish to the table. They ate it in silence. After the meal – the minced remains of a tapir – the priest swallowed two Maloprim tablets and retired to his room.

Gabriel walked to the village a hundred yards away. Some children were kicking a ball. When they saw Gabriel they hopped across the grass, struggling to push their arms and heads into their brown cushmas.

They re-emerged in a long orderly line led by their father. He smiled. He had an arrow in his hands which he pointed to a hut in the trees. Three women sat in the shade of this hut. They were joined by the children who stood shyly by a boiling kettle. Behind, some ceramics dried in the sun. A calendar for 1968 – eighteen years old – flapped from a beam overhead. March showed Christ on the cross and an advertisement for tractors.

A girl washed out a gourd bowl. She gave it to her mother who poured masato into it. The girl offered the bowl to Gabriel.

Another girl offered sticks of yucca on a white tin plate. The man spat and sat on his haunches. He laughed as he watched Gabriel eat and drink.

When he had finished eating, Gabriel thanked him in Quechua. The man continued to laugh. He didn't understand a word, thought Gabriel. He asked something else, in Spanish. The man looked bashfully down at his arrow. He poked its tip between his toes.

Gabriel thought of the years he had spent in the villages around Ayacucho. Cleaning irrigation ditches, clearing the terraces of paddle-shaped cactus, claiming the people's serrano confidence inch by inch until the time he could plant in their minds the idea that life was a much longer thing than the span of their generation.

Gabriel thought of these Chinese years in the field, working, working, working, interring in that same ungenerous soil his own identity, his own past, his own passions in order to understand the customs and the ways and the language of those Ezequiel wanted to liberate. Yet here in the jungle, in the department of his birth, he couldn't exchange a sentence.

The man raised his arrow. He pointed it at Gabriel's chest.

"Elena," he said. The word unlocked the children behind him. They came forward on their hands and knees.

"Elena," they repeated. Elena, Elena, Elena.

"What would you say to a drink?" Father Maby stood in the kitchen wearing a clean pink shirt.

"Perhaps you'd like a Bourbon. I think we'd both of us could do with a Bourbon."

He handed Gabriel a large tumbler and took a gulp from his own. This he kept in his mouth before swallowing.

"That's better. That's what I call high-class holy water."

Dinner was a repetition of the same dish they had eaten at lunch, with rice. For a time the only sound on the verandah was that of cutlery on china. Somewhere in the night a bird called. After a while Gabriel cleared his throat.

"More?"

Gabriel held up his hand.

"Father, why did she come here?"

Father Maby did not answer immediately. Then he said: "Perhaps because I was the first person who believed her. And I doubt she had anywhere else to go." He broke a ryebread cracker. "She also wanted a safe place, where she could wait until you came out of prison. I don't know whether or not she had forgiven you for Don Miguel, but she didn't want that to be a barrier. She hoped you might make the same sacrifice that she had made for you."

He swallowed more of his muddy holy water. There was a burr in his words when he spoke again.

"She was living for you, dammit. For the life you would have together, for the children that would come of it."

He heard her voice as she knelt on the grass with his photograph album. "Everywhere I looked, Father, there were frescoes of the Virgin with a child in her lap." She had looked up from the photographs they had sent him from Tulsa of a niece he was unlikely to see. "I was surrounded by reminders of the children I couldn't have."

His speech sweltered with fever and Bourbon. A drop of sweat trembled on the tip of his beard. He forked up some food. It fell to the table.

"Goddam," he cursed, brushing it to the floor with his napkin. "I never could eat rice." He dabbed his forehead and retucked the cloth under his chin.

"Tell me, Gabriel Lung, why *have* you been released?"

So Gabriel told how he had discovered the newspaper cutting; how he had arranged a palanca on the remote chance it might be Elena who had escaped the convent in Silar, how he had followed the trail from Bishop Barrantes to this mission on the Yagua.

At the mention of Barrantes, Father Maby changed colour.

"Barrantes wouldn't say shit if his mouth was full." He waved his fork in the air. "That man was so mean he wouldn't have given a rice grain to Saint Peter's cock. But tell you something, that was one weird situation. I think a small part of him wanted to believe in Elena's vision, but another part, the larger part, the part that collected those crosses, felt he shouldn't. Anything that fouled up his relations with Rome or the big-wigs in Lima was out, out, out. And there was I who didn't want to believe it, whose whole training and instinct was hostile to believing it, but who came to believe it. He saw me off, though. Chased me back to the back of beyond." He spoke the last words in English.

"It can't have cost him a minute's sleep to make her disappear into a closed order while he sat back and reaped the unofficial benefits. It takes no fool to work out how he bought his crosses. What he had going with Don Miguel would have filled the Prado."

His hand jutted out to the bottle.

"You know, when your people burnt down the mission here, he

refused to visit me. He felt it would be 'badly interpreted' – as if what you had done was God's way of punishing me. He didn't give me anything, not a jumping bean, even though my vestments had gone up in flame."

"What burning?" said Gabriel.

"Don't, don't, don't." Father Maby's voice rose. "At least be decent enough to take responsibility for your actions."

"I know nothing of this," Gabriel insisted. "What burning?"

In the poor light, Father Maby could see the palpitating scar. What the hell, perhaps he didn't know. If so, it only confirmed his experience that after twenty-six years in this country, he had met no one outside the jungle who knew their butt from their elbow.

"OK, buddy." He pushed away his unfinished plate, and lit a cigarette. He had sat on the packet of Hamilton Lights and it poked from his lips like a broken pencil.

"Since you continue to plead ignorance, I'll tell you what happened here while you were fiddling with the masses."

It had happened two years ago. They had come at six in the evening, forty or fifty of them. He had been in Lima, seeking advice on a hydraulic pump to bring water from the Yagua to a reservoir nearer the village.

"Elena was delivering anti-biotics to a hamlet an hour away. When she heard the explosions, she hurried back. She was found on the path by a group of children. Fortunato, the village elder, had sent them to hide her. She was concealed in one of the pits used for trapping wild boar.

"They were looking for both of us. Instead they found an empty village. The people had fled like chickens. All except an old father, quivering behind the altar. He told them the two gringos were in Lima.

"They started burning the mission. They set fire to the house. They set fire to Elena's room. They set fire to the hut with the medical supplies. Last of all they threw dynamite at the tabernacle.

"It was a woman who led them. The children saw her through the grass. They said she had war paint on her face. She stood back from the others as her henchman kerosened the church. She was watching a nest on the roof. She was watching the birds as they tried to rescue their young.

"When the church collapsed the sky was filled with birds on fire."

He poured more Bourbon.

He closed his eyes.

He drank.

"I arrived two days later. The Indians were gathering. They came down from the hills all painted black and stamping their bows on the ground while a drink was mixed which wound them into a state in which they either had to kill those responsible or kill each other.

"They gathered in the square. There were so many that they spread into the compound here. Fortunato said to me 'Do you agree Father, we should kill them.' 'Fortunato,' I said, 'remember when you asked me to baptize you, what you promised? No vengeance. You too, Román. Egalimento, Leonidas, José, Pablo,' I said, looking at those I had baptized. 'Remember what you promised.' Suddenly Fortunato let his spear fall. He burst into tears. One by one the others followed. You can cut an Indian's arm off and he won't show emotion, but there they all were, weeping like a lot of willows."

Father Maby rubbed an eye stung by his smoke. "One way and another, you can say I saved a few lives that day. Theirs, as well as your friends'."

He shook a finger at Gabriel. "But lighten my darkness, will you? What did you have against us? What possible threat was posed by a middle-aged nun and a Yankee priest who for no reason he could explain, except his whole heart told him so, believed that a long time ago this woman saw the Mother of God?"

Gabriel was not listening.

"Edith . . . " he mouthed. Anger squalled his face.

Father Maby sniffed and carried the plates to the kitchen. His voice came through the kitchen window. "Tomorrow I'll show you what's left of the damage." A moth floundered against the wire mesh. Inside a plate clattered.

"Dammit, dammit, dammit."

Father Maby appeared in the doorway.

"I've spilled that tapir all down my front."

*

Gabriel spent the night in a wooden outhouse twenty yards from the main quarters. It had been built for Elena after the burning down of the mission. The room was empty except for a bed. Gabriel ran his hands several times over the blanket. Then he lay down and slept.

In his dreams he dreamt of Elena and Ezequiel. Their faces alternated. But the face of Ezequiel was the clearer. It was the morning after Ezequiel's lecture twenty-one years before. Gabriel was knocking on a door in Calle Libertad. The door opened and there stood the professor. The sky was cloudless, but he still wore his jacket. He was chewing a pen. (He had been marking a thesis.) Behind him a hose was watering the grass, its damp crackle the only sound in the garden.

Gabriel was shown to a white wickerwork chair. He told Ezequiel that listening to his lecture was like listening to himself. He confessed he had been one of those in the room with Fuente. He described his involvement with the northern foco in '65.

"I want to join you."

Ezequiel heard everything Gabriel had to say. He removed the pen from his mouth. Come back in a week, he said.

A week later they were walking by an empty river bed.

"Do you really know what's required of you?" Ezequiel scooped up a handful of pebbles. He threw them into the ditch where the water should have been.

"I'm prepared."

"You have to be a lost man. A man without interests. A man without belongings. A man without a name."

"I know."

"You'll have to live without your family, your friends, your girl." He threw the last stone. "You have a girl?"

"No."

"But you did have."

"There was one . . . "

"I know."

"How do you know?"

"Edith told me." Edith.

Then Gabriel saw them together. They were walking out of a café in the slanting square where the students drank pisco with tea. Ezequiel stumbled. Edith helped him. "Thank you," he said. That was all, just those two words, which caused no suspicion until the day when Gabriel discovered Ezequiel had vanished.

But that was more than ten years later, years which he had spaded into the soil, with his head down, his eyes on the terraces, never thinking of his own life, only of the harvest the revolution would bring.

A week after Ezequiel's absence all those years later she turned up in the "thank you" café. Gabriel was sitting with Julio and Bonifacio. The two men had come to join him in the fields near Chuschi. Julio brought him news of his step-mother's death. Bonifacio scratched a crop of spots on his shoulder as he told how he had burned down the church the Bishop had started building, then desecrated the altar. There wasn't much other news. Pía Zumate was thought to be having an affair with Dr Lache. The Bishop had decided after all not to move into his new palace. Don Miguel was going to stand for the council.

"And that aunt of Elena's, remember," said Bonifacio.

"What about her?"

Bonifacio gloved his answer with a smile. "She died." That was when Edith entered. She had driven Ezequiel and his wife to Arequipa. They had gone underground, she explained. For the final stage.

Gabriel woke.

He saw a smear like lipstick on the pillow where his gums had bled. Since his torture, they bled all the time.

He dressed and walked outside. Father Maby crouched in the stiff grass with a butterfly net.

"Catching the Holy Ghost, Father?"

The priest made a fisherman's gesture with his hands. "The biggest swallow-tail I ever saw – and I missed it." He put down the net. His fever was passing.

Later, they walked to the Yagua, to where the river was fed by a tributary from an overhead cliff. They stripped, leaving their clothes on a rock and entered the sparkling barley-stick of water.

"Sorry I lost my cool last night," shouted Father Maby. He raised his face to the spray. The water pummelled his head. A bird swooped into the fall. It disappeared behind the dazzling curtain.

Gabriel didn't reply. He shouted again. Gabriel muttered something.

"What?" yelled Father Maby.

"It's I who am sorry."

Father Maby looked at him, standing in the roaring white mist, his ribs a shipwreck covered by sand, his scars shiny in the sun. This was the man who had been chosen over God, he thought.

"I believe you."

They dressed, except for their shoes, which they held, and walked back. Half way up the hill, Father Maby left the path and made into the trees.

"There," he said. "Our old church. Where the rubber station used to be." He indicated a statue of the Virgin on a stretch of concrete cracked by roots and creepers. Her crown was melted, her head a black char brushed by grasses.

"I couldn't bear to throw it away. Don't you think her expression is . . . beautiful's not the right word, but can you see what I mean?"

They stood looking at the twisted shape which had been her face. As they stood, a large blue butterfly danced like broken paper over the concrete.

"Sonofabitch," said Father Maby. He watched it disappear into the trees.

They continued uphill. "I've been thinking more about that stingless bee, Barrantes. He's like all those for whom the means are the ends. They miss the bolt. OK, we've got the Pope's infallibility. OK, we've got the Immaculate Conception, but where does that take us? I'll tell you where." Father Maby dropped his shoes to the ground. He wiped the sand from between his toes.

"It takes us to a world where everyone's a Catholic and no one's a Christian, where everyone celebrates the cross but forgets the Christ. When Elena saw what she saw, the Church was still in diapers. A father had more confidence in his sixteen-year-old son than the Roman Catholic Church in a man of sixty. It was a triangle of Pope and Bishop and People – which meant that everything was translated into inaction.

"Much of it hasn't changed. Barrantes' Church still likes to force-feed its people with dogma as if they are Strasbourg geese. It makes them swallow the idea of an invisible God when they already have the sun and the moon.

"And what happens? They come to think Holy Water is a medicine they can buy. They come to think that prayer is something to mouth, like an American pop song they don't know the words of."

He wriggled his feet into his shoes.

"That's not my Church. In my Church the people matter more. Put character at the centre of your faith and all the obstacles fall away."

"Even sin?"

"I don't believe many people sin. What we want is a consciousness of sin, not a list of sins. It used to be like a Sears Roebuck catalogue. I would have men say to me, Father, I've committed a sin. I'd look at them and say Do you really believe that? They'd shake their head and say No, Father. And I'd say, Come back when you believe you have."

Father Maby turned to Gabriel. "No good explaining this to you, of course." He held out his hand to a girl who had run onto the path. When she saw Gabriel she chewed her fingers.

"Do you honestly think these people give a monkey's about Mao or Mariátegui? Any more than they care about Catholic dogma. I tell you, I came here to teach the Indians Christianity, but I found they had more to teach me. They don't steal. They don't lie. They don't covet their neighbour's wife. The only thing I've been able to teach them is money — so they're not robbed by the rivereños. Hardly something to be proud of.

"But I also learnt something else. You can't impose anything on them, politics or religion. It's like putting a plaster on a dog's nose. The dog just scratches it off."

He sent the girl gently away. "I don't know, perhaps we're both clawing at the moon."

"I hate God," Gabriel said. "I hate him so much I used to dress as a priest."

"You only hate what you fear."

"Don't tell me you've never had doubts."

"I have had doubts," replied the priest. "But I'm almost certain – no, no almost – that God exists and that I will have to tell Him what I have done and that in staying here I will have made the right choice."

"Why here?" asked Gabriel. "Why not the shanty-towns in Lima? Why not the pueblos jóvenes in Piura or Puno or Trujillo?"

"If I'm not here, soon no one will be. Unless someone protects these people, they will be chased out, corrupted, murdered by the mestizos from the mountains, the narcos from upriver, you lot. They haven't much time. But they've all the time I've got."

They faced each other on the path, their hands spidering their hips. Gabriel thought of Fuente and Ezequiel in the drawing room, by the empty fireplace.

He smiled. "And women?"

Father Maby laughed. "You know what they call a Franciscan? A man who fucks well. When women ask me why I'm not married, I tell them I am. I have been tempted, naturally."

"What do you do?"

"My job is not to do anything."

"What do you feel?"

"I feel I must pray harder."

They reached the top of the hill where children were playing football. When they spotted Father Maby, they kicked the ball towards him. He returned it awkwardly so it bounced off the pitch. A boy running to retrieve it said something. It included the word Elena. Father Maby shook his wet head.

"They'll have to know the truth," he told Gabriel.

"Which is?"

"That she's not coming back."

"How do you know?"

"After a lifetime in the Styx, one knows these things. Like one knows one will never catch that homerus swallow-tail. Like one knows there is no man in the moon."

"Like one knows that she saw what she saw?"

Father Maby didn't answer.

"I'm going to have to tell you something," he said at last, "for which I will rot in hell." He rubbed his malarial eyes. "But it involves us both."

It was something that happened the day before Elena left Delicias. A rivereño had beached his boat on the sand and walked to the house. He wanted to sell the priest a case of sorghum whisky. Fortunato had interrupted their negotiations. He had a query about the ditch they were digging for the reservoir. Father Maby had left the rivereño with Elena.

"She was milking him for news of the big wide world."

After dealing with Fortunato, Father Maby came back to pay for the whisky. When the rivereño had gone, Elena came into the kitchen. She wished him to take her confession. Not in the morning. There and then. Father Maby was surprised, but said nothing. They went into the church. Elena knelt. She nodded to the altar. Then turned her blue eyes on him.

She had something to tell him. Something she had kept secret for twenty years, since the night of her first vision. She spoke her words deliberately, with the care of one who had thrust their arm into a deep hole and one by one drawn a nest of eggs to the surface.

The vision Elena had seen was not of the Virgin Mary.

It was the vision of a man.

She had been too ashamed to admit this at the time. She had accepted the version put upon her first by Gabriel, then, imperceptibly, by everyone else. By the third day, it was too late to say anything.

She hadn't felt fraudulent about it. Nor had there been any reason to. The voice she had heard and the visions she had seen were obviously those of the Archangel, whose effigy was the first image to meet her eyes when she heard the sound of guns as she prayed in the cathedral.

She remembered the initial apparition at Fátima had not been the Virgin. It had also been an Angel. And that anyway, Saint Teresa had always impressed on everyone the unreliable nature of visions.

It was years later at Santa Clara, listening to the music from the river that Elena came to realize that what she had heard and seen was not a vision of the Archangel Gabriel, but instead a revelation and an affirmation of the beauty of human love . . .

The priest looked at the children playing. He looked at the church he had rebuilt with his own hands. He looked at Gabriel's hand gripping his shoulder. His eyes were heavy with tiredness.

"Yes?" stammered Gabriel.

Father Maby heard the words flutter from her caged mouth.

"It was a vision of you," he told Gabriel, "dressed as the Archangel."

Chapter 25

GABRIEL LEFT DELICIAS on a raft of logs nailed together in an open semi-circle. He stood at one end, his ankles washed over by the water rising through the beams. The river soon carried him out of sight of Father Maby on the sandbank.

At the point where the tributary joined the Amazon he caught a launch to Dos de Mayo. From there he boarded an empty packet to Belén.

The boat was one of the old steamers used to carry barbasco and curare in the days after the rubber boom. The blades of its paddles were rotten and splintered. The paint had flaked from its hull, removing its name.

For most of the passage Gabriel stood alone at the stern rail. Occasionally he spat into the Amazon.

To the captain he seemed a figure from a book, a figure of romance. To the captain's mate, a man with one green eye, one brown eye and a face pitted by verruga fever, he looked like a howler monkey.

"Engineer, missionary or gun-runner?"

The captain, a man of semitic appearance, scratched his chin. "None," he said. "I'd say he was a man down on his luck. A musician who has lost his instrument."

Pleased with the image, he spread some tinned fish onto a slab of bread. He opened the cabin door and offered it to the *Libertad*'s only passenger, who refused.

"Gun-runner," said the mate. "Definitely."

Gabriel was not hungry. He gazed at the stern rail into the wake, smelling the sharp scent of foliage on the afternoon breeze. He was remembering his call to arms and the death of Don Miguel six years before.

*

One March morning he walked into a small hotel in the town of Satipo. He climbed the uncarpeted stairs. He thought how long it had been since he had seen Ezequiel's handsome face. He knocked. The door was opened by Augusta, Ezequiel's wife.

He entered.

Someone was standing by the window with their back to him. Gabriel recognized the outlines of Ezequiel. He was wearing slippers. He appeared to be reading. His body has thickened, he thought, looking at Augusta looking at him and becoming aware of her implacable stare.

"It's Chino," she said.

Ezequiel turned.

In the light from the window, Gabriel saw a face covered with pustules. Its mouth, nose and eyes were hardly recognizable as features. Somewhere in the white and scarlet sores, Gabriel detected the professor from Ayacucho.

Ezequiel walked towards him.

"What's the matter," he said. His voice was the same soft voice. "Don't you like my face?" He made another step towards him. Suddenly Gabriel understood. Ezequiel was going to kiss him.

"I'll leave you together," said Augusta. She edged past and descended the staircase with her black and white dress swelling in the air.

"Psoriasis universalis." Gabriel felt the rough vegetable skin on his cheeks. Ezequiel drew back. That's why he had gone underground when he did. "It had reached my face." He took Gabriel's hand.

"Something to show you." He brought Gabriel to the window. He held up a piece of paper. Even the skin under his fingernails was affected.

"The final decision of the Central Committee," he said. "To begin the revolution."

Gabriel breathed out. "At last," he said.

Ezequiel explained. He wanted Gabriel to return to Belén to prepare a cell. He needed someone who understood the Soretanas and their jungle. He didn't want a recurrence of the mistakes that were made in '65. Edith would help him.

"I've told the others," Ezequiel said, scratching his elbow.

"I wanted to do so personally because, for security reasons, they are unlikely to see me again. And that goes for you too."

"I understand, Comrade Ezequiel."

"Not Comrade, Chino." It was a mild chide. "Nor Professor." There was a trace of humour on the mother-of-pearl scales where his lips should have been. "Presidente."

"When do we begin?"

Ezequiel gave a date. "The day Túpac Amaru was pulled apart in Cuzco." He referred to the last great Indian revolutionary and the belief, common in the Andes, that Túpac Amaru's severed body had been regrowing underground until the day he would rise to liberate his oppressed people.

"The choice of date is Augusta's," said Ezequiel. It was merely a coincidence that it was the date of the presidential election.

"And remember, Chino, if ever you have a creeping doubt, as you will do, as I have done, as we all have done, it's not numbers that are important. It's faith." Pizarro, he reminded him, had taken a continent with 180 men. Columbus, with 90, a hemisphere.

"What we are about to make isn't just a revolution for Peru." His smile was a compass indicating he was no longer concentrating on Gabriel.

"This is an example to the whole world. This is the start of a people's war to liberate all humanity."

Gabriel left the hotel in a trance. He paused at the bottom of the staircase to steady himself. He took several breaths, then walked out.

As he crossed to the square, Gabriel heard the words of a song. He stopped in the middle of the street. The words were in English, the singer American. The voice was familiar. Turning, Gabriel followed the music back to its source on the third floor of the hotel.

A light was on. It haloed the dark shape of Ezequiel, motionless but for a blur where his fingers scratched. The words drifted down from his window.

"I'll find you in the morning sun," Frank Sinatra was singing.

"And when the night is new,

I'll be looking at the moon,
But I'll be seeing you . . . "

When Ezequiel sent Gabriel back to Bélen, it was his first visit since Hipólito's death. Much had changed. His step-mother's house had become part of a school. San Agustín College had moved premises to a modern building in the Plaza Clavero. Señora Guzmán's house was shuttered and ambulantes sat on the steps among the dry fruit peel, no longer admonished.

Posters papier-mâchéd the front door and the tiled wall. They showed the thick lips and beseeching smile of Don Miguel who was standing for Mayor.

Gabriel noticed the changes but they didn't trouble him. He had returned for a purpose. He had come back as an active participant in the people's war. The theoretical part of his life, the years of preparation were over. The time had now come to bloody his hands.

For two weeks he stayed in a hut on the red road to the zoo. He rarely left it. He spent his time planning several operations and organizing leaflets. The leaflets exhorted the people to avoid deception by a presidential election which would prolong a brutalizing oligarchy. But he was angry. At Edith, for never having confided in him about Ezequiel's illness. At Ezequiel, for, among other things, having confided in Edith. He was also angry with Julio and Bonifacio who turned up from Ayacucho a week later than expected.

At the end of April, Gabriel sent a message to Satipo. He was ready.

In May 1980, the Belén cell of the Shining Path attacked the Banco de Crédito in Calle Morona. The cashier, a niece of Pía Zumate, saw a mother enter the main hall, pushing a pram. The baby was crying so much that the mother gathered the bundle in her arms and walked up and down, whispering soothing words in its ear and humming a ballad. The cries grew louder so she went outside leaving her pram unattended.

Four minutes later it blew up.

When the police arrived, the bank had been robbed of 50 million soles by two men who materialized through the smoke. One was dressed as a priest. The other wore a military uniform. Both carried guns. On the wall above the upturned filing cabinets and their smoking contents was daubed: EZEQUIEL OR DEATH.

It was November before Gabriel's unit captured Don Miguel. By then the man cured of terminal cancer by Elena Silves had been sworn in as Mayor of Belén.

Edith drove the car – a blue Peugeot – to Don Miguel's house behind the university canteen. It was past eleven at night. Two men sat on the steps of the billiard hall on the corner of Ucayali. The streets were quiet. The evening air smelled of oil from the refinery.

Bonifacio stood at the entrance to a lane on the left of Don Miguel's door. Down that lane, men would walk to the soggy meadow known as the Colchón Verde. On the Green Mattress, on nights when it had not rained, candles lit the feet of prostitutes waiting for clients in the long grass.

Bonifacio was dressed as a colchona. He wore a wig of loose blonde hair, a brown cape and a bag over his shoulder. When he saw the car, he waved.

"Park by that Ford," said Gabriel, adjusting his dog-collar. He drew back a sleeve to look at his watch. "Fifteen minutes." He looked out of the window. A girl with red hair was crying in the front seat of the parked car. He watched her for a while. Then he said, "Let's go."

Don Miguel opened his door. He had been at dinner and his mouth was full of chicken. He was surprised to see the two figures of a priest and a woman in a brown cape. The woman was moaning uncontrollably. She had thick calves, he noticed approvingly. He was less sure about the purple lipstick.

He swallowed his food.

"Yes?"

"Don Miguel?" said the priest.

"What you want?"

"The señora, she's had a terrible experience."

Through his confusion, Don Miguel absorbed the priest's appeal.

"You'd better come in," he said. As he shut the door behind them, the woman reached into her bag. Instead of a handkerchief, she drew out a hand-gun. Don Miguel said nothing, perhaps because he felt nothing. The priest held him by the wrist. It was already slack, as if he had given up the moment he realized his mistake.

The car headed out of the city. On the windows a mist formed, smeared there by the tension of the occupants. Every time Gabriel wiped the windscreen with his sleeve, the mist returned.

"Wind down your window," said Edith.

A kilometre beyond the electricity works, Edith turned off the road. She braked in front of a two-storey building. She kept the headlights on until Gabriel and Bonifacio had disappeared inside.

The house was used as a metal forge for the plywood factory. Near the window an anvil was bolted to the floor. Saws and soldering irons hung on the wall.

Don Miguel was placed in a chair. From his seat he watched the girl with thick calves transform herself into Bonifacio. In front of him the priest defrocked into the person of Gabriel.

A damp patch grew under his arms.

His captors sat behind a table, a plywood sheet on trestles.

"Don Miguel Minero," Gabriel began, his dog-collar loose around his neck. "You have been arrested by the members of the Peruvian Communist Party. This is a revolutionary trial." Edith raised a camera and took a photograph. Bonifacio toyed with a metal-worker's mask. Don Miguel said nothing. Under his arms the patches spread.

Gabriel looked into the Mayor's face. Until this moment the man had been not much more than a shape behind the frosted glass of Eden Expeditions. Yet this was Elena's miracle, he suddenly realized. This was the living proof of her vision.

Gabriel was reminded of a badly stuffed animal in the museum at Quistacocha. A long nose dented with wide pores, hair tumbling from his ears like moss on a dead tree and still, grey, artificial eyes. He imagined the faded label. Common name – Don Miguel Minero. Scientific name – Mayor of Belén. Family name – Bourgeois Reactionary.

"By executing you," he thought to himself, "I'm beginning to topple the whole structure. With your death, nothing can be the same again."

Gabriel listed the charges against Don Miguel. The shooting of the early martyr Comrade Hipólito. Corruption of Customs, corruption of Police, corruption of the Church . . . Occasionally Don Miguel answered "I don't remember that." It was when Gabriel mentioned the circumstances surrounding his father's death that Don Miguel appeared to recognize him. His face went the colour of a man who has swallowed cordite.

"Don Miguel Minero," said Gabriel. "The tribunal has found you guilty of treason against your nation and your people. You will be executed shortly."

The vest showed through Don Miguel's shirt like a girl's swimming costume.

"Could I shave?" he faltered.

"We have no razor," replied Gabriel.

"You must let me have a priest. A real priest."

"There's no time."

Don Miguel wiped his forehead. Even the Rotary Club badge on his lapel had lost its glint. He took a comb from his shirt pocket and ran it through his damp hair. The gesture seemed to tranquillize him.

"What about my family?"

"No charges exist against them."

"She will never forgive you for this, you know," he said.

For an instant, Gabriel did not understand. When he registered what was being said he stood up.

"Gabriel!" Edith held him back. "No. Not now."

"Let's get this over with," he said.

He pulled Don Miguel to his feet and led him to the staircase.

"Down," he said.

"You're not going to kill me in the basement?"

"Bonifacio, the anvil."

In the basement, Gabriel stood Don Miguel against a wall. More tools hung on a rack behind him. Snapped saws, bent drills, blunt screwdrivers. Bonifacio's hammering began. The noise came through the ceiling, reverberating about the small underground room – not in a natural beat but in a steady metallic rhythm of its own.

"Faster," shouted Gabriel. "For God's sake tell him to go faster."

Edith handed Gabriel her pistol. She disappeared up the stairs.

The secret was not to look at the eyes.

"At least tie my laces?" Don Miguel's words had a reasonableness about them. With his shoes undone, the Mayor of Belén seemed ludicrously unready for death.

Gabriel pointed the pistol at Don Miguel's stomach. He lowered himself onto his haunches. When he saw the shoes and their trailing laces he realized he would have to use both hands. It was during that hesitation, to Bonifacio's quickening tempo, that the stuffed animal came alive. Don Miguel jerked a knee into Gabriel's face, grabbed a saw blade from the wall and lunged out, slashing Gabriel in the cheek. His arm was raised to strike again when there was a shot.

Don Miguel turned casually to the floor.

Gabriel looked at him through fingers squeezed against the pain in his face. He knew Don Miguel was hurt as well. It was the first time he had seen him with a finished smile.

Edith placed the pistol to his forehead. She timed herself against two of Bonifacio's strokes on the anvil. In tune with the third she fired. The body went limp. The blade fell to the floor. It was followed by Don Miguel's comb.

Edith spoke. "When the snake is dead, its poison is dead."

They dropped his body by a rubbish heap near the airport. Bonifacio placed a week-old edition of *El Oriente* over his head. Edith pinned a notice to his shirt.

"There is no town, no home, no bed where you can hide if you are an enemy of the people. The armed struggle will always find you because no one can hide from the people. They are the eyes of Presidente Ezequiel."

They drove to the Malecón. Edith parked the car above the Requena wharf. She saw the night ferry at the bottom of the bank. Sparks from the funnel fireworked into the night. The decks milled with people. The boat was on time. By tomorrow morning they would be another world away.

They got out of the Peugeot. Edith and Bonifacio supported Gabriel between them. His arms lay over their shoulders like broken wings. The blood fell from his ripped cheek. It fell over his dog-collar, his shirt, his shoes.

"Wait," said Edith. She slipped away. She walked back to the car. From the boot she took out the brown cape Bonifacio had worn as a colchona. She draped it over Gabriel's head and shoulders.

"We'll say he has la uta."

The boat paddled on through the dusk. On either bank, the orange fires of the river-dwellers flickered through the trees. Once or twice a fish dented the silver river.

Looking into the wake, Gabriel thought of Ezequiel who wanted to change the face of the world. Was it vanity which fuelled his secrecy, a vanity only someone like Edith would understand? He thought of Elena's vision. Had it, in fact, been as flawed as his own?

Above all, he thought of Elena.

A light went on in the wheelhouse. From a cupboard, the captain's mate produced a bottle of cachaza and two tumblers filigreed with dirty fingerprints. He placed them on the varnished sill. He splashed out the dark rum. Behind the glass, in silence, the two shapes began drinking.

And the boat moved on towards Belén, a ghost boat gliding beneath the full moon.

The police picked up the trail next day.

It was Abel Fonseca, the cine-projectionist, who alerted them. He was carrying three reels of *The Rubber Man's Daughter* from the Cinema Bolognesi, where the film had enjoyed a long run, to the Cinema Grau, where it was about to open.

He was walking along the Malecón in the early hours of the morning, the romance of Luis Sintra balanced on his head, when he noticed, at irregular intervals, marks on the mosaic pavement.

Abel Fonseca was not the most intelligent of projectionists, and it was a bother to have to put down the heavy cans. But he had spent a life watching popular films and he had no doubt that what he saw when he crouched on the pavement and dipped his finger into it was blood.

He told a police sergeant who told Lieutenant Velarde who followed the drops along the Malecón and down the path to where they disappeared by the empty berth of the *Victoria Regia*.

Lifting his eyes to the Amazon, Velarde cursed. He would bet a week's whoring in the Teletroca that whoever had murdered Don Miguel was no longer in Belén.

He returned to his office. He removed his sunglasses. He rubbed his eyes, then his chest. Sacramento. Just when he hoped for promotion. Just when he'd expunged from his record the disaster of that episode with the poet.

Velarde's failure then had set back his prospects of promotion for a good ten years. Whatever benefits had come by way of Don Miguel's handout – the mountain of jerseys, the daughter's school fees in America, his four thousand shares in Electro-Peru – that thirty-year salary cheque had not helped his career. He hadn't tracked down a single one of those terrucos with Hipólito Mercedes, not one. Of course, given time, he would have found them all, but then the military suddenly burst in on the scene, removing the president from his palace, still wearing pyjamas, and handing out pardons to every mother-fucking cholo criminal in sight as if they were tickets for the lottery.

Since when Velarde had eaten shit with the patience of a novice. And after all the shit he'd eaten, it was looking as if finally, finally things might be paying off. Only last month his superior got brandy-drunk in the Club de Leones and told him he was being considered for Deputy Police Chief.

Then this had to happen.

He knew his duty as a policeman. He rang the station in Requena.

"If you know the difference between a jerk-off and a fuck," he told his opposite number, "you'll be on that wharf when the Belén ferry comes in. And, Pablo, careful. Whoever this Presidente Ezequiel is, he's just made chicken crap of our Mayor." Velarde put down the receiver. Later he would hear how a man had been apprehended, hiding under a blanket, without so much as a fistfight, and how pleased Lima was, even though they hadn't found anyone else and how Pablo must make it back to him sometime . . .

Don Miguel, he thought. His dead Mayor. Did he feel sorry? No, he didn't. The man had been a braying, stubborn, corrupt, unpleasant ass. For more than twenty years he'd made Velarde follow him. The Lieutenant picked his nose. He inspected the result. He turned it into a very small ball and rubbed it on the wall behind him.

Twenty years. And all that fucking time he'd had to smell his wind.

The sun had finally set. The sky was the pink of a dolphin's belly, leaping to swallow the moon. In the wheelhouse the two men raised their glasses again.

Gabriel moved towards the bow. They were rounding the Padre Isla. Soon they would see the lights of the city. He lowered his head until it rested on an arm. Seeing Gabriel lean like that on the bowsprit, the captain opened the wheelhouse door. He slopped down the steps to join him.

"Señor." He swallowed before speaking again. When he opened his mouth his breath was sweet. "Señor, a drink."

He held the bottle out to him. There was something placatory in the gesture, as if he might be afraid of rejection a second time by the musician who had lost his instrument.

Gabriel was on the point of waving a flat hand to say no when he changed his mind. He looked at the bottle, the surface of its brown liquid bobbing with greasy slicks. He reached out and held it.

"It's good," slurred the captain. He watched Gabriel's Adam's apple rise and fall as he swallowed the rum. "The best."

He rested his arm on the rail and looked at the night. "Tell me, señor, what do you play?"

"What do I play?" asked Gabriel. He wiped his mouth.

"Yes, what do you play. Guitar. Pipes. Drums. Clarinet?"

"Ah, what do I play. I play . . . " He thought a second. "I play the flute."

"The flute?" The captain was pleased.

"Not any old flute," said Gabriel, raising the bottle again. "Not one of those cane flutes that go peep peep peeep. No. My flutes are made of bone."

"Bone?"

"Yes, human bone." He stared joylessly at the captain. "Have you ever heard the sound of such a flute, Captain?"

"No, señor." The captain drew back.

"But it is a beautiful noise, Captain. Once you have heard it, I promise you never forget."

"Indeed," said the captain stiffly. "And how does it sound, this flute of yours?"

Gabriel took a deep breath. He screwed his face in preparation. But the captain was not listening. He was staring into the dark.

"Strange," he said.

Gabriel's face went slack. He let the air out through his teeth without a whistle.

"What's strange?"

"Belén."

"What about it?"

"Look."

"But there are no lights."

"That's what I mean."

And sure enough, gazing into the night, the phosphorescent waves beneath him, Gabriel saw that where the town should have been was a blackness as dark as Sebastián's hood.

Chapter 26

THE MAN KNOWN TO his followers as the Fourth Sword of the World Revolution woke earlier than usual.

He lay in a cold, bare room. A loose wire ran down the wall beside his bed. There was a framed photograph of Paris on the wall and a lithograph by Cossio del Pomar of six Apristas who had been executed at Chan Chan in April 1932. The only furniture was a side table and a red chair, grey with dust.

He rose from his bed and unbolted his door. He felt his way to the lavatory over the landing, careful not to stub his toes. The building was silent, like the jungle outside. Thinking of those asleep below, he did not flush the bowl.

He returned to his narrow bed and swallowed a pill containing a solution of potassium arsenite. He shook the bottle. Only half a dozen remained, and his psoriasis was worse, definitely. He felt himself possessed by a powerful alien. The disease had a life of its own, overtaking his own. He raised a hand to his elbow and began scratching.

He slept.

A dog barked.

He woke.

He raised himself from the bed. His face corrugated with the effort. He limped to the shutters. He looked down through the slats onto the roof of the next-door building, the café. A ladder connected the flat roof, one storey below, with his own building. The ladder was out of sight from the square and led to a door at the rear of the landing.

He concluded it was someone he knew. Already the dog was scraping a tongue along its back searching for fleas. He stood in the centre of the room facing the closed door. In the fragment of mirror hanging from a nail he saw the cravat around his neck and an expanse of red shirt. He lowered his head to complete the reflection.

Behind his lips he still had perfect teeth.

There was a knock on the door. "Ezequiel? Presidente Ezequiel?"

Recognizing the voice, he unbolted the lock.

"I don't know why I bother," he said half to himself. He rattled the bolt back and forth. "There is no gun."

Edith came into the room. She walked to the table. "Here," she said. She produced two batteries, then a small bottle from a bag.

"Sorry they've taken so long. Dr Lache wanted a fortune."

He sat down on the bed and inspected the pills.

"Everything fixed for this evening?"

She nodded. "I'll go straight there from the meeting. I have the keys. The explosives are ready."

"You approve?"

"Yes. It'll mean another move for you. But we're not throwing anything away. Not after Cabaña," she said.

"What about the meeting? Can everyone be there?"

Edith's eyes fixed on the collar of his red shirt.

"Everyone except Chino." The words were devoid of emotion.

"Chino?" he frowned. "But he was in the dormitory?"

"He'd arranged a palanca with Julio Medina."

"And why can't Comrade Chino be with us?" asked Ezequiel. He shook his bottle.

"A woman."

"A woman. That's unlike Chino."

"Bonifacio will take his place. He'll come with me to the plant." She raised her eyes above the collar. "Ezequiel, is there anything else?"

"What?"

"Can I get you anything?"

"No, no." The man shook his head.

"If that's all, I'll see you this afternoon."

"Yes."

"Chau, Ezequiel."

"Chau, Edith," he said as the door closed. Then, remembering something, he shouted, "Edith?"

The door opened.

"The tapes. Did you bring any?"

She looked miserable. "I found one in Sargento Lores, but you already have it."

"Which one?"

"*Point* of something."

"*No Return,*" he acknowledged. "You're right."

"But Augusta promised she'd bring some from Lima."

The door closed. He waited until she had disappeared from the roof. Then, careful not to be seen from the street nor dislodge a row of batteries recharging on a sheet of tin foil, he pushed open the shutters.

The sun burst in, thickly, as if it had been accumulating against the wood. He took off his shirt. He threw it on the bed. In the light he examined his body; the psoriatic patch returning below his arms, the scaly lesions coalescing about his elbow like a pile of silver coins thrown carelessly onto a gaming table. His fingers moved gingerly down the soft felt of his skin.

"I must not scratch, I must not scratch," he told himself. If he didn't scratch, his skin built up a dry white crust. If he did, it became red and shiny. If he pulled off a flake too near the new skin, it wept.

He moved to the side table, slapping his chest with alternate hands. He picked up the two new batteries. He fitted them into the bottom of a small cassette recorder and inserted a cassette. He pressed Rewind, then Play.

"I'll be seeing you
In all the old familiar places
That this heart of mine embraces
All day through . . . "

It was twenty years since Ezequiel's discovery of Frank Sinatra. He possessed most of his recordings, and a dim understanding of the words. It was an insidious passion, he knew, one that irritated and amused him. But in the songs, which he played when no one could hear and which he accompanied unmelodically, he found things that had continued to stir him.

For a man not allowed to eat cebiche – his favourite food – nor smoke, nor drink, nor take tea or coffee, it was a harmless pleasure.

"I'll be looking at the moon," he told himself as he limped up and down, a half-naked man pottering through the shadows. "But I'll be seeing you."

But his mind today was not on Frank Sinatra. It was on the man with Chinese eyes who had risen from the dead. The man who couldn't attend his meeting this afternoon because of a woman.

A funny thing, but last night he'd dreamt of Chino. He was turning down Lima's Washington Street on his way to visit José Mariátegui when out of the night loomed Gabriel Rondón Lung.

"Where are you going?" asked Gabriel. Ezequiel told him. "Can I come too?" It was vaguely appropriate. He had detected a similarity between the young man and the socialist. The same green eyes, the same pale, wasted face, the same falsetto voice. Or perhaps he didn't have a falsetto voice. He couldn't recall.

They found Mariátegui lying on a chaise-longue, a tartan blanket over his leg, a curl of hair making a black cedilla on his forehead, a bow-tie drooping over a starched collar.

There were others in the room. Mariátegui was telling them of the night he saw Naska Rouskaya dance in the cemetery to the strains of Chopin's funeral march. How the girl from Buenos Aires had whirled her indigo dress against the tombstones and lifted her Porteña chin to the stars.

"That was the night I gave up believing in God," he whispered. He glanced at Ezequiel. And then all of a sudden it wasn't Mariátegui who lay along the chaise-longue looking into his eyes, but Gabriel Rondón Lung, the man who had pleaded his way into Ezequiel's house in Ayacucho twenty years before and through that door, two steps up off Calle Libertad, into the revolution.

A woman, he told himself.

He stopped his pacing and looked out over the glittering calamina roofs to the jungle.

A woman. The psoriasis had put paid to that.

"To be a lost man. A man without a name . . . " How aware had he been of the sacrifices he demanded? Here he stood, a man debilitated by illness, a man trying to restore the past, yet for ten years without a past of his own – just the memory of hotel rooms in Piura, Chimbote, Puno, Arequipa, Satipo, Belén.

Wasn't that why he'd come to Belén, because it was the safest of the lot? No one in the square below, nor the houses beyond nor the country beyond that knew if he was alive.

Only the dog on the ledge below, catching sight of him at the window gave a whimper of recognition.

"In the small café,
The park across the way,
The children's carousel,
The chestnut trees, the wishing well . . . "

Ezequiel closed his eyes and raised his face to the sun, recharging his batteries.

They sat, the seven of them, cheek by jowl in Ezequiel's room around the table which rocked whenever anyone moved.

A poster hung on the door, covering the mirror – which made a bump beneath. It showed a line of soldiers firing at a mass of prisoners. The prisoners carried the communist flag and they rose from out of the sun. The sun was Ezequiel's unblemished face.

"Glory to the fallen heroes. Long live the revolution!" went the inscription. Ezequiel thought he detected the influence of Goya and Delacroix in the design.

Augusta was talking. She sat on a stool opposite, her face between her hands. She was speaking for him.

The prison massacre was a tragedy. But they must avoid panic. Comrade Edith's operation at Cabaña was a fine example. What they needed now was a single concerted action. That night the whole country would witness it.

She outlined Ezequiel's plan: a simultaneous blackout in all the major cities. The only light would come from bonfires. They would burn on the mountain-sides of Piura, Puno, Lima, Arequipa and Trujillo. They would blaze out the name of the man opposite.

She crossed her legs and made the table rock. Ezequiel leant back on his chair. He picked an empty cassette box from the side table where he kept his Dead Sea salts and violet bergamot that smelt of tea. He slid the cassette box under the guilty leg.

"Are we together on this?" he asked, speaking for the first time.

"Abimael?"

"Yes."

"Emilio?"

"Yes."

"Edith?"

"Yes."

"Bonifacio?"

"Yes."

"One final item," said Augusta. "The case of Comrade Chino."

There was silence. Then Bonifacio spoke. "His behaviour puts us all in jeopardy. I recommend he be tried by the Central Committee."

Several elbows descended in the murmur of consensus. Ezequiel was pleased to notice the table did not move. He fastened his gaze on the poster, stroking the folds beneath his chin.

"Comrade Edith," he said, displaying his perfect teeth. "You find him."

One by one the members of the Central Committee embraced Ezequiel and left. Only Augusta remained. She touched his cheek. She didn't bother to hide her concern. He wrapped her in his arms, embarrassed.

"I'll get us something to eat," she said.

Ezequiel walked to the balcony. The sun was setting. He looked at his watch. They had been talking for four hours. A plastic box flickered into life on the right of his balcony. The blue neon letters illuminated the corroded ironwork and the empty plant holders. LIBERTY they flashed. From where he stood, the letters read back to front.

He watched his wife bob across the square and into a shop. Reminded of something, he went inside and opened her bag. What was the name she said? Jones? Not a name he knew. He switched on the cassette recorder. For the first time in three years he dragged a chair to the balcony. He would catch the last of the sun which his ancestors had worshipped. It was meant to be good for his skin.

"The green, green grass of home . . . "

From inside the room came the voice on Augusta's cassette.

Whoever this Jones was, he didn't bear comparison, thought Ezequiel, looking down through the ironwork, onto the roof where the dog was dream-shivering in its sleep and the corner of the iron house where Sebastián was rattling his bowl and the square beyond where three old men sat watching him.

Chapter 27

Now NIGHT APPROACHES the square. The sun is setting. The sky is full of masato. One by one the lights come on in the Hotel Liberty, in the Bishop's palace and in the fountain where the water shines bright green like Inca Kola.

The square is an ovation of flowers. The smell of copa de oro which has pervaded it since early morning now mingles with acetylene as Don Vásquez ignites his lamp. Suspended from a coat hanger, the lamp illuminates his bottles of red alcohol, his steaming tray of chicken pieces and his newspaper, folded to a syndicated article on Bolívar's journey into exile and an interview, in her Fort Lauderdale home, with a former lavandera from Iquitos.

With the exception of Don Wenceslau and Don García, no one has bought anything all day, but now they queue for chicken; girls rubbing insect-repellent on their shins, a mother wiping her daughter's face, a pair of shoe-shine boys arguing over a sheet of lottery tickets.

In the middle of the square, the benches fill with smartly dressed couples. They watch the flies cluster the lights, they whisper comments about those passing by and, tapping their polished shoes, they listen to the naval band facing the town hall. As the white uniforms break into "Sin ritorno", the younger men snake an arm around necks dabbed with Caliope, Caribe, Madame D'Orly.

"Ah, look!" says Don Wenceslau. "La Palometa!"

Her mouth leafed in red, her hair piled in a hennaed bun, her moustaches swirling, Pía Zumate crosses the square towards the islamic pillars of the Sociedad Española de Beneficiencia. Dreaming of the evening ahead, she smiles manically.

"Tut, tut," says Don García. "Stockings."

"Look!" says Don Wenceslau. "The British lord!"

They follow his quivering hand to the balcony where Ezequiel sits, partially obscured by the ironwork. Don Leopoldo reaches down into his green bag. He produces a leather spectacle case. From it he extracts a pair of half-moon glasses.

In the dark the three men peer, Don Leopoldo most of all.

"There's something not quite right with his face," he says.

But suddenly Don Wenceslau is not interested.

"Look!" he says. "A shoe-shine boy!" He inserts a finger to his mouth. He whistles. At long last he feels ready for his second polish of the day.

Don Leopoldo removes his glasses. The lenses have also brought Eiffel's iron house into focus. He adds another line to his cheeks as he thinks of himself in fine Scotch tweed, drinking rum-coloured beer in the Club of the Dead Parrots. He folds his spectacles and slides them back into their case.

At the other end of the bench, Don García nurses his disappointment as a man joins the girl opposite. It is a disappointment only a visit to the Teletroca will cure.

Next to him Don Wenceslau stretches out his Doocares. "Now that's red, boy, and you know it is . . . "

The three of them are too far from the electricity station to hear the bomb. When the power cuts out, cowling the city and causing the monkeys to howl in their cages behind the Meloka Restaurant, the clock in the cathedral tower is striking half past eight.

They come into the square from Raimondi, round the corner of Fitzcarrald's house and along the pavement towards the town hall. Three of them lurching in a flip-floppy walk.

"Tell you what," says the captain.

"What?" asks Gabriel.

"Let's go to the Teletroca."

"The Teletroca?"

The mate's face creases in a gargoyle grin. He snuffles his approval and elbows Gabriel in the side. Gabriel looks at him. On his pock-marked cheeks, he seems to be wearing make-up.

"Don't you like girls, señor? Or is it boys you like?"

"No," hiccups Gabriel. "I like girls." The statement is bent with tiredness. To his companions it acknowledges arousal.

"Sometimes," says the captain, "the only thing that keeps me going are my balls."

"Echo!" says his mate.

"He can get through two or three a night," the captain tells Gabriel. "It builds up, when you've been on the river."

"To the Teletroca, then," says Gabriel.

"To the Teletroca," the others roar.

They begin crossing the road as a car turns the corner. It yelps to a halt in front of them. Capitán Velarde leans out of his window. "Hey, there! Sh-sh-sh-shift it," he screams, raising his Ray-Bans because he cannot see, then realizing the blackout has put dark glasses over the whole town. Still chanting, the figures move from the road onto the central square.

Furiously, Velarde thrusts his car into gear. His mind is on a million things as he drives out to the municipal electricity station near the airport. His promotion, his shares in Electro-Peru, the news that his wife wants to leave him for a young man she met at a party to celebrate the publication of Jaime Regan's *Hacia la Tierra Sin Mal*. It will be an hour before something triggers the image of the face frozen in his Datsun's headlight, the face of a man who has dogged his steps since more or less the moment he put on a policeman's badge, a man he had imagined to be lying safely in the ground at San Bartolo.

In the square, the captain, the captain's mate and Gabriel walk past the statue of Admiral Grau. They are propelled by the full moon at their backs. They are hauled by their shadows. They walk by without noticing the singer, the drinker or the local historian.

Gabriel trips on the verge, causing a flutter of feathers and a scratching of feet from the pigeons on the calamina roof of the Club de Leones. The others steady him and head off down Calle Nauta.

"It's him," observes Don Wenceslau. "The Chino."

"I would say," adds Don Leopoldo after a certain passage of time, "he has been drinking."

"I would say," says Don Wenceslau, "he has every good reason. What do you think García?"

At first there is no reply to the drinker's question. Then the bench creaks. Don García stands up. He appears to smell the air, but he is eyes glitter – "it comes out lit."

They pass into a room pulsing with music. When his eyes are used to the low light, Gabriel makes out a bar, some cane chairs along the wall and a short corridor leading into another courtyard. The only source of illumination is a large television on the bar. Five European girls, dressed up as nurses, fellate a bearded doctor on a surgical couch.

"Playing the cornet," giggles the captain. He orders three beers from the barman. "Hey, this is my friend," he tells the man. "He plays the human flute." The barman nods. He lifts the lid on a fridge and produces the bottles.

The captain drinks. He beams tipsily at the television set. Gabriel finishes his bottle. Then he drains the bottle ordered for the captain's mate. The man has vanished.

"Look!" The captain doesn't turn his head. "Pucha . . ." he swears. He cannot believe his eyes. Gabriel tries to look but he is dazzled by the light. Instead, he focuses on the men who stand with arms crossed staring at the screen.

Some of them are old, like Don Tonsurans and the man he speaks to who wears a grey hat and a red handkerchief. Others he recognizes from school: Alberto, who has become a hydrologist. Abel Fonseca who works in the film business. The manager of the plywood factory, José da Silva. Gonzalo Mego, the administrator of the Club de Leones. Dr Lache, the bigamist.

On their faces, like underwater patterns on sand, are the reflections of whatever makes the captain gasp.

Gabriel orders another beer. As he waits for it, his eyes stray to a movement on the green wall behind the fridge, below a rack of Gigi toilet paper. He looks at a small frog. It rests its panting belly on the acrylic O of Dora, one of several names painted in stencilled letters. With another hop it lands on Carmen. With another, on Gloria.

"Angels," he tells the barman. "Lovely angels."

"You should see the girls when they look at this," says the captain. He juts his chin at the screen. "They get really excited, I tell you."

"Where are the girls?" asks Gabriel. He squeezes his palm. It still contains his Sultan.

The captain nods his head at the corridor. "Let's go inspect the merchandise."

The courtyard is a red glow. A cone of multi-coloured light projects the same television scenes onto a wall. In the centre of the wall is a basin, above it painted the words "I fuck. And you?"

There are twelve rooms on either side. In two of them a girl leans with hand on hip against the doorframe. The remaining doors are closed.

The captain leaves Gabriel's side. He stands in the middle of the film, looking at one of the two open doors.

"An open door tempts a saint," he says. As he moves towards it, a penis the size of a paddle ejaculates on his back.

At the end, on the right, a door opens. A man walks to the basin. Gabriel recognizes the captain's mate. A figure takes up her position at the low entrance of the room he has vacated.

Lazily she scratches one leg with another.

Gabriel stumbles towards her. He feels a hand between his legs. He looks up.

It is her.

Chapter 28

THE STORIES DIFFER about what happened that night.

After mulching on it, Don Leopoldo has come down on the side of Capitán Velarde. It is only luck that made him visit the Club de Leones on the very afternoon that Velarde's report is suppressed. "In the interests of the municipality and the Roman Catholic Church," sneers the policeman.

Until Don Leopoldo turned up with that bag of his, which he somehow manages to trip over every time, the policeman could find no one to lend an ear.

"Hey, Leopoldo, come here. You interested in that crazy business? Two brandies, Gonzalo. No one else gives a whore's kiss for what happened. You know what Barrantes said about Elena Silves? He said hers was the love of a bad woman. I mean, shit!"

If Velarde is to be believed, shortly after 9.45 p.m. – the time given by Cleopatra Zumate at the door – a man and a woman forced their way into the Teletroca. They were dressed from head to toe in black. At the time, Señora Zumate passed them off as security police.

"I thought they were looking for the terrorists who blew up the power-station. Either that, Capitán, or they had come to clean their pistols – like you boys do on a Friday night. I didn't know what the woman wanted. It didn't cross my mind they were terrucos."

The two of them scanned the faces at the bar, then walked into the courtyard. According to one of Señora Zumate's girls – one of the vaunted new girls from Nauta – a client was pressing his face against a door by the basin. The door was closed. The girl thought she heard crying on the other side and what could have been the sound of a head knocking against the doorframe.

The man in black approached the client from behind. He put an arm round his neck and jerked him away. The client seemed very groggy, so groggy that he could hardly walk as he was pulled from the courtyard.

The other person, the woman, took his place at the door. She said something through it. A few minutes later the door opened and a girl emerged, wearing a shirt and a pair of trousers. She was weeping hysterically.

Despite the low red light from the bulb above the room, despite the shifting beams from the projector, painting her in the colours of the spectrum, the girl from Nauta recognized the person who had joined them on the journey down river.

"Describe her," said Velarde.

"She was a woman . . . " began the girl.

"Of course she was a woman," said the policeman. "What do you think this is, the Club de Leones?"

But a much older woman.

"She was also a gringa."

The girl saw nothing else. She was watching the two of them disappear into the television room, when her vision was blocked by a man with a toothpick in his teeth and one eye different from the other.

She laughed. "He fucked like a tunchi."

Five weeks later, two bodies were discovered twenty kilometres down stream from Belén, tied together at the wrist and ankle and eaten by fishes. Both had red scarves tied about their skulls. Both scarves contained a powder-burned hole. The bodies were described by Dr Lache, the elderly pathologist, as being "in their late thirties/early forties."

Don Leopoldo's belief that these are the bodies of Gabriel Rondón Lung and Elena Colina Silves is shared by Don Wenceslau. Where Don Wenceslau parts company with Capitán Velarde's version is in the timing of their death.

According to an article Vásquez showed him in *El Oriente*, they were found five weeks later – but they had only been in the river two weeks.

"That leaves three weeks, right?"

"Two weeks and five days."

"Two weeks and five days. But that was the time they had to themselves."

"Why on earth, Wenceslau, would they have had time to themselves?"

"Until it was decided what to do with them." That was why they had died with Pía Zumate's smile on their faces.

Don Leopoldo says there has never been any mention of a smile.

"Yes, there has," says Don Wenceslau. "It was there in Vásquez's paper."

Don Leopoldo cannot conceal the contempt that forms on his lips.

"Journalism," he spits.

Don Wenceslau disregards him. In the end it all comes down to Edith. (He bets a day without masato that her breasts are stunted – so she might shoot arrows, like the Amazon she evidently was. "Only the right breast was stunted," Don Leopoldo points out.)

Obviously, it was Edith who spared them initially. But in the end it had been she who recommended their execution.

"She couldn't live with the knowledge of their happiness," he says dramatically. His voice imitates Don García. He inspects Don García to see if the singer recognizes this, but he doesn't. In the shape of Elena Silves' life Don García sees something worthy of an opera by Donizetti or Verdi. His version of that night differs from the others in one crucial aspect.

Don García believes the lovers are still alive.

But to begin with, he wishes to exonerate Elena from what he interprets as disapproval on the part of at least one of his companions on the bench. His chromatic mind can easily picture how she came to arrive at Señora Zumate's establishment by the river.

He sees the expression on Elena's face when the rivereño mentions the prison massacre. He watches the man produce from his dirty jacket a copy of *El Oriente* with the details of those killed by the military. He feels the fuse inside her go when she sees the name of Gabriel Rondón Lung. He sees it all.

She walks through the stiff grass of Father Maby's lawn and into the carob trees. She doesn't know where she is walking. For one hour, for two hours, for three hours she walks. She goes deeper still into the jungle. She has lost all motive except to walk. The trees rip her clothes. They tear at her face, her hair, her hands which take on the colour and texture and smell of the branches. Towards evening she enters a Devil's Farm, a clearing made by a poisonous tree, full of dead leaves like a park she once visited in Lima. She sits among them. A wind comes up and the leaves rise slowly as if they are snowflakes in the paperweight shaken by her father when he lies on the bed of his sick wife, not knowing what to do. They rise against her where she sits, each leaf a jigsaw piece of memory; and she thinks of her father and mother, who read Kipling to each other and never quarrelled about anything except the properties of hair oil, and her aunt who was always talking of the day she would live in Óbidos, in a house with blue and gold stripes on its outer wall to ward off flies and witches who might think they had flown too close to Heaven, and Madre Ana who smelt of Vaseline and Nivea and who could never pass the reproduction of Saint Bernadette without admiring herself in the glass, and pigeons flying from a bell tower, and the lines of a song, and Gabriel whom she had last seen on the cold concrete floor of Hipólito's hut, his face austere with desire. And these fragments swirl against her and about her, rising in a vortex until they become indistinguishable from the vultures who have begun to wheel and eddy on the evening air, waiting to see if she is dead, like the leaves. She closes her eyes.

She sleeps, she doesn't know how long. One morning she reaches a river. On the bank she finds a raft. She takes the raft to what is Dos de Mayo. The current is strong. It carries her past the village. It carries her into the Amazon. A small boat with a thatched roof, like a floating hut, approaches from upstream. It brims with cheerful Indian girls. They have come from the jungle near Nauta, recruited by the man who sits at the engine. They wave. They smile. They reach out their hands and flick water at her. When Elena doesn't respond, they call to the man. The long boat turns, making a wave like a scythe. The girls stretch out to the raft. They hold it. They lift her aboard. She allows them to do this without struggling. She lets them surround her. She lets them embrace her. After three years in the jungle, she knows their ways. Only this time she has no instructions, no comfort, no hope to give them.

No longer sustained by the God she deserted or by the promise of finding again the man she loved, she now wants their simplicity for herself.

In the late afternoon, the noise of the engine dies down. The boat slides onto the bank. The girls step ashore. The man points to a path and they begin walking into the trees. He sees Elena standing back. Go on, he tells her. Go on, you'll lose them. She sets off after them in a trance. Soon they arrive at a building with a large courtyard and a wire mermaid on its roof.

Someone takes off the remnants of her wet, muddy cushma. She is given a bath. Then a new dress. Then shown to a room.

When the man with the strange coloured eyes fills her doorway, she is clean and ready. Like someone quenched with absinthe, thinks Don García, not that he has ever tasted the wormwood spirit.

But it is the sighting of a Venezuelan engineer six months after that night in the Teletroca which convinces Don García the two lovers are alive and reunited.

On a tributary of the Putumayo, a day's journey from the village where he was constructing a new school, the engineer, Firmino Rojas, came upon a group of Indians engaged in clearing the forest.

Recognizing a minga – the custom of gathering neighbours into a work party – Rojas was surprised to see the foundations of an unusually sophisticated building. Curiosity combined with a professional admiration caused the engineer to stand up in his boat.

Directing the Indians was a tall man without a shirt. On his thin chest he had a series of scars. Beside a large bonfire, on which the felled trees were burning, he was talking to someone.

At first the distortions created by the veil of hot air made it difficult for the engineer to see this other person. As the boat moved on he recognized a woman. The woman was white. When the man said something, pointing at the trees, she threw back her head and laughed. When she laughed, it was with her whole body. She was very beautiful.

Neither of them noticed the Venezuelan.

"A romantic extravaganza," says Don Leopoldo.

"Could have been anyone," says Don Wenceslau.

Don García thinks otherwise. For Don García everything ends in song.

In his mission in the jungle, Father Paul Maby hears nothing of this. Along with his flock, he continues to lament the absence of Elena, instinctively looking up whenever a wind moves the carob trees. Somewhere in his secret heart he hopes that Gabriel will find her, but he doubts it. He writes several letters to Eucario Barrantes urging him to make representations to the appropriate authorities. (In passing, he informs Barrantes of strange men who warn that if his Indians show their faces on a certain stretch of water they will be shot. Of late, his Indians have stopped eating fish. Too many bodies, they say, have been found in the river, and they have never been cannibals.)

As expected, Father Maby receives no reply.

At night he often has dreams of being thrust down a dark well by a toothless Virgin Mary who admonishes him with a shake of the egret feathers on her trousered head – sometimes for betraying the secrets of the confessional, sometimes for not trying harder.

In a hotel room somewhere in the country, Presidente Ezequiel continues to scratch the silver dollars proliferating on his arm. The happenings in a jungle town are of little moment to him now the revolution is at hand.

Against the gathering rhythms of early Sinatra, he contents himself with the knowledge that on a given evening his people are able to black out the capital cities of every department in the land, leaving only his bonfired name to vie with the stars and the moon.

In the blackout, Don Leopoldo is dreaming of Cochrane, the gringo, the scientist's son, the firework-maker known up and down the coast as El Diablo, the dashing peer who beat Drake's drum and slipped one midnight with a "Viva el rey" into the Callao fog.

He hears small boats grating the side of Spanish frigates and warm wind in the rigging.

He sees the sky explode with fantastic rockets that zig-zag crazily in all directions, and in all colours, because they have been filled by royalist prisoners with rags and sand and birdshit.

And he smiles at the sight of Spain's great flagship slipping cable into the agitated night, its liberator on deck, his face elated in the saltpetre blaze.

As he dreams the lights come on again in the square.

He finds himself in painful contiguity with Don Wenceslau, scratching his crotch.

"Have patience, fleas, the night is long," says the drinker. He looks at his watch. "You still going to this film, García? If so, I might join you."

He stretches out his arms. He yawns. He examines his feet and the two red shoes shining there.

He gives out a cry.

"I'm sure it wasn't intended," says Don García. "You can tell him tomorrow."

"Just look at that," says Don Wenceslau, leaping from the bench. He is sulphurous with anger.

"Just look," he says.

Don Leopoldo gathers up his bag. He ignores Don Wenceslau, whose feet squirm in their crimson brogues. He ignores Don García, the man who believes Caruso sang in a chicken yard. His mind is on the man opposite, sailing forever in his legendary iron-clad.

He sees the horizon in his eyes, the vertebrae of smoke from six enemy funnels, one of them the *Cochrane*'s. Watching the lamps glint on the face of Admiral Grau, who died outnumbered and outgunned but who has never been more alive, he fancies that he sees Peru's sole hope rise again to give his orders.

A NOTE ON THE TYPE

The text of this book was set in Sabon, a type face designed by Jan Tschichold (1902–1974), the well-known German typographer. Because it was designed in Frankfurt, Sabon was named for the famous Frankfurt type founder Jacques Sabon, who died in 1580 while manager of the Egenolff foundry. Based loosely on the original designs of Claude Garamond (c. 1480–1561), Sabon is unique in that it was explicitly designed for hot-metal composition on both the Monotype and Linotype machines as well as for film composition.

Composed in Great Britain
Printed and bound by The Haddon Craftsmen,
Scranton, Pennsylvania
Title page and binding design by Irva Mandelbaum

ANGELS. Small golden pins on lapels. *Angels.* Trumpeting china figures on coffee tables. *Angels.* Accounts of unknown friends performing unmistakable acts. *Angels.* They seem to be everywhere. From clothing to furniture to testimonies.

How are we to interpret this phenomenon? A flurry of heavenly kindness? A demonic counterfeit? How can we be sure of the good without indulging in the evil?

David Jeremiah has set out to offer some guidance. What a welcome work from his pen. David has that uncanny ability to be deliberate without being dull. You get the details and you don't get sleepy!

How thankful we are to God that he has turned his skills toward this vital issue of angels. His words will deepen your gratitude for God's messengers in light of God's Word.

—MAX LUCADO
author and pastor
San Antonio

SIMPLY PUT, this is an outstanding book! As one would expect from David Jeremiah, this book reflects a theologian's concern, a pastor's heart, and a Biblicist's accuracy.

But more than anything else, this book reflects the power of the pulpit! It preaches in the best and most honored sense of the word, carrying the reader toward convincing closure, chapter after chapter. In a day of many choices, I would recommend this book as a first—and maybe last—selection on angels.

—DR. BRUCE WILKINSON
author and director of Walk Thru the Bible Ministries
Fort Mill, South Carolina

WITH ALL the curiosity and excitement over angels these days, David Jeremiah presents a refreshing and encouraging look at *What the Bible Says about Angels.* Thank you, David, for drawing me closer to God through this wonderful book.

—DAVE DRAVECKY
author and director of Outreach of Hope,
Colorado Springs

DR. DAVID JEREMIAH has written a powerful and insightful book about angels. He shifts the focus from contemporary "angel hype" to the fascinating biblical truth about God's powerful messengers and what their miraculous presence reveals about our loving Creator. It is a "must read" for anyone interested in the dramatic truth about angels.

—DR. JOHN C. MAXWELL
founder, INJOY, Inc.
San Diego

WHAT

THE BIBLE

SAYS ABOUT

ANGELS

Christmas 1996

WHAT THE BIBLE SAYS ABOUT ANGELS

Powerful Guardians
A Mysterious Presence
God's Messengers

DR. DAVID JEREMIAH

MULTNOMAH BOOKS • SISTERS, OREGON

WHAT THE BIBLE SAYS ABOUT ANGELS
published by Multnomah Books
a part of the Questar publishing family
© 1996 by David Jeremiah

International Standard Book Number: 0-88070-902-2

Cover design by David Uttley
Cover illustration by Douglas Klauba
Printed in the United States of America

Most Scripture quotations are from:
The Holy Bible, New International Version (NIV) © 1973, 1984 by International Bible Society,
used by permission of Zondervan Publishing House
Also quoted:
New American Standard Bible (NASB) © 1960, 1977 by the Lockman Foundation
The New Testament in Modern English, Revised Edition (Phillips) © 1972 by J. B. Phillips

For information:
Questar Publishers, Inc. · Post Office Box 1720 · Sisters, Oregon 97759

Library of Congress Cataloging-in-Publication Data

Jeremiah, David.
  What the Bible Says About Angels: Powerful Guardians, A Mysterious Presence, God's
  Messengers/David Jeremiah.
    p. cm.   Includes bibliographical references and index.
  ISBN: 0-88070-902-2
  1. Angels--Biblical teaching.   I. Title.
  BS680.A48J47 1996
  235'.3--dc20
                                                        96-16251
                                                           CIP
      96 97 98 99 00 01 02 03 — 10 9 8 7 6 5 4 3 2

to my wife's mother

ANNIE THOMPSON

who at ninety years of age
still prays for us every day
and every night

CONTENTS

All glory be
to the God of the angels

Chapter One

WHAT IN THE WORLD
ARE ANGELS DOING?

I N A DOCTOR'S OFFICE one fall day last year, I was told I had cancer. I'm sure you'll understand when I say I was fearful. It was one of those times when I would have cherished having an angel with me in the room, assuring me everything would be okay.

In the months that followed I felt the same fear when I prepared to have surgery on two occasions. An angel's hand holding mine as I was wheeled into the operating room would have been treasured comfort.

But as far as I knew, I'd never seen an angel. Never. Did that mean something was wrong with me? Why did only other people have that privilege? Wasn't I spiritual enough?

Maybe you've asked the same questions. And maybe you're dissatisfied with the answers you've received. The explosion of interest in angels has thrown a lot of information your way — but also confusion and contradiction and flimsy speculation. Where can you go for solid, meaningful information? How can you gain a balanced and accurate perspective that's built on God's reality and eternal truth?

That's what this book is all about.

Welcome Wonders, or a Waste of Time?

Suddenly in the 1990s you found angels everywhere — or rather you found them *talked about* everywhere, from major magazines and bestselling books and popular TV shows to kitchen conversations and university seminars. Lots of people said they had actually seen or felt the presence of an angel. Never in history, I suppose, had so much attention been directed at these heavenly beings.

So what's the significance of it all? Is the Lord delighted by this burst of curiosity and belief? And does he want you and me to join in the fun — or at least to take a bit more notice of angels than we did before? Should we be looking around on earth for these heavenly beings? Should we be confident of daily care and protection from angel guardians?

Or is all this a waste of time? Maybe the angel craze of the 90s has been at best just another trivial fad, and at worst a deceptive tactic of Satan's to divert people's spiritual attention away from real truth. Like young children at the Grand Canyon who can't see beyond the spoiled chipmunks darting along the rim seeking tourist handouts, if we start focusing on angels, we might miss the grand, sweeping view of God.

On the other hand, could more attention on angels actually be God's desire and plan for his people at this moment in history? Is it perhaps a clue and signal that we're on the threshold of something bigger in God's timetable for the world? Is the present age about to end? In God's mercy and love for sinners, is he suddenly causing a belief in spiritual angels to be more respectable so people can better accept the spiritual message of the gospel — before it's too late?

Or as some highly respected Bible teachers say, is there no such thing as angelic activity in our world anymore, since the close of Bible times?

The questions go on and on. (I wonder if the angels are asking them too.)

Probably no major theological issue has received as much secular attention in modern times as the doctrine of angels has in the 1990s. You would expect Christians to be delighted at this, and start rushing in to make the most of this fresh opportunity for spiritual dialogue with the non-Christian world. But a good many Christians don't know what (if anything) to think about angels.

At least when the "God is dead" notion grabbed headlines a few decades ago, Christians were united in their response: No, they proclaimed, God is alive! But now when headlines along the grocery checkout lane talk about widespread angel activity and belief in personal angels, the typical Christian reaction is: Well, maybe — or maybe not.

The Dangers

We've probably moved beyond the giddiest heights of the angel craze. We may not see many more major magazines with front-cover features on angels, since the topic isn't as fresh and new-fashioned as it was in the years just past. But there does seem to have been a major shift in thinking for the general population. In the popular mind, what was once mostly a myth is now a mysterious and fascinating reality.

This all seems to fit into a greater openness to spirituality that's been building for years. Few people think anymore that all of life's important answers can be found in science and rational thought and reasonable logic. They know reality has another dimension — a spiritual dimension beyond science and reason. And this "other" side of reality keeps growing bigger in popular thought.

What does all this mean? Is it good or bad?

The biggest danger may well be greater susceptibility to spirituality's dark side. Mankind's mental doorway may be open wider to thinking about religion and eternity, but it's probably also open wider to Satan's influence.

Scripture warns us that "Satan himself masquerades as an angel of light" (2 Corinthians 11:14). Perhaps this strategy of deception wasn't so effective in the generations just before us. People weren't as open to believing in angels then, and if you talked about seeing one or wanting to, you might have been called flighty or foolish or weird.

Now the situation has changed. It's acceptable and even fashionable to believe in angels, and millions around the world are looking for angelic activity as never before.

But a stronger belief in angels is no guarantee of greater understanding of God's truth. The devil can ensnare us as much through "angelism" as he can through materialism or sexual lust or power-hunger. In fact he has scored some of his greatest triumphs in the disguise of angels. In the year 610 the oppressive religion of Islam was born when Muhammed received the contents of the Koran in a series of visions from someone he believed to be the angel Gabriel. Twelve centuries later, the deceptive cult of Mormonism supposedly arose when an angelic being called Moroni got Joseph Smith connected with the Book of Mormon.

Is Satan doing the same thing again? Or instead of launching a big new anti-Christian religion or cult, perhaps he and his demons are simply using angelic disguise — a little here and a little there — to flirt with people's fascinations and to create a curiosity and craving for angelic presence. By influencing the right people with the right connections to get the right books and magazine articles published and the right TV shows on the air, he can lure millions into a false sense of spiritual experience and security. The syrupy-sweet, spirit-tingling taste of a little angelism can ruin people's appetite for the good, solid food of God's Word and his gospel of grace and truth.

Even secular publications have recognized at least partly this aspect of angelmania. They note the easy lure of preferring angels over God. "For those who choke too easily on God and his rules," *Time* magazine stated, "angels are the handy compromise, all fluff and meringue, kind, nonjudgmental. They are available to everyone, like aspirin."

"Angels offer a form of spirituality devoid of Jesus and God," wrote Joan Webster Anderson in her book *Where Angels Walk: True Stories of Heavenly Visitors*. "Belief in God has been so depopularized in America that now belief in anything can happen. The search is on for spirituality, but without God."

Life magazine attached the label "God Lite" to the angelism movement. The magazine's reporter visited a conference of angel enthusiasts. Unlike the mighty heavenly beings described in the Bible, the reporter said the angels described to him at the conference were

> a more benign and bite-size species, cuddly as a lap dog, conscientious as a school crossing guard. I heard angels likened to spiritual kissing cousins, flower delivery messengers… and just a nice feeling of warmth and love that washes all over you. Today's angels seem to spend a lot less time praising God than serving us. While they are still making super-hero, nick-of-time rescues, they are also showing up in less dire emergencies to track down a set of lost keys or make a chicken casserole more flavorful. Indeed, nearly all the angel believers I met got around to mentioning their parking space angel whom they call upon while cruising crowded city streets.

If some of your neighbors or friends or family members become attracted to an empty and frivolous but potentially dangerous angelism, will you be able to steer them out by showing them God's truth about angels? It's my prayer that this book will help you do just that. There's nothing that deals with error like a good dose of truth.

Meanwhile let's remember God is sovereign. He's shown in history that he uses even the mistakes and tragedies and follies of mankind to accomplish his higher will. Could it be that in our day he's using angelmania — even though it's often excessive and eccentric — to give his people a certain push? Does he want to sharpen our sensitivity toward spiritual realities? After all, it looks as if angels will be a big part of our eternal environment, which will be far more substantial than our short and shadowy presence on this earth. Being eternal themselves, angels have a greater claim to "reality" than our homes and jobs and hobbies. And unlike our homes and jobs and hobbies, the holy angels are always pointing us in the right direction: toward God.

Just thinking about angels can give us a fresh reminder that there's another world besides this one that clings so closely all around us. Angels already experience the fullness of that other world—God's eternal, heavenly kingdom—where God's rule goes entirely unopposed and unquestioned. Someday we'll experience it with them.

Jesus was turning our eyes toward this other, unseen world when he taught us to pray, "Thy will be done on earth as it is in heaven." Hearing those words, we easily assume that right now in heaven angels are doing God's will perfectly and gladly. So we ask the same for us, here and now. And when we sincerely pray "Thy kingdom come" to our heavenly Father, we show him that we long for something better than the enemy territory which our world is today, infested by sin and filled with deceptions from the fallen angel Satan.

The Real Thing

Before preaching and writing on this subject I read hundreds of stories describing angel sightings and encounters. Many are far-fetched and go beyond the bounds of what Scripture allows as being reliable. For example, the Bible gives no indication angels will respond if we pray directly to them for help. In fact in Scripture we don't find any instances of people even asking God to send them an angel's protection. And the only person in Scripture who tried persuading someone else to seek help from an angel was Satan, who quoted an Old Testament verse about angelic protection while tempting Jesus in the wilderness (Matthew 4:6).

More importantly, Scripture gives no basis for assuming angels will serve and help non-Christians. The Bible describes angels as "ministering spirits sent to serve *those who will inherit salvation*" (Hebrews 1:14). Who are these people destined to "inherit salvation"? The Bible makes it clear that this refers only to those who come to know Christ as Savior. It's to serve only them that angels are sent. If someone claims to have seen an angel yet that person professes no allegiance to Jesus Christ, it's likely that any angel he saw (if he truly saw one at all) was a fallen one — one of the devil's messengers, not the Lord's. Not every angel is from God.

A book far larger than the one in your hands would be needed to discuss all the circulated opinions and beliefs about angels which down through history have either been highly questionable or in flat opposition to biblical truth. But what about angel stories that fit within Bible parameters and which are reported by trustworthy sources, by people we would never expect to make things up? Should we believe them?

In his landmark 1975 book *Angels* (which has sold more than two and a half million copies and continues as a bestseller), Billy Graham collected and retold many reputable stories of experiences with angels, including this family account of his maternal grandmother's death:

> The room seemed to fill with a heavenly light. She sat up in bed and almost laughingly said, "I see Jesus. He has his arms outstretched toward me. I see Ben [her husband who had died some years earlier] and I see the angels." Then she slumped over, absent from the body but present with the Lord.

Billy Graham said he believed in angels not only because of the Bible's testimony about them, but also "because I have sensed their presence in my life on special occasions." He wrote:

> As an evangelist, I have often felt too far spent to minister from the pulpit to men and women who have filled stadiums to hear a message from the Lord. Yet again and again my weakness has vanished, and my strength has been renewed. I have been filled with God's power not only in my soul but physically. On many occasions, God has become especially real, and has sent his unseen angelic visitors to touch my body and let me be his messenger for heaven, speaking as a dying man to dying men.

He also recounted such exciting stories as this one from pioneer missionary John G. Paton in the New Hebrides Islands, in the South Pacific:

> Hostile natives surrounded his mission headquarters one night, intent on burning the Patons out and killing them. John Paton and his wife prayed all during that terror-filled night that God would deliver them. When daylight came they were amazed to see that, unaccountably, the attackers had left. They thanked God for delivering them.
>
> A year later, the chief of the tribe was converted to Jesus Christ, and Mr. Paton, remembering what had happened, asked the chief what had kept him and his men from burning down the house and killing them. The chief replied in surprise, "Who were all those men you had with you there?" The missionary answered, "There were no men there; just my wife and I." The chief argued that they had seen many men standing guard — hundreds of big men in shining garments with drawn swords in their hands. They seemed to circle the mission station so that the natives were afraid to attack. Only then did Mr. Paton realize that God had sent his angels to protect them. The chief agreed that there was no other explanation.

One of the most popular angel stories of this century happened in a gruesome Nazi prison camp in the Second World War, as told by Corrie ten Boom in *A Prisoner — And Yet*. She and her sister Betsie had just arrived at Ravensbruck, where new prisoners were being searched. Corrie was hiding a Bible under her dress.

> It did bulge out obviously through my dress; but I prayed, "Lord, cause now Thine angels to surround me; and let them not be transparent today, for the guards must not see me." I felt perfectly at ease. Calmly I passed the guards. Everyone was checked, from the front, the sides, the back. Not a bulge escaped the eyes of the guard. The

woman just in front of me had hidden a woolen vest under her dress; it was taken from her. They let me pass, for they did not see me. Betsie, right behind me, was searched.

But outside awaited another danger. On each side of the door were women who looked everyone over for a second time. They felt over the body of each one who passed. I knew they would not see me, for the angels were still surrounding me. I was not even surprised when they passed me by; but within me rose the jubilant cry, "O Lord, if Thou dost so answer prayer, I can face even Ravensbruck unafraid."

Christianity Today reported a story of angelic intervention told by the editor of *Leadership,* a magazine for church leaders. One night the editor's young daughter was in a coma and near death. A hospital staff worker looked into the girl's room and witnessed an astonishing sight: Angels were hovering over the girl's bed.

Amazingly, the following morning the daughter had recovered. Her father, a man not prone to sensationalism, did not hesitate to believe angels had truly visited his daughter. Meanwhile the hospital worker renewed her commitment to God as a result of what she had seen in the girl's room that night.

A Reliable Source

Stories like these are from sources we've come to trust. So do people really see angels today? If so, who are these angels, and what in the world are they doing?

We'll look at these and many other questions in this book. And the Bible will be our guide. Actually there's nowhere else reliable to look. We would know nothing dependable about angels if it weren't for the fact that God himself has told us. Apart from divine revelation, science and human wisdom can't come close to answering our questions on this topic, and would only mumble and stumble along through speculation. The Bible, however, as Lewis Sperry Chafer reminds us,

> reflects God's knowledge of the universe rather than man's; therefore in the Scriptures the angels, concerning whom man of himself could know nothing, are introduced with perfect freedom.

Scripture is our source and standard. Much that goes on in the name of angels in our world isn't biblical; we need caution not to get caught in the web of angelmania. Whatever our past experiences or beliefs or opinions regarding angels, they must be checked against the principles of Scripture. They must spring from Scripture, not from what we've conjured up in our minds that we'd *like* to believe about angels.

Don't worry that limiting our authority to God's Word will make this a dull subject. In that "perfect freedom" of disclosure that Chafer noted, what the Bible says about angels is stirring and eye-opening and heart-opening.

Therefore we can enter gladly and easily into an experience with angels any time we like. God has given us rich and inspired messages in Scripture that usher us right into the essence of what angels are all about. God's Book is the thrilling place and the trustworthy place to learn about them. We can see them and hear them and watch them work, and find out all that their examples can teach us. Through careful study, anyone who truly seeks the Lord with a good and honest heart can find these riches.

And yet for all that the Scriptures tell us about angels, the serious Bible student soon gets the feeling God has been guarded in what he's revealed. Everything Scripture says concerning angels is in connection to something else as the main theme. There are no pages or passages whose central purpose is to spell out a doctrine of angels. So we can't uncover as much about them as we might like. Unfortunately those who don't understand or appreciate the Bible's wisdom and authority have been quick to jump in and try to fill all the gaps with fanciful conjecture. We ought to try to know as much about angels as God has determined to reveal to us — and then be content to leave it at that. Someday we'll understand more. But try crossing that line now and you can end up doing yourself damage.

It's like our knowledge of heaven. We really don't know much about it. The bottom line is that heaven is where God is, which is all that should be important. The writer of Psalm 73 shows the right heart when he tells God, "Whom have I in heaven but you? And earth has nothing I desire besides you." Besides God there is no one on earth and no one in heaven — not even angels — who can give your soul true fulfillment.

So make sure God sets your agenda, whatever knowledge you seek. John Calvin worded it this way as he launched his own discussion of angels:

> Let us here remember that on the whole subject of religion one rule of modesty and soberness is to be observed, and it is this — in obscure matters not to speak or think, or even long to know, more than the Word of God has delivered.

So what does the Word of God deliver to us about angels? How much does God really want us to comprehend about this mysterious subject?

Let's explore the answers together.

Angels and Me and You

But first come back with me to last year, when I found out I had cancer. I never did see or hear an angel in the room with me, as much as that might have encouraged me then. But I did feel God's presence. And who's to say seeing an angel would have been better than that?

Both times that I went into surgery, I found a peace in my heart that was born out of my relationship with God. Looking back now on these recent months I wonder what an angel could have added to that peace — except perhaps another exclamation point to my belief that God was there, caring for me.

So as I think about why some people see angels and others don't, I wonder if God doesn't withhold the sight of angels from most of us so we'll understand where our trust should truly be and where we really should focus our attention. Maybe we don't need all the sensations and excitement that so many people clamor for. Wonderful as the presence of an angel might be, God has given us something better. In fact he's given us the greatest gift of all: his presence through his Holy Spirit, and in his Word.

Maybe it's even possible that the lack of an angelic manifestation in my life is like a backhanded compliment. God may be telling me, "Jeremiah, you don't need an angel. You'll be fine. You know who you are and Who is with you—and that's enough for now."

If an angel has never made himself known to you either, maybe you can take it as God's affirmation of your trust in him. And if someday in the future God deems it wise and good to dispatch an angel to me or to you, I'm sure he will. I don't have a fixation on angels, but I'm more convinced than ever that they are far more involved in our world than most of us realize. I believe they certainly do intervene here, both visibly and invisibly.

Meanwhile, whether or not we ever see an angel before we're carried home to heaven, there's great value in exploring what God has to say about them. As C. F. Dickason reminds us in his biblical handbook *Angels: Elect and Evil,*

> Though angelology is not a cardinal doctrine, its acceptance opens the mind to a better understanding of the Bible, God's plan of the ages, the Christian life and ministry, as well as world conditions and the course of world affairs.

If studying this subject has anything close to the impact on you that it already has had on me, your mind and heart will soon be opened to believe a host of things you may never before have realized. There's a lot more to this "strange" topic of angels than we imagine. Once we honestly investigate the amazing things Scripture tells us about them, we actually find ourselves drawn closer to God, instead of being distracted and turned away from him.

Anyone who goes into a study of angels with a high view of God will come away with an even higher view.

That, in fact, is the only sufficient aim in a study of angels: that you might draw closer to God. If you study angels and the result is anything less — if you build up only a file of information about angels or a fascination with them or even a supposed relationship with one, but haven't encountered at least a tug toward humble submission to the Almighty God…you've totally missed what angels are all about.

Chapter Two

IN THE PRESENCE
OF ANGELS—Part I

D O YOU *really* believe in angels?

Walt Shepard does. His angel story is a favorite among hundreds I've read lately.

Walt had become depressed over a broken relationship and was ready to end his life. In the dark, predawn hours one Sunday he accelerated his Sunbeam sports car to 120 miles per hour on Interstate 10, north of New Orleans.

Ahead, on the side of the road, he saw what appeared to be an abandoned car. Here was his chance, he decided.

He plowed into the back of the parked car. There was an explosion. Both vehicles burst into flames.

The manager of a nearby motel heard the crash and called rescue authorities.

Walt had been thrown through his windshield and was lying on the mangled engine, trapped by the crumpled hood. Fire surrounded him. He lost consciousness.

The highway patrol quickly arrived but the fire was so intense it kept officers from getting within fifty feet of the wreckage. With amazement, however, they and the hotel manager suddenly saw two figures approach the car without hesitation. They pulled Walt from the flames, then helped a rescue team load him in an ambulance. The ambulance sped away.

The officers wanted to interview the two unknown helpers to find out more about the accident and to write up reckless driving charges against Walt. Though no other cars had been parked nearby, the two had mysteriously disappeared.

Walt began months of painful recovery. He struggled with bitterness and anger. But he began reflecting on his upbringing as the son of Presbyterian missionaries.

One day he decided to pray. He was in a body cast and couldn't kneel, but he rolled over in his bed and faced the wall. He said to the Lord, "I can't take it. I need your forgiveness.... Come into my life and clean me up."

The next morning he woke up after the best night's rest he could remember in five years.

His father, meanwhile, had talked with those who witnessed his son's rescue. They agreed that two unidentified figures had boldly approached the car as though there were no fire at all. The rescue continued to baffle police.

A short time after Walt prayed his prayer, he was talking with his dad about the unusual circumstances of the accident. His father proposed a supernatural explanation.

"Son, I think you were saved by two angels," he said, "so you'd have the opportunity to do what you did this week — to get your life right with God."

At first Walt was skeptical. But now, after maturing from youth to middle age, he says, "I believe angels are simply part of God's natural dealings with us. It's amazing, but I believe angels rescued me from the fire that morning. And I believe they haven't stopped working."

Do you believe Walt Shepard's story? I can't verify it, but in my opinion his account fits the context of everything the Bible tells us angels can do and will do. Walt's story is strong because it has the right focus. It gives glory to God — as angels do — and credits God with using angels to help bring salvation through Jesus Christ to a man's soul.

A Settled Question

Some people might criticize you believing in angels or even expressing interest in them. Maybe you've already heard from critics like that. But don't let them worry you. You're in better company than they are.

In the Scriptures—from Genesis to Revelation—the existence of angels is simply assumed. The Bible contains more than three hundred direct references to them.

The same assumption about the reality of angels has always been widespread throughout our civilization. "There is nothing unnatural or contrary to reason" about a belief in angels, wrote J. M. Wilson earlier in this century. "Indeed the warm welcome human nature has always given to this thought is an argument in its favor. Why should there not be such an order of beings...?" In 1952 the editorial board of the classic series *Great Books of the Western World* included "Angels" as one of the 102 most important topics and ideas that the famous authors of these great books have discussed down through the ages. Throughout the full length of history, skepticism about angels has been the minority view, though it began to swell when faith in science replaced faith in God.

Those who have doubts might run the risk of suffering the same fate as the Sadducees, the only group of folks identified in the Bible as not believing in angels (Acts 23:8). Such "gross ignorance," as John Calvin called it, was a point that put even the hypocritical Pharisees ahead of them. The Sadducees disappeared from history without a trace before the first century ended, though in Jesus' day they were Israel's most powerful Jews. They controlled both the high priesthood and the Sanhedrin, the Jewish ruling council. They were aristocratic, pragmatic, and arrogant—quite a contrast to the childlike faith that so easily believes in angels.

It's richly satisfying to see in Acts 5 how God chose to thwart the Sadducees in their actions against his apostles. After seeing the apostles heal the sick and powerfully proclaim the gospel, we read in Acts 5:17-18 that "the high priest and all his associates, who were members of the party of the Sadducees, were filled with jealousy. They arrested the apostles and put them in the public jail."

Now God's chosen method for correcting this injustice is unveiled in verses 19-21:

> But during the night *an angel of the Lord* opened the doors of the jail and brought them out. "Go, stand in the temple courts," he said, "and tell the people the full message of this new life." At daybreak they entered the temple courts, as they had been told, and began to teach the people.

The apostles might have held back a few laughs shortly after this episode when they were summoned once more before that no-such-thing-as-angels crowd. The powerful Sadducees spurned angels, and would drop from history within a generation; the imprisoned apostles simply obeyed God's message delivered by an angel, and they would change history's course forever.

An equally ironic but more poignant picture of the hardened Sadducees comes later in Acts, when Stephen was dragged before the Sadducee-dominated Sanhedrin. Stephen, "a man full of God's grace and power" (6:8), had been falsely accused of blasphemy. At his trial, "all who were sitting in the Sanhedrin looked intently at Stephen, and they saw that his face was like the face of an *angel*" (6:15). But angelic appearance wasn't enough to prevent the blinded Sadducees from stoning Stephen to death.

One last word before dropping for good the fundamental but easily answered question of whether angels exist. J. M. Wilson states it well:

> For the Christian the whole question turns on the weight to be attached to the words of our Lord. All are agreed that he teaches the existence, reality, and activity of angelic beings.... We have the guarantee of Christ's word for the existence of angels; for most Christians that will settle the question.

Yes. For you and me and our brothers and sisters who follow Christ—as we acknowledge the lordship of Jesus and the "guarantee of Christ's word"—the question is settled already. For the rest, doubts will surely evaporate on the day "when the Son of Man comes in his glory, *and all the angels with him*" (Matthew 25:31).

No Other Choice

Okay, our critics may respond, so angels exist. But why should that interest us?

There are some, for example, who suppose there's no angelic activity on earth today since we live in the time of the Holy Spirit. However, a quick look at Acts 8 should answer their objection. Notice who helps and guides Philip into a life-saving mission. First we read, "Now *an angel of the Lord* said to Philip, 'Go south to the road—the desert road—that goes down from Jerusalem to Gaza.' So he started out...." (8:26-27).

Down that desert road Philip spotted someone riding in a chariot and reading a book. Philip was now ready for further guidance from God. Would the angel reappear? No. Now we read, "*The Spirit* told Philip, 'Go to that chariot and stay near it.' Then Philip ran up to the chariot..." (8:29-30).

Here we see the Holy Spirit and an angel working together, and Philip responding correctly, just as the jailed apostles had done earlier. The result for Philip was the privilege of leading the chariot-rider—a visiting dignitary from Ethiopia—to salvation.

Perhaps the Spirit himself directed the angel on that occasion. We know God the Father commands angels, and we also see in Scripture that his Son Jesus can. While facing arrest, Jesus claimed he could just say the word and his Father would "at once put *at my disposal* more than twelve legions of angels" (Matthew 26:53). Before Jesus ascended he told his disciples, "All authority *in heaven* and on earth has been given to me" (28:18)—certainly his authority in heaven includes authority over angels.

So if God can direct angels and Jesus can direct angels, it's easy to believe that the third Person of the Trinity can as well. The Holy Spirit is eternal God, not just a modern-day substitute for angels. And I see no clear indication in Scripture whatsoever that angelic activity will decline or cease in this day, the age in which Jesus Christ is building his church through the Holy Spirit's power.

Meanwhile other critics accept the possibility of modern angelic activity but don't think the topic is worth close study. Sure, angels are out there somewhere, these people say, and we can all be pleasantly impressed with them when we get to heaven and actually see them. But why bother *now* to scrutinize what the Bible says about them?

Why? Because ultimately God leaves us no other option. As theologian M. J. Erickson declares,

> The teaching of Scripture is that he has created these spiritual beings and has chosen to carry out many of his acts through them. Therefore, if we are to be faithful students of the Bible, we have no choice but to speak of these beings.

We run the risk of insulting God if we aren't truly open to appreciate every single thing he's made — including angels — as well as to *learn* about God from everything he's made — including angels, and perhaps *especially* angels. "If we desire to know God by his works," wrote Calvin, "we surely cannot overlook this noble and illustrious specimen."

The great hymn from Stuart K. Hines captures the right mindset:

> O Lord my God, when I in awesome wonder
> Consider *all* the works Thy hands have made...
> Then sings my soul, my Savior God, to Thee:
> How great Thou art, how great Thou art!

"Awesome wonder" is the perfect phrase to describe a person's frame of mind after a true biblical exploration of angels.

But enough of the awesome wonder talk, some would say. What about *pragmatic* value?

This is probably the most deeply founded objection to studying about angels. Always faithful to watch out for number one, our down-to-earth spirit demands: What's in it for me?

Well—quite a lot, as we'll see. A. C. Gaebelein's conviction in *The Angels of God* points the way:

> Like every truth, the truth of the angels of God—their presence on earth and their loving ministries—has a practical value. As we real-ize in faith…that they are watching us, ready to walk with us as we walk with him in his ways, ready to serve us as we serve him, ready to shield us and help us in a hundred different ways, a solemn feel-ing will come into our lives. Surely we will walk softly in the pres-ence of the Lord and his holy angels.… Thus this truth will assist us in a holy life.

Finally, there's another big point to make about the *why* of studying angels before we continue on to taste the riches. It's a point that's truer today than it was yesterday, and will be truer tomorrow than it is today.

Most Christians agree demonic activity will increase as we near the last days. It's a viewpoint grounded not only in simple observation of what the world is coming to, but also in Scripture. "The Spirit clearly says," Paul reminds us in 1 Timothy 4:1, "that in later times some will abandon the faith and follow deceiving spirits and things taught by demons."

Here in our own church's counseling ministry we see this more and more. After reviewing some of the powerful and mystifying disorders people are manifesting, we look at each other and say, "Something's going on here that isn't human." It's true for Christian ministry throughout the world too: We have seen and will probably continue to see greater attacks from the forces of spiritual evil.

So I ask you: Isn't it reasonable to expect that as demonic activity increases while we near the day of the Lord's return, angelic activity will also increase? It makes sense. As Billy Graham says, "God is still in business too."

Warriors and Agents of Wrath

So hold on to your book and let's go for a ride — a journey at the speed of heavenly light across the ages and pages of Scripture.

We have a guide going with us, both to pilot our invisible craft and to explain things along the way. He's a stranger, but he seems a nice enough fellow. In a cheerful voice he tells us we'll be watching the angels at work. "Put everything else out of mind," he says. "Use all your mental powers to catch the clearest impression of what angels do and how they do it. We'll take several spins through the territory, and each time our perspective will change a little, so there's something new to learn at each turn." It sounds like an interesting trip.

"Ready?" he says. We nod.

"Let's go!"

Our first stop is at the eastern gateway to the Garden of Eden. Our guide tells us this is the first glimpse in Scripture of angelic creatures. It's by no means a peaceful, pleasant scene. What catches our attention first is a flaming sword flashing back and forth. These heavenly beings are armed soldiers placed here by the Holy God because his holy creation has just been contaminated by the sin of Adam and Eve. The soldiers' mission: "to guard the way to the tree of life." We can tell they mean business. We have no intention of even a peek over their shoulders at the tree. *(Genesis 3:24)*

Now we zoom forward across the centuries. We look down on a small city crowning a hill. This is Jerusalem, city of David. Between the town's largest buildings we see a figure kneeling in the street, looking up at the sky. Yes, our guide tells us, that's David himself.

Our eyes blink, catching a movement in the clouds above. We turn to look where David looks. We gasp, overcome by what we sense and see, something words can't fully describe: The angel of the Lord is there. At once we're given insight to know the situation. In the angel's hand is a sword holding the power of the plague. Throughout the land of Israel this day, sickness from that sword has already killed seventy thousand people.

Now the angel stretches his hand over Jerusalem. The sword is poised to strike.

In the street below, a voice cries out. David confesses in agony: "I am the one who sinned!"

Another voice shouts like thunder, far above the angel: "Enough! Withdraw your hand." The angel puts the sword back in its sheath. (2 Samuel 24:15-17, 1 Chronicles 21:14-17)

We move forward again through time to a different scene. Now we see more soldiers—human soldiers—massed as an army, countless thousands upon thousands. Outside the gates of Jerusalem their camp stretches as far as we can see in the evening light. These are Assyrians, living legends for their battle-skill and their cruelty as conquerors.

Night comes on. In time the campfires and the boasting voices die down. The vast camp grows quiet. The soldiers sleep, resting for tomorrow's work of war against the besieged city.

The darkness deepens. Suddenly we look up and cringe. There he is again—the angel of the Lord, come to slay.

His deed is done in only a moment. Then the angel is gone.

We watch. The camp is cloaked in quietness as before, only more so. Dawn's first grayness marks a faint line in the sky behind the city. Still the camp does not awaken. The light grows, revealing nothing in the sprawling Assyrian camp except dead bodies. Their number is more than would later be killed at Hiroshima and Nagasaki combined. In a single night, an angel has slain one hundred eighty-five thousand Assyrians. (2 Kings 19:35, 2 Chronicles 32:21, Isaiah 37:36)

Forward again, seven hundred years. We see another king over Israel. He wears rich robes and is seated on a throne while addressing an admiring throng. The people shout: "This is the voice of a god and not a man! Long live the god King Herod!"

Herod's plump face glows. He extends his open, meaty palms to acknowledge the acclaim. He does not see what we see: An angel of the Lord suddenly stands behind the throne, and touches the king's body. Herod's smile slackens. He bends over in pain. He feels but does not know what is happening: Worms are devouring him from within. (*Acts 12:21-23*)

Forward, forward again we go, to view a raging battlefield. The time and scene are hazy—we're beyond earth and outside earthly time. The fiery, deafening intensity of the fight is beyond anything we've imagined or could ever explain. In fact we can bear only a moment of it before the image disappears. But we remember what we saw: "There was war in heaven. Michael and his angels fought against the dragon, and the dragon and his angels fought back." (*Revelation 12:7*)

The next scenes in our journey come as fleeting glimpses into the future. They flare into our view for only a second or so. After the last picture has dissolved, we struggle to express in words what we saw and perceived.

First, four angels stood on a riverbank and "were released to kill a third of mankind."

Then seven angels appeared and were given "seven golden bowls filled with the wrath of God."

Seven more scenes followed immediately. In each brief picture, one of the seven angels poured out his bowl upon a world in rebellion against God. Instantly, calamity struck. We trembled as we saw the unleashed angelic power: "Ugly and painful sores broke out on the people." "Every living thing in the sea died." "The rivers and springs of water...became blood." "The sun was given power to scorch people with fire." There was darkness. There was drought. There was an earthquake more powerful than any in history, and a storm of hundred-pound hailstones. (*Revelation 9:14-15, 15:1, 15:6, 16:1-21*)

And now another scene. This one lingers in view for a longer while. We look up. Out of a golden brightness that we know is heaven, an angel rapidly descends. In one hand he holds a huge key. In the other is a massive chain. He carries the chain effortlessly enough, but it looks as if it must weigh tons.

Now we see where the angel goes. Below, a serpentine dragon lashes about, breathing fire and fury. If it weren't for the presence of the descending angel we would scream in horror, for the dragon is Satan, revealed in all his raw and ugly power.

The angel nears. With only one hand he casts out a short length of the chain and snares the dragon at once. Satan is paralyzed, powerless before him. Still using only one hand, the angel wraps the chain around and around and around the dragon. The mighty chain seems endless; not until the angel makes exactly a thousand loops does the last link lock in place.

Now the angel touches the key to the ground. The surface cracks wide and a gaping hole opens. With his free hand the angel picks up the bound dragon and tosses him into the bottomless blackness. (Revelation 20:1-3)

In silence, this final picture fades. Our guide tells us that the first leg of our journey is over. Soberly we tell each other that all this has done something to our view of angels. Divorced from any credibility forever in our minds are the thoughts of plump baby "cherubs" or pale ladies with see-through wings traced in glitter across our Christmas cards.

No, real angels have been and are and shall forever be awesome *warriors* for God, agents of his wrath and power. We don't wonder in the least why people in the Bible who see angels are so often struck with terror at the sight.

And we look forward to what we'll discover on the next stretch of our journey.

Chapter Three

IN THE PRESENCE
OF ANGELS—Part II

O UR HEARTS are still thumping, but our guide says it's time to
move again.

We race to another scene from centuries past. Not far away
we see a walled city dotted with palm trees — Jericho. At a distance outside the city, a man crouches behind rocks and bushes. He keeps
himself hidden from the watchmen on the walls as he moves in closer. This
is Joshua, scouting out the scene for the battle he expects shortly between
Jericho's defenders and the army of Israel camped nearby.

But he's not alone. Another warrior arrived here first. As Joshua parts
some branches to pass through a clump of shrubbery, he sees the man, and
stops cold. It's too late to slip back undetected. The warrior is looking right
at him, with drawn sword in his hand.

Bravely Joshua moves closer. He plants his feet only five paces from the
warrior. Joshua's hand rests on his sword hilt. Somehow he is sure this man
knows his identity. But Joshua is filled with a strange uncertainty about the
man.

Joshua gets to the point: "Are you for us, or for our enemies?"

"Neither," the warrior answers. "But I have come as the commander of
the army of the Lord." Joshua knows at once what he means. This is the captain of the Lord's angelic host, the holy army whose service transcends any

earthly allegiance, even to Israel. A rush of fear mixed with hope surges through him. Will God's angels fight for Israel against Jericho?

Joshua throws himself down. With his face bowed to the ground he asks for a message from the Lord.

"Take off your sandals," the commander says, "for this place is holy." Joshua removes his sandals.

"Jericho is delivered into your hands," the commander continues. Then he outlines step by step what Joshua and the armies of Israel must do to bring to pass the victory God has already ordained. (*Joshua 5:13–6:5*)

Onward again. Centuries later we're in rugged forest country in the south of Judah. Nearly hidden on a hillside is a cave. At its mouth, and as far inside as the late afternoon light will reveal, we can see a few men — they are from David's band. A few of them stand watch, but most are resting from their latest flight from the soldiers of King Saul. They are weary but thankful to be safe.

From the depths of the cave David himself walks out. The few men outside greet him and slap his shoulders. David laughs with them, then saunters down the hill away through the trees to a place where he can be alone. He carries a simple harp. By a small stream at the foot of the hill he sits down. He's silent for a long time as he looks from the trickling water to the wind-tossed trees and up to the clouds. Sometimes he bows his head and closes his eyes. We sense a divine presence around this man. In quiet respect we hardly dare to breathe as we watch.

Finally David takes up his harp and his fingers pluck forth a melody. In his strong, pleasing voice he begins a new song. He sings praise and thanksgiving. And he sings his faith in God's protection:

> *The angel of the Lord*
> *encamps around those who fear him,*
> *and he delivers them.*

With a smile David looks to either side, trusting in the angel's invisible presence. Then he sings his new song again. *(Psalm 34:7)*

Forward now five hundred years and five hundred miles. We're in Babylon, where the Jewish people have been taken captive. King Nebuchadnezzar is seated on a portable throne set up near a towering furnace —a furnace built for executions. At the bottom of the furnace-tower is a door, and cut into it is a window of thick Phoenician glass. The throne is positioned so the king can look through the glass and watch the flames torture the offenders whom he has judged.

Suddenly the king leaps to his feet, his arm outstretched, his hand pointing. Three Jews who refused to bow down and worship Nebuchadnezzar had been dropped into the flames from the top of the tower. Yet now the king sees not three figures but four. All stand calm amid the flames, unharmed. And the fourth figure is surrounded by a whiteness that shines even brighter than the flames. He looks like a being from heaven! And his arms reach out to enfold the others.

The king orders the furnace door opened. He shouts inside: "Shadrach, Meshach, and Abednego, servants of the Most High God, come out!" They do. As soon as the third man emerges, the fourth figure inside disappears.

Shadrach, Meshach, and Abednego stride forward and stand before the king's throne. The ropes with which they were tied have burnt off, but nothing else about them has even the smell of smoke.

Nebuchadnezzar takes a step toward them, then drops to his knees and cries, "Praise be to the God of Shadrach, Meshach, and Abednego, who has sent his angel to rescue his servants!" *(Daniel 3:13-30)*

We go forward to another day under another king in Babylon. In the first light of dawn, King Darius rushes to the great stone-and-iron enclosure where Babylon's lions are kept. He orders the servant with him to pull back the stone that was rolled over the opening to the den. Before the stone is halfway back Darius rushes forward and grips the iron bars on the grated gate. "Daniel," he cries, "your God whom you always worship — has he been able to rescue you from the lions?"

From the darkness in the den comes a man's calm and confident voice with a greeting for the king. And he adds, "Yes, my God sent his angel, and he shut the mouth of the lions." (Daniel 6:19-22)

Forward again to see another gate with iron bars, the door to a cell in a Jerusalem prison. In the flickering light of a nearby torch we see the apostle Peter asleep between two soldiers. Each of his arms is bound by a separate chain. Suddenly the cell fills with light. An angel of the Lord stands there, but neither Peter nor the soldiers stir from their sleep. The angel reaches out and delivers a good whack to Peter's side. The chains fall from Peter's wrists and drop noisily to the floor. Peter's eyes slowly open, but we're amazed to see the guards still sleeping.

"Get up!" the angel loudly commands Peter. "And get dressed." Peter obeys and silently follows the angel out of the cell and past two sets of guards, but he still seems half asleep. The last iron gate separating the prison from the city streets opens by itself. Peter and the angel walk through. The cool night air is bracing. Peter's eyes open wider.

Without a word they walk side by side to the end of the street. Peter turns to look down a side street leading to the house where he last saw his friends and fellow disciples — before he was hauled off to jail.

He turns back around. He's alone. His companion is gone.

In the deserted street, under stars shining in the blackness, Peter speaks aloud: "The Lord sent his angel to rescue me." (Acts 12:11)

The second part of our journey is finished, our guide announces. We've been inspired and encouraged to see how God sends his angels to *deliver* and *protect* and *defend* his people. We smile and say that already we expect to sleep more soundly tonight.

"But first," says our guide, "there's still much more to see as well as to hear. In fact, on this next leg of the journey, your ears will be of more value than your eyes."

Guidance from God

He's taking us faster now. We're on a desert road near a spring where a woman kneels to drink from the water. Suddenly we see an angel approaching on the road.

"Hagar, servant of Sarai," he calls. "Where have you come from and where are you going?"

Hagar looks up. "I'm running away from my mistress Sarai," she answers.

"Go back to your mistress," the angel commands, "and submit to her." (*Genesis 16:7-9*)

The scene changes to an early morning on the plain west of the Dead Sea. Two angels rush out the city gate of Sodom. They're holding the hands of Lot and his wife and his daughters, pulling them along. At a good distance from the gate they finally halt and let go of the hands of Lot and his family. "Now flee for your lives!" one of the angels commands. "Don't look back and don't stop anywhere in the plain! Flee to the mountains or you'll be swept away!" (*Genesis 19:15-17*)

Next we see the shepherd Jacob asleep in the land of the eastern peoples, where he works for his father-in-law. We can see into Jacob's dream. God's angel speaks to him: "Leave this land at once and go back to your native land." (*Genesis 31:10-13*)

Now we're startled by thunder and lightning and smoke. We're on Mount Sinai with Moses. God calls to him from the thunder: "See, I am sending an angel ahead of you to guard you along the way and to bring you to the place I have prepared. Pay attention to him and listen to what he says." (*Exodus 23:20-21*)

Next we're on a path between two walled vineyards. The angel of the Lord stands with drawn sword. The man Balaam bows to the ground before the angel. Balaam's donkey, with a satisfied look on his gray, gnarly face, is nearby. The angel says to Balaam, "Go, but speak only what I tell you." (*Numbers 22:22-35*)

We're on a hilltop now along the ridge of Mount Carmel. Dressed in a hairy garb tied with a leather belt, the prophet Elijah waits. A captain with fifty soldiers approaches in the valley below, sent by the wicked King Ahab. This is the third of Ahab's captains and the third set of fifty men to come up this valley on the same mission. Both times before, they demanded Elijah's surrender to Ahab. Each time, Elijah called down fire from heaven to destroy them all.

The third captain is more humble. He falls on his knees and calls up to the prophet, "Please have respect for my life and the lives of these fifty men!"

Immediately the angel of the Lord comes to Elijah's side and speaks: "Go down with him; do not be afraid of him." Elijah gathers his cloak and steps down the hillside to go with Ahab's captain. (2 Kings 1)

Now we're in Jerusalem once more, in the time of the plague that struck the entire land during David's reign. We're in the house of an older man who kneels in prayer. He's a prophet named Gad. He's a longtime friend of the king's, and first helped him many years ago when the young David was fleeing from Saul.

As Gad prays, the angel of the Lord comes to him with clear instructions: "Tell David to go up and build an altar to the Lord on the threshing floor of Araunah the Jebusite." The angel leaves, and the prophet goes to find his king. (1 Chronicles 21:18)

Next we're in a small and simple house in the town of Nazareth in Galilee, at night. A worried young man tosses in restless sleep. In his dream an angel of the Lord appears and says, "Joseph son of David, don't be afraid to bring Mary home as your wife. The child conceived in her is from the Holy Spirit." (Matthew 1:20)

Later we see the same man resting deeply and peacefully in a house in Bethlehem. Again in his dream he sees and hears the angel: "Get up! Take the child and his mother and escape to Egypt. Stay there until I tell you, for Herod will look for the child to kill him." Joseph opens his eyes. He's on his feet at once. (Matthew 2:13)

Forward now to another house, larger and better furnished. We're in the Mediterranean port of Caesarea, headquarters of a Roman regiment occupying Palestine. A man wearing a centurion's uniform is kneeling in prayer.

Suddenly an angel in shining clothes is standing in the room behind him. "Cornelius!" he calls.

The centurion turns and stares in fear. "What is it, Lord?"

"Your prayers and gifts to the poor have come up as a memorial offering before God," the angel replies. "Now send men to Joppa to bring back a man named Simon Peter. He's a guest in the home of Simon the tanner, who lives by the sea."

The angel departs. With quick, military-like obedience to the angel's words, Cornelius calls in two servants. He also calls one of his aides who, like Cornelius, believes in God. Cornelius tells them everything the angel said and sends the three on their way to Joppa. (Acts 10:3-33)

More thunder now. We're back in the future, where the apostle John is in the middle of a blinding revelation. He sees an angel "robed in a cloud, with a rainbow above his head; his face was like the sun." The angel has his right foot planted on the sea; his left is on the land. He holds a scroll, looking so small in his massive hand.

John hears a voice from heaven: "Go, take the scroll that lies open in the hand of the angel who is standing on the sea and on the land." Somehow John is empowered to move and to reach into the cloud-robed angel's hand. The angel looks down to him and says, "Take it and eat it. It will turn your stomach sour, but in your mouth it will be as sweet as honey." (Revelation 10:1-10)

Another portion of our journey has ended. "What have you learned from your listening?" the guide asks.

We answer, "That angels give *guidance* from God, with clear and specific instructions."

Our guide nods. Then he starts us out again.

Comfort and Encouragement

We're going even faster now. "This time watch the angels' hands," the guide says.

We're back in the desert again, with the woman we saw earlier at the spring. This time no water is in sight. The woman is seated in the hot sand, her face buried in her hands, her shoulders heaving. A few steps away under the meager shade of a scrub bush, a boy cries with a parched, rasping voice.

Suddenly, high above us in a stark blue sky, an angel appears. He calls down, "What is the matter, Hagar? Don't be afraid. God has heard the boy crying as he lies there. Lift the boy up and take him by the hand." Hagar rises. Clutching her own dry throat, she shuffles in a daze through the sand to her crying son.

Above her the angel sweeps his hand over the scene. Hagar turns. She sees for the first time what we hadn't noticed before either: a well of water close by. (*Genesis 21:14-19*)

Now we move on to another desert scene where we see Elijah again. He hurries with stumbling steps, as if he's run a long way. Finally, in the shade of a broom bush, he falls to the ground. Gasping, he prays: "I've had enough, Lord. Please take my life!" He collapses into an exhausted sleep.

All at once an angel is bending over Elijah, touching his shoulder. "Get up," the angel says, "and eat."

Elijah weakly lifts himself from the ground. He's as surprised as we are at what the angel points to: a fire of hot coals, with a pan of bread baking over it. A toasty brown crust and a delicious aroma tell us that it's ready to eat. A pottery jar of water is nearby, cool enough to be covered with beads of moisture.

"Eat and drink," the angel tells Elijah, "for your journey ahead is too much for you." *(1 Kings 19:3-7)*

Once more we're with Daniel in Babylon. He's become an old man, though still strong. He and a few companions stroll along a bank of the great Tigris River. Suddenly there's a roar and a blaze of light. His companions flee in terror, but Daniel stays to see a blinding, thundering vision of a heavenly being. As he gazes, he feels his strength draining. He falls, fully outstretched on the ground along the riverbank.

The angel touches Daniel and helps him to his hands and knees. "Daniel," he says, "you're a man highly esteemed. Stand up and consider carefully the words I will speak to you." Somehow Daniel stands.

The angel tells him not to be afraid. He says he's come in response to Daniel's prayers, though he had to overcome demonic opposition on the way. "Now I'm here," the angel adds, "to tell you what will happen to your people in the future."

Once more Daniel swoons and falls to his knees. His head lowers to the ground. He wants to talk, but words will not come. Again he is helped by an angel's touch — this time to his lips. Daniel opens his mouth. In halting words he explains the anguish and weakness he feels. "My strength is gone," he whispers. "I can hardly breathe."

The angel touches him again and says, "Do not be afraid, O man highly esteemed. Peace! Be strong now. Be strong!"

Soon Daniel's shoulders pull back, his chin lifts, and his chest begins to rise and fall in the rhythm of regular breathing. "Speak now, my lord," he tells the angel, "since you've given me strength." *(Daniel 10:4-19)*

Again we're in the desert, in a specially rocky and barren tract. For the first time on this journey we see Jesus Christ, Son of Man and Son of God. He stands on a shadeless, stony hill.

Over the horizon a shadowy form is departing. Satan was here, tempting Jesus, but for now he's gone.

Our Master's body and face are thin from forty days of fasting. His skin is darkened by the sun.

Now, coming in visible form—just as the devil came—a group of angels appear at the side of Jesus. They kneel before him and reach out to him with food. (*Matthew 4:10-11; Mark 1:13*)

Forward now, but we're still with Jesus. It is night, and we're in an olive grove. A stone's throw away we see the huddled forms of sleeping men. Closer to us, Jesus is awake, kneeling in prayer. We look into his face and shudder. It's lined with agony from some deeper ordeal than we can imagine. "Father!" he cries, his head leaning back and his eyes lifted to the black sky. "O Father, if you're willing, take this cup from me. Yet not my will, but yours be done." The moonlight shimmers in the sweat on his brow.

Suddenly an angel kneels beside him and reaches out to him. In slow, soft strokes, the angel's hand wipes the sweat from our Savior's brow and his temples. Jesus appears strengthened. He closes his eyes and draws a deep breath. (*Luke 22:43*)

The scene fades from our sight, but we watch intently as long as we can, straining at the barest outline of our Lord praying under the olive trees. We know he was there for us. How we wish we could have helped the angel serve him. But instead, he was serving *us*.

When at last we can see no more of Gethsemane, we wipe tears from our eyes and remark to our guide that angels are great *comforters* and *servants,* bringing encouragement and strength in their hands and in their voices.

Messengers to Enlighten Us

Our guide takes us onward, increasing the speed again. "Stay with me," he urges us, "and keep listening."

So we listen. We hear the angel of the Lord call down to Abraham from heaven. He promises descendants to Abraham, "as numerous as the stars in the sky and as the sand on the seashore." (*Genesis 22:15-17*)

We hear the angel of the Lord say to Hannah, "You are barren and child-less, but you will conceive and bear a son." *(Judges 13:1-5)*

Centuries later we're inside the temple in Jerusalem, where a priest applies incense to the altar in the Most Holy Place. Suddenly he sees an angel of the Lord and is gripped with fear. The angel says, "Don't be afraid, Zechariah. Your prayer has been heard. Your wife Elizabeth will bear you a son, and you're to name him John." *(Luke 1:11-13)*

With the blink of an eye we're six months forward in time. We're again in Nazareth in Galilee. A young girl is frightened by the sight of the angel Gabriel, and is troubled by his greeting. But Gabriel says, "Don't be afraid, Mary. You've found favor with God. You will be with child and give birth to a Son, and you're to name him Jesus." *(Luke 1:26-31)*

Now nine months later: We're on a hillside outside Bethlehem in Judea, where shepherds struck with fear are crouched on the ground. An angel has appeared and the glory of the Lord lights up the sky and the hill and the shepherds and the sheep. "Don't be afraid," the angel says. "I bring you good news of great joy that will be for all the people. Today in the town of David a Savior has been born to you. He is Christ the Lord." *(Luke 2:9-12)*

A lifetime later: In Jerusalem two women approach a tomb. They're shocked to see the stone rolled back from the tomb's entrance, and a white-robed angel sitting on the stone. "Don't be afraid," the angel tells the women. "I know you seek Jesus, who was crucified. He isn't here; he has risen, just as he said." *(Matthew 28:1-7)*

A quarter-century later: We're on a battered ship in a howling storm on the Mediterranean Sea. It is night. Below decks where a prisoner has been trying to sleep, an angel stands beside him. "Don't be afraid, Paul," the angel says. "You must stand trial before Caesar; and God has graciously given you the lives of all who sail with you." *(Acts 27:13-26)*

And finally, to another glimpse of the future: In the middle of the sky an angel is soaring. He has the eternal gospel to proclaim to everyone on earth. And he calls in a loud voice, "Fear God and give him glory, because the hour of his judgment has come. Worship him who made the heavens, the earth, the sea and the streams of water." *(Revelation 14:6-7)*

Yes, we tell each other — angels are *messengers* who inform and enlighten us with tidings from God.

Our journey is over. We give warm thanks to our guide for taking us on this incredible voyage through the Bible. He accepts our invitation to join us for a meal, and over a fine dinner we discuss our discoveries from the trip. We're grateful the guide has joined us because he continues to offer helpful explanations here and there, while eating heartily. During dessert you and I briefly become engrossed in comparing impressions of the soaring angel we saw at our last stop, the one who had the gospel to proclaim. Suddenly we notice the guide has disappeared. Beside his plate is a slip of paper. We pick it up and read these handwritten words in gold ink:

> *"Do not forget to entertain strangers,*
> *for by so doing some people have entertained angels*
> *without knowing it."*
> —Hebrews 13:2

Three Warnings

A trip like that will give anyone a healthy respect for angels. But before looking longer and closer at them, we need to get a few guidelines out on the table. These principles are key warnings that will serve us well as we move forward.

The first principle: *We must not create or reshape angels according to our own fancy.* Countless multitudes have fallen into this error. In today's spiritual smorgasbord an angel can be anything you make it out to be. A majority of the angel representations we see—in paintings and giftbooks, or as lapel pins and china figurines, or gracing a host of other varieties of merchandise—are merely the product of human imagination. The word "angel" used in marketing these items is from a totally different vocabulary than the one used in the Bible. These so-called "angels" could just as well be labeled "fairies" or "phantoms" or even "devils" and be closer to the truth.

When *Time* magazine speaks of angels as "all fluff and meringue, kind, nonjudgmental," and "available to everyone, like aspirin"—you can be certain that God's angels aren't being described, but only the modern counterfeit whose roots go no deeper than foolish fantasy, pure commercialism, or even deliberate deception.

Bestselling author Sophy Burnham (*A Book of Angels*) says that angels have become popular "because we created this concept of God as punitive, jealous, judgmental," and she assures us that "angels never are. They are utterly compassionate." She must have never read the Bible, especially the book of Revelation. She's describing not God's angels, but the modern fraud. Too bad she wasn't with us on our journey.

When it comes to spiritual reality (including angels), the Bible is the only entirely reliable source of information. And the Bible gives clear depictions that pull the rug out from under the modern phonies that people call angels.

For example, whenever gender is indicated in reference to angels in the Bible, they're always masculine. Sometimes people say they've seen female angels, but the Bible never points them out. Nor do angels ever appear in Scripture as an animal or bird, as we sometimes see in angelic folklore.

According to the Bible, angels are a created class of beings and are never represented as spiritually progressed humans. In other words, humans don't evolve or transform into angels. In a children's book on angels is this quote: "Heaven is a place where girls get turned into angels and then God tries to do the best he can with the boys." But actually, sweet little girls have no more chance of becoming angels than the rowdiest boys. Likewise, imagining that a departed loved one now glides around as an angel is only a hollow comfort, and not in keeping with the pattern of God's Word.

Nor does the Bible indicate that these heavenly beings ever dwell inside human beings. There is no "angel within you," even on your best days.

There isn't the remotest hint in Scripture that angels spend time trying to earn their wings, like Clarence in the Jimmy Stewart movie *It's a Wonderful Life*. In fact, except for two classes of heavenly beings known as cherubim and seraphim, there isn't a lot of evidence in Scripture that angels even have wings. (Perhaps sometimes they do and sometimes they don't.)

Nor is there indication in the Bible that angels age — there are no "littlest angels" going through their growing-up years among the clouds. God's angels exist eternally. The angel Gabriel who appeared to Daniel was the same unchanged Gabriel who appeared more than five hundred years later to Mary the mother of Jesus, and to Zechariah the father of John the Baptist.

So I repeat: Steer clear of modern make-believe about angels, and trust only the Bible's perspective.

The second warning principle: *We must never let angels replace God in our lives.* This is a giant snare today for those who don't understand Scripture's teaching. I'm convinced that spiritual fads and tangents like those we see in angelmania are a tool of the enemy to keep us from following hard after God, as the deer pants for streams of water (Psalm 42:1).

All of us have a sense of spiritual destiny — a deep longing for eternity — placed within us by God. Long ago Paul reminded the pagan Greeks in Athens that God has even ordered human history "so that men would seek him and perhaps reach out for him and find him, though *he is not far from each one of us. For in him we live and move and have our being*" (Acts 17:27-28). But that spiritual framework and longing is easily misdirected or perverted, because our sin makes us love darkness rather than God's light. People who want a spiritual plaything or placebo are quick to bring their search for God to a dead end, and to search instead for angels.

Christianity Today warned, "Angels too easily provide a temptation for those who want a 'fix' of spirituality without bothering with God himself."

Professor Robert Ellwood, a specialist in unorthodox religions at the University of Southern California, observes, "With angels around, people feel they don't have to bother an Almighty God in order to get help."

This preference for angels over their Creator (and ours) is an insult to God. The very thought that we would have an angel's help *instead of* God's should fill us with grief, as it once did to the people of Israel. After they were rescued from Egypt but then sinned against God by making the golden calf (Exodus 32), God mentioned to Moses a new plan for the rest of Israel's trip to the Promised Land. *"I will send an angel* before you," he said. "But I will not go with you, because you are a stiff-necked people and I might destroy you on the way" (33:1-3).

Did the Israelites jump for joy when they heard about this change in leadership for the journey? Did they consider an angel a more companionable guide than God? No. "When the people heard these distressing words, they began to mourn..." (33:4).

Tragedy awaits anyone who turns for spiritual help in any direction away from God. Whatever spiritual reality that person encounters will most likely be from Satan, who would just as soon come to the party dressed as an angel of light as anything else. A desire for angels that's greater than a desire for the Creator can only lead to trouble. An infatuation with angels can be as wrong as any other infatuation with anything except God. Angels are not the Creator; they were created by the Creator, just as food and sex and ourselves and other people were.

The Ten Commandments begin with warnings about turning away from God. It's enlightening to think how heaven's angels fit in when we go back and read the first two commandments:

> You shall have no other gods before me.
> You shall not make for yourself an idol *in the form of anything in*
> *heaven above* or on the earth beneath or in the waters below. You
> shall not bow down to them or worship them... (Exodus 20:3-5).

Even something as holy as an angel in heaven above is never to be turned into an idol.

That leads directly to the third warning principle: *Angels must never receive our worship.* Scripture hits this one head-on. In Colossians 2:18, Paul speaks against "anyone who delights in false humility and the worship of angels." Worshiping angels is another exhibition of the basic idolatry charged against sinful mankind in Romans 1:25 — "They exchanged the truth of God for a lie, and worshiped and served created things rather than the Creator."

One of the most devoted men of God in Scripture had to be reprimanded twice on this point. John was the apostle of love, noted for his teaching on love and his deep bond of love with Jesus. In the concluding line of his letter which we know as 1 John, he penned these words: "Dear children, keep yourselves from idols." Who would suspect that John himself would soon come up short in resisting idolatry?

Late in his life, while in exile on the island of Patmos, he was given the visions recorded in the book of Revelation, visions filled with angels throughout. After one ecstatic scene of heavenly worship at the wedding supper of the Lamb (Revelation 19), a guiding angel turned to John and asked him to write these words: "Blessed are those who are invited to the wedding supper of the Lamb!" The angel added, "These are the true words of God."

At once, John "fell at his feet *to worship him.*"

The angel's rebuke was quick: "Do not do it! I am a fellow servant with you and with your brothers who hold to the testimony of Jesus. *Worship God!*" (19:10).

But this temptation is dangerous enough that we'll see John warned about it once more. In the climax of his visions, an angel showed and described to John the heavenly New Jerusalem and its inexpressible glory. "These words are trustworthy and true," the angel said to him (22:6). John also heard Christ's promise to come soon. Then again we read John's honest account:

> I, John, am the one who heard and saw these things. And when I
> had heard and seen them, I fell down *to worship* at the feet of the
> angel who had been showing them to me.
>
> But he said to me, "Do not do it! I am a fellow servant with you
> and with your brothers the prophets and of all who keep the words
> of this book. *Worship God!*" (22:8-9)

John's weakness on this point is a good reminder of how easy it is to sin through idolatry. Worshiping angels is as wrong as giving control of our lives to anything or anyone else other than God. Angel worship is no more acceptable to God than the worship of money or power or self-indulgence. The Lord says, "You shall have *no other gods* before me."

We're to cultivate the same devotion to him that the writer of Psalm 73 attained. He could say to God, "Whom have I *in heaven* but you? And earth has nothing I desire besides you" (73:25-26). Can you pray these same words in all honesty?

Most of us find John's fall into angel-worship quite understandable. Who would not be tempted to fall down before these majestic beings, especially after seeing all that John had seen them do in Revelation. The sight of God's true angels must be awe-inspiring beyond anything we can imagine. Perhaps one reason angels are almost always invisible is so that we won't be tempted to do what John did. We're tempted enough as it is to worship the work of our own hands. What would we do if we saw angels every day?

But even if we could see them, angels pale into insignificance in relation to a glimpse of God. A. W. Tozer helps us see the comparison:

> Forever God stands apart, in light unapproachable. He is as high
> above an archangel as above a caterpillar, for the gulf that separates
> the archangel from the caterpillar is but finite, while the gulf between
> God and the archangel is infinite. The caterpillar and the archangel,
> though far removed from each other in the scale of created things,
> are nevertheless one in that they are alike created. They both belong

in the category of that-which-is-not-God and are separated from God by infinitude itself.

Such majestic beings as angels can help lift our eyes from this troubled and temporal earth. But they are meant to draw our gaze to the Lord, not to themselves. All glory is due to God, and he has no intention of sharing it with angels. Angels deserve no more worship than caterpillars.

We, too, are spiritual beings, and as we go honestly and carefully into a deeper study of angels, our spirits cannot help but experience the desire to worship. So as we go on, if you remember any words at all that you've heard angels speak in Scripture, remember especially these two:

Worship God!

Chapter Four

THE ANGELS AND GOD

W E'VE SEEN SOMETHING now of what angels do in the Bible. Impressive, I'm sure you'll agree. But you might ask, what evidence is there (and you hope there's plenty) that angels are still doing all those things today?

The right starting place for answering that question is to look closely at the character of God himself. God had his reasons for creating angels. And just like his reasons for creating you and me, those reasons spring from *who God is*.

Communication Channels

As we prepare for that closer look at God, let's first tighten up a bit our understanding of what we mean when we speak of "angels." A basic, stripped-down definition of angels is that they are spirit beings from outside this world.

Within that loose meaning are two broad categories of angels: good and bad. The good ones we call God's angels. They have always served and obeyed him, and always will. The bad ones are fallen angels — Satan and his demons. They are evil spirits who disobeyed God and continue to do so. They have a story all their own, one we can learn much from. We'll look at it later. Until we do, when we speak of "angels" here we mean only the good kind.

In the Bible, our English word "angel" translates the Hebrew word *mal'ak* in the Old Testament and the Greek word *angelos* in the New. The core meaning of both those words is *messenger.* That's the essence of who and what angels are. They are couriers for Someone other than themselves. They're Someone else's ambassadors, Someone else's agents. They represent only him, and never themselves. They are channels to carry only his information. They speak and act according to his instructions and they bear his authority.

The next time you read a Scripture passage about them, try substituting the word *messenger* for *angel* to get a good feel for this crucial aspect of their essence. Apart from God, angels can do nothing and are nothing. Their very food and drink is to do his will and accomplish his work. And God's will and work for angels is to *communicate his messages,* both by what they say and what they do.

They are *his* messengers. When they give us strength or enlightenment, it is God's strength or enlightenment that they impart. Their encouragement is God's encouragement. Their guidance is God's guidance. Their protection is God's protection. When they bring comfort, it is God's comfort they offer. And when they bring wrath, it is God's wrath they inflict.

That's why the right understanding of angels must go back to God's character. God himself is a communicator. *Word* is one of his right and proper names: "In the beginning was the Word ... and the Word was God" (John 1:1). God "reveals his thoughts to man," the prophet Amos says (Amos 4:13). God makes himself known. He's always talking to you and to me. "The whole Bible supports this idea," writes A. W. Tozer:

> God is speaking. Not God spoke, but *God is speaking.* He is, by his nature, continuously articulate. He fills the world with his speaking voice.

Angels are only one of many ways he does this. He has also communicated through human messengers: "In the past God *spoke* to our forefathers *through the prophets* at many times and in various ways" (Hebrews 1:1). Our Scriptures are the living and active record of those past prophecies from God. We also hear God calling in the life of Jesus Christ: "In these last days he has *spoken* to us by his Son" (Hebrews 1:2).

Even the sky above is a 3-D screen showing God's constant communication: "The heavens *declare* the glory of God; the skies *proclaim* the work of his hands. Day after day they pour forth *speech.*..." (Psalm 19:1-2). In fact the same stream of divine expression comes through unceasingly in all of nature. It's so steady and continual that those who miss the message are "without a rag of excuse," as J. B. Phillips words it in his paraphrase of Romans 1:19-20.

> It is not that they do not know the truth about God; indeed he has made it quite plain. For since the beginning of the world the invisible attributes of God, e.g., his eternal power and deity, have been plainly discernible through things which he has made....

Nature is God's mouthpiece; the design reflects the Designer. And since true science is the observation and understanding of nature, science's full and proper purpose is to point us toward God.

Angels have a wonderfully unique role in God's communication, yet their work is interwoven with these other ways in which he speaks. How we got the book of Revelation is a good picture of this. We're told that God revealed the book's message to Jesus. Jesus then revealed it to a human messenger (the apostle John), but he did it *through an angel.* Lastly, John revealed the message by recording it in the book we now read in the back of our Bibles.

So the sequence here was:

God → Jesus → angel → John → Scripture → you and me.

Look carefully to see if you catch all that in the opening lines of Revelation:

The revelation of Jesus Christ, which God gave him to show his servants.... He made it known by *sending his angel* to his servant John, who testifies to everything he saw — that is, the word of God and the testimony of Jesus Christ.

The majestic ending of Revelation makes the same point. First the angel tells John,

These words are trustworthy and true. The Lord, the God of the spirits of the prophets, *sent his angel* to show his servants the things that must soon take place. (22:6)

Then we hear these words from Jesus himself:

I, Jesus, have *sent my angel* to give you this testimony for the churches. I am the Root and the Offspring of David, and the bright Morning Star. (22:16)

As messengers, angels had a special part in giving us the Old Testament. Both Stephen and Paul speak of the Old Testament law as being "put into effect through angels" (Acts 7:53, Galatians 3:19), and the writer of Hebrews calls it "the message spoken by angels" (2:2). Apparently a huge number of angels were involved. When Moses remembers how God came to Mount Sinai to give him the law, he says God arrived "with myriads of holy ones" (Deuteronomy 33:2). Both *myriad* and *holy ones* are words often used in the Bible in connection with angels. *Myriad* can mean ten thousand or simply an exceedingly vast number, and *holy ones* reflects the purity of the angels' devotion to God.

Angels are just as prominent in the New Testament. We'll see that especially when we study their role in the earthly life of Jesus, as well as in Revelation.

So God is always communicating in a multitude of ways, and his angels play a big part.

Of course you and I are also communicators. So are the people you most enjoy being around. Suppose you received a letter today from a favorite friend who's far away. What would you do with it first? Would you stare at the stationery for hours, to analyze and admire it? Would you obtain a chemical analysis of the ink, to learn exactly what it's made of? Would you investigate where the paper came from, and how it was woven and cut?

No — paper and ink are simply the means of your friend's communication. What you're interested in is your *friend* and your friend's *message*. The paper and ink fully serve their intended purpose by simply bringing that personal message to you.

The same logic applies in our approach to angels. Angels are just a means of communication from the God who communicates. Through what angels say and do, God personally expresses his friendship to us and his fatherhood and much more. What's important is the message angels bring — not the messengers themselves.

To a Deeper Love for Christ

Remember, however, that angels are always *one-way* messengers. They are God's messengers to us, and never our messengers to God. No one in Scripture ever prays to an angel, and neither should we. They are not go-betweens or mediators between us and heaven.

They are not mediators because there is Another who already fulfills that role — and praise God for that! "For there is one God and *one mediator* between God and men, *the man Christ Jesus*" (1 Timothy 2:5). Christ's mediation brings us what any mediation of angels could never begin to accomplish: the freedom and eternal salvation of our souls. "Christ is the mediator of a new covenant, that those who are called may receive the promised eternal inheritance — now that he has died as a ransom to set them free" (Hebrews 9:15).

That's why in the New Testament the mention of angels is so completely dominated by a focus on the excellence of Christ in every way.

Now that angels have been on our minds so much, this New Testament focus is a perfect stimulus for letting angels lead us to a deeper love for Christ. Come along with me through a few of these angel passages, and keep asking yourself: How well does my own devotion and esteem for Christ and his gospel match up with what's being taught here?

Paul is so struck by Christ's unconquerable love that by comparison he lumps angels together with demons, as well as "anything else in all creation." He exclaims that none of these "will be able to separate us from the love of God that is *in Christ Jesus* our Lord" (Romans 8:38-39).

Paul's commitment to the gospel of Christ is great enough that by contrast he is ready to invoke a curse upon angels. Listen to his intensity:

> But even if we or *an angel from heaven* should preach a gospel other than the one we preached to you, let him be eternally condemned! As we have already said, so now I say again: If anybody is preaching to you a gospel other than what you accepted, let him be eternally condemned! (Galatians 1:8)

If you think such a harsh attitude toward angels is too extreme, remember that Paul is willing to apply the same curse to himself (as well as to "anybody" else) if ever he should fail to stay true to Christ's gospel. Absolutely everything is at stake in our answer to the good news. To be right with God through Christ is heaven; by comparison, to be right only with an angel is hell.

Paul proclaims how God raised Christ and seated him "in the heavenly realms, far above *all rule and authority, power and dominion*" (Ephesians 1:20-21). In those heavenly realms he surely had in view the glorious ranks of angels — powerful and stately, yet so very far below Christ.

When Paul tells us to set our minds and hearts "on things above" in Colossians 3:1-2, he points out specifically that heaven is "where Christ is." Angels are there too, but Paul doesn't put them in the spotlight. It's Christ who can make us heavenly minded, not angels. When Paul later warns against worshiping angels, in the same breath he reminds us that "reality...is found *in Christ*" (Colossians 1:17-18).

In Philippians 2:9-10 he tells us that God exalted Christ

> to the highest place and gave him the name that is above every name, that at the name of Jesus every knee should bow, *in heaven* and on earth and under the earth.

Angels, men, and demons must all alike bend the knee someday to acknowledge the glory and supremacy of Jesus. (Have you done so today?)

The most extensive treatment of angels in the entire Bible stretches over the first two chapters in the book of Hebrews. But the whole discussion makes one resounding point—Christ is utterly superior to angels. With reason after reason, the author drives his message home:

- God calls Jesus his Son, a title angels never wear. (1:4-5)
- God commands angels to worship Jesus. (1:6)
- God gives Jesus a solid eternal throne from which to rule as King, while the work of angels is like fleeting breezes or flickering flames. (1:7-8)
- Jesus knows more gladness than angels. God set him high above his companions (the angels) by anointing him with "the oil of joy." (1:9)
- Jesus himself created the world—a temporal world with an appointed end. Meanwhile he himself stays unchanged and eternal, highly honored by God, and with all his enemies crouched underfoot. Angels, on the other hand, are only servant spirits whose job is to wait upon the human beings rescued from that temporal world. (1:10-14)
- In the world to come it isn't angels who'll be in charge, but Jesus. (2:5-9)

On this foundation the author of Hebrews moves on to a more subtle point in the heart of chapter 2. It dawns on us with breathtaking fitness. The author has earlier stated that angels are spirits, and are like wind and fire.

Now he reminds us that Jesus for a short time was made "a little lower than the angels" — he embodied himself in human form. He who is eternal Spirit was instead given "flesh and blood" like men and women, and in so doing "he shared in their humanity." He was made "like" us — "in every way."

It was in that human body that "he suffered when he was tempted."

And it was in that body that he would "taste death."

As spirits, angels cannot bleed or die. Christ could, and did — for you and for me.

And for you and for me, it's that distinction between Christ and angels that makes an eternity of difference. For by it, Christ was able "to destroy him who holds the power of death — that is, the devil" (2:14).

Angel Stairway

But don't let me mislead you into writing angels off. All this discussion is not to put down angels, but to exalt Christ. And that's a necessary step. Nothing in all creation can truly be understood aright until seen in proper relationship to Christ. Exalting Jesus will not make us shrug off angels. No, it will allow us to really comprehend angels, and to actually receive their best help.

One more sketch from Scripture will help root this rich perspective of Christ and the angels even deeper in our hearts. Remember the dream the man Jacob had the night he slept on the ground with a rock for his pillow? In that dream

> he saw a stairway resting on the earth, with its top reaching to heaven, and *the angels of God were ascending and descending on it.* There above it stood the Lord. (Genesis 28:12-13)

Nineteen centuries later, near the Jordan River, Jesus was having a first conversation with a few men who someday would be his apostles to the world. "I tell you the truth," he told them, "you shall see heaven open, and *the angels of God ascending and descending on the Son of man*" (John 1:51). His words would easily bring to their minds Jacob's dream. But instead of a stairway, Christ spoke of himself. What did he mean?

Perhaps the meaning of our Lord's words will not come fully alive until we see him return from heaven "in his glory, and all the angels with him" (Matthew 25:31). But in the interplay between those Scriptures in John and Genesis, John Calvin found this clue: "that it is solely by the intercession of Christ that the ministry of angels extends to us."

Even now angels may come and go between heaven and earth only by way of Christ. Solely in obedience to his will are they sent to serve us. His own ministry to us, his plans for us, and his protection of us are the busy stairway they use in their daily diligence of attending to our needs.

Lord of Heaven's Armies

God is the Great Communicator, speaking to us through Christ, through whom also the angels are sent to serve us. God sends the angels to show us his love for us, and his power.

To help us understand this he identifies with angels in a special way— through one of his names.

More than 250 times in the Bible, God calls himself "the Lord of Hosts," meaning "the Lord of Heavenly Armies." The Hebrew term is *Yahweh Seba'ot*. Occasionally in the King James Version it's given as "Lord Sabaoth." Many modern English translations render the name as "the Lord Almighty" to rightly help us focus on the power it implies—God sovereignly commands all the forces of heaven. But perhaps a little is lost in that translation. Keeping the word "hosts" brings quicker to mind the innumerable and powerful angels who make up heaven's armies. It's as if God wants us to envision those robust ranks of troops whenever we hear him called by that name.

This name instantly gives us a royal and military picture of the Lord leading his celestial soldiers. One day soon we'll surely think of this name again and shout it in praise "when the Lord Jesus is revealed from heaven in blazing fire with his powerful angels" (2 Thessalonians 1:7).

Interestingly enough, this name for God seems to be used most often in Old Testament books where overt angelic activity is less prominent. It's as if God wanted his people to especially remember the angels at his instant command even when these heavenly beings weren't being seen or heard from.

In the New Testament the Greek version of the name "Lord of Hosts" is used in James 5:4 in a frightful warning to the rich who hoard their wealth. This passage, too, looks ahead to the time of Christ's return with his angels. But notice how it recalls the judgment and wrath they will bring, rather than redemption:

> Look! The wages you failed to pay the workmen who mowed your fields are crying out against you. The cries of the harvesters have reached the ears of the *Lord of Hosts.* You have lived on earth in luxury and self-indulgence. You have fattened yourselves in *the day of slaughter.*

The appearance of the Lord and his fighting forces will be overwhelming enough for everyone, but a terrifying sight indeed for the wicked. Until then, he wants us all to bear the picture in mind.

With all the evil occurring today, it's easy to wonder if God has lost control. If this world is going to hell in a handbasket, can't somebody do something about it? But even in times of apparent chaos, the Lord of Hosts is still in charge. The Lord of the Armies is still the Sovereign God, the ultimate Victor, our Captain of Salvation. And he and I are on the same side. That gives me comfort.

At the same time it inspires in me a great reverence, which is something the angels won't let us forget.

Both Near and Far Away

When you ponder angels in Scripture you quickly lock in on two things: majesty and awe. The majesty is always there in who they are, and the awe is constantly inspired in the people who are exposed to them.

We know the source of this is not the angels themselves, but God. His majesty and his capacity to inspire awe far surpass theirs. His glory is exalted *"above the heavens,"* the psalmist announces. "Who is like the Lord our God, the One who sits enthroned on high, who *stoops down to look on the heavens and the earth?"* (Psalm 113:4-6). In a real sense God looks downward even upon heaven where the angels are. They, too, are merely his creation.

In fact, the more we think about it, the more we experience two separate and conflicting reactions to this image of God as the Lord of Hosts, the Lord of angel armies. We're glad to think of such powerful help available on our behalf. What a privilege it is that God would come down from heaven and intervene for us.

But just to visualize such a scene of holy splendor and unearthly force only emphasizes our own smallness and weakness and unworthiness. Suddenly, with more clarity than ever, we can see how much mightier and holier he is than we've imagined. He's so different and distant from us.

Yes, he comes — but even in his coming, he creates a bigger gap. We see how close God draws, but also how far apart from us he remains. He's always near, yet always far. It's a mystery to our souls!

The angels only accent the paradox. How gracious and thrilling it is that they come to us with the Lord's messages, opening a window for us into God and his heaven. Yet the very sight of them causes even the best of people to shrink back in fear, thinking only of the great gulf between God and themselves.

Isaiah is one of those who had that experience, and his account of it is one of the most awesome passages in Scripture.

It was "in the year that King Uzziah died" (6:1). The long, eventful reign of that remarkable monarch had come to an end. But Isaiah got a glimpse of a greater King. He says he saw "the Lord seated on a throne, high and exalted."

Above him, Isaiah saw glorious angelic beings called seraphs. These seraphs had to cover their faces with their wings, for even they could not gaze straight at God's glory. Isaiah heard them calling, "Holy, holy, holy is the Lord of Hosts." They gave triple emphasis to the fact that God is separate and set apart over all else. Theologians like to call this God's "transcendence." He is holy and high and exalted, forever above and beyond and outside all his creation.

And yet Isaiah also heard these seraphs cry out, "The whole earth is full of his glory." Somehow this Holy God is also actively present in all of his creation. This is what theologians call God's "immanence."

Both God's transcendence and his immanence are always true at the same time. In our limited human thinking we tend to lean first one way and then the other as we think about God. But in reality the two are always in perfect balance — he is always near, and he is always far.

> "Am I only a God nearby," declares the Lord, "and not a God far away? Can anyone hide in secret places so that I cannot see him?" declares the Lord. "Do not I fill heaven and earth?" declares the Lord. (Jeremiah 23:23-24)

Paul instructed the wise men in the marketplace of Athens on the same point: "The God who made the world and everything in it is *the Lord of heaven and earth*," he said, "and does not live in temples built by hands." God is above and beyond all that. But this same God, Paul went on to say, *"is not far* from each one of us. For in him we live and move and have our being" (Acts 17:22-28).

Angels, too, come near, and yet also keep their distance. They're like that because of the One who created them and who designs their work. They can be as winsome as serving baked bread to Elijah or helping Daniel to his feet. They can be as repellent as a flaming sword to shut out man and woman from their perfect garden.

So — back to this chapter's original question: Today, do angels still do all that the Bible shows them doing in the past?

I see no biblical reason why they cannot and will not, because God has not changed. He still communicates. He is near to us. He is our Savior and our loving Father. "He who did not spare his own Son, but gave him up for us all — how will he not also, along with him, graciously give us *all things?*" (Romans 8:32). Surely that "all things" must include angels.

But their services can never be summoned by you or me, and their presence can never be predicted. They're as near as they've ever been, but they're also just as far away.

It's a mystery. In fact, mystery saturates this whole topic. But mystery is good and healthy for us, and maybe more now than ever. So many Christians today are lacking in awe and a sense of mystery when they consider the things of God. We think we have as much of him figured out as is practical and approachable—and isn't the rest only small potatoes anyway? My prayer is that this presumption will start to be corrected as we gain respect for the secrets surrounding God's angels.

God hasn't told us everything about them, and never will. Even what he *has* revealed can't be entirely comprehended by us, because of our mental and spiritual limitations. But the treasures he has shown us are there to be discovered and possessed. "The secret things belong to the Lord our God, but the things revealed belong to us and to our children forever" (Deuteronomy 29:29).

Chapter Five

WHAT ANGELS ARE

WHAT EXACTLY *are* angels, anyway? What are they made of, where did they come from, where do they stay? How are they like me? How are they different? If an angel should appear — if I should somehow become acquainted with one — what should I expect?

With so much misinformation accumulating today on the subject of angels, let's go back and begin where the Bible begins.

Angels are first of all *created beings* — like you and me, and like caterpillars, as we noted earlier. They are not the result of the Big Bang. They did not come about in the hierarchy of some evolutionary process. God made angels.

And just like you and me and the caterpillar, angels were made *in* Christ and *through* Christ and *for* Christ. In Colossians 1:16 we read that "*all things were created*" with those same intricate connections to God the Son. Christ was the *cause* of all created things, he was the *way* and the *means* in which they were fashioned, and he is the *purpose* for their very existence. For all created things, he is the where from, he is the how, and he is the why. Christ is their King and Master, just as he is ours.

But is there any reason to believe Paul was thinking beyond earthly creation in this passage? Did he really have angels in mind, any more than caterpillars?

Evidently so. In the same verse Paul rushes into an overview of what he's including:

> ...things *in heaven* and on earth, visible and *invisible,* whether thrones or powers or rulers or authorities; *all things* were created by him [by Christ], and for him.

In this deeply bonded created order, Paul takes care to include what is heavenly and invisible. Those characteristics definitely fit angels, as we'll soon see. Paul's purpose in including them here may well have been to counter the spread of angel worship in the Colossian church which he refers to later (2:18). He knew that a focus on Christ is the corrective for all drifting.

Angels apparently have no problem going astray by worshiping each other. They know better. They know they were created only by the Lord's will and pleasure. Angelic beings themselves declare this while worshiping God in Revelation 4.

> They lay their crowns before the throne and say:
> "You are worthy, our Lord and God,
>   to receive glory and honor and power,
> for *you created all things,*
>   and by your will they were created
>   and have their being."

In those last four words these angelic creations confess a further truth: Only by God's will and pleasure does their existence continue even now. This, too, is as true of us as of angels: Why we were born is the same reason as why we're still kept alive, and that reason is wrapped up in the will and pleasure of God.

This foundational fact demands one simple response above all: praise to God. Psalm 148 begins by calling on everything in the "heavens" and "the heights above" — specifically including sun, moon, stars, *and angels* — to give God praise. "Let them praise the name of the Lord, *for he commanded and they were created.*" This, too, is as true for us as for angels and stars. The angels and stars are continually and joyfully meeting this requirement of praise. How about you?

Created for Us

But *why* would God create these troops of heavenly messengers when he certainly doesn't need them? As Calvin says, "Whenever he pleases, he passes them by, and performs his own work by a single nod."

So Calvin comes to this conclusion: In creating angels, God must have had *our* interests in mind. God employs angels simply as "a help to our weakness," in order to "elevate our hopes or strengthen our confidence."

Calvin admits that God's offer of his own personal protection ought to be enough for us. He says it's "improper" for us "still to look round for help." He adds, however, that if God in his "infinite goodness and indulgence" chooses to provide angels for our weakness, "it would ill become us to overlook the favor."

His conclusion reflects the teaching of Hebrews 1:14, a verse we keep coming back to: Angels are "ministering spirits sent to serve those who will inherit salvation." Angels are here for us.

Angels aren't named in the creation account in Genesis 1, where the narrative focuses on visible creation. Their omission in that passage could be another indication that angels are not under human authority. In the climax of creation week, God gave mankind the privilege and responsibility of ruling "over the fish of the sea and the birds of the air, over the livestock, over all the earth, and over all the creatures that move along the ground" (Genesis 1:26). But that list doesn't include angels. We can herd cattle and cage canaries and grow cantaloupe and cauliflower in our gardens, but we can't make angels do our laundry or warm up the car.

Created in the Beginning

When did God create angels?

The Lord told Job that angels were already on the scene to celebrate when the earth was created. He asks Job in 38:4, "Where were you when I laid the earth's foundation?" Job, of course, wasn't around, so for his benefit God adds a few details of what that ground-breaking was like: It was "while the morning stars sang together and all the angels shouted for joy" (38:7). Job wasn't there when the earth was formed, but the angels were, and having a good time of it too.

Therefore angels were made apparently before the third day of the creation week, the day when God gathered waters into seas and the dry land appeared (Genesis 1:9-10).

Psalm 104 seems to reflect the same timing for the angels' appearance. It's a psalm praising God's greatness for how he made and sustains all creation. In richly poetic imagery, the opening lines give a broad overview of what God created. The psalm seems to follow the same sequence as in Genesis 1: first of all light, then the heavens and the gathering of heavenly waters, then the land, seas, animals, and man.

Coming along naturally in this procession is verse four which reads, "He makes winds his messengers, flames of fire his servants." These lines often are taken as referring to angels. That's the way the New Testament writer quotes them in Hebrews 1:7. And in Psalm 104, this reference to angels comes immediately before the first mention of the earth in verse five: "He set the earth on its foundations."

Creation scientist Dr. Henry Morris is my good friend and a member of our church, and he believes angels were formed on the second day of creation. He points to Psalm 104 and its implication that angels came as "the next act after the creation of the space-time cosmos and the establishment of God's light-arrayed throne therein." Very likely the angels are older than anything in the world as we see it.

In one of Daniel's visions in Babylon, he saw God (whom he called "the Ancient of Days") on a flaming throne surrounded by angelic beings: *"Thousands upon thousands attended him; ten thousand times ten thousand stood before him"* (Daniel 7:10).

The same language is echoed in John's vision of God's throne in Revelation 5:11.

> Then I looked and heard the voice of many angels, numbering *thousands upon thousands, and ten thousand times ten thousand.* They encircled the throne....

Taken literally, "ten thousand times ten thousand" angels would be a hundred million of them. That's enough to fill the California Angels' baseball stadium in Anaheim for every home game for nearly twenty years, without anyone going back a second time.

In using such numbers the Scriptures are probably describing simply an inexpressibly large host, far more angels than any of us could look at and count. That's not to say *God* doesn't know their number. The Scriptures say he's counted the hairs on our head (Matthew 10:30). And he's numbered and named all the stars (Psalm 147:4) and knows that "not one of them is missing" (Isaiah 40:26). If he's calculated totals for the stars and our hair, he surely has the angels tallied.

Since a certain portion of the angels became fallen angels along with Satan, some Bible scholars have speculated that perhaps every place in heaven vacated by a fallen angel will be filled in eternity by a redeemed human being. That would bring heaven's population back to its original number when the angels were first formed.

Angels Are Heavenly

Angels — the good angels, that is — definitely call God's heaven their home. We see this especially in the gospels and the book of Revelation. The one who ministered to Jesus while he prayed in Gethsemane is called "an angel *from heaven*" (Luke 22:43). Three days later an angel "came down *from heaven*" to roll back the stone guarding his tomb (Matthew 28:2). Jesus himself refers often to "angels *in heaven*" (Matthew 18:10, 22:30, 24:36). The angels who announced his birth are called "the *heavenly* host" (Luke 2:13), and when they left the shepherds they returned "into *heaven*" (2:15).

Heaven is their dwelling place because angels belong exclusively to God. The best definition of heaven is that it's God's dwelling place. "*Heaven is my throne,*" God says in Isaiah 66:1, and that is where angels work and live. If you tend to picture angels going through life lounging on fluffy clouds or cruising from star to star, you've missed a big truth. They inhabit the throne-room of God, because they belong to God.

Jesus specifically referred to them as *God's* angels (Luke 12:8-9, 15:10). He promised the disciples that when they saw "heaven open," they would also see "the angels *of God*" ascending and descending on himself (John 1:51).

Because Jesus is God, he also referred to the angels as belonging to himself, especially when he spoke of his return to earth and his coming judgment (Matthew 13:41, 16:27, 24:31).

The holy angels — the good angels — belong only to the God of the Bible, and therefore to his heaven. They do not belong to earth or to any earthly religion or philosophy.

Angels Are Spirit Beings

Someone once asked me, "Do you know why angels can fly?" I said, "No. Why?" He answered, "Because they take themselves lightly."

In a way he's right. Angels are spirit beings, without permanent material bodies to haul around. They are specifically called "ministering *spirits*" (Hebrews 1:14).

So each angel is a *spirit*. But what does that mean?

A. W. Tozer defines the word this way:

Spirit means existence on a level above and beyond matter; it means life subsisting in another mode. Spirit is substance that has no weight, no dimension, no size nor extension in space. These qualities belong to matter and can have no application to spirit. Yet spirit has true being and is objectively real.

Angels are real, but without material substance as we think of it. They apparently have no physical nature, no breath or blood. If they occupy some form of permanent bodies, these would be spiritual bodies, perhaps like the ones we'll wear someday in eternity (1 Corinthians 15:44). The angels do not marry, as we saw earlier from Jesus' words, and do not procreate.

You and I are spiritual beings too. But unlike angels, we're also physical beings. And unfortunately, here on earth our physical nature tends to overshadow our spiritual nature.

It must be their spiritual nature — as well as their spiritual holiness — that allows angels the continual proximity to God they enjoy, for in this they are like God. Jesus said, "God is spirit, and his worshipers must worship in spirit and in truth" (John 4:24).

Spirit Beings — Yet Limited

But we can't assume that the spiritual nature of angels is identical to God's spiritual nature. Some theologians even say that although angels don't have material bodies in comparison to man, they *do* have material bodies in comparison to God, for God's self-existent spirituality is on such a higher level than theirs. Here we come again to more mystery surrounding angels.

In their spiritual state, angels have many limitations that God can never have. For example, angels cannot be in more than one place at once, unlike God, who is everywhere at once. Only God is infinite in his whereabouts; he is *omnipresent*. David's awe-struck confession to God in Psalm 139 is that no matter where he went or imagined himself to go, *"You* are there."

Angels are also limited in knowledge. Jesus said the angels don't know the time of his second coming to the world, and that this was knowledge even he himself did not possess while on earth (Matthew 24:36, Mark 13:32). But God in heaven always knows "the end from the beginning," and can communicate his plans to whomever he chooses (Isaiah 46:10). He is *omniscient,* all-knowing, infinite in knowledge.

Angels are also limited in power, though their power is indeed staggering to behold. In Revelation 7:1, we see how only four of them can stand and hold back destructive winds ready to rip across the earth. Three times in Revelation John says he saw a *"mighty* angel." The one in 18:21 "picked up a boulder the size of a large millstone and threw it into the sea."

The force of the angels in unleashing destruction and violence is especially evident in Revelation as Christ opens the seven seals. In case you hear of anyone rejecting this destructive picture because it's inconsistent with Jesus' teachings on peace and gentleness and love, point out to them that as Christ opens these seals, he's always described as "the Lamb." People who like soft, delicate angels are usually after a soft, delicate God as well. God is never that way, however, and neither are his heavenly servants.

But powerful as angels are, they are not all-powerful like God. They have no force of their own, and are impotent without God. They can exercise only the energy God channels through them. They operate within the divine allowance that A. W. Tozer describes so carefully:

> God has delegated power to his creatures, but being self-sufficient, he cannot relinquish anything of his perfections and, power being one of them, he has never surrendered the least iota of his power. He gives but he does not give away. All that he gives remains his own and returns to him again. Forever he must remain what he has forever been, the Lord God *omnipotent.*

As Jesus stood before Pilate awaiting the sentence of crucifixion, he told the governor, "You would have no power over me if it were not given you from above" (John 19:11). The same is as true of angels as of men. Angels would have no power if it were not given them from above. And what they have been given is limited.

Angels can face struggles. The angel who spoke with Daniel mentioned being "detained" by an encounter with what was apparently a demonic ruler, and he said the angel Michael "came to help me." Apparently this angel needed the archangel Michael's assistance to overcome the evil power he met.

God, and God alone, is infinite in power. The angel Gabriel said it best: "*Nothing* is impossible with God" (Luke 1:37).

Another mystery is how the holiness of angels is also limited and lesser than God's. We see this in the fact that some angels fell along with Satan from their original state of goodness. But God will always be perfectly holy, just, righteous, and loving. He is infinite in goodness. "Taste and see that the Lord is good" (Psalm 34:8). Jesus tells us, "Your heavenly Father is perfect" (Matthew 5:48).

In a dramatic scene in Revelation 5 we glimpse the limitation of angels in both power and holiness. Angels in splendor are circled around God's throne. God himself holds in his right hand the scroll with writing on both sides, sealed with the seven seals. A "mighty angel" shouts, "Who is worthy to break the seals and open the scroll?" Surely one of the majestic angels would be deserving of this task. "But *no one in heaven or on earth or under the earth* could open the scroll or even look inside it." Only the Lamb — Jesus Christ — is worthy of that. Angels were no more worthy of this honor than you or I, or the inhabitants of hell.

Spirit Beings — Like Wind

Angels are described in Scripture as being like "winds" and like "flames of fire" (Psalm 104:4, Hebrews 1:7). Wind and fire may be the best things on earth to help us picture the spiritual make-up of angels.

The word *wind* brings to mind their spiritual nature. In both Hebrew and Greek the words for "spirit" can also mean "breath" or "wind." And even when the words are translated "wind" as the Bible describes some breeze or storm, it's easy to imagine that maybe angels had something to do with it.

Sometimes the connection is stated and obvious, as in David's Psalm 18. He writes this about God sending angelic beings (called cherubim) to his rescue:

> He parted the heavens and came down;
>> dark clouds were under his feet.
> He mounted the cherubim and flew;
>> he soared on the wings of the *wind*.

David saw the wind and the angels together.

A thousand years later, Jesus told Nicodemus, "The *wind* blows wherever it pleases. You hear its sound, but you cannot tell where it comes from or where it is going" (John 3:8).

Then Jesus added, "So it is with everyone born of the Spirit." To that we might also add, "So it is with the angels." For angels are already spiritual beings attuned to God, and in at least that sense we become like them when we're born again.

Many Old Testament passages describe strong winds blowing on the day of God's judgment. These verses anticipate the judgment passages in Revelation, where angels are so active in accomplishing God's wrath. Remember how powerful we saw them in this work? In the verses below, think about angel power and see if you can imagine God sending angels to do the "blowing":

> When you cry out for help,
>> let your collection of idols save you!
> The *wind* will carry all of them off,
>> a mere breath will blow them away.

But the man who makes me his refuge

 will inherit the land and possess my holy mountain.

 (God's words in Isaiah 57:13)

Oh, the raging of many nations…!

Oh, the uproar of the peoples…!

Although the peoples roar like the roar of surging waters,

 when he rebukes them they flee far away,

driven before the *wind* like chaff on the hills,

 like tumbleweed before a gale.

In the evening, sudden terror!

 Before the morning, they are gone! (Isaiah 17:12-14)

The Lord will dry up

 the gulf of the Egyptian sea;

with a *scorching wind* he will sweep his hand

 over the Euphrates River. (Isaiah 11:15)

At that time this people and Jerusalem will be told, "A *scorching wind* from the barren heights in the desert blows toward my people…. Now I pronounce my judgments against them." (Jeremiah 4:11-12)

This is what the Sovereign Lord says: In my wrath I will unleash a *violent wind*, and in my anger hailstones and torrents of rain will fall with destructive fury. (Ezekiel 13:13)

Perhaps an angel worked up the storm that sent Jonah overboard and into a big fish's mouth: "The Lord sent a *great wind* on the sea, and such a violent storm arose that the ship threatened to break up" (Jonah 4:8).

It's even possible that the Holy Spirit commanded angels to provide the great noise heard on the birthday of the church — the day of Pentecost — when "a sound like the blowing of a *violent wind* came *from heaven*" (Acts 2:2).

We don't know for certain that angels were involved in all these situations, but it isn't hard to see how they could be.

Spirit Beings — Like Fire

"Flames of fire" are the other image we get of angels in Psalm 104 and Hebrews 1. Angels are connected with flames often enough in Scripture that you may want to pack along a fire extinguisher while we explore a few of these passages. Notice in how many different ways their fire is manifested.

You'll remember how the cherubim who guarded the gates of Eden were accompanied by "a flaming sword flashing back and forth."

Later, the angel of the Lord appeared to Moses "in flames of fire from within a bush" (Exodus 3:2).

The angel of God asked Gideon to prepare a sacrifice of meat and unleavened bread, and to set it on a rock. When the angel touched the tip of his staff to the sacrifice, "fire flared from the rock, consuming the meat and the bread. And the angel of the Lord disappeared" (Judges 6:20-21).

Manoah and his wife (the parents of Samson) were visited by an angel, and Manoah also offered a sacrifice on a rock that was then consumed by fire. "As the fire blazed up from the altar toward heaven, the angel of the Lord ascended in the flame" (Judges 13:19-21).

Isaiah saw a seraph flying toward him "with a live coal in his hand" (Isaiah 6:6).

The appearance of the cherubim whom Ezekiel saw "was like burning coals of fire or like torches. Fire moved back and forth among the creatures; it was bright, and lightning flashed out of it" (Ezekiel 1:13).

The angel that overwhelmed Daniel on the banks of the Tigris River had a face "like lightning" and eyes "like flaming torches" (Daniel 10:4-6).

In John's vision he saw an angel with "legs...like fiery pillars" (Revelation 10:1).

Perhaps one of the busiest creatures in heaven is the one John mentions in Revelation 14:18 — "another angel, who *had charge of the fire....*"

Where do the angels get all that fire?

From God, of course. "Our God is a *consuming fire*" (Hebrews 12:29). When the Lord met with Moses on Mount Sinai, it was "covered with smoke, because the Lord descended on it *in fire*" (Exodus 19:18). His fire gets our attention, so we'll listen: "Our God comes and will not be silent; *a fire devours* before him" (Psalm 50:3). The Lord once promised to be "*a wall of fire*" around his people (Zechariah 2:5). And now we look forward to the time "when the Lord Jesus is revealed from heaven *in blazing fire* with his powerful angels" (2 Thessalonians 1:7).

We associate fire with hell, and frequently think of flames as the devil's instrument. But hell is set afire by God and his angels, who will toss both Satan and all who belong to him into the torturing flames of "the lake of burning sulfur" (Revelation 20:10,15). Jesus speaks of "the eternal fire prepared for the devil and his angels" (Matthew 25:41). Hell's fire isn't something Satan devised for human beings; God prepared it for Satan.

Isaiah 66:15-16 gives a good preview of the coming fiery judgment. Here as in other Scriptures, the reference to "chariots" is probably a picture of angels. We see them associated once more with both wind and fire:

> See, the Lord is coming with *fire,*
>> and his chariots are like a *whirlwind;*
> he will bring down his anger with fury,
>> and his rebuke with *flames of fire.*
> For with *fire* and with his sword
>> the Lord will execute judgment upon all men,
>> and many will be those slain by the Lord.

Fire is God's tool, and he makes it the property of angels.

Spirit Beings — Like Stars

Yes, angels are spirit beings. But since they're called "flames of fire" and since Scripture sometimes associates angels with stars, is all this a hint that the substance of angels is more like that of stars — orbs of fire — than anything else?

That's a possibility put forward by my friend Henry Morris, who says,

> This concept is beyond our naturalistic comprehension, but that is no reason for us to reject or spiritualize it prematurely. We do not know the nature of angels. Man was made of the natural chemical elements and is therefore subject to the electromagnetic and gravitational forces which control these elements. But angels are not so bound. They can fly swiftly from God's throne to earth when God commands them and they are not limited by gravity or other natural forces.

Maybe he's on to something there. Often people today who report sighting an angel have described it in terms of a brilliant light or a luminescence they couldn't describe and had never seen before.

Certainly angels in Scripture are often associated with bright light. The angels at Jesus' tomb had "clothes that gleamed like lightning" (Luke 24:4). The angel that Cornelius saw wore "shining clothes" (Acts 10:30). When an angel came to get Peter out of jail, "a light shone in the cell" (Acts 12:7). In Revelation we read of an angel whose "face was like the sun" (10:1), and about seven angels dressed in "shining linen" (15:6).

It appears to be this particular aspect of angelic demeanor — their shining brilliance — that Satan tries to counterfeit. For Paul warns us that "Satan himself masquerades as an angel *of light*" (2 Corinthians 11:14). But as with their flame, so it is with their light — it's safe to say that whatever the glow surrounding angels, it comes straight from the light of God. When the angel appeared to Bethlehem shepherds to announce Christ's birth, "the *glory of the Lord* shone around them, and they were terrified" (Luke 2:9). It was the Lord's glory that was shining, not the angel's glory. Satan can never duplicate this. Only God's holy angels are truly "angels of light."

Now back to the stars. Take a look at a few places in Scripture where the angels are associated specifically with stars. Earlier we looked at Job 38:7, where God mentions angels looking on when he laid "earth's foundation"—

> ...while the morning stars sang together
> and all the angels shouted for joy...

If this refers to the third day of creation, then "the morning stars" could not be the lights we see in a clear night sky, since these weren't created until the fourth day. Instead it's more likely that "stars" here is another designation for the angels, joyfully singing over the works of God.

John says that in his vision,

> I saw a *star* that had fallen from the sky to the earth. The star was given the key to the shaft of the Abyss. When he opened the Abyss, smoke rose from it like the smoke from a gigantic furnace. (Revelation 9:1-2)

This star is generally interpreted as another of the angels in Revelation who are part of God's final, awful disclosure of his wrath against evil.

In Israel's war with the Canaanites, one dramatic battle against the commander Sisera was won only by supernatural intervention (Judges 4:15). After the battle, one line in Deborah's victory song goes like this:

> From the heavens *the stars fought,*
> from their courses they fought against Sisera. (5:20)

Perhaps this is a hint of warrior angels who assisted in the battle.

It could be that even the miraculous star that brought the wise men to Bethlehem was in actuality an angel, faithfully serving God in his appointed task of guiding worshipers to the newborn King.

Stars and Angels and Us

It's easy to imagine a peaceful scene for David in the Psalms in which the stars reminded him of angels. Perhaps he was lying on his back out on a hillside one clear night near his home in Bethlehem. (Maybe it was the same hill where shepherds would hear good news from an angel a thousand years later.)

As David looked up, inspiration came to him for a new song, a song that would someday become our Psalm 8.

First David sang his praise to God, whom he could imagine far out of sight, at a distance even beyond the stars:

> O Lord, our Lord,
>> how majestic is your name in all the earth!
>
> You have set your glory
>> *above the heavens.*

His voice continued ringing in a river of words as he addressed a searching question to God:

> When I consider your heavens, the work of your fingers,
>> the moon and the stars, which you have set in place,
>
> *what is man* that you are mindful of him,
>> the son of man that you care for him?

David had his mind on man, even as he gazed at the star-host shining from horizon to horizon. They made him think of angels — heavenly beings who were above him like the stars, and yet not so very far.

In the song's next line, he added another thought about man:

> You made him a little lower than the heavenly beings
>> and crowned him with glory and honor.

How amazed David was that the majestic God would bring his care and concern down to man. For David knew that angels and men are closer to each other than either of them is to the Holy God.

The stars, the angels, the quiet hillside, the deep questions for God— it's a wonderful scene to get lost in.

The clear night sky may be one of our best pictures right now of the host of angels arrayed like stars around God's throne-room, radiating praise and worship. Go outside some night soon, and put your focus in that direction, especially if earthly concerns and difficulties are weighing you down.

Gratefully accept the Lord's invitation in Isaiah 40:26 — "Lift up your eyes and look to the heavens," and remember the one "who created all these" and who "brings out the starry host one by one, and calls them each by name."

You might recall the example of Abraham from Genesis 15. Just as you and I often do, Abraham needed something. He asked God, "O Sovereign Lord, what can you give me?" (15:2) — which is a lot like our questions of "How can you fix this problem, God?" Or, "Lord, when will you get me out of this tight spot?" Or especially, "Father, when will you do what you promised?"

In response, God took Abraham outside under a blazing night sky. He said to Abraham, "Look up at the heavens and count the stars — if indeed you can."

Maybe that's a picture of how we should think of angels. We can't count them, any more than we can count the stars. (The stronger our telescopes, the more stars there are to count!)

But like David, we can see in those stars an amazing picture of God's care and concern for us. It's a love coming through not only by way of thousands or millions of angels whom God created to serve us, but also in a thousand or a million other ways as well. His grace is "one blessing after another" (John 1:16).

Look up at the stars and be amazed. Then trust God and find his reward, as Abraham did: "Abram believed the Lord, and the Lord credited it to him as righteousness" (15:6).

So the stars are a good reminder of angels, but also of something more.

The book of Revelation opens with John's vision of the glorified Jesus Christ. John saw Jesus holding something: "In his right hand he held seven *stars*" (1:16). What are these stars? Jesus himself tells us: "The mystery of the seven stars that you saw in my right hand ... is this: The seven stars are the *angels* of the seven churches" (1:20).

The next few pages in Revelation give us messages from Jesus Christ to each of these "seven churches," located in seven cities in Asia Minor where Christians were established. Each message is addressed identically: "To the *angel* of the church...." Who are these seven "angels," who are also pictured as seven stars?

The best explanation seems to be that they're the pastors leading and shepherding those seven churches. They're charged by the Lord Jesus with faithfully communicating his Word to the people in these seven churches. They were his messengers, his ambassadors.

In this sense, we too can be more like angels than we might have thought possible. For we, too, have been charged by the Lord Jesus with faithfully communicating his divine message — the gospel.

> God was reconciling the world to himself in Christ, not counting men's sins against them. And *he has committed to us the message of reconciliation.* We are therefore Christ's ambassadors, as though God were making his appeal through us. (2 Corinthians 5:19-20)

That's why we too can be like stars, as long as we don't let our grumbling selfishness get in the way of our testimony. Paul says it like this:

> Do everything without complaining or arguing, so that you may become blameless and pure, children of God without fault in a

crooked and depraved generation, in which *you shine like stars* in the
universe as you hold out the word of life…. (Philippians 2:14-16)

If you want to be like an angel — even to the extent of shining like a
star — then stop your grumbling and wrangling, and let God mold you into
a faithful sharer of the Word of Life. The world out there is dark, and des-
perately needs your starlight.

The next time you see a night sky charged with stars, think about
angels…and think about yourself.

Chapter Six

WHEN ANGELS
APPEAR

THERE'S NO WAY to fathom how often angels have been involved in your life. One may be at your side right now, helping you turn the pages of this book. (What an honor that would be for both of us!)

But we can't know for sure, because angels are mostly invisible. That can seem bothersome, but Billy Graham helps us see it in perspective:

> While angels may become visible by choice, our eyes are not constructed to see them ordinarily any more than we can see the dimensions of a nuclear field, the structure of atoms, or the electricity that flows through copper wiring. Our ability to sense reality is limited: The deer of the forest far surpass our human capacity in their keenness of smell. Bats possess a phenomenally sensitive built-in radar system. Some animals can see things in the dark that escape our attention. Swallows and geese possess sophisticated guidance systems that appear to border on the supernatural. So why should we think it strange if men fail to perceive the evidences of angelic presence?

Sometimes, though, angels show up in Scripture in ordinary human form. Gideon at first didn't seem to recognize the person standing before him as an angel (Judges 6:12-13). Nor did Samson's father, Manoah (Judges 13:16) — though Manoah's wife was quicker on the uptake. "A man of God came to me," she told her husband. "He looked like an angel of God, very awesome" (13:6).

When angels came to rescue Lot and his family from Sodom, Lot assumed they were only men as he greeted them, then invited them into his home and off the wretched streets of Sodom, and showered them with hospitality (Genesis 19:1-3).

Before rescuing Lot, these same heavenly beings had been calling on his famous uncle. "While he was sitting at the entrance to his tent in the heat of the day," the passage tells us, "Abraham looked up and saw three *men* standing nearby" (18:1-2). Abraham also lavished hospitality on these visitors whom he first perceived as men, and after they washed up they ate Sarah's cooking. But Abraham, the man of faith and the friend of God, seemed quicker to grasp the Lord's presence in these "men" than Lot was.

The New Testament implies that it's still possible to receive angelic visitors who appear to be only human. Remember that bit about this in Hebrews 13:2? We're told, "Do not forget to entertain strangers, for by so doing some people have entertained angels without knowing it." If you really believe in angels and would enjoy entertaining or honoring them (as a thank-you gesture perhaps for everything they do for you), consider improving your hospitality to strangers. Not until eternity will you know if any of them were angels, but the possibility anyway is exciting. (Of course, there's an even stronger motive for being gracious and giving to those you don't know well. Jesus said in Matthew 25:35, "I was a stranger and you took me in." If we respect and serve strangers, the Lord counts it as service done to *himself*.)

More frequent in Scripture than the undetected appearances of heavenly spirits are the times when there's no mistake about it: There's an angel on the scene.

Jacob was certain. He was heading home to the land of his grandfather Abraham and his father Isaac, when on the way, "the angels of God met him" (Genesis 32:1). And his response when he saw them? It was a shout: "This is the camp of God!" (32:2). Jacob still had some wrestling to do with the Lord, but his sensitivities were on the right track. He knew God was with him.

Daniel was even more certain about what he saw. His report in Daniel 10 of the awesome figure he saw on the riverbank has been called Scripture's most detailed description of an angel's appearance. Notice how much Daniel observed:

> I looked up and there before me was a man dressed in linen, with a belt of the finest gold around his waist. His body was like chrysolite [a yellow or golden stone], his face like lightning, his eyes like flaming torches, his arms and legs like the gleam of burnished bronze, and his voice like the sound of a multitude. (10:5-6)

You can tell Daniel took more than a brief look, and it's no wonder the experience drained him. "I had no strength left," he says; "my face turned deathly pale and I was helpless" (10:8). The squinting alone would have given anyone a headache.

We've already seen in lots of other Scriptures how angels appear in various degrees of light and fire and glory. But it's worth another dazzling look. Notice, for example, what's recorded about the color of their clothing after Jesus had risen from the dead:

The angel who rolled back the stone from Jesus' tomb had an appearance "like lightning, and his clothes were white as snow" (Matthew 28:3). As various women came to the tomb, the angels they saw are described as "a young man dressed in a white robe" (Mark 16:5), and "two angels in white" (John 20:12), and "two men in clothes that gleamed like lightning" (Luke 24:4).

Forty days later the angels on the ground when Jesus ascended into heaven appeared to the disciples as "two men dressed in white" (Acts 1:10).

Years later, the angelic and worshipful creatures whom John saw as twenty-four elders "were dressed in white and had crowns of gold on their heads" (Revelation 4:4).

The color white in Scripture is associated not only with purity but also with joy. "Eat your food with gladness, and drink your wine with a joyful heart," we're advised in Ecclesiastes 9:7-8, "for it is now that God favors what you do. *Always be clothed in white,* and always anoint your head with oil."

The soul-stirring fulfillment of that instruction for God's people is foretold in Revelation 7. In his vision John saw a countless multitude from among all the world's ethnic groups standing before God. "They were *wearing white robes* and were holding palm branches in their hands."

The angels joined in their joyful praise to God. Then one of those elders dressed in white told John that these human worshipers "have washed their robes and made them *white* in the blood of the Lamb" (7:14).

Joy was assured for this white-robed multitude, because the elder promised John that "God will wipe away every tear from their eyes" (7:17).

The whiteness gets even more dazzling as we picture the Lord's ride to final victory with his angels. Enjoy this scene with John:

> I saw heaven standing open and there before me was *a white horse, whose rider is called Faithful and True.* With justice he judges and makes war. His eyes are like blazing fire, and on his head are many crowns. He has a name written on him that no one knows but he himself. He is dressed in a robe dipped in blood, and his name is the Word of God. The armies of heaven were following him, *riding on white horses and dressed in fine linen, white and clean.* (Revelation 19:11-14)

Pure, snow-white joy is what awaits us as we share in the pure, snow-white victory of the Lord and his angels.

Our Eyes Opened to See Them

Getting a glimpse of angels doesn't depend solely on what form God happens to give them. Scripture lends support to the fact that the Lord must open our eyes before we can see them.

Sometimes in Scripture — as in the case with Daniel and his companions on the bank of the Tigris (Daniel 10) — one person could see the angel, but the people beside him couldn't.

And one time a donkey could see the angel, but the person riding him couldn't.

That was Balaam's donkey. The greater miracle in that story isn't so much a donkey getting to *talk* about an angel, but a man like Balaam getting to *see* an angel.

Remember the story? Balaam was internationally known as a diviner — part magician, part prophet, so to speak, and the king of curses and blessings. He was a "seer" — he was supposed to "see" what others couldn't. If anybody in the world should have been expected to spot angels, it was Balaam.

One day he was invited by the King Balak of Moab to call down curses on Israel. God communicated his thoughts on that subject right away. He commanded Balaam not to return with the Moabite princes who had hand-delivered the king's invitation. He said Israel was blessed, not cursed.

That should have been the end of it for Balaam.

But the king of Moab sent his invitation again, this time by way of princes "more numerous and more distinguished than the first" (Numbers 22:15). Plus, the king upped his promised payment for Balaam's curses. "I will reward you handsomely," he said (22:17).

Balaam, therefore, said he would check things out again with God.

Fifteen centuries later, the apostle Peter would precisely define Balaam's character this way: He "loved the wages of wickedness" (2 Peter 2:15).

The Lord had a plan for accomplishing something through Balaam far bigger than this heathen diviner could comprehend. "Okay," God said that night to Balaam. "Go." A money-hungry celebrity was about to be humbled.

At sunup, Balaam was saddled and off on the road to Moab to join King Balak. Little did he know how angry God was with him.

How angry was he?

Angry enough to station his angel with drawn sword across the middle of the Moab road (and in a narrow spot at that, with no place to swerve). The poor donkey must have been as terrified as any human being ever was to see such a sight. She tried all she could to get herself and her master away from that awesome presence.

But Balaam — world-famous seer — didn't notice his visitor.

What he did notice was his donkey's strange behavior. Balaam was angry now, and he beat her with his staff. (Who's the jackass in this story anyway?)

God now performed a two-step miracle of opening what was closed. Each step was just as easy for him to do as any other miracle.

First he opened the donkey's mouth and let her speak. Balaam was enough beside himself with fury that he fell right into an argument with her. "If I had a sword in my hand," he told her, "I would kill you right now" (Numbers 22:29).

Step Two: God opened Balaam's eyes to see where a sword really was — and whose hand it was in. "He saw the angel of the Lord standing in the road with his sword drawn" (22:31).

"That donkey," the angel told him, "just saved your life."

As anybody might with a sword aimed at his neck, Balaam suddenly exhibited meekness — to all appearances anyway. God showed him amazing visions of just how blessed the people of Israel really are. Balaam remained docile long enough to pass those visions on to a very frustrated King Balak. The whole time, the image of that upraised angelic sword must have been flashing in Balaam's mind. At any moment, it just might become visible again. Balaam took no chances.

Soon, however, his fear of God wore off. What Balaam and the king of Moab couldn't do to Israel by divination, they tried to accomplish by seduction. Jesus himself uncovers their crime while speaking to John in Revelation 2:14 — "Balaam...taught Balak to entice the Israelites to sin by eating food sacrificed to idols and by committing sexual immorality." That sordid story is told in Numbers 25.

Balaam also got involved with the Midianites, another group of Israel's enemies, in a further attempt to seduce Israel (25:14-18). This time it cost him his life. God commanded his people to take vengeance on the Midianites. The victims' list in Numbers 31:8 is headed by the names of five Midianite kings killed by the Israelites. Then comes this entry: "They also killed Balaam son of Beor with the sword." Seeing the sword of the Lord's angel wasn't enough to reform Balaam for good. So the sword of man sent him to his eternal reckoning.

But there's a happier story in Scripture about God opening up someone's eyes to see angels. What a delight it is to hear it again.

Six hundred years after Balaam's time, Israel was at war with Syria. Elisha, the prophet of the Lord, had the power to discern all of Syria's military secrets. Naturally he would promptly share these discoveries with the king of Israel.

The Syrian king figured that kind of leak had to be fixed. He sent his forces out to capture Elisha. They located him in the town of Dothan, and surrounded the place by night with soldiers, horses, and chariots (2 Kings 6:8-14). There could be no escape.

Early the next morning Elisha's servant went out and discovered the dreadful trap. With despair he reported their predicament to his master. "What shall we do?" he cried.

Elisha told him not to fear. "Those who are with us," he said, "are more than those who are with them" (6:16).

The prophet knew that, frankly, the servant would find such optimism hard to swallow. Israel had no armies in Dothan.

So Elisha prayed: "O Lord, open his eyes so he may see."

God answered his prayer. "The Lord opened the servant's eyes, and he looked and saw the hills full of horses and chariots of fire all around" (6:17). That was *God's* army in them thar hills — his host of angels.

In the rest of the passage, the servant isn't mentioned anymore. He must have mostly been staring in wonder at what happened next. As it turned out, the sight of those angel warriors might have been only to instill brave confidence in Elisha and his companion. The angels never entered the battle. As the Syrian soldiers closed in on him, Elisha prayed for God to blind their eyes. In this condition Elisha led the Syrian troops down the road ten miles to Samaria, and into the hands of Israel's king and army. Not until then did Elisha pray for the Syrians' eyes to open. Then they discovered that instead of having Elisha for a prisoner, they were prisoners themselves. The glory for the victory was God's.

Seeing those angels must have persuaded Elisha that the strength of an enemy army is never an actual threat when you're on God's side. When Israel's king asked if he should kill the Syrian captives, Elisha said no. "Feed them instead, and send them home." The king followed Elisha's advice. The Syrians were guests at Israel's feast, then they returned to Syria. And for a time at least their warfare with Israel ended.

A modern yet similar story is told by Doug Connelly in his book *Angels Around Us.* In the early 1950s, a missionary group in Kenya learned of an imminent attack on their mission by Mau Mau warriors. To defend their families as well as they could, the men put up a barbed wire barricade and turned on the few floodlights. With what few weapons they had they stood guard along the mission's perimeter, while their wives and children prayed inside.

They waited. But no attack came.

Months later a converted Mau Mau tribesman explained that just as he and his fellow warriors prepared to attack the mission from all sides, large fiery figures appeared from out of the night. They stood between the Mau Mau and the missionaries, racing in a circle around the barricade. Frightened by the sight of these creatures, the Mau Mau fled.

"The missionaries may not have seen them," Connelly writes, "but God opened the warriors' eyes to what normally would have been invisible — His band of holy angels."

Sometimes when angels intervene on the fields of human conflict, God opens the eyes of both sides to see his heavenly beings at work. In her book *Angels,* Hope Price records two hopeless situations in World War I related by a British captain. The first occurred early in the war near Mons, France, where outnumbered British troops had been fighting for days without relief.

> They had lost many men and guns, and defeat looked inevitable. Captain Cecil W. Hayward was there and tells how suddenly, in the midst of a gun battle, firing on both sides stopped. To their astonishment, the British troops saw "four or five wonderful beings, much bigger than men," between themselves and the Germans. These "men" were bare-headed, wore white robes and seemed to float rather than stand. Their backs were to the British and their arms and hands were outstretched toward the Germans.
>
> At that moment, the horses ridden by German cavalrymen became terrified and stampeded off in every direction.
>
> Hayward also told of another battle sometime later in World War I when matters again seemed hopeless for British soldiers, who were surrounded by German troops. Suddenly the heavy enemy fire stopped completely, and everything grew strangely quiet.
>
> Then "the sky opened with a bright shining light, and figures of luminous beings appeared floating between the British and German lines."

German troops retreated in disorder, allowing the Allied forces to reform and fall back on a line of defense farther to the west.

German prisoners were taken that day, and when they were asked why they surrendered when they had the British troops surrounded, they looked amazed, saying, "But there were hosts and hosts of you!"

Hope Price comments in her book that the British government officially sponsored national days of prayer during the conflict. She believes the government's commitment to prayer played a role in the angelic intervention on behalf of the British soldiers.

No doubt the key event in the missionaries' story from Kenya during the Mau Mau uprisings was the praying being done inside the mission by the women and children. Many a godly teacher has reminded us over the centuries that all that the Lord does on our behalf is in answer to someone's prayer. That surely includes sending angels to our rescue, plus opening our eyes to see them.

There must be quite a lot of intervening angels around that we just never notice — but sometimes, when the time is right, God takes the scales off our eyes so we can see them.

Appearing in Dreams

Before moving on from angels' visibility, remember too that angels can show themselves in our dreams. Jacob saw angels that way at two crucial times in his life. He saw them first on a stairway to heaven when he was alone and camping out while running away from home (Genesis 28). Many years later they appeared in a dream in which God told him it was time to go back (31:10-13).

The New Testament story of Joseph the husband of Mary contains the most dream appearances by angels in the Scriptures. It also contains some of the strongest examples of obedience. Joseph didn't get into angel-mania from all of his supernatural experiences. He just did what God's angel told him to do.

While we study his story, let's ask ourselves these questions: *How is my own track record in obedience? Is it strong enough that God could trust me to obey his special instructions delivered through an angel in a dream?*

Notice what thorough and specific directions Joseph receives on the first night an angel comes to him.

> An *angel* of the Lord appeared to him *in a dream* and said, "Joseph son of David, do not be afraid to take Mary home as your wife, because what is conceived in her is from the Holy Spirit. She will give birth to a son, and you are to give him the name Jesus, because he will save his people from their sins." (Matthew 1:20-21)

Joseph gets the what and the how and the why. Now see for yourself how thorough Joseph is in his response.

> When Joseph woke up, he did what the angel of the Lord had commanded him and took Mary home as his wife. But he had no union with her until she gave birth to a son. And he gave him the name Jesus. (1:24-25)

Joseph has proven himself. God has his man, and he can use the same, intimate channel again to communicate to him. Look closely at the next directions Joseph obtains by night courier, this time after the wise men had left Bethlehem:

> An *angel* of the Lord appeared to Joseph *in a dream*. "Get up," he said, "take the child and his mother and escape to Egypt. Stay there until I tell you, for Herod is going to search for the child to kill him." (2:13)

Again, judge his response, and notice how Joseph fulfills prophetic Scripture by simply obeying God.

So he got up, took the child and his mother during the night and left for Egypt, where he stayed until the death of Herod. And so was fulfilled what the Lord had said through the prophet: "Out of Egypt I called my son." (2:14-15)

Watch the process a third time...

After Herod died, an *angel* of the Lord appeared *in a dream* to Joseph in Egypt and said, "Get up, take the child and his mother and go to the land of Israel, for those who were trying to take the child's life are dead."

So he got up, took the child and his mother and went to the land of Israel. (2:19-21)

And a fourth, with prophetic fulfillment again:

But when he heard that Archelaus was reigning in Judea in place of his father Herod, he was afraid to go there. Having been warned *in a dream*, he withdrew to the district of Galilee, and he went and lived in a town called Nazareth. So was fulfilled what was said through the prophets: "He will be called a Nazarene." (2:22-23)

In this last situation, an angel isn't mentioned as being in the dream. If an angel did appear to Joseph, obviously it isn't important enough to be recorded. What was important for Joseph is what's also crucial for all of us: We're to obey, whether or not God's instruction comes through an angel.

The Sound of Angels

Learning about angels and dreams helps us see that these heavenly beings can access us through senses other than sight.

Sometimes it may be only the *sound* of angels that human beings can perceive. It was that way once for David and his fighting men (2 Samuel 5:22-25). With the enemy Philistines spread out before him in a valley,

David asked God what to do. God told him not to try a direct attack, but instead to have his men circle behind the enemy, to a place where balsam trees were growing.

And there, the Lord told David, they should listen for the sound of angel warriors.

> As soon as you hear *the sound of marching in the tops of the balsam trees,* move quickly, because that will mean the Lord has gone out in front of you to strike the Philistine army.

Men don't march in treetops, but angels can. David did what the Lord told him, and the result was another in Israel's string of victories through David's obedience to God.

Angels definitely know how to make noise. The angel in Revelation 10:3 "gave a loud shout like the roar of a lion. When he shouted, the voices of the seven thunders spoke." Seven thunders is no whisper.

In Isaiah's vision, the seraphs are calling to one another, "Holy, holy, holy is the Lord Almighty." But they weren't just murmuring a phrase or humming their way through a hymn. "At the sound of their voices," Isaiah says, "the doorposts and thresholds shook." That's real vibes.

"Strange," says H. A. Ironside on this verse, "that inanimate pillars should thus be moved while the hearts of men remain obdurate and motionless!" Amen.

Angels apparently have their own spiritual languages, though 1 Corinthians 13 makes it clear that these "tongues of angels" are not as important or as beautiful in God's eyes as the simple human language of our love in action.

Do angels sing? Usually we assume that they do, and many a Christmas pageant includes a musical number from an angel choir.

Surprisingly, however, the Scriptures don't clearly indicate the angels singing as often as you might think. In a passage such as the Christmas story in Luke 2, some English versions and paraphrases say that the angels were "singing" their praises of "Glory to God in the highest," but the Greek word simply means that they were "saying" these words. The same is true of the word sometimes translated "singing" in Revelation 5:13, where "every creature in heaven and on earth and under the earth and on the sea" joins in an exalted expression of praise to God and to the Lamb.

A stronger reference to angel song might be a passage we looked at earlier—Job 38:7, where "the morning stars *sang* together and all the angels shouted for joy." The Hebrew word translated here as "sang" is usually used in reference to singing.

But mostly in the Bible when it comes to singing, it's God's people who make the music, not angels.

My friend and great preacher W. A. Criswell explores an interesting reason for this, one that reminds us of Paul's words in Romans 8:22 that "the whole creation has been groaning...right up to the present time":

> Music is made up of major chords and minor chords. The minor chords speak of the wretchedness, death and sorrow of this fallen creation. Most of nature moans and groans in a plaintive and minor key. The sound of the wind through the forest, the sound of the storm, the sound of the wind around the house, is always in a minor key. It wails. The sound of the ocean moans in its restlessness, in its speechless trouble. Even the nightingale's song, the sweetest song of the birds, is the saddest. Most of the sounds of nature are in a minor key. It reflects the wretchedness, the despair, the hurt, the agony, the travail of this fallen creation.
>
> But the angel knows nothing of it. An angel knows nothing of wretchedness, nothing of despair, nothing of the fall of our lost race....
>
> Our sweetest songs with deepest sorrows are fraught. Somehow it is the sorrow of life, the disappointment of life and the despair of life that makes people sing, either in the blackness of its hour or in the

glory of its deliverance. That is why the redeemed sing and angels just speak of it. They see it, they watch it, but they know nothing about it. For it takes a lost and fallen man — who has been brought back to God, who has been forgiven of his sin, who has been redeemed — it takes a saved soul to sing!

Yet it's fine to believe that angels can and do sing, because just as Scripture doesn't pointedly show them singing their praises, neither does it insist that they *can't*. Billy Graham says the idea of angels never singing "seems inconceivable." He reminds us that angels certainly "possess the ultimate capacity to offer praise," and that music has always been a universal language for praise. He also points to the testimony of dying believers who said they "heard the music of heaven."

He concludes: "I believe that angels have the capacity to employ heavenly celestial music." He suggests that "in heaven we will be taught the language and music of the celestial world." But he also notes that

> before we can understand the music of heaven we will have to go beyond our earthly concept of music. I think most earthly music will seem to us to have been in the "minor key" in comparison to what we are going to hear in heaven.

The question of angels singing is linked to our own nature and destiny as human beings. It's time to look closer at that now — to understand better how angels are like us, and how they're different.

Chapter Seven

THE ANGELS AND US: HOW MUCH ALIKE?

E'VE SEEN ENOUGH by now to know God's angels differ from you and me in many remarkable ways. But one distinction towers above all others. It's a desperate difference, a contrast that has rocked the course of universal history. We have to understand this profound difference before we can fully appreciate the ways in which we and angels are alike — and how we'll be alike in the future.

That difference is this: God's good angels are still what they were created to be; you and I are not.

Ever since the flaming sword of the cherubim flashed across Eden's gate, the life God created for our enjoyment has been out of our reach. All human flesh has fallen short of the Lord's intended purpose for mankind. Sin infected us all, enslaved us all, and cursed us all with death and the fear of it. You and I were ruined. As Adam and Eve's children we were conceived in sin and born only to die. As we grew, each of us only confirmed our condemnation by selfish, destructive choices.

Throughout human history no father's son and no mother's daughter was born outside this predicament. Humanly speaking there was no escape, no hope for a cure. You and I were utterly doomed.

But then — *God* sent his Son to be born into human flesh and to take upon *himself* all the curse and the death and the doom that was ours. Then with power he proved his total victory over all of it by rising from the dead.

When by faith you and I grasp what really happened here, we too rise up from our chains. We stand amazed and forever grateful and filled with unspeakable joy.

And what do the angels think about all this?

The apostle Peter tells us they are gripped with an abiding curiosity about it. And I suppose they always will be.

Our Salvation Makes Them Curious

After Peter warms our hearts in 1 Peter 1 with a description of our salvation, he adds, "Even angels long to look into these things" (1:12). What exactly are "these things"? Don't angels already understand the details of our salvation better than we do? Surely they have a better vantage point than we do down here.

Peter's words are a good reminder that what counts in the Christian life is personal experience, not head knowledge. Yes, angels certainly have intellectual awareness — "head knowledge" — of our salvation. But they haven't *felt* salvation or feasted on it. Therefore they "long to look into these things" because they understand that personal acquaintance is far better than mental comprehension. They have no pride about what they merely know; they long instead for *experience*.

Just look back over the first eleven verses of 1 Peter 1. See how much of it must be outside what angels can personally encounter.

As people chosen for salvation in Christ we have been "sprinkled by his blood" (1:2). Angels have never known this cleansing that's available to us constantly.

We've been given "new birth" (1:3). Angels can never know the freshness of being born again.

This new birth comes our way through God's "great mercy" (1:3). Angels have never needed his mercy because they've never sinned.

God promises us a rich and indestructible inheritance that's being "kept in heaven for you" (1:4). Angels already have what's theirs. As far as we know there's nothing for them to inherit. The riches they see stacked and stored in heaven are for us.

We have "a living hope" (1:3). Our hope is that our faith will "result in praise, glory and honor when Jesus Christ is revealed" (1:7). The angels have no need of hope since Christ's glory is already a present reality to them.

Peter tells us this about Jesus: "Though you have not seen him, you love him" (1:8). The angels *do* see Jesus, and surely they love him too. But tell me: Which do you think is more precious — true love from those who already see the Lord, or true love from those who still must wait to get their first glimpse of his glorious face?

Peter drives deeper. He tells us, "Even though you do not see him now, you *believe* in him" (1:8). We believe. We have no choice but to walk by faith because the Lord is not within our sight. But angels have no need of belief. They know the Lord by sight, not by faith.

Because of our faith, Peter says, we're "filled with an inexpressible and glorious joy" (1:8). It seems obvious in Scripture that angels know plenty about "glorious joy." But which would you say is more wonderful—the rejoicing of those who stay by God's throne, or the rejoicing by faith of those who can only imagine what heaven is like?

Peter tells us more. During this "little while" that we live on earth we must endure "all kinds of trials," and these trials cause us to "suffer grief" (1:6). As far as we know, angels lose no loved ones, nor experience lingering trials of personal grief and loss.

All our own sufferings, however, have a greater purpose, one that allows us to be thankful for them:

Has God created any more angels since then? I have no biblical reason to believe he has. And apparently there's been no reduction in their number either (except for the dismissal of the fallen angels, which we'll take up later). Nor has there been any increase, since angels don't reproduce — according to Jesus' statement that angels don't marry (Matthew 22:30, Mark 12:25, Luke 20:34-36). We have as many angels today as we've ever had.

Angels Are Innumerable

And exactly how many angels is that?

No precise count is given in Scripture, but there's plenty of evidence that they make up a mighty multitude.

On that dark night of agony when an angel came to minister to the Son of God as he prayed in Gethsemane, Jesus had to stop his disciples from fighting against soldiers who came to arrest him. Christ admonished his men with these words: "Do you think I cannot call on my Father, and he will at once put at my disposal more than twelve legions of angels?" (Matthew 26:53). That's enough for each disciple to have his own entire legion for his personal bodyguards. A typical Roman legion numbered from three to six thousand men, often with the same number of backup troops. So the total host Jesus brought to mind would be as great as 144,000 heavenly soldiers.

In a majestic and timeless picture in Hebrews 12:22, we're told that we've come to *"thousands upon thousands* of angels in joyful assembly." In various English translations this assembly is called "the gathering of *countless* happy angels," or *"innumerable* angels in festal gathering," or *"millions* of angels gathered for the festival." Here again is a form of the Greek word *myriad,* the word we saw earlier with a meaning of ten thousand or a vast number.

In Psalm 68:17, David probably is thinking of angelic warriors when he says, "The chariots of God are *tens of thousands and thousands of thousands."*

These have come *so that your faith* — of greater worth than gold, which perishes even though refined by fire — *may be proved genuine....* (1:7)

Proven, genuine faith in God is what you and I really want, isn't it? Right now we long for the day when we can shout, "See, it really is true! I was right to believe! I was right to take God at his word!" We know that day is coming. So right now we rejoice — "for we are receiving the goal of our faith, the salvation of our souls" (1:9).

No wonder Peter adds the line about the angels wanting to explore this salvation inside-out. When he says that "even angels long to look into these things," the single Greek word translated as "to look into" is a term with intensity. It pictures someone "stooping over to look." This is not a quick glimpse, but a calculated, close-up analysis — a deliberate gaze, a studied observation. That's what angels wish they could do with our salvation.

In the Gospels this same verb is used three times for someone actually bending over to look inside Jesus' empty tomb on that first Easter Sunday morning: Peter himself (in Luke 24:12), the apostle John (John 20:5), and Mary Magdalene (John 20:11). You can easily imagine with what intense curiosity all three of them stared at the place where they fully expected the dead body of their Lord to be, but where now they plainly saw it was not.

Maybe that's a hint of another picture: Today the angels wish they could bend over and look inside what was once as empty and cold as a tomb — our spirits — and see and feel and experience just how the living Christ can be there inside us through his Holy Spirit.

Angels can only long to experience this — but we already can!

Thank God he had the answer for our enslavement — a cure for the curse and the doom. That answer is my salvation through Christ. But the joy of it can be fully known only because of the despair that came first.

Until I discovered last year I had cancer, I never seriously doubted I would live out a full life on this earth. Then, after I had looked death in the face, being told that my disease was in remission was the greatest news I could imagine. Being saved is like that too. If we didn't know the hopelessness of being lost we could never appreciate the hope of being saved.

I remember what it was like to go to bed at night and worry about what would happen to me if I woke up somewhere other than that room where I'd gone to sleep. Then one day I trusted Jesus as my Savior, and knew my sin was forgiven. That worry went away.

To their benefit, angels have never known such worry or any depression or despair. But they've also never known the stunning power of the hope that can come after the hopelessness. Since they can't say, "I know what it's like to be lost," they also can't say, "I know what it's like to be found." They can't imagine being overwhelmed with a burden of failure and guilt, then one day to be overwhelmed with joy as the Holy Spirit ignites the discovery in our heart that Jesus has come and forgiven it all.

A great hymn I heard often in my childhood comes to mind here. I remember our singing "Holy, Holy, Is What the Angels Sing" in special services and evangelistic crusades in the church my father pastored. It was written in 1924 by Rev. Johnson Oatman Jr. and John R. Sweeney, and the chorus goes,

> Holy, Holy, is what the angels sing.
> And I expect to help them make the courts of heaven ring.
> But when I sing redemption's story, they will fold their wings,
> for angels never felt the joy that our salvation brings.

As great and mighty as angels are, they can only guess at the joy of a single moment when the Lord Jesus wipes a tear from our eye and the stain from our heart.

It kind of feels good to be one up on the angels, doesn't it? Isn't it wonderful to be redeemed! Isn't it wonderful to be forgiven!

So that's a strong explanation for why angels long to explore the hope of our salvation. But there's another reason that may be even stronger.

Our Salvation Makes Them Rejoice

When we see what angels possess in power and light and constant closeness to God, it's easy to envy them. We're tempted to prefer an angel's existence to our own. It makes us wonder which would be better: to be sinless and never need salvation, or to be a sinner who's found the joy of being saved and forgiven?

I suppose there's been more than one discussion about that through the years. We could debate it for eternity. But it wouldn't make any difference. I was born into a fallen race as a lost human being, and trying to assume what it would be like to never have sinned is ridiculous. I don't even have the option.

Angels, likewise, can't fully imagine what's it's like to be in my condition. Redemption for them is not a personal reality to enjoy. But they can be excited about it on *my* behalf.

Jesus says, "There is rejoicing *in the presence of the angels of God* over one sinner who repents" (Luke 15:10). It sets off a party in heaven whenever someone on earth recognizes his need for the Savior and responds correctly.

Revelation 5:9-14 provides an awesome picture of angelic joy over our salvation, and points clearly to what may be the deepest reason for their elation. In this passage the "twenty-four elders" praise Christ for being worthy to open the scroll and break its seven seals, something no one else could do. *"You were slain,"* these angelic beings cry out to Christ, "and *with your blood* you purchased men for God from every tribe and language and people and nation."

Suddenly their worship is joined by "the voice of many angels, numbering thousands upon thousands, and ten thousand times ten thousand." This massive angel choir offers up its praise "in a loud voice":

> *Worthy is the Lamb, who was slain,*
>   to receive power and wealth and wisdom and strength
>   and honor and glory and praise!

Here in the high places which have always been their home, the angels' praise centers on this: the entrance into God's holy heaven of those who don't deserve to be there, *all through the blood of the murdered Son of God.*

This sacrifice of Christ must bring angels the most astonishment of all. How in the vastness of eternity could the Lord of Heaven's Armies ever be killed? How in all divine infinity could there be reason enough for God to take on human flesh and blood in the first place, let alone to have it pierced and spilled, and surrendered to death at the hands of wicked rebels?

I can imagine the angels thinking, "If the redemption and rescue of human beings is worth *that much* to the Lord — if it's worth the pure and precious life-blood of the eternal Son of God — then this salvation demands our eternal attention and our unceasing contemplation."

And think about this: Angels are able to rejoice over what they do not fully understand and experience. What an example for us! If they rejoice over a salvation they don't even get to share in and can't even fully understand — how much more should we, the saved ones, live in constant joy!

It's true of course that there are many deep wells in the Christian life we haven't yet dipped into, and many deep mysteries we haven't understood. But can't we go ahead with joy and offer God the worship he deserves for all his riches, even if we haven't embraced them all ourselves?

That's something we can learn from angels.

And now that we've got a good grasp of the big differences between human beings and angels, let's look more at how we're alike.

Angels Are God's Servants (And So Are We)

Scripture directly mentions at least three ways in which we're like angels. Together they point especially to our eternal future, which we'll enjoy in the angels' presence.

When the apostle John wanted to worship an angel, the point the angel made in his reply (after telling John, "No, don't do it!") was how alike he and John were. It happened both times. First:

But he said to me, "…I am a *fellow servant with you* and with your brothers who hold to the testimony of Jesus." (Revelation 19:10)

And then:

But he said to me, "…I am a *fellow servant with you* and with your brothers the prophets and of all who keep the words of this book." (22:9)

The angel was God's servant, just as John and the prophets were God's servants, and just as all of us are God's servants when we speak a word of testimony for his sake and on his behalf.

Servant is one of the most commonly used names in Scripture for those who follow the Lord — and especially those whom we might more readily call "leaders." The apostles didn't deck themselves out with lofty titles. Their favorite term to describe themselves was simply God's "servants." Paul, Peter, James, Jude, and John himself all used it (just check out the opening verse in Romans, 2 Peter, James, Jude, and Revelation).

Likewise in the Old Testament, Moses, Joshua, Samuel, David, and Elijah are all called God's servants (Exodus 14:31, Joshua 24:29, 1 Samuel 3:10, 2 Samuel 3:18, 2 Kings 9:36).

The "higher" you go in God's family the more you're called upon to serve. Even if somehow you reached the equivalent of angel status in this life, you would still be simply a servant doing your duty to God. Angels, too, are servants — "ministering spirits sent to serve."

Paul once complimented the Galatians for treating him like an angel: "You welcomed me as if I were an angel of God," he said, and "as if I were Christ Jesus himself" (4:14). The Galatians probably didn't fall down in fearful awe and worship at Paul's presence; more likely they simply showed him heartfelt gratitude and respect for his service to them, which was just as the angels and Christ himself had served them.

But service isn't for leaders and angels only. "Serve one another in love," Paul says to all of us. When we reach heaven we all want to hear the commendation, "Well done, good and faithful servant!" from the Lord's lips. So we serve others now as we serve God, since that's the example Jesus set for us. "Whoever serves me must follow me," he tells us, "and where I am, my servant also will be" (John 12:26).

Our privilege of being able to offer service to God will continue in eternity. John saw my future and yours in his vision: Those who've been washed in the Lamb's blood "are before the throne of God and serve him day and night in his temple" (Revelation 7:15). When the new Jerusalem comes, "The throne of God and of the Lamb will be in the city, and *his servants will serve him*" (22:3).

Let's grow in learning and loving to serve him now, that we may all the more enjoy serving him then.

Angels Are Immortal (And So Are We)

Jesus mentions two other ways in which we will be like the angels in eternity.

First, we'll no longer experience marriage as we do now. Jesus said, "When the dead rise, they will neither marry nor be given in marriage; they will be like the angels in heaven" (Mark 12:25). The gladness and fulfillment we will know in our perfect, heavenly union with Christ will transcend any satisfaction we've known in marriage. Human marriage, after all, is a temporary picture reflecting an eternal reality—which is Christ's relationship with his bride, the Church (Ephesians 5:25-32). Our joy in the future reality will far exceed our pleasure in the present scenario.

The second way we'll be like angels is that we can then no longer experience death. Jesus says in Luke 20:36 that those who are raised to eternity "can no longer die; for they are like the angels." As spiritual beings, angels know nothing of what it's like to get ill, grow old, and eventually die. Someday we, too, will be beyond the reach of those afflictions.

God's angels are known as the "elect" angels (1 Timothy 5:21), indicating that God chose to let them live eternally in his heaven. Christians are also are called "the elect" (2 Timothy 2:10). The angels themselves will be sent by God to "gather his elect from the four winds" (Matthew 24:31), for we too are chosen for eternal life. We and the angels will share permanent citizenship in God's heavenly kingdom forever.

The difference is in how and why we get to stay there. C. F. Dickason explains that angels were elected "unto perseverance," while Christians have been elected "unto redemption." He says the good angels who did not fall in Satan's rebellion "remain fixed in holiness." They are incapable of sin, just as we will be in eternity. But we will be there in heaven only because the blood of Christ has washed away our sins. The "perseverance" and "fixed holiness" that God provides the angels helps assure us that in heaven we also will be truly free from "this body of sin" (Romans 6:6).

Like us, angels are not eternal from of old, as Christ is. Their immortality is like ours: They are merely created beings who were given eternal life in heaven by God (and never lost it). Even in eternity, in the presence of the eternal God, neither we nor the angels will ever be on God's level. M. J. Erickson explains this from the human point of view:

> Even when redeemed and glorified, we will still be renewed human beings. We will never become God. He will always be God and we will always be humans…. Salvation consists in God's restoring us to what he intended us to be, not elevating us to what he is.

It's the same conclusion from the angels' perspective. Angels are always just angels, while God will always be God.

Since angels never die, the ones we see in heaven will be the same angels we read about in the Bible. Won't it be thrilling to meet Gabriel and Michael, and the angel who locked the lions' jaws for Daniel, and the one who set aside the stone from Jesus' tomb, and the one who sprang Peter out of jail, and all the others?

But even today, just think: Those same angels are carrying on their invisible ministry to us right now.

Angels Have Personality (And So Do We)

Since Jesus indicates that our heavenly existence will be like that of the angels in some essential ways, this could well be our signal to consider other similarities also.

The most logical assumption along this line is that as spiritual beings we'll continue to have personality, just as the angels do. In fact we'll doubtless have a much stronger and more fulfilled sense of personhood than we have now. We should never fear that in heaven we'll turn into wispy wallflowers with little to say or do. That certainly doesn't describe the angels.

Have you picked up just how powerful their personalities are? Listen to some snatches of angel speech, and ask yourself: Do these sound like slow drifters talking, or like strong, action-oriented personalities with intelligence and purpose? What do their words tell you about their mental and communication abilities?

> "Look with your eyes and hear with your ears and pay attention to everything I am going to show you, for that is why you have been brought here."

> "I have now come to give you insight and understanding."

> "I have come to explain to you what will happen to your people in the future, for the vision concerns a time yet to come."

> "I will tell you what is written in the Book of Truth."

> "There will be a time of distress such as has not happened from the beginning of nations until then.... Multitudes who sleep in the dust of the earth will awake: some to everlasting life, others to shame and everlasting contempt."

"We have gone throughout the earth and found the whole world at rest and in peace."

"Your wife...will bear you a son.... He will go on before the Lord... to turn the hearts of the fathers to their children and the disobedient to the wisdom of the righteous — to make ready a people prepared for the Lord."

"I am Gabriel. I stand in the presence of God, and I have been sent to speak to you and to tell you this good news. And now you will be silent and not able to speak."

"Do not be afraid. I bring you good news of great joy that will be for all the people."

"Why do you look for the living among the dead? He is not here; he has risen!"

"There will be no more delay!... The mystery of God will be accomplished."

"The kingdom of the world has become the kingdom of our Lord and of his Christ, and he will reign for ever and ever." (*Ezekiel 40:4, Daniel 9:22, 10:14, 10:21, 12:1-2; Zechariah 1:11, Luke 1:13-17, 1:19, 2:10, 24:5-6, Revelation 10:6-7, 11:15*)

These angels certainly have their wits about them. They don't just have personality — they've got *class* and *style*, even while they're being so direct and businesslike. I'm guessing that in heaven, you and I will be something like them.

Already Up There with Them

Yes, it will be thrilling to be around these fellows all the time.

But there's a sense in which we're already in the presence of angels. I'm referring not to the fact that they're "here" watching over us, but rather that we're already "up there" with them.

Wait a minute, you're thinking. *Has this author got his head in the clouds?* Perhaps, but maybe that isn't so bad. Look with me at these profound verses.

Paul says in Ephesians 1:3 that God "has blessed us *in the heavenly realms* with every spiritual blessing in Christ." He's not speaking in future tense here. He doesn't say God *"will"* give us these blessings, but that he *"has* blessed us." He's already blessed us *in heaven.*

Notice how this picture gets even clearer in the next chapter:

> And God raised us up with Christ and seated us with him in the heavenly realms in Christ Jesus. (2:6)

Paul speaks in terms of what's already happened. We've already been raised up with Christ and placed with him (and *in* him) in the heavenly realms. There's a real sense in which we're in heaven already.

I know what you're thinking: Maybe we're already in heaven in some symbolic or mystical way, some imagined way that removes the distinction between future and present and past. But let's face it: Our feet are very much planted on solid earth. Tomorrow morning we've got tough hills to climb, tough bills to pay, and tough pills to swallow. That's reality, and it isn't heaven by a long shot.

But Paul won't let us off so easily. He tells us to deliberately fix our focus on those "blessings in Christ" up there:

> Since, then, you have been raised with Christ, *set your hearts on things above,* where Christ is seated at the right hand of God. *Set your minds on things above, not on earthly things.* (Colossians 3:1-2)

"Things above" must surely include angels, since they're such a fixture in the heavenly landscape. Our *hearts* are to be set in that direction, and so are our *minds*. That doesn't leave much of us to get engrossed in matters here on earth, does it?

Why does Paul gives us such impractical instructions? I think it's because he knows there's only one who can truly meet our every need down here, and it's the One who's worshiped day and night by angels. Our marriages, our children, our friends, our careers, our hobbies, our weekends, our retirement — none of that will meet those deepest needs that are such a reality in our life. Only Christ can meet them, and his reality is a place at the throne of his Father, where he prays for us and prepares a home for us in the sight of angels.

Paul knows what aching disappointment we'll experience if our affections aren't up there with Christ. I have the greatest wife a man could have, and a wonderful family, and a great job most of the time, and so many other gifts from God. But there's no way I could honestly say that these meet every need of my life.

I think that's why Paul wants us to make sure we're looking into heaven for fulfillment. And the harder the struggle down here, and the older you get, the more your heart begins to think about what it's like up there.

The man who wrote Hebrews left us some amazing words to help us visualize a heavenly focus. Near the end of his letter he says,

> You have come [not "you *will* come" — we're there already] to Mount Zion, to the heavenly Jerusalem, the city of the living God. You have come to *thousands upon thousands of angels* in joyful assembly.... (12:22)

That's part of the eternal picture we're to look at *now*. Not only have we come "to God, the judge of all men" (12:23) and "to Jesus the mediator of a new covenant, and to the sprinkled blood that speaks a better word than the blood of Abel" (12:24) — but we've also come to all those happy angels.

In our heart of hearts, in our deepest thoughts, we can be there — now.

The Angels Observe Us

For thinking that way, it may help us to realize what the angels up there are looking at, besides God.

The apostle Paul mentions how the apostles were on display "as a spectacle to the whole universe, *to angels* as well as to men" (1 Corinthians 4:9). Later he gave solemn instructions to his helper Timothy *"in the sight of God and Christ Jesus and the elect angels"* (1 Timothy 5:21).

Paul was certain he was in the angels' line of sight, and it seemed to really *matter* to Paul that the angels were watching him. Should we assume they're watching us too? And should it be just as important to us?

Paul seems to think we should. When he tells us to be orderly in our worship, for example, one reason he gives is simply, "because of the angels" (1 Corinthians 11:10). They themselves are the worship champions, and they're quite involved in watching how we do it. (You might remember that next Sunday morning.)

Paul touches on angel observation to a more staggering degree in Ephesians 3:10. In this letter Paul hits on high and lofty themes that strain our understanding. In chapter three Paul says God was now shedding light on a "mystery" which he had kept hidden "for ages past." This mystery had to do with the birth of the Church, which now included both Jew and Gentile in the composition of God's holy people. Why did God follow this strategy of suddenly revealing what he had earlier kept hidden?

J. B. Phillips translates Paul's answer this way:

> The purpose is that *all the angelic powers* should now see the complex wisdom of God's plan being worked out through the Church,

in conformity to that timeless purpose which he centered in Christ Jesus our Lord.

God is showing something to the angels! And that something is his wisdom on display in the Church — in us! We are the stage where God's new production is performed before a heavenly audience. We are the show-room where his latest masterpiece is unveiled to angelic applause. We are the arena where his matchless feats of skill are exhibited to the sound of angel cheers.

All this had been screened from the angels before, but not anymore. God wants the angels to see his wisdom at work in a miraculous new way —through the gospel.

They were already peering through heaven's windows when Jesus walked among us. When Paul once listed the wonders of Christ to Timothy, he included the fact that Jesus "was seen *by angels*" (1 Timothy 3:16). Jesus, too, was under their observation. They had their eyes glued on the Word who became flesh. "Beyond all question," Paul concluded, "the mystery...is great."

Paul sensed the angels watching everything about us. And they'll still be watching in the very end. Jesus lets us know that in Luke 12:8-9, as he speaks of the judgment day:

> I tell you, whoever acknowledges me before men, the Son of Man will also acknowledge him *before the angels of God.* But he who dis-owns me before men will be disowned *before the angels of God.*

When that day comes, what do you want the audience of angels to see and hear about *you?*

Maybe it's time to pray about it. In Revelation 5:8 we see the angels holding "golden bowls full of incense, which are the prayers of the saints." What precious prayers from you have gone up today to help fill those bowls as they rest in the holy hands of angels? Have you prayed today for God's kingdom to come? Have you prayed for his kingdom to be born in the lives of your family and friends and neighbors whom you love, but who are not yet believers? Have you prayed for his will to be done in your life, just as it's already done by the angels in heaven? Have you asked him to show you his specific will for your life today?

Later in Revelation we see an angel standing at God's altar with a golden censer. What an honored privilege this angel received:

> He was given much incense to offer, *with the prayers of all the saints,* on the golden altar before the throne. The smoke of the incense, together with the prayers of the saints, went up before God from the angel's hand. (8:3-4)

What fragrant prayers from you today will be offered on that altar, to rise up in sacred smoke to the God of the angels?

Chapter Eight

ANGELS YOU'VE HEARD ABOUT (AND MORE)

NGELS GO by lots of names. Even before you picked up this book you'd probably heard of *cherubim* (or cherubs—but "cherubim" seems to fit these awesome creatures better) as well as *seraphim*. As far as individual angels go, you can easily recall the two most famous: Gabriel and the archangel Michael.

What else is good to know about angel groups or individuals and the names Scripture gives them?

Names mean more in the Bible—and meant more in Bible-time cultures—than they usually mean today. We grow in appreciating that when we look long and hard at what these heavenly beings are called in addition to "angels" (which, you'll remember, means "messengers").

Thrones, Powers, Rulers, Authorities

Some of the Scripture names for angels suggest that they're organized in an orderly way. Angels don't just go about their business at their own whim, and independently of one another. You'd think that if any group of beings could rightly do their own thing their own way, angels could. But apparently God carefully organizes them so they can best carry out his will. (And if that's true for the angels, do you think it's true for us too?)

Our evidence for angel organization includes a handful of terms in the New Testament referring to someone or something as "thrones," "dominions," "powers," "rulers," and "authorities." This terminology seems to imply different groupings or levels of angelic beings. Let's see what we discover as we scan some passages containing these terms.

Sometimes the references seem to be only to evil angelic forces—to Satan and his demons:

> The end will come, when [Christ] hands over the kingdom to God the Father after he has destroyed all *dominion, authority* and *power.* (1 Corinthians 15:24)

> Our struggle is not against flesh and blood, but against the *rulers,* against the *authorities,* against the *powers* of this dark world and against the spiritual forces of evil in the heavenly realms. (Ephesians 6:12)

> And having disarmed the *powers* and *authorities,* [God] made a public spectacle of them, triumphing over them by the cross. (Colossians 2:15)

Other references might have only God's good angels in view:

> [God] raised him from the dead and seated him at his right hand in the heavenly realms, far above all *rule* and *authority, power* and *dominion,* and every title that can be given, not only in the present age but also in the one to come. (Ephesians 1:20-21)

> His intent was that now, through the church, the manifold wisdom of God should be made known to the *rulers* and *authorities* in the heavenly realms.... (Ephesians 3:10)

Still other references could easily be to both good and evil beings, though in the larger picture the meaning could ultimately apply differently to God's angels than to demons:

For by [Christ] all things were created: things in heaven and on earth, visible and invisible, whether *thrones* or *powers* or *rulers* or *authorities;* all things were created by him and for him. (Colossians 1:16)

You have been given fullness in Christ, who is the head over every *power* and *authority.* (Colossians 2:10)

We see one of these terms again in Romans 8:38-39, though here Paul seems to be actually distinguishing angels from "powers."

For I am convinced that neither death nor life, neither *angels* nor demons, neither the present nor the future, nor any *powers,* neither height nor depth, nor anything else in all creation, will be able to separate us from the love of God that is in Christ Jesus our Lord.

On the other hand, "powers" in this passage might simply be a broader designation that encompasses both angels and demons as well as perhaps the time forces of present and future. (We're definitely feeling our way through the mist of mystery here!)

The most important point to make about these passages is that they all proclaim the vast superiority of Christ in relation to these angelic "powers." Paul seems to bring up these terms only to show how much greater Christ is than anyone or anything else. Paul's focus here certainly does *not* seem to be on providing a complete picture of angel hierarchy.

So a timely word of caution: It's possible to get carried away in imagining the details of angelic organization.

Some theologians in centuries past delighted in working out elaborate systems of angelic groupings. One popular arrangement in the Middle Ages was a ranking of nine different levels of angels.

Thomas Aquinas, the great thirteenth-century theologian, laid hold of this traditional nine orders of angels but also went beyond it. In his masterpiece, the *Summa Theologica,* he admitted that "our knowledge of the angels is imperfect" and that therefore "we can only distinguish the angelic offices and orders in a general way." But he added,

> If we knew the offices and distinctions of the angels perfectly, we should know perfectly that each angel has his own office and his own order among things.

Aquinas believed each angel is his own "species" (unlike mankind, which is all one), and that each angel stands alone on his own level in a perfectly ranked ordering of all of them.

Aquinas, by the way, wrote many thousands of words about angels, and was so esteemed for his intellect that in all of history, only he was known by the academic title "Doctor of Angels." But about the time of his forty-ninth birthday he had a vision that redirected his life. This preeminent scholar suddenly stopped writing altogether, and said, "Such things have been revealed to me that all I have written seems as straw." Perhaps he even saw an angel in his vision, and that one glimpse of heavenly reality made his volumes of intellectual discourse seem as nothing by comparison. He died before he reached age fifty.

Aquinas had been influenced and inspired by an earlier writer who went by the name of Dionysius, though his real identity was unknown. In one of his works, *Celestial Hierarchy,* Dionysius pushed forward his detailed ideas of angel organization. A thousand years later John Calvin found reason to suspect the suppositions of Dionysius, and to put the question of angel hierarchy in better perspective.

Calvin wrote,

> None can deny that Dionysius (whoever he may have been) has many shrewd and subtle discussions in his Celestial Hierarchy; but on looking at them more closely, every one must see that they are merely idle talk.

Calvin counseled his readers to "renounce those vain babblings of idle men concerning the nature, ranks, and number of angels, without any authority from the Word of God." He said the path of discipleship taught by Jesus discouraged this kind of "superfluous speculations," and that we, "being contented with him for our master," should do the same.

"When you read the work of Dionysius," Calvin reflected, "you would think that the man had come down from heaven, and was relating not what he had learned but what he had actually seen."

Calvin contrasted that with Paul's example. We know from Scripture that Paul was actually "caught up to the third heaven" and "caught up to paradise" (2 Corinthians 12:2,4). But instead of coming back and chattering about heaven's furnishings or about the setup of the angels there, Paul affirmed simply that he had encountered "inexpressible things, things that man is not permitted to tell" (12:4). Paul, whom we assume could have shared many secrets about angelic arrangement, instead was constrained to silence.

In the centuries leading up to Jesus' ministry on earth and the birth of the Church, many popular ideas of extensive angelic organization had developed among the Jews. They conjectured a variety of angelic positions and functions. Paul may have had this in mind when he said Christ is seated "far above" not only "all rule and authority, power and dominion," but also above "every title that *can be given*" (Ephesians 1:21). We can strain our imaginations to the breaking point in describing multi-layers of angelic superstructure, but it doesn't matter. Regardless of how dignified and dazzling and detailed the angel forces may be, and regardless of how powerful and wonderful angels will appear when we see them in the age to come, their glory is always as darkness compared to Christ. And Christ is all that matters.

Order and Harmony

Nevertheless there's something worth learning from angels when Scripture calls them by these exalted titles. Calvin himself was willing to say the terms *powers, authorities,* and *rulers* indicated that God's government of this world "is exercised and administered" by angels. To him these words also show "the dignity of angelic service."

As for the name *thrones,* Calvin said perhaps it's used for angels "because the glory of God in some measure dwells in them." But with typical caution Calvin hastened to add, "As to this last designation I am unwilling to speak positively, as a different interpretation is equally if not more congruous."

So the Scriptures don't make a big deal of a detailed angelic organization, but they do seem to allow for it.

It makes sense that there's order and organization among the angels, "for God is not a God of disorder but of peace" (1 Corinthians 14:33). Throughout God's visible creation, even amid all the wondrous variety of it, we see an amazing orderliness, a profusion of patterns all interlocking with symmetry and logic. It's a master design that brings glory to the Master Designer, because he not only made it but also sustains it. It's his active energy that keeps it running moment by moment and season after season.

It seems only reasonable that the angelic realm, which God also created and sustains, is just as masterfully designed, however limited we are now in understanding it.

So what difference should all that make to you and me? Why should we care whether the angel domain is well-ordered and humming smoothly? For that matter, why should we care whether nature is well-ordered and humming smoothly?

Our first concern should be to recognize that this orderliness is a reflection on God. We learn about him from what we see in the creation which he made and continues to hold together. Creation is complex and intricate and harmonious and orderly because that's the way God is.

Our second focus should be on ourselves. Unlike the angels and nature, we human beings have deliberately turned away from God's original design for us. So now we have to go through the struggle of rediscovering that orderly design, then understanding and applying it.

Let's ask some hard, specific questions: Have we really recognized the master design God set up for our churches? Do we understand it, as proved by the fact that we're living it out in peace and harmony?

And the same at home: Have we really recognized the master design God set up for our families? Do we prove we understand it by the way we live it out in peace and harmony?

Yes, orderliness is just as important in church and at home as it is in nature and in the angelic sphere.

Satan understands this, which is why he constantly attacks the God-ordained chain of love and authority established for our churches and our homes. Whenever there's disorder in these places, someone other than God is behind it, because God is not the author of confusion.

Are you experiencing disorder now in your home or church? If so, can you pinpoint the ways God's design is being overlooked or opposed?

And how about your personal life, your inner reality? God is not a God of disorder but of peace. Is peace the dominant note inside you, or has it been disrupted by disorder and confusion and instability?

Spirituality implies an orderliness in our lives.

Hosts and Chariots

Another name we've seen used for angels collectively is "hosts." We discovered earlier that this one's especially important because of God's personal identification with it—he so often calls himself "the Lord of Hosts."

This word *hosts* also implies order and organization among the angels, especially in the sense that angels are organized for battle. It's a military picture. *Hosts* is the primary scriptural word for God's heavenly armies. We can picture well-trained troops, their loyalty unquestioned, their obedience instantaneous. They're in perpetual readiness to respond to their Commander's call. Angels must surely be more tightly ordered than any army, any military machine on earth.

Angels are called hosts, Calvin writes,

> because they surround their Prince as his court—they adorn and display his majesty. Like soldiers they have their eyes always turned to their leader's standard, and are so ready and prompt to execute his orders that the moment he gives the nod they prepare for work, or rather are actually at it.

The name "Lord of Hosts" for God is first used at a military low-point in Israel's history—at the beginning of First Samuel (1:3), which opens at a period when the Philistines were oppressing God's people. Matthew Henry says this title of God was probably introduced by the prophet Samuel here "for the comfort of Israel" at a time when "their hosts were few and feeble and those of their enemies many and mighty."

This name would soon be encouragement indeed to a shepherd boy called David. He shouted to his mighty Philistine enemy Goliath,

> You come against me with sword and spear and javelin, but I come against you *in the name of the Lord of Hosts, the God of the armies of Israel,* whom you have defied. (1 Samuel 17:45)

With the honor and presence of the Lord of Hosts on their side, Israel won the battle that day.

But they lost another one centuries later when a king was determined to lead his soldiers into battle without the Lord and his hosts on the king's side. Not that Israel's King Ahab wasn't warned. The prophet Micaiah stood before him and said, "I saw the Lord sitting on his throne with *all the host of heaven* standing on his right and on his left" (2 Chronicles 18:18). And what were God and all these angels discussing? Not how to give victory to Ahab, but how to bring disaster and death to this corrupt ruler (18:19-22).

Ahab refused to heed Micaiah's vision. His men charged into battle against the Syrians, and the king was wounded when a randomly shot arrow pierced him between the sections of his armor. Ahab propped himself up in his chariot to see the rest of the day's battle, while his blood covered the chariot floor. He died at sunset, as the battle turned against Israel.

The strategies of God and his armies can never be thwarted.

We saw earlier how this military side of the Lord and his hosts is strong enough that sometimes the presence of angels need only be implied by mentioning their chariots. We heard David's song of praise: "The chariots of God are tens of thousands and thousands of thousands" (Psalm 68:17). We heard Isaiah's warning: "See, the Lord is coming with fire, and his chariots are like a whirlwind" (66:15-16). We saw God answering Elisha's prayer by opening up his servant's eyes to see "the hills full of horses and chariots of fire all around" (2 Kings 6:17). Even the "chariot of fire and horses of fire" that swooped down to carry Elijah to heaven were most likely an angel squadron on special assignment: to bring an old soldier home (2 Kings 2:11-12).

This military aspect of the angels is as much an example for us as is their orderliness. When David shouts to the Lord, *"Your troops* will be willing on your day of battle" (Psalm 110:3), both angels and men may well be the Lord's ready soldiers on that day.

Are you his willing soldier? The more you learn about angels—the more clearly you see what spiritual reality in this universe is all about—the more you'll hear the call to arms. For heavenly battle lines are drawn, and you and I cannot escape the fight. We must be steeled for the fray.

> *Put on God's complete armor* so that you can successfully resist all the devil's craftiness. For our fight is not against any physical enemy; it is against organizations and powers that are spiritual. We are up against the unseen power that controls this dark world, and spiritual

agents from the very headquarters of evil. Therefore *you must wear the whole armor of God....* (Ephesians 6:11-13, J. B. Phillips)

Hear the trumpet's alarm! "Be on your guard; stand firm in the faith; be men of courage; be strong" (1 Corinthians 16:13). Victory is assured (won by Christ himself!) and you have only to stand and see it. But you can't even do that if you're defenseless, if you're a naked target for the enemy. Don't leave yourself open to a fall! Strap on the Lord's full armor, "that when the day of evil comes, you may be able to stand your ground, and after you have done everything, *to stand*" (Ephesians 6:13).

This is warfare like no other. So go for the best protection there is:

Put on *the armor of light....*
Clothe yourselves with *the Lord Jesus Christ....* (Romans 13:12-14)

Holy Ones

Remember: Names *mean* something in the Bible. With that in mind let's look at more Scripture names for angels. Some of these may refer to all God's angels and others only to special classes of them.

Angels are called "holy ones." They're separated, set apart for God's use. This holiness *comes* from God's holiness and *points* to God's holiness. A statement about them in Psalm 89:7 is a strong picture of this:

In the council of *the holy ones* God is greatly feared;
he is more awesome than all who surround him.

The angels assembled around God are holy. But their awesome holiness doesn't compare with God's, so the angels "greatly fear" him.

"Holy ones" is also what the angels are called when Moses describes them coming to Mount Sinai when God gave the law to Israel (Deuteronomy 33:2). Job's friend Eliphaz calls angels "holy ones" (Job 5:1, 15:15). So does Daniel in recounting his visions:

Then I heard *a holy one* speaking, and *another holy one* said to him, "How long will it take for the vision to be fulfilled...? (Daniel 8:13)

Notice how in three other passages—one in the Old Testament and two in the New—the Lord is seen as "coming with his holy ones" on some future day. In all three verses the "holy ones" mentioned may refer to both redeemed believers and unfallen angels:

You will flee as you fled from the earthquake in the days of Uzziah king of Judah. Then *the Lord my God will come, and all the holy ones with him.* (Zechariah 14:5)

May he strengthen your hearts so that you will be blameless and holy in the presence of our God and Father when *our Lord Jesus comes with all his holy ones.* (1 Thessalonians 3:13)

See, *the Lord is coming with thousands upon thousands of his holy ones* to judge everyone, and to convict all the ungodly of all the ungodly acts they have done in the ungodly way, and of all the harsh words ungodly sinners have spoken against him. (Jude 14-15)

Once again our human destiny is linked with angels.

Mighty Ones of God

Emphasizing their power, angels are even called "gods" and "sons of God" and "sons of the mighty." Just as their holiness does, their might points back to God. The King James Version of Psalm 89:6 captures this well: "Who among *the sons of the mighty* can be likened unto the Lord?" Angels are mighty, but their might is nothing compared with God's.

The angels must surely follow with gladness what David says to them:

Ascribe to the Lord, *O mighty ones,*
    ascribe to the Lord glory and strength. (Psalm 29:1)

Praise the Lord, you his angels,

you *mighty ones* who do his bidding,

who obey his word. (103:20)

In Psalm 8:5, where David says that man was made only "a little lower than the heavenly beings," the Hebrew word for these beings is actually the word *elohim* or "gods." We see their exalted power but also their reflection of God's glory. Calvin says angels are "more than once called gods, because the Deity is in some measure represented to us in their service, as in a mirror."

We can see another measure of divine power mirrored in the angels of Revelation. John saw and heard "a *mighty* angel" asking in God's throne-room, "Who is worthy to break the seals and open the scroll?" (5:2). It's "another *mighty* angel" who "planted his right foot on the sea and his left foot on the land" (10:1-2). And it's "a *mighty* angel" who "picked up a boulder the size of a large millstone and threw it into the sea" (18:21).

In 2 Thessalonians 1:7, Paul says the Lord Jesus will be "revealed from heaven in blazing fire with his *powerful angels.*" Bible scholars say this last phrase might best be translated as *"the angels of his power."* It could refer to a special group of angels with special power from God, or it could be another way of showing the great power all his angels have.

Holy Watchers

A different perspective on angels comes through when we see them referred to as "watchers" by King Nebuchadnezzar as he talked with Daniel, his royal advisor. The Hebrew word translated here as "watchers" or "watchmen" (or "messengers" in some versions) is used nowhere in the Bible except in Daniel 4. It comes from a verb meaning "to be wakeful" and "on the watch."

Nebuchadnezzar was telling Daniel about a dream he'd had while in bed in his palace, "contented and prosperous" (4:4). In that dream he saw a large, healthy, fruitful tree with birds in its branches and animals resting in its shade.

> I was looking in the visions in my mind as I lay on my bed, and behold, an angelic *watcher*, a holy one, descended from heaven. (4:13, NASB)

This holy watcher from heaven gave orders for the tree to be cut down, and the stump and the roots bound with iron. The watcher also described someone (it turns out to be the king himself) who was sentenced to being "drenched with the dew," living outside with animals, and having an animal's mind. "This sentence," said the watcher,

> is by the decree of the angelic *watchers*, and the decision is a command of the holy ones. (4:17, NASB)

So there were other "watchers" besides the one talking to Nebuchadnezzar, and they were entrusted in some manner with pronouncing God's judgment. They could be a particular class of angels with special duty related to communicating God's decrees.

In Nebuchadnezzar's case the watcher gave the reason for this particular verdict:

> so that the living may know that the Most High is sovereign over the kingdoms of men and gives them to anyone he wishes and sets over them the lowliest of men.

Nebuchadnezzar became that "lowliest of men" as he took on an animal's existence, living outdoors and eating grass. His hair grew out and his unclipped nails became like claws. When God finally restored his sanity, Nebuchadnezzar was ready to give honor and glory to God as the one who "does as he pleases with the powers of heaven and the peoples of the earth" (4:35).

The watchers were right.

Cherubim and God's Throne

The background of the name *cherub* is something of a mystery. Some scholars suggest that it's related to words meaning "intercessor" or "guardian." Others see a connection to words meaning "to grasp or hold fast," or "to plow or till the ground" or "to be diligent." Perhaps cherubim (the Hebrew plural of *cherub*) are the real workhorses among the angels as they fulfill their role as royal guards in service to the King. For sure they're a far cry from naked valentine babies.

We originally encountered cherubim in Genesis 3 as the first angelic beings mentioned in Scripture. Cherubim guarded Eden's gate with a flaming sword after Adam's fall, showing us vividly that sin can never be a part of paradise.

The next mention of cherubim is when God is giving Moses directions for making the ark of the covenant and the tabernacle. The ark was to have a pure gold "atonement cover" or "mercy seat" on top, and this cover included two hammered-gold cherubim. The author of Hebrews calls them "cherubim of the Glory" (9:5).

Note the reverent pose God told Moses to give these figures:

> The cherubim are to have their wings spread upward, overshadowing the cover with them. The cherubim are to face each other, looking toward the cover. (Exodus 25:20)

Since the ark represented God's throne and his royal presence, the gold cherubim figures with upraised wings remind us that God on his throne is surrounded by glorious, worshiping angels. Their faces turned toward the "atonement cover" or "mercy seat"—which itself is suggestive of Christ's atoning sacrifice—could indicate that the destiny of angels is also caught up in what Christ accomplished on the cross. Or it might be a strong picture of the angels "longing to look" into the things of salvation (1 Peter 1:12).

Or perhaps, as some scholars venture to say, the cherubim are a picture of the ideal future state of redeemed mankind, and their gaze at the mercy seat represents their eternal gratitude and praise for Christ's sacrifice. The cherubim are what *we* might be like someday.

This cherubim motif was carefully repeated in other tabernacle furnishings as well. The Lord commanded that ten tabernacle curtains be made "of finely twisted linen and blue, purple and scarlet yarn, *with cherubim worked into them* by a skilled craftsman" (Exodus 26:1). A curtain dividing the inner chambers of the tabernacle was also to have *"cherubim worked into it* by a skilled craftsman" (26:31).

In connection with the cherubim-shadowed ark, God promised his presence to Moses:

> There, above the cover *between the two cherubim* that are over the ark of the Testimony, *I will meet with you* and give you all my commands for the Israelites. (25:22)

God right away made good on this promise:

> When Moses entered the Tent of Meeting to speak with the Lord, he heard the voice speaking to him *from between the two cherubim* above the atonement cover on the ark of the Testimony. And he spoke with him. (Numbers 7:89)

From then on many in Israel remembered this sign of the Lord's presence and earthly kingship among them, for God was often called the one "enthroned between the cherubim" (1 Samuel 4:4, 2 Samuel 6:2, 2 Kings 19:15, 1 Chronicles 13:6, Psalm 80:1, 99:1).

When a massive Assyrian army was camped outside Jerusalem waiting to destroy it, King Hezekiah began his prayer this way: "O Lord of Hosts, God of Israel, *enthroned between the cherubim,* you alone are God over all the kingdoms of the earth..." (Isaiah 37:16). It was in answer to this prayer that the angel of the Lord put to death 185,000 Assyrian soldiers in a single night.

A different glimpse of the cherubim comes in David's song of praise and victory in 2 Samuel 22, "when the Lord delivered him from the hand of all his enemies and from the hand of Saul." It's an amazing picture of the cherubim actually carrying God's presence down to David's rescue:

> He parted the heavens and came down;
>> dark clouds were under his feet.
> *He mounted the cherubim* and flew;
>> he soared on the wings of the wind. (22:10-11)

Since the cherubim signify the angelic presence around God's throne, David felt that when the Lord rescued him it was just as if God had packed up his heavenly throne and come down with it to be the liberating King in David's life.

You and I can have that same picture of our own situation. We can be confident of God's kingly help coming to our rescue exactly when needed:

> Let us then approach *the throne of grace* with confidence, so that we may receive mercy and find grace to help us in our time of need. (Hebrews 4:16)

Yes, "The Lord is our king; it is he who will save us" (Isaiah 33:22).

Cherubim in the Temple

When David's son Solomon built the temple to replace the tabernacle, cherubim were again featured in the furnishing, but this time even more so.

The temple followed closely the pattern God had shown Moses for the tabernacle. In 1 Chronicles 28:11-12 we learn that David gave his son Solomon the plans for every part of the temple, and these were plans "that the Spirit had put in his mind." That's important to remember. The figures of cherubim adorning the tabernacle and the temple were *God's* idea—they were not human-conceived decorations.

Imagine yourself being there in Solomon's reign, some three thousand years ago. You're walking up the steps before the east entrance of the new temple, the world's most famous building. To visitors from other lands this is the centerpiece in the capital city of the world's wisest and richest king. But it means much more than that to you and your countrymen. This is the chosen earthly dwelling of the Lord of Hosts, and today is his Day of Atonement. Today is the only day of the year that *any* person can enter into the Most Holy Place—the Holy of Holies.

And you are that person, for you are the high priest.

You and your fellow priests have already offered the special sacrifices for this day upon the great altar in front of the temple. Now you carry a golden bowl filled with the blood of a goat that was slaughtered as a special sin offering for the people. You are to take this blood inside the Holy of Holies and sprinkle it on the atonement cover on the Ark of the Covenant.

At the top of the steps you walk between two giant cast-bronze pillars into a portico. Before you are two huge doors. Carved into them are intricately formed figures of cherubim. Your eyes go at once to their wings, then to their lion-like shoulders, then to their solemn, mysterious faces. All these features are highlighted in hammered gold, glittering in the brilliant midday sun of Israel. As you look long into one of their faces, suddenly a chill runs down your neck. With a twinge of terror you imagine the reality of their presence at God's home in heaven.

Bravely you reach out a hand. One of the doors swings back smoothly to your touch. You hold your breath. You sense that the cherubim on the open door are watching as you enter a large room.

A gold-covered floor gleams before you. Away on either side are gold-covered walls soaring up nearly fifty feet. The light from golden lampstands on both sides of the room reflects off the carvings covering the walls— countless more cherubim. Their awesome forms are set off with palm trees and flowers, all covered in gold. You stand for several moments staring at one cherub, then another, and another. Each one seems alive. You almost fear to go forward.

Finally you move. Your bare feet step slowly and silently across sixty feet of golden floor until you stand before a square, gold-covered altar. The smoke of sacred incense rises from it.

Behind the altar two more gold-covered doors tower above you, and these too are covered with carved cherubim, plus palm trees and flowers. You kneel before the incense altar and pray, then stand again and step behind the altar.

You reach out to touch one of the cherubim-covered doors. You close your eyes. Only after you swing both doors open wide do you open your eyes as well—to gaze upon this, a room untouched and unseen for a full year: the inner sanctuary, the Holy of Holies.

The gleaming light from the main hall pours in through the doorway into the gold-covered sanctuary. Facing you and towering above you are two gleaming statues of magnificent golden cherubim, each one fifteen feet high. Their wings are raised up and out. Their outer wings touch the wall. Their inner wings touch one another, forming an arch, fifteen feet across. Below the winged arch is the Ark of the Covenant, with its atonement cover— where two more cherubim with outstretched wings overshadow the Ark.

In the silent majesty of that room you feel your hands and legs quivering. You fall to your knees. The familiar opening of the ninety-ninth psalm leaps from your heart to your lips:

> The Lord reigns,
>> let the nations tremble;
> *he sits enthroned between the cherubim,*
>> let the earth shake.

Centuries later the Babylonians destroyed this beautiful temple. The grieving Jews must have had those beautiful cherubim-covered walls in mind in Psalm 74 as they lamented what the invaders had done:

They behaved like men wielding axes
  to cut through a thicket of trees.
They smashed all the carved paneling
  with their axes and hatchets.
They burned your sanctuary to the ground;
  they defiled the dwelling place of your Name.

But already the vision of a new temple was given to the priest and prophet Ezekiel, who was with the Jewish exiles in Babylon. The new temple would also be filled from floor to ceiling with cherubim "at regular intervals all around the inner and outer sanctuary" (Ezekiel 41:17), and interspersed again with palm trees. This is what the cherubim looked like:

Each cherub had two faces: the face of a man toward the palm tree on one side and the face of a lion toward the palm tree on the other. (41:18-19)

And once more the doors to the sanctuary would be filled with "carved cherubim and palm trees like those carved on the walls" (41:25).

But even in this exalted vision, the sight of those cherubim probably would not have been quite as awesome to Ezekiel as they would be to you or me—because not long before, Ezekiel had been privileged to see *the real thing*. God opened the heavens and gave to Ezekiel a vision of his throne and the cherubim surrounding it.

The power and beauty of these angelic beings cannot be fully conveyed within the limits of human language, but Ezekiel does the best he can. His descriptions in Ezekiel 1 push us beyond human imagination, yet they include much detail. It's worth our while to include nearly all this chapter here with its awesome presentation of these heavenly beings. (Ezekiel first calls them "living creatures," and not until chapter ten are they identified as cherubim.)

First the scene for the vision. Ezekiel sees

a windstorm coming out of the north—an immense cloud with flashing lightning and surrounded by brilliant light. The center of the fire looked like glowing metal, and in the fire was what looked like *four living creatures.*

What stands out first to Ezekiel is their faces, their wings, and their fire.

In appearance their form was that of a man, but each of them had four faces and four wings. Their legs were straight; their feet were like those of a calf and gleamed like burnished bronze. Under their wings on their four sides they had the hands of a man. *All four of them had faces and wings,* and their wings touched one another....

Their *faces* looked like this: Each of the four had the face of a man, and on the right side each had the face of a lion, and on the left the face of an ox; each also had the face of an eagle. Such were their faces.

Their *wings* were spread out upward; each had two wings, one touching the wing of another creature on either side, and two wings covering its body....

The appearance of the living creatures was *like burning coals of fire or like torches.* Fire moved back and forth among the creatures; it was bright, and lightning flashed out of it.

Ezekiel also is fascinated by their movements:

Each one went straight ahead; they did not turn as they moved....

Each one went straight ahead. Wherever the spirit would go, they would go, without turning as they went....

The creatures sped back and forth like flashes of lightning.

Then he sees a spellbinding dance-like motion of sparkling, intersecting wheels full of eyes. But notice how the wheels are not independent of the living creatures, but somehow are spiritually a part of them. Try to imagine the sight:

As I looked at the living creatures, I saw a wheel on the ground beside each creature with its four faces. This was the appearance and structure of the wheels: They sparkled like chrysolite, and all four looked alike. Each appeared to be made like a wheel intersecting a wheel.... Their rims were high and awesome, and all four rims were full of eyes all around.

When the living creatures moved, the wheels beside them moved; and when the living creatures rose from the ground, the wheels also rose. Wherever the spirit would go, they would go, and the wheels would rise along with them, because the spirit of the living creatures was in the wheels. When the creatures moved, they also moved; when the creatures stood still, they also stood still; and when the creatures rose from the ground, the wheels rose along with them, because the spirit of the living creatures was in the wheels.

Ezekiel also lets us hear with his ears:

When the creatures moved, I heard the sound of their wings, like the roar of rushing waters, like the voice of the Almighty, like the tumult of an army.

God's angels always point us to God, and that now becomes clear in Ezekiel's case as well. He isn't being shown this vision just to learn about cherubim, but rather to hear a word from the Lord.

Ezekiel glances "above the heads of the living creatures" and sees "what looked like an expanse, sparkling like ice, and awesome." He hears a voice from the expanse, then looks up to see this overwhelming vision:

Above the expanse over their heads was what looked like a throne of sapphire, and high above on the throne was a figure like that of a man.... From what appeared to be his waist up he looked like glowing metal, as if full of fire... and from there down he looked like fire;

and brilliant light surrounded him. Like the appearance of a rainbow in the clouds on a rainy day, so was the radiance around him.

This was the appearance of the likeness of the glory of the Lord. When I saw it, I fell facedown, and I heard the voice of one speaking.

After all these preliminaries, God now gives Ezekiel his calling and instructions, as recorded in Ezekiel 2 and 3.

Ezekiel must have recalled this vision every day for the rest of his life as he faced the struggles and pressures of living out his calling. It must have brought constant motivation and encouragement to think that this was the God he served.

How many of us would enjoy having had a majestic and mysterious vision like that to keep us going in our own specific calling from God? But the fact is, we *do* have it. Through his Word the Lord has given it to us for keeps. The God whom Ezekiel saw surrounded and served by flaming cherubim will always be the same. Ezekiel's vision is for you and me even more than it was for Ezekiel.

In Scripture we never see the cherubim serving as messengers from God to men—at least by their words. But their appearance must have communicated a great deal to Ezekiel, to God's people who saw the figures in the temple and tabernacle, and to Adam and Eve fleeing from Eden.

Seraphim

The name *seraph* means "burning one" or "shining one" (reminding us again that God makes his angels "flames of fire"—Psalm 104:4, Hebrews 1:7). The seraphim dwell so close to the presence of God that they burn with holy brilliance.

They are mentioned by name in only one passage in the Bible, but what an awesome scene it is. Let's return again to the vision where Isaiah sees God on his throne and hears voices around him crying "Holy, holy, holy is the Lord of Hosts" (Isaiah 6:1-4).

Isaiah says these are seraphs who sound that continual praise. He describes them as having six wings. With two wings they cover their faces in reverence. This reminds us of God's majestic glory. The Bible says no man has ever seen God and lived, and even these angels protect themselves from the brilliance of God's glory when they're in his presence. Matthew Henry expressed it this way:

> Though angels' faces doubtless are much fairer than those of the children of men (Acts 6:15), yet in the presence of God they cover them because they cannot bear the dazzling luster of the divine glory, and because, being conscious of an infinite distance from the divine perfection, they are ashamed to show their faces before the holy God.

Isaiah notices also that with two other wings the seraphs cover their feet. This speaks of their humility and their reverence in waiting on God for his next directions.

With their other two wings the seraphs fly. These two wings propel them with speed to do whatever God calls them to do.

Notice the proportion: Four wings for worship and only two for work —twice as much attention to being in God's presence as compared to carrying out other responsibilities. It seems like we today often reverse this ratio. We would do well to be more like the seraphim.

Like Ezekiel's vision of the cherubim, Isaiah's vision of the seraphim provides another picture of reverence and adoring awe to help us in approaching our heavenly Father. Trying to follow their example in this may seem uncomfortable and even threatening. But if it felt only cozy and comfortable, God would not be God.

Isaiah knew this tension. While the seraphs sang "Holy, holy, holy," he was thinking how much he was "unholy, unholy, unholy." He cried out, "Woe, I am ruined!" (6:5). But through the touch of a live coal from a seraph's hand to Isaiah's lips, the prophet was able to continue in his encounter with the holy God. The Lord will give the right grace for us to do it too.

Just as in Ezekiel's case, Isaiah after this experience was able at once to hear God's specific calling. Isaiah responded gladly. "Here am I," he said. "Send me!" Our own understanding of God's will for our lives will open up as well after an extended experience of worship in the fear of God.

Living Creatures and Elders

At the end of Scripture, in John's vision on Patmos Island, he saw "four living creatures" who have similarities to both the seraphim in Isaiah 6 and the cherubim in Ezekiel 1. Their name—"living creatures"—quickly tells us that they have life and that they're created beings.

Like the cherubim, these living creatures number four and have the likenesses of lion, ox, man, and eagle (Revelation 4:7). And like the seraphim they have six wings, and honor God with their continual praise of "Holy, holy, holy is the Lord God Almighty"—to which they add a new phrase: "who was, and is, and is to come" (4:8).

They're able to praise God in this new way because of two things which we learn about them right away. The first is that in God's presence they stand "in the center, around the throne" (4:6). They may well be closer to God than any other angelic beings.

The second thing we learn about them is that they're "covered with eyes, in front and in back," reminding us of the cherubim's wheels in Ezekiel 1, which had eyes all along the rims. These living creatures in Revelation are fully alive to see everything, past and future, front and back. Perhaps they can actually see that God was, and is, and is to come.

The four living creatures are involved not only in worshiping God but also in bringing about his final wrath upon the earth. As John watches the Lamb opening the first of the seven seals, he says,

I heard one of the four living creatures say in a voice like thunder, "Come!" (6:1)

This authoritative shout summons a rider on a white horse who "rode out as a conqueror bent on conquest" (6:2). As Christ opens the next three seals, the other three creatures each in turn also calls out, "Come!" Again their simple command immediately brings forth a horse and rider bearing destruction to the earth. The living creatures know how to make their words count.

Later John says he saw

> seven angels with the seven plagues.... Then *one of the four living creatures* gave to the seven angels seven golden bowls filled with the wrath of God, who lives for ever and ever. (15:6-7)

Closely associated with the four living creatures in Revelation are the "twenty-four elders." When John first sees them they're seated on twenty-four thrones that encircle God's throne. "They were dressed in white and had crowns of gold on their heads" (4:4).

This name *elders* implies "leadership by example." These elders are like our "older examples," the ones we look up to as models for our behavior. As "elders" they bear the same name that the highest Scripture-ordained leaders of our churches have. So perhaps their worship and service to God is especially meant to be an example to those in church leadership—who in turn are meant to be "examples to the flock" (1 Peter 5:3).

The elders in Revelation are especially involved in proclaiming God's saving acts toward men. One of their most glorious moments is when "the seventh angel sounded his trumpet" (11:15) and loud heavenly voices announce that at last the world is completely and forever under the reign of Christ.

The elders are now in John's focus, setting the example for the rest of us in responding to Christ's kingship: "The twenty-four elders, who were

seated on their thrones before God, fell on their faces and worshiped God."
Just listen to their praise (in 11:17-18), and how it involves you and me and
all the Christians we know, small and great:

> We give thanks to you, Lord God Almighty,
>> the One who is and who was,
> because you have taken your great power
>> and have begun to reign.
> The nations were angry;
>> and your wrath has come.
> The time has come for judging the dead,
>> and for rewarding your servants the prophets
> and your saints and those who reverence your name,
>> both small and great—
> and for destroying those who destroy the earth.

Notice the assurance here that God *will* take care of us! The elders know
this, and they want us to know it as well.

Now look what happens next—and let your mind recall those cherubim in the temple and what they represented:

> Then God's temple in heaven was opened, and within his temple was
> seen the ark of his covenant. And there came flashes of lightning,
> rumblings, peals of thunder, an earthquake and a great hailstorm.

These elders definitely know what it means to get a response when they
worship! No wonder they love doing it all the time.

We see the elders and the four living creatures worshiping together
often—in fact we could almost say the living creatures set the pace as
heaven's worship leaders, while the twenty-four elders are their assistants
showing us how to rightly respond. An example is in 4:9-10.

> *Whenever the living creatures* give glory, honor and thanks to him who
> sits on the throne and who lives for ever and ever, *the twenty-four*
> *elders* fall down before him who sits on the throne, and worship him
> who lives for ever and ever.

At this point the elders "lay their crowns before the throne" and praise
God for his worthiness as Creator and Sustainer of all things. What an example for us—actually setting aside their own honor (their crowns) in order to
give more glory to the One who alone is worthy of it all.

Notice also the elders and the living creatures working together in the
scene with the unopened scroll in Revelation 5—when John was weeping
"because no one was found who was worthy to open the scroll." It was "one
of the elders" who told John to stop crying, and turned his attention to
Christ. Then John saw the slain Lamb "standing in the center of the throne,
encircled by the four living creatures and the elders" (5:6).

After Christ had taken the scroll from God's hand,

> *the four living creatures* and *the twenty-four elders* fell down before the
> Lamb. Each one had a harp and they were holding golden bowls full
> of incense, which are the prayers of the saints. And they sang a new
> song: "You are worthy to take the scroll and to open its seals, because
> you were slain, and with your blood you purchased men for
> God...." (5:8-9)

The scene reaches a climax when "every creature in heaven and on
earth and under the earth" sings praise to God and to the Lamb (5:13). Then
look again at our worship team in action:

> *The four living creatures* said, "Amen," and *the elders* fell down and
> worshiped. (5:14)

And after that "Amen" I'm sure everyone there was feeling, "What a
wonderful worship service we've had!" It couldn't be better.

If these heavenly beings really will be our future worship leaders up there, isn't it great that God's already introduced them to us?

Meanwhile let's meet some particular angels one by one. "One by one" is actually as far as we can go right now, because only two angels in Scripture are individually named. Both are justifiably famous.

Gabriel

Gabriel's name means "Mighty One of God." Gabriel would probably easily win the award for "Most Admired Angel." He always seems to be bringing important news, and usually quite good news.

Gabriel met Zechariah inside the Holy of Holies in the temple to tell him that his prayers had been answered (that's always good news!) and that he would have a son. And not just any son, but the forerunner of the Christ (Luke 1:11-17).

Shortly afterward Gabriel went to a girl named Mary to tell her the best news the world has ever heard: God was sending his Son to earth in the flesh, to establish a kingdom that would never end (1:26-37).

Five hundred years earlier, the news Gabriel brought to Daniel was more complicated, with its visions of future world-shaking events. But his welcome word to Daniel in 9:23 reminds us of the news Zechariah heard and that we all long to hear—"As soon as you began to pray, an answer was given...."

Gabriel has good news to give because he stays in the right place to learn it. As he told Zechariah, "I am Gabriel. *I stand in the presence of God.*" If you want good news to give people you love, stay long in the presence of God.

No doubt Gabriel will be quite an awesome sight for us to behold in heaven, but when he came to Daniel he seems to have taken on a more normal human aspect. Daniel says he "looked like a man" (8:15), and later calls him "the man I had seen in the earlier vision" (9:21).

Gabriel is perfect at the job of being God's messenger. Notice how concisely and helpfully he explains to Daniel what he's up to: "I am going *to tell you* what will happen later," he says in 8:19. And on his next visit he says,

> Daniel, I have now come *to give you insight and understanding.* As soon as you began to pray, an answer was given, which I have come *to tell you.*... (9:22-23)

Likewise he makes his mission plain to Zechariah:

> I stand in the presence of God, and I have been sent to speak to you and to tell you this good news. (Luke 1:19)

He also knows how to be positive and encouraging, a great skill to have in communication. He tells Daniel, "You are highly esteemed" (9:23). And listen to his encouragement for Mary:

> Greetings, you who are highly favored! The Lord is with you....Do not be afraid, Mary, you have found favor with God. (Luke 1:28-30)

Gabriel is also quite a mover. Daniel tells us, "While I was still in prayer, Gabriel...came to me *in swift flight* about the time of the evening sacrifice" (9:21).

Michael

Michael's name means "Who Is Like God?" While Gabriel is more of an announcing and preaching angel, Michael is more involved in protecting and fighting. Even individual angels seem to have their special gifts and responsibilities, just as members of the body of Christ do.

In Revelation, for example, besides seeing Michael at his task of fighting, we read of an angel "who had charge of the fire" (14:18), "the angel in charge of the waters" (16:5), and an angel who had "the key to the Abyss" (20:1). Apparently angels and believers alike all have their own perfect jobs in carrying out God's perfect will.

Only three times in the Scripture do we see this particular Michael mentioned (there are other Michaels in the Old Testament, but they're men, not angels).

Michael is a royal champion of God's people Israel. He's referred to three times in Daniel, and his tagline gets progressively more exalted and more personal toward Israel:

First he's called "one of the chief princes" in 10:13.

Then it's "Michael, *your* prince" in 10:21.

Finally it's "Michael, the great prince who protects your people" in 12:1.

In the New Testament, Michael is mentioned twice. In Revelation 12:7 he's the leading warrior in the great heavenly battle against Satan—"And there was war in heaven. Michael and his angels fought against the dragon, and the dragon and his angels fought back."

In Jude 9 he's called "the archangel Michael." This title "archangel" means the angel who is "first, principal, chief." Only Michael is given that name in Scripture (Gabriel isn't), and so Paul may be referring to Michael as *"the* archangel" in 1 Thessalonians 4:16—

> For the Lord himself will come down from heaven, with a loud command, with the voice of *the archangel* and with the trumpet call of God, and the dead in Christ will rise first.

Michael's voice may be the one we'll hear on the day of the rapture.

Is Michael the one angel who is above all others? He may well be, though the reference to him in Daniel 10 as *"one of* the chief princes" is enough to keep us from being dogmatic about it. Revelation 8:2 speaks of *"the* seven angels who stand before God." If these are the seven leading angels, it's possible that Michael is one of them and perhaps even the chief of the seven. This is all another mystery we'll learn more about later.

If Michael is the foremost of all angels, then his name is quite appropriate—"Who Is Like God?" The answer, of course, is "No one." Nobody compares to God, not even the mighty captain of the angelic host. Regardless of the great battles Michael wins, or whatever great things any angels do, our only praise must go to the Lord, "who *alone* does marvelous deeds" (Psalm 72:18).

Yes, having a name that's meaningful is a great way to let others know what's significant about you. That's certainly the way it is with angels—who are messengers, and powers, and warrior hosts, and holy ones, and mighty ones, and watchers, and hard-working guardians, and burning and shining ones, and living creatures, and elder examples—but still, nothing much in comparison to God.

And what about you and me? Do our names reveal the best truths about us? Of course they do! We're saints, and Christians ("little Christs" or "Christ Ones"), and believers, and brothers and sisters in the Lord, and children of God, and disciples, and—well, and quite a lot more.

But that's all a chapter in another book, by another name.

Chapter Nine

THE GREATEST ANGEL

THERE ARE ANGELS—and then there's The Angel.

Now we come to the greatest mystery of all in our study here together: the one who is called *"the* angel of the Lord."

No doubt you've already noticed that often in an Old Testament passage the "angel" who's speaking is identified directly with God himself. The angel seems not just to be *from* the Lord, but actually to *be* the Lord.

As we walk again through Scripture, let's focus our mental lens on this question: Could this be the Lord himself appearing in these encounters?

God or Angel?

We're back along that desert road where a woman kneels by a spring. She is Hagar, Egyptian maidservant to Sarai, the wife of Abram. Here by the spring *"the angel of the Lord* found Hagar" (Genesis 16:7).

In their conversation the angel makes a promise that sounds straight from God: *"I* will so increase your descendants that they will be too numerous to count" (16:10). As Hagar heard this promise, who did she think she was seeing and hearing? Verse 13 tells us:

> She gave this name *to the Lord* who spoke to her: *"You are the God who sees me,"* for she said, *"I have now seen the One* who sees me."

Was he an angel, or was he God?

Now let's climb Mount Moriah, at a time not many years later. On the mountaintop, following God's instructions, Abraham is about to bring down a knife into the cord-bound body of a boy lying on an altar. It's his beloved son Isaac. Abraham's arm is upraised.

> But *the angel of the Lord* called out to him from heaven, "Abraham! Abraham!... Do not lay a hand on the boy." (22:11-12)

At once the angel tells Abraham, "Now I know that you fear *God*, because you have not withheld from *me* your son, your only son." A grateful Abraham then offers a different sacrifice on the altar—a ram instead of his son. And then:

> The *angel of the Lord* called to Abraham from heaven a second time and said, "*I* swear by *myself*, declares *the Lord*, that because you have done this and have not withheld your son, your only son, *I* will surely bless you...." (22:15-17)

Was he angel or God?

Years later, Isaac's son Jacob is telling his family about a dream.

> *The angel of God* said to me in the dream, "Jacob." I answered, "Here I am." And he said, "...*I am* the *God* of Bethel, where you anointed a pillar and where you made a vow to *me*. Now leave this land at once and go back to your native land." (Genesis 31:11-13)

Was this an angel in Jacob's dream, or God?

But soon Jacob would do more than dream about this heavenly being. As he followed the angel's instructions and traveled back to his native land, he was camping late one night along the Jabbok River. Earlier that evening he had sent his family and his belongings across the ford of the river. For a God-appointed reason, Jacob stayed behind. "Jacob was left alone, and *a man* wrestled with him till daybreak" (32:24).

Who was this man, this endurance wrestler?

The prophet Hosea tells us that he was an "angel," and Hosea summarizes what happened to Jacob that night: "He struggled with *the angel* and overcame him; he wept and begged for his favor" (12:4).

We get more details in Genesis. When this "man" wrestling with Jacob "saw that he could not overpower him, he touched the socket of Jacob's hip so that his hip was wrenched" (32:25). At daybreak the "man" gave Jacob a new name—Israel, which means, "he struggles *with God*."

Then Jacob said, "Please tell me *your name.*" The "man" avoided answering Jacob's question, and instead "he blessed him there."

In the light of the morning sun, Jacob—tired and now limping—said, "I saw *God* face to face, and yet my life was spared."

Was the "man" Jacob saw an angel, or was he God?

Four centuries later, Moses is herding sheep "on the far side of the desert" near Horeb, the mountain of God. "There *the angel of the Lord* appeared to him in flames of fire from within a bush" (Exodus 3:1-2). Then "*God* called to him from within the bush" (3:4). Moses would never forget what this "angel" told him:

> I AM WHO I AM.... This is *my* name forever.... Go, assemble the elders of Israel and say to them, "*The Lord,* the *God* of your fathers— the *God* of Abraham, Isaac and Jacob—appeared to me...." (3:14-16)

God or angel?

Another four centuries later, in an Israelite town called Zorah, "the angel of the Lord" appeared to the barren wife of a man named Manoah. The angel promised her that she would bear a son (he would later be called Samson).

When she told this exciting news to her husband, she described the messenger as "a man of God" who "looked like an angel of God, very awesome. I didn't ask him where he came from, and he didn't tell me his name" (Judges 13:6).

Soon afterward the angel came again. This time Manoah saw him too, but he "did not realize that it was the angel of the Lord" (13:16).

> Then Manoah inquired of the angel of the Lord, "What is your name, so that we may honor you when your word comes true?"
>
> He replied, "Why do you ask *my name?* It is *beyond understanding.*" (13:17-18)

Following the angel's instructions, Manoah prepared a burnt offering to offer on a rock altar to the Lord.

> And *the Lord* did an amazing thing while Manoah and his wife watched: As the flame blazed up from the altar toward heaven, *the angel of the Lord* ascended in the flame. Seeing this, Manoah and his wife fell with their faces to the ground. When the angel of the Lord did not show himself again to Manoah and his wife, Manoah realized that *it was the angel of the Lord.*
>
> "We are doomed to die!" he said to his wife. "We have seen *God!*" (13:19-22)

At about the same time, the angel of the Lord even made a kind of cross-country trip across a stretch of Israel to broadcast an urgent message to the entire nation. It was urgent because the people had backslidden so far, neglecting to tear down the pagan altars in the land. God in his mercy went all-out to get his people's attention:

> *The angel of the Lord* went up from Gilgal to Bokim and said, "I brought you up out of Egypt and led you into the land that *I* swore to give to your forefathers.... Yet you have disobeyed *me....*"

As punishment, the angel warned that he would not drive out the pagan peoples from Israel's land, but would leave them to become "thorns in your sides."

When *the angel of the Lord* had spoken these things to all the Israelites, the people wept aloud, and they called that place Bokim [which means "weepers"]. There they offered sacrifices to the *Lord.* (Judges 2:1-5)

And so it happened, again and again in the Old Testament. "The angel of the Lord" came on the scene with reproof or guidance or encouragement. He appeared to Gideon as he threshed wheat in a winepress, and to David at the time of the punishing plague, and to the prophets Elijah and Zechariah, and even to Balaam's donkey. And it was "the angel of the Lord" who went out at night and slaughtered 185,000 Assyrians camped outside Jerusalem.

In these passages, did the people (as well as the donkey) actually see *God?*

But Scripture is clear: *No man or woman can ever see God.* The Lord himself told Moses this in the wilderness: "You cannot see my face," he said, "for *no one may see me* and live" (Exodus 33:20).

Jesus said it too, as he claimed for himself a unique relationship with God: *"No one has seen the Father* except the one who is from God," he told the Jews; "only he has seen the Father" (John 6:46).

Paul's teaching holds consistent with this. He calls the Lord "the invisible God" (Colossians 1:15) and praises him as the one "who lives in unapproachable light, *whom no one has seen or can see"* (1 Timothy 6:16).

The apostle John agrees. *"No one has ever seen God,"* he says twice, first in his gospel (1:18), then in his first epistle (4:12).

Moses carefully reminded the people of Israel that when the Lord's presence came with fire and thunder on Mount Sinai, *"You saw no form of any kind* the day the Lord spoke to you" (Deuteronomy 4:15). God cannot be seen.

So who *was* "the angel of the Lord"?

Though the angel of the Lord seems in some ways to be *distinct* from God, there can be no denying that in some mysterious way he was also clearly identified *with* God and *was* God—and therefore not at all like other angels.

Therefore you might be saying right now that this chapter doesn't even belong in a book about angels. Others would probably agree with you. Lewis Sperry Chafer reminds us that the title "Angel of the Lord"

> belongs only to God and is used in connection with the divine manifestations in the earth and *therefore is in no way to be included in the angelic hosts.*

M. J. Erickson writes,

> It is not possible, then, to draw from the nature of the angel of the Lord inferences that can be applied to all angels.

By looking at the angel of the Lord we're in some definite way looking at God. And God, as we know, is set apart from angels just as he is from all the rest of creation. There's a sense in which the actions and behavior of the angel of the Lord in these amazing passages doesn't tell us any more about angels than it does about our crawly friends the caterpillars.

Yet God in his wisdom does use the word *angel* to identify this particular manifestation of himself in these passages. And since the deepest purpose of the book you hold in your hands isn't just to teach us about angels, but rather to help us learn *through* angels what we can about God himself, let's go ahead and stick with the topic for a few pages.

Could He Be Christ?

The angel of the Lord certainly must be more than just an angel with special credentials. Did God the Father himself somehow come down to be represented in temporary human form?

Or—since the angel of the Lord appears to be both distinct from God in heaven as well as identified with him, and seems to possess his deity—is it possible that this could actually be *Christ?* Did God the Son, the second person of the Trinity, come and walk on earth centuries before he was born a baby in Bethlehem?

Some Bible scholars and teachers have been reluctant to come to that conclusion, especially since the New Testament doesn't clearly insist on it. J. M. Wilson says that of the various proposed explanations for the angel of the Lord, identifying him with God the Son "is certainly the most tempting to the mind." Then he adds,

> Yet it must be remembered that at best these are only conjectures that touch on a great mystery.... The appearances of the angel of the Lord ...culminated in the coming of the Savior, and are thus a foreshadowing of, and a preparation for, the full revelation of God in Jesus Christ. Further than this it is not safe to go.

But over the centuries, many who have searched the Scriptures feel it is safe to go further—including Calvin, who wrote:

> I am rather inclined...to agree with ancient writers, that in those passages wherein it is stated that the angel of the Lord appeared to Abraham, Jacob, and Moses, Christ was that angel.

"According to all the evidence," says C. F. Dickason, the angel of the Lord "seems to be the preincarnate Son."

"Christ," wrote Lewis Sperry Chafer, "is the Angel of Jehovah."

And Billy Graham writes,

> There are no grounds for questioning the very early and traditional Christian interpretation that in these cases there is a preincarnation manifestation of the second person of the Trinity.

But rather than take someone else's word for it, let's look at some of the evidence ourselves.

First of all we know that Christ is indeed eternal. His existence did not begin at Bethlehem. He was "with God in the beginning" (John 1:2). "Before Abraham was born, I am!" he told the Jews (8:58). He had glory in God's presence "before the world began" (17:5), and a loving relationship with his Father "before the creation of the world" (17:24).

So we know that Christ was at least around and available for ministry during Old Testament times.

Now consider how Christ is different from the Father and the Spirit. Of the three persons of the Trinity, the second is the one most involved in manifesting God to man.

We've looked already at Scriptures that tell us no one can see God the Father. Likewise the third person of the Trinity is also associated with an invisible ministry. The Holy Spirit is like the wind, and "the wind blows wherever it pleases. You hear its sound, but you cannot tell where it comes from or where it is going" (John 3:8). Jesus implies that though believers will know the Spirit's indwelling work within them, the Spirit himself will be invisible both to them and to the world, which "neither sees him nor knows him" (John 14:17).

But Scripture emphasizes that the second person of the Trinity is God become flesh, God in human form. He is "Immanuel—which means, 'God with us'" (Matthew 1:23). He's the one and only Son of God who is both "at the Father's side" and "has made him known" (John 1:18). "He appeared in a body" and "was seen by angels" (1 Timothy 3:16).

John describes him with his senses:

> That which was from the beginning, which we have *heard*, which we have *seen* with our eyes, which we have *looked at* and our hands have *touched*. . . . We have *seen* it and testify to it. (1 John 1:1-2)

And someday, "men *will see* the Son of Man coming in clouds with great power and glory" (Mark 13:26).

Christ is God in our sight. Christ is God seeable and touchable and knowable. And the Old Testament ministry of the angel of the Lord is consistent with this. Even the personality of the angel of the Lord seems consistent with what we know of Jesus. Some of the phrases spoken by the angel of the Lord to Gideon remind us of what Christ tells his disciples in the Gospels—"Am I not sending you?" (Judges 6:14). "I will be with you…" (6:16). "Peace! Do not be afraid…" (6:23).

In the last book of the Old Testament—the last book written before the coming of the Christ—the promised Messiah is described as "the Messenger of the covenant, whom you desire" (Malachi 3:1). In Hebrew this word "messenger" is the same term commonly translated as "angel," so the phrase in Malachi is often rendered "the *angel* of the covenant." This title could be a designation that bridges "the angel of the Lord" with Christ, here on the final pages before the old covenant gives way to the new. Jesus could be the "Angel of the Lord" just as surely as he is the "Angel of the Covenant."

Another intriguing passage that may speak to this topic is 1 Corinthians 10:1-4. Paul is recalling the Hebrews who followed Moses out of Egypt. Think back to those days for God's people: We read how "the angel of God" traveled with them in connection with a pillar of cloud and fire (Exodus 14:19). And on Mount Sinai the Lord made this promise to them: "My angel will go ahead of you and bring you into the land" (23:23). Notice what God says about this faithful guide:

> See, I am sending an angel ahead of you to guard you along the way and to bring you to the place I have prepared. Pay attention to him and listen to what he says. Do not rebel against him; *he will not forgive your rebellion, since my Name is in him.* (23:20-21)

This angel is definitely a cut above ordinary angels, for God's very "Name" was in him. Also, he could forgive sins—and "who can forgive sins but God alone?" (Mark 2:7). The angel of the Lord was personally guiding the Israelites from Egypt to the Promised Land.

Paul now recalls the Hebrews' wilderness experience in spiritual terms:

> They were all baptized into Moses in the cloud and in the sea. They all ate the same spiritual food and drank the same spiritual drink; for they drank from the spiritual rock that accompanied them, and *that rock was Christ.* (1 Corinthians 10:2-4)

The "spiritual rock" that accompanied Israel in the wilderness, Paul says, was Christ. Christ was there!

It could be that late on the first Easter afternoon, when the resurrected Jesus walked unrecognized with Cleopas and his friend on the road from Jerusalem to Emmaus and "explained to them what was said in *all* the Scriptures concerning *himself*"—it just might be he had something to say that afternoon about once making a promise to Hagar beside a desert spring, and once keeping Abraham from killing his son, and once talking to Moses from a burning bush, and once rising up in flames before Manoah and his wife, and even once flashing a sword to a frightened donkey and his unsuspecting rider.

God Was There

But what difference does all this make to us?

First of all, it shows us God's love. In Old Testament times the Scriptures were not yet complete, the Son of God had not yet lived out his sacrificial ministry, and the Holy Spirit's indwelling ministry had not yet given birth to the Church. How privileged we are today to have all these!

But God in his love still provided a special grace to his people through the ministry of the angel of the Lord. God *cared deeply* for them in their condition, and he did something about it. Isaiah puts it well:

In all their distress he too was distressed,

   and *the angel of his presence saved them.*

In his love and mercy he redeemed them;

   he lifted them up and carried them all the days of old. (63:9)

In so many critical moments of Old Testament history, God was there in the form of his angel, providing his loving guidance: when the seed of the nation was begun in the lives of Abraham, Isaac, and Jacob; when the people were led by Moses out of bondage and across the wilderness; and as they faced many trials and enemies in the land God had chosen for them.

Appearances of the angel of the Lord ceased after the birth of Jesus Christ—a further bit of evidence that he may indeed have been that angel. That fact also teaches us the supreme importance of Christ's incarnation, and of the ministry of the Holy Spirit, and of the revelation of Scripture in its entirety. Now that we have those, we do not need the angel of the Lord.

Understand especially that Christ could not have saved us as the angel of the Lord. To accomplish our redemption, he had to become flesh. He had to become *one of us*—not an angel.

> Since the children have flesh and blood, he too shared in their humanity.... For surely it is not angels he helps, but Abraham's descendants. For this reason he had to be made like his brothers in every way...that he might make atonement for the sins of the people. (Hebrews 2:14-17)

It's seems highly possible that in the Old Testament, Christ came to earth in the form of an angel—the greatest Angel. But it's the most absolute, most dependable and undeniable fact in all history that in the New Testament Christ came to earth as a man—the greatest Man, even God himself among us.

Chapter Ten

SHOWING US
HOW TO WORSHIP

I N HIS WISE and warm book *Somewhere Angels,* Larry Libby tells children (and their parents) about two important things in particular we can learn from angels.

One of them is this: "We can learn how to worship the Lord with all our heart."

Angels worship not only wholeheartedly, but also all the time, Libby suggests.

> I think angels have been worshiping from the time they first opened their eyes and saw God's smile....
>
> There are even special angels around God's throne who never, ever stop praising His name. They don't have rest time or recess. They don't go home at night because there is no night—and they wouldn't want to leave God's side even if there was. Shouting and singing praise to the Lord is all they do—and all they *want* to do—forever and ever.

Jesus spoke of angels who "always see the face of my Father in heaven" (Matthew 18:10). I'm sure the result of their unbroken gaze into his face is lots of rich, genuine *worship.*

Wouldn't it be exciting to be a part of that?

Of all the things we've bungled over the years in the Church, worship is maybe the biggest. If giving glory to God is mankind's chief purpose, somehow Satan has gotten us caught up in other agendas. What goes on in lots of places in the name of worship is not really that at all. We've lost the sense of what it means to truly worship God.

The angels can help us rediscover it.

When we first met angelic beings in Scripture, they guarded the gate to the earthly Paradise, keeping Adam and Eve from the tree of life. But several hundred pages later, when we reach the last chapter in Revelation, John actually gets an angel-guided tour of heavenly Paradise, with the tree of life thriving in the middle of it. After the tour the angel says to John, *"Worship God!"*

Between the Garden of Eden in Genesis and the New Jerusalem in Revelation, lots of angelic worship takes place. And the angels' kind of worship is the *real* kind. We have lots to learn from them.

Angels worship so well because they always obey God perfectly, and worship is one of the things he's commanded them to do (and us too). We can actually hear him commanding every single angel to worship his Son Jesus Christ in Hebrews 1:6—

> When God brings his firstborn into the world, he says, *"Let all God's angels worship him."*

Angels live in the presence of God, and stay focused on God, and this is where they get their majesty and awe. With that kind of lifestyle, how could they be anything *but* majestic and awesome? I wonder what you and I would be like if we camped each night beside God's throne in glory, and stayed full of his presence even when we went out into the world to do his work?

I've been around a few people like that. Haven't you? When you're with them you're almost unsure what to say. There's something so different about them. So you reach the same conclusion that was made about the disciples in Acts 4:13—they've "been with Jesus." The Lord is all they seem to want to talk about, and they make you want to think more about him too.

Maybe they've taken lessons from an angel, like the one A. W. Tozer reflects upon:

> If some watcher or holy one who has spent his glad centuries by the sea of fire were to come to earth, how meaningless to him would be the ceaseless chatter of the busy tribes of men.... And were such a one to speak on earth would he not speak of God? Would he not charm and fascinate his hearers with rapturous descriptions of the Godhead? And after hearing him could we ever again consent to listen to anything less than theology, the doctrine of God? Would we not thereafter demand of those who would presume to teach us that they speak to us from the mount of divine vision or remain silent altogether?

As we go to the "mount of divine vision" in Scripture, I think especially of two lessons about worship that angels teach us most: The *fear of God* in worship, and *freedom* in worship.

Fear of God

Remember Psalm 89:7? God's holy angels don't just fear him. They fear him *greatly:*

> In the council of the holy ones God is *greatly feared;*
> he is more awesome than all who surround him.

Here is Scripture using that word *awesome,* which you've seen popping up again and again in this book. It's a shame that through overuse and misuse in our culture this word has lost nearly all the power it once had. With its older meaning, there's really no word quite like it for describing what we encounter so often in this book. *Awesome* means "inspiring awe," and *awe* in turn means "fear mingled with reverence; a feeling produced by something majestic and sublime." Keep that classic meaning in mind as you picture the angels looking around in their "council" in heaven and across the horizon of the universe, and seeing nothing and no one that even remotely approaches the awesomeness of God. They know he's sublimely and majestically holy—awesomely holy. Therefore they show him "fear mingled with reverence."

The richest scenes of heavenly worship in all of Scripture are in Revelation. Here the angelic beings demonstrate their reverence for God, and make a point of doing so again and again. "Day and night" the four living creatures "never stop saying, 'Holy, holy, holy is the Lord God Almighty'" (4:8). And "whenever" those living creatures offer up that praise, "the twenty-four elders *fall down* before him who sits on the throne, and worship him," and they "*lay their crowns before the throne*" (4:10).

In John's vision, after Christ had taken from God's hands the scroll with seven seals, "the four living creatures and the twenty-four elders *fell down* before the Lamb" (4:8). There were more songs of praise, and then "the four living creatures said, 'Amen,' and the elders *fell down* and worshiped" (4:14).

After six of the seals on the scroll had been opened,

> *All the angels* were standing around the throne and around the elders and the four living creatures. *They fell down on their faces* before the throne and worshiped God.... (7:11)

The opening of the seventh seal brings out seven angels with seven trumpets, and after the last of these has been sounded, "the twenty-four elders, who were seated on their thrones before God, *fell on their faces* and worshiped God...." (11:16).

From all we can tell in Scripture, these spirit beings right now are worshiping in this very manner the same God whom you and I claim as our Lord. If these holy creatures, awesome as they are, cry out in praise of his holiness day and night, how much should we? If they who are pure and splendid fall down before God again and again, how often should we?

Have we had the wrong idea about worship? Are we leaving out too much reverence? Are we trying in vain to get cozier with God, when we should instead be mindful of the distance that must forever stand between us?

M. J. Erickson writes,

> Some worship, rightfully stressing the joy and confidence that the believer has in relationship to a loving heavenly Father, goes beyond that point to an excessive familiarity treating him as an equal, or worse yet, as a servant.... While there are room and need for enthusiasm of expression, and perhaps even an exuberance, that should never lead to a loss of respect. There will always be a sense of awe and wonder.... Although there are love and trust and openness between us and God, we are not equals. He is the almighty, sovereign Lord. We are his servants and followers.

In a sense, fear is simply our honest recognition of the facts. God is holy in and of himself. We are not. And holiness being what it is—exclusive, set apart, untouchable, unknowable, fiery and consuming—we cannot be simply casual and carefree and comfortable around it.

Angels practice the fear of God because they're already in his presence. We must have fear of God because someday we'll be there too, to see God's holiness up close.

We grow in fearing the Lord as we think more clearly about the moment when *we'll* appear before him. When the time comes to receive our rewards, we'll stand wholly accountable to God for the responsibilities he's given us as his children here. Whatever I'm planning right now, or whatever I'm thinking, or whatever I'm doing, or whatever I'm saying will either count for God's kingdom or count for nothing. I'll find out about it all on that day I stand before him.

When Paul said, "Since, then, *we know what it is to fear the Lord,*" it was immediately after he had warned us,

> For we must all appear before the judgment seat of Christ, *that each one may receive what is due him* for the things done while in the body, whether good or bad. (2 Corinthians 5:10-11)

The standards by which we'll be measured at Christ's judgment seat are the perfect standards of the holy God. Therefore we fear him.

But fear of God is bigger than that. In fact our fear of him will continue even in heaven, even after judgment. In a great scene of worship in Revelation 19, after the twenty-four elders and the four living creatures cry "Hallelujah," a voice comes from heaven's throne to God's redeemed people: "Praise our God, all you his servants, you who *fear him,* both small and great!" This takes place as we're called to the great wedding supper of the Lamb.

Even in eternity we'll still be gratefully redeemed human beings, fearing God with good, perfect fear.

Earlier we looked briefly at Psalm 99, a celebration of the one who "sits enthroned between the cherubim." Three times in this brief song we're reminded of something about God: "he is *holy*" (verse 3); "he is *holy*" (verse 5); "the Lord our God is *holy*" (verse 9). The cherubim understand this truth. We must also understand it, and fear.

"In olden days men of faith were said to 'walk in the fear of God' and to 'serve the Lord with fear,'" A. W. Tozer reminds us. "However intimate their communion with God, however bold their prayers, at the base of their religious life was the conception of God as awesome and dreadful." Why and how have we lost this "healing fear," as Tozer goes on to call it?

We eagerly desire wisdom, and we search for life-knowledge, yet we forget what the Bible gives as the only starting place for it: "The *fear of the Lord* is the beginning of wisdom, and knowledge of the *Holy One* is understanding" (Proverbs 9:10).

In Psalm 36, the first fault David finds with the sinner is that "there is *no fear* of God before his eyes." Perhaps it's also the first fault the angels would find with our worship—and the first fault we should repair, "because of the angels" (1 Corinthians 11:10).

Freedom in Worship

Although angels are so perfect in their fear of God, we don't sense at all that they're *frozen* in fear. Instead they demonstrate great freedom in their worship. They're free to worship God the way he wants to be worshiped.

Reflect again on the Scripture scenes below, and this time notice the indications of the angels' energy and movement and emotion in their relationship with God:

In Ezekiel's vision he saw the cherubim moving "wherever the spirit would go" (1:12), and they *"sped back and forth* like flashes of lightning" (1:14).

In Jacob's dream he saw the angels *ascending and descending* on the stairway leading into the Lord's presence (Genesis 28:12). Jesus describes them *"ascending and descending* on the Son of Man" (John 1:51).

In Job 38:7, the heavenly beings sing together and *shout for joy* in recognition of God's work.

In Hebrews 12:22 the myriads of angels are described as being "in *joyful* assembly."

Throughout Revelation we see not only the angels' continual acts of great reverence for God and the Lamb, but also their exuberant outbursts of freely given praise. In 5:8-9 the four living creatures and twenty-four elders all have harps, and John hears them singing "a new song."

One of the most memorable pictures is in Revelation 7. After a great multitude of the redeemed (in white robes and holding palm branches) has praised God, the angels and living creatures and elders have another turn at doing this themselves. We hear their shouts of worship like pealing bells or salutes of cannon-fire:

Amen!
Praise and glory
and wisdom and thanks and honor
and power and strength
be to our God for ever and ever.
Amen! (7:12)

As John stared at this vision, he might have thought it impossible for worship to get any richer and more powerful and triumphant. But the crescendo keeps building.

In chapter 19 there's an overflowing of joy marked by four great shouts of "Hallelujah!" from the "great multitude in heaven." They shout to God, "Let us rejoice and be glad and give him glory!" as the Lamb's wedding supper is announced. They rejoice especially that the Lamb's bride is given "fine linen, bright and clean" to wear. The angels know these wedding clothes represent "the righteous acts of the saints," and they share our joy over them.

It's no wonder that at this point John fell down to worship the angel who was showing him all this.

What a freedom and fullness of joy we see here—and to think it's all because of what God did for *us!* So weren't *we* made to worship this deeply too? If the angels shout "Hallelujah!" on our behalf, surely we can feel free to do it in our own worship as well.

Mature believers know that a heart full of thanksgiving is the most fertile soil for freedom in worship. But offering thanks isn't reserved just for redeemed mankind. We see the twenty-four elders demonstrating this for us in 11:16-17. They fall on their faces and say,

We *give thanks* to you, Lord God Almighty,
the One who is and who was,
because you have taken your great power and have begun to reign.

Just as Psalm 99 promotes fear in worship by reminding us of God's holiness, the next psalm promotes our freedom in worship through thanksgiving. *"Shout for joy* to the Lord," Psalm 100 begins. We're warmly invited to "worship the Lord with *gladness,"* to "come before him with *joyful songs,"* and to "enter his gates with *thanksgiving."*

Just as God's holiness is the reason for our fear, so God's good and faithful love is the reason for our freedom and thanksgiving. The psalm concludes,

> *Give thanks* to him and praise his name.
> For *the Lord is good* and his *love* endures forever;
> his *faithfulness* continues through all generations.

Soaring in Freedom

The cherubim give us another strong angelic picture of liberated worship.

God gave specific instructions that the sculpted cherubim on the atonement cover of the Ark of the Covenant were "to have their *wings spread upward"* (Exodus 25:20). Centuries later, when the Ark was moved from the tabernacle into Solomon's temple, the wings of the great fifteen-foot-high cherubim in the Holy of Holies were also crafted "with their wings spread out" (1 Kings 6:27). Wings are for flying, and the cherubim's wings gave God's people a picture of free flight in the presence of God.

We can understand why the wings of the cherubim sculptures were designed as they were when we meet the real cherubim through Ezekiel's vision: "Their wings were spread out upward" (Ezekiel 1:11).

Wings are moving parts, and one of the strongest impressions upon Ezekiel in this vision was the loud noise made by their motion. The noise always reminded him of God:

When the creatures moved, I heard *the sound of their wings,* like the roar of rushing waters, *like the voice of the Almighty,* like the tumult of an army. (1:24)

The sound of the wings of the cherubim could be heard as far away as the outer court, *like the voice of God Almighty* when he speaks. (10:5)

The cherubim in God's presence aren't locked into silent stillness, but are engaged in free and active (and noisy!) worship.

Perhaps the six-winged seraphim in Isaiah 6 show something of the same picture. Isaiah says that with two of their wings "they were flying," and their flight may be as much an expression of free worship as of carrying out their work.

In his commentary on this passage, Matthew Henry asks us,

If angels come upon the wing from heaven to earth to minister for our good, shall not we soar upon the wing from earth to heaven, to share with them in their glory?

We too "will soar on wings like eagles" (Isaiah 40:31) as we hope in the Lord and let his strength renew us. Our soaring can take place as much in worship as anywhere else, when our hearts and hands and voices rise freely above personal and cultural inhibitions.

God's sovereign rule for us now is the "perfect law that gives freedom" (James 1:25), and in that freedom we must have the liberty to "lift up our hearts and our hands to God in heaven" (Lamentations 3:41). For "where the Spirit of the Lord is, there is freedom" (2 Corinthians 3:17).

Summon the Angels to Worship

So the angels help us worship. Can *we* help the angels worship?

Maybe we can!

Occasionally in the Psalms, the human writer invokes praise for God from the angels. David does it in Psalm 29 and 103—

Ascribe to the Lord, *O mighty ones,*
    ascribe to the Lord glory and strength.
Ascribe to the Lord the glory due his name;
    worship the Lord in the splendor of his holiness. (29:1-2)

Praise the Lord, you his angels,
    you mighty ones who do his bidding,
    who obey his word.
Praise the Lord, all his heavenly hosts,
    you his servants who do his will. (103:20-21)

The unknown author of Psalm 148 makes the same request:

Praise the Lord from the heavens,
    praise him in the heights above.
Praise him, all his angels,
    praise him, all his heavenly hosts. (148:1-2)

Would the angels really listen to a mere man asking them to praise God?

Why not? As Larry Libby says in *Somewhere Angels,* "They'll praise the Lord for any reason at all, and love doing it."

Maybe God has worked out something special with them in advance. Knowing how thrilling and fulfilling worship is for angels, maybe he's told them, "As I work in the hearts of my people on earth, and they call out the Scriptures that summon you to praise me, I'll gladly allow you the privilege of responding to their words. You can take their cue to make your songs to me even sweeter and your shouts even louder!"

It's probably worth a try. Go ahead and look up sometime, and ask the angels to pour on the coals in their worship intensity. But make sure you're doing the same to yours.

Fire and Wind Again

To get the most from the angels for our worship, we can go back once more to fire and wind, the apt imagery for angels that God gives us in Psalm 104 and Hebrews 1.

In our worship, the fire reminds us of fear. Like the angels, we fear God, for our God is a consuming fire. His blazing holiness leads us onward into accountability and fear.

Likewise in our worship, the wind reminds us of freedom and the Spirit. Like the angels we want to be free as the wind, as bold as a breeze in Spirit-directed worship. For "the wind blows wherever it pleases," and "so it is with everyone born of the Spirit" (John 3:8). God's soaring love leads us onward into thanksgiving and freedom.

To stay balanced in your worship and devotion to God, saturate your heart with both aspects: Fear and freedom. Fire and wind. God's great holiness and God's great love.

Tomorrow, as you meet with the Lord of the morning for your personal and private devotion, lock into both sides of worship.

And remember both sides as well next Sunday when you meet with the family of God. You can't cause others there to dive deeper into worship, but you can be responsible for your own heart, and have it ready to meet God more fully in public, corporate worship than you ever have before.

And that, in turn, will make you better fitted for the day up there when we unite in perfect praise with the angels.

Chapter Eleven

SHOWING US
HOW TO WORK

NOTHER GOOD lesson we can pick up from angels, according
to Larry Libby in his children's book *Somewhere Angels,* is this:
"We learn the great joy of obeying God quickly."

Calvin reflects that "in accommodation to us," Scripture has
shown us the wings of seraphim and cherubim "to assure us that when
occasion requires they will hasten to our aid with incredible swiftness, wing-
ing their way to us with the speed of lightning."

Once more the fire and wind illustration suggest a potent picture: The
angels in their obedient service are as intense as flames, and as quick as the
wind. Angels are just as good at the *work* God gives them as they are at *worship.*

God can count on them, and so can we. There's no sloppy workmanship or laziness or negligence on their part.

When David summons the angels to praise God in Psalm 103, he calls
them "you mighty ones who *do his bidding,* who *obey his word…* you his servants who *do his will.*"

Angels get so absorbed in their work that even their appearance is gov-
erned by their assignment. Depending on the task God gives them in serving us, they may remain invisible to our eyes, or appear in ordinary human
form, or take on some more glorious aspect. Their form—what they *are*—

depends on their function—what they *do*. As J. M. Wilson says, "In general they are simply regarded as *embodiments of their mission.*"

Here again let's recall Hebrews 1:14. It's a rich verse, and we can draw truth and implications and reflections about angelic work from every phrase: (a) the angels are *sent forth* (they're on assignment); (b) they're sent forth *to minister* (that means *service,* and service means *work*); (c) *all* angels are thus sent forth (no loafers among them); and (d) they go only *to those who will inherit salvation* (their labor benefits us!).

With David's words in Psalm 34:7 in mind—"The angel of the Lord encamps around those who fear him"—Matthew Henry comments on several aspects of angelic work. He notes that God uses angels

> for the protection of his people from the malice and power of evil spirits; and the holy angels do us more good offices every day than we are aware of.
>
> Though in dignity and in capacity of nature they are very much superior to us . . . though they have constant employment in the upper world, the employment of praising God, and are entitled to a constant rest and bliss there—yet in obedience to their Maker, and in love to those that bear his image, they condescend to minister to the saints, and stand up for them against the powers of darkness; they not only visit them, but encamp round about them, acting for their good. . . .

Angels get different instructions for different people in different circumstances. The angels appearing to Daniel told him to "seal up" the vision and prophetic words he'd been given (Daniel 8:26, 12:4), because "it concerns the distant future." (By the way, scholars think this may be why Daniel's visions are recorded in his own Hebrew tongue, while the rest of Daniel is written in Aramaic, the most common language of the Babylonian Empire.) But in Revelation, the angel speaking with John specifically told him, "Do *not* seal up the words of the prophecy of this book, because the time is near" (22:10). No doubt angels have to be careful to follow their instructions exactly.

As we noted earlier, the word *angel* means "messenger," so messenger-work appears to be a big part of an angel's job description. And angels are *trustworthy* messengers. In Luke 2 the shepherds went into Bethlehem to see the baby Jesus, and they found everything "just as they had been told" (2:20). Who had given the shepherds such an accurate picture of what to expect? It was an angel.

When the angel tells John in Revelation, "These are the *true words* of God" (19:9), and "These words are *trustworthy* and *true*" (22:6), we don't doubt it for a minute. Angels tell the truth.

We looked before at how these truth-telling messengers were especially involved in communicating God's law to mankind, which was "put into effect through angels" (Galatians 3:19, Acts 7:53). As holy beings who have always obeyed God perfectly, the angels probably have total comprehension of God's law for mankind. They know it and understand it better than you and I do the alphabet. The Bible never says angels desire to know more about the law; what they "long to look into" is the matter of our salvation (1 Peter 1:12), our redemption as those whom the law condemns but whom Jesus died for. Since we as human beings didn't live up to the law the angels brought to us, I'm sure they were thrilled out of their wings to also be assigned messenger-duty in communicating the coming of our Savior, who saves us from the law's curse.

Another angelic service to us is shown in Revelation 7:3-4. Angels put a seal "on the foreheads of the servants of our God," and this seal marks believers as belonging to the Lord. It's in contrast to the "mark of the beast" worn by those who belong to the devil (13:16-17), and who thus are destined to receive God's tormenting wrath (14:9-11). We can be thankful that the angels will be accurate and thorough in this service. (Wouldn't you hate to be a believer whom the angels inadvertently forgot to seal that day?)

As we've seen many times, everything good or noble or noteworthy about angels is directly attributable to something good or noble or noteworthy about God. Their faithfulness in their work is no exception.

The angels are faithful at work because they see the faithfulness of God in *his* work. A man in the Bible named Ethan knew this for sure. "Who's Ethan?" you may be saying. He isn't as well known as Daniel or John or Ezekiel, but perhaps of all human beings who have walked the earth, none had greater insight into angels than Ethan—Daniel and John and Ezekiel being the only exceptions, by virtue of their stunning visions.

Ethan the Ezrahite was noted for his wisdom (1 Kings 4:31) in the days of Solomon. He's likely the same Ethan who was originally appointed by Solomon's father David as one of the leaders among the temple musicians (1 Chronicles 15:19). Part of his job in the celebrations at the house of the Lord was "to sound the bronze cymbals."

He also was the writer of the 89th Psalm. We quoted it earlier. It's the one that mentions how God is "greatly feared" in "the council of the holy ones." Ethan also specifically says that God's *"faithfulness* too" is praised "in the assembly of the holy ones." And after citing the angelic praise for this faithfulness, Ethan adds his own:

> O Lord God of Hosts, who is like you?
>> You are mighty, O Lord,
>> and your *faithfulness* surrounds you. (89:8)

Ethan knew that angels are faithful to us because God is faithful to us.

Throughout this book we've seen plenty of examples of the angels at work—from defending Eden to feeding Elijah, and healing Isaiah's sinful lips, and springing Peter out of jail, and showing John around New Jerusalem, and lots more. Now that we've highlighted so much of their labor, some particular questions about it are worth delving into.

Do I Have My Own Guardian Angel?

Is there one particular angel whose God-given assignment is serving me—just *me?*

There are plenty of folks who think that. Guardian angels are mainstream America these days. "GET IN TOUCH WITH YOUR OWN GUARDIAN ANGEL!" screamed a recent full-page advertisement in a leading magazine.

Many years ago, before I was ordained to the gospel ministry, I had to go through an ordination council in Haddon Heights, New Jersey. As a pastor, my father was on the ordination committee. My mother had also been invited to be in the room and watch the proceedings.

The committee reviewed a paper in which I outlined my doctrinal beliefs, then called me up for questioning on all the different levels and aspects of theology. When they came to the subject of angels, one of the committee members asked me, "David, do you believe in guardian angels?"

Before I could answer, my mother (I couldn't believe she did this) raised her voice and said, "Well if he doesn't, I do."

When she heard that question, who knows how many close calls during my growing-up years came flashing into her mind?

One of them I still remember as vividly as if it happened yesterday, though it occurred more than forty years ago.

My uncle had a farm near Binghamton, New York where I visited in the summertime. I was a city boy and didn't know much about a farm, but I learned a lot from my uncle.

One summer I was intrigued by the silos that towered up beside the barn. There were two of them. At that time one was full nearly to the top with silage, and the other was still empty, waiting to be filled.

I got the idea I wanted to climb up the outside of the silo that was full. I would slip through the little metal door at the top and land on the silage. Up there I could be in my own little world for a while.

So I climbed the ladder that scaled the outside. I don't know their exact dimensions, but man, those silos are *high*. As you go up you feel you're just hanging out in the middle of nowhere. I was stepping real slow, trying to be careful.

At the top I opened the door and swung my foot into the darkness. Just as I leaned in, I looked down and realized an awful fact: I had climbed the wrong silo! The one I was about to fall into was empty. There was nothing there—all the way to the ground.

I think that's the closest I ever came to not being here to write this book for you. I hung on with both hands and slowly eased myself back out to the ladder. Shaking like a leaf, I climbed down.

I've always believed that an angel saved me up there. That's one of the encounters that comes to my mind when I'm asked if I believe in guardian angels. Anyway, my mother believes in them.

What does the Bible say about them?

Psalm 91:11-12 gives a general overview of the angels providing protection for God's people:

> For he will command his *angels* concerning you
>> to guard you in all your ways;
> they will lift you up in their hands,
>> so that you will not strike your foot against a stone.

But that verse speaks of angels, plural. What about the concept of *one* particular angel assigned only to me?

Many theologians over the centuries have believed this way, including Thomas Aquinas, who thought everyone has a guardian angel assigned to him at birth. But what does the Bible say?

Two passages are pointed to most often in discussing the question of guardian angels. In the first, Jesus tells his disciples,

See that you do not look down on one of these little ones. For I tell you that *their angels* in heaven always see the face of my Father in heaven. (Matthew 18:10)

From these words some would assert that a number of God's angels are assigned to stand ready before the Father to respond instantly to his command for protection and care over these "little ones." Jesus calls them *"their angels."* But others would point out that the passage doesn't say these angels do any "guarding" of the "little ones"—in fact, they apparently "always" stay in God's presence. Nor does the passage specifically match one angel to each "little one."

The second passage that supporters of the guardian angel concept point to is Acts 12, where Peter is miraculously delivered from prison. It's one of everyone's favorite Bible stories. When we retold it earlier, we left Peter standing in the middle of the street. The angel had awakened him in his prison cell, ordered him to get dressed, slipped him out past guards and through gates, then led him out into the cool night air of freedom. Now the angel disappeared. Peter "came to himself." No longer groggy, he acknowledged what the Lord's angel had done, then went to a house where some of the believers had gathered and were praying.

The scene awaiting him there "was one of confusion and joyful humor," as one commentator describes it, and "must have led to hilarity every time it was repeated among the early believers."

Peter knocked at the outer entrance, and a servant girl named Rhoda came to answer the door. When she recognized Peter's voice, she was so overjoyed she ran back without opening it and exclaimed, "Peter is at the door!"

"You're out of your mind," they told her. When she kept insisting that it was so, they said, *"It must be his angel."*

But Peter kept on knocking, and when they opened the door and saw him, they were astonished. (12:13-16)

The believers praying for Peter thought it was "his angel" that the flustered servant girl had encountered at the door. Surely, some would say, they were referring to his guardian angel. But Rhoda had only heard a voice at the door. Why would Peter's guardian angel have a voice that sounded like Peter's? What the believers really were thinking, some say, is that Peter had been killed, and "his angel" was their way of referring to his disembodied spirit. No wonder they were hesitant to open the door.

Besides these passages, there's no other obvious scriptural evidence for *individual* guardian angels, so the case for them isn't a strong one.

But if this is disappointing news to you, and you're dismayed to think there may not be a specific angel responsible for your protection, you need not jump up in fear to check the locks on your doors and windows. There's plenty of evidence that God himself is looking out for you, in addition to all the angels he chooses to use in carrying out the job.

I love John Calvin's thoughts on this:

> Whether or not each believer has a single angel assigned to him for his defense, I dare not positively affirm.…
>
> This, indeed, I hold for certain, that each of us is cared for *not by one angel merely,* but that all with one consent watch for our safety.

"After all," he adds,

> it is not worthwhile anxiously to investigate a point which does not greatly concern us. If anyone does not think it enough to know that all the orders of the heavenly host are perpetually watching for his safety, I do not see what he could gain by knowing that he has one angel as a special guardian.

One thing we know for sure: Our God uses his awesome power in a compassionate, loving way to help those who need help. I like that about God. I've felt His love and compassion in many ways in recent months, and I know he's that kind of God. While on the one hand he's holy, there's the other side of it too: He condescends to be concerned about such as us, and will even dispatch one angel or an army of them for our service and protection.

There's great hope in that.

This is a good time to remind ourselves again that angels are created beings—*God's* created beings. He's told us much about them, but he's also withheld much. Even if he told us everything, however—even if we knew all there is to know about angels—the simple truth still would stand that they belong to God. They're his, and he can do with them whatever he wills. They aren't ours to control or to use. They aren't ours to satisfy either our physical and emotional needs or our intellectual curiosity.

They serve us, but they are not our servants. God alone is their Master. When they minister to us, it's because God has so directed, and not because we have commanded or even requested their service.

Are Angels Still Involved in Warfare?

Now back for a moment to the military aspect of angels. There's no way around it: A big part of angel work is warfare.

The angels are warriors because God is. *"The Lord is a warrior; the Lord is his name"* (Exodus 15:3). David, the man after God's own heart, tells us in song that God *"expresses his wrath every day"* (Psalm 7:11).

Here's a picture David gives of God getting ready for this daily work:

> He will sharpen his sword;
>> he will bend and string his bow.
> He has prepared his deadly weapons;
>> he makes ready his flaming arrows. (7:12-13)

Psalm 78 shows God on the warpath in his plagues against Pharaoh. This psalm by Asaph recounts the rivers of blood and the swarms of flies and frogs, the pestilence of grasshopper and locust, and the storms of hail and sleet and lightning bolts that devastated the Egyptians. The Lord "unleashed against them his hot anger, his wrath, indignation and hostility" (78:49).

In the same verse Asaph tells us who God used for this angry work: "a band of *destroying angels.*"

But God the Divine Warrior isn't only an Old Testament concept. Look again at the picture of Christ that was revealed first to John, and through him to us:

> There before me was a white horse, whose rider is called Faithful and True. With justice he judges and makes war.... Out of his mouth comes a sharp sword with which to strike down the nations.... He treads the winepress of the fury of the wrath of God Almighty. (Revelation 19:11-15)

And look again at who is with Christ in this scene:

> The *armies of heaven* were following him, riding on white horses.... (19:14)

Yes, God is a warrior and he wins every battle. Because of that, the angels also never lose.

If this thought of a Warrior God and warrior angels is disturbing—if you'd rather think of peace—then remember that your peace is possible only because of powerful protection (both by angels and through the Holy Spirit) that shields you from Satan and his wicked hosts. Battle is being waged on your behalf. If it wasn't, just how long do you think you could withstand the devil's attacks, fighting alone? Could you hold out even half a minute? And once you were conquered, as you inevitably would be, how much mercy could you honestly expect from this enemy, considering his character and background?

Thank God he is a Warrior!

Does God Do All His Work through Angels?

In a letter addressed to God, a little girl wrote,

> Dear God,
>
> Do you get your angels to do all your work? Mommy says that
> we are *her* angels and we have to do everything.

I think God's answer would be that no, he doesn't get angels to do *all* his work. (And they won't do all of ours, either.)

God *could* do everything himself, without ever using angels or nature or Christians or anything else. Or God can use those agents to accomplish whatever he wants, without in any way limiting his sovereignty. As M. J. Erickson reminds us, "God is not limited to working directly to accomplish his purposes."

God always does what he wants to do, and he does it the way he wants. He may use an angel to do some service one moment—a word of encouragement to a stranger perhaps, or locating a lost item for someone, or providing a needed gift of finances or food—and the next moment use a Christian to do an identical deed—and the next moment accomplish the same purposes by using neither angel nor man.

Therefore if God the Almighty can indeed send angels—or anything else—to our aid, then let's never stop praying for his help. Remember that the angel Gabriel came to Daniel specifically in response to his prayer (9:23), though Daniel was *not* praying to see or be served by an angel.

If I Sense an Angel's Presence, How Can I Be Sure?

When Gabriel appeared to Daniel, he told him, "Therefore *consider* the message, and *understand* the revelation." Daniel saw the angel and heard him, but Daniel was still required to put his own mental energy into evaluating all that the angel communicated to him.

This could well be God's command to us about angels as well— first in regard to what his Scripture says about them, and second in regard to our own experience.

"*Consider*…and *understand*…." How much are you doing that even now, as you study this topic? Are you really putting your mind to work as you look over the scriptural record?

"*Consider*…and *understand*…." How much are you prepared to do this as well if you encounter the presence of a totally spiritual being?

The Bible is clear: We are to "test the spirits" (1 John 4:1-3)—and angels are spirits. Paul said it too: "Test everything. Hold on to the good. Avoid every kind of evil" (1 Thessalonians 5:21-22).

Your best test is to keep Jesus Christ before the eyes of your heart:

> Every spirit that acknowledges that Jesus Christ has come in the flesh is from God, but every spirit that does not acknowledge Jesus is not from God. This is the spirit of the antichrist, which you have heard is coming and even now is already in the world. (1 John 4:2-3)

And suppose an angel did appear to you with some message from God. What would you honestly be more excited about—God's message, or getting to see an angel?

Again and again in the Scriptures we see this pattern: Those who are given the privilege of a direct visible or audible ministry from angels are those with mature hearts who want to encounter God—not angels.

The gospel accounts of the resurrection are a good example. The women and the disciples believed the angelic report of the good news of Jesus' resurrection, but not once did any of them turn their attention and their focus upon the angels. No one got excited about seeing angels. They were excited about what the angels *said*.

Notice what Mary did in John 20:10-18. She carried on a fairly calm conversation with two angels dressed in white, then turned away from them to converse with someone she thought was nothing more than a gardener.

It turned out to be Jesus himself. When she returned to tell the disciples, she didn't say, "I've seen angels," but, "I have seen the Lord." Her heart was right, and therefore God was able to let her see angels.

As a side-note on the angels' work, let's take up a couple of perplexing questions that often arise because of two unusual passages in Scripture.

Do God's Angels Ever Deceive Us?

We noted before how King Ahab died in his bloody chariot on the battle-field after failing to heed the angelic vision recounted to him by the prophet Micaiah. The prophet told Ahab he had seen the Lord "sitting on his throne with all the host of heaven standing on his right and on his left" (1 Kings 22:19, 2 Chronicles 18:18), and that these angels and God were discussing the disaster and death that would soon come to Ahab if he went into battle against Syria. What we didn't mention before is that four hundred other prophets around Ahab didn't agree with Micaiah's outlook. These other prophets told Ahab he *should* go into battle because he was sure to be victorious.

Micaiah told Ahab that these other prophets were liars. Furthermore, he said that their lies had been allowed in the sovereignty of God, and even influenced by one of the spiritual beings conversing around God's throne. Did God actually tell an angel to bring about such deceit?

This time let's listen in on that heavenly conversation as Micaiah relates it to Ahab:

> And the Lord said, "Who will entice Ahab king of Israel into attacking Ramoth Gilead and going to his death there?"
>
> One suggested this, and another that. Finally, *a spirit* came forward, stood before the Lord and said, "I will entice him."
>
> "By what means?" the Lord asked.
>
> "I will go and be *a lying spirit* in the mouths of all his prophets," he said.

"You will succeed in enticing him," said the Lord. "Go and do it."
(1 Kings 22:20-22, 2 Chronicles 18:19-21).

"So now," Micaiah tells Ahab, "the Lord has put *a lying spirit* in the mouths of these prophets of yours. The Lord has decreed disaster for you."

We might ask, how could an angel stoop to such a trick? And how could God be a part of it? Wasn't this unfair to Ahab, tyrant and idolater though he was? And are angels pulling this kind of stunt all the time?

But before jumping to any uncomfortable conclusions, remember first of all that Ahab is told *everything*—and he finds out all this *before* he goes into battle, not afterward, when it would be too late to do anything about it. When Ahab died in his blood-soaked chariot at sunset, he was not the victim of an angelic deception, but the victim of his own foolishness in not heeding what God revealed to him. In fact, the shocking vision from heaven might well have been God's merciful way of using every available means to grab Ahab's attention and try to turn him around. God held nothing back from him. However, only Ahab could choose his response. And Ahab chose wrongly.

We know that God himself is perfectly good, truthful, and holy. Repeatedly in Scripture we hear that he hates evil in every form (Psalm 11:5; Proverbs 6:16-19, 17:15; Isaiah 61:8; Jeremiah 44:2-4; Zechariah 8:17; Malachi 2:16). God's character is affirmed in a prayer of the prophet Habakkuk: "Your eyes are too pure to look on evil; *you cannot tolerate wrong*" (1:13).

It's possible that the "lying spirit" sent to the four hundred prophets was a demon or the devil, in a situation similar to the time when Satan appeared before God and asked for permission to afflict Job. But regardless of the identity of the spirit Micaiah described, we know that nothing God was responsible for in Ahab's life could have been evil, nor were his angels responsible for any evil in that situation. And since God never changes, he and his servants the angels can never be responsible for evil in our lives either.

Did the Angels Intermarry with Mankind?

This second perplexing question springs from Genesis 6. Just before we begin the story of God's mercy in saving Noah from the flood, we read this:

> When men began to increase in number on the earth and daughters were born to them, *the sons of God* saw that the daughters of men were beautiful, and they married any of them they chose.... in those days—and also afterward—when *the sons of God* went to the daughters of men and had children by them. (6:1-4)

Who were these "sons of God"? Since the Hebrew term here is used to refer to angels in the opening chapters of Job, some have thought that the Genesis passage is an instance of angels—perhaps even fallen angels—marrying human beings. Jesus' statement that the angels in heaven do not marry (Matthew 22:30, Mark 12:25) may rule out that interpretation.

Another suggested interpretation is that "the sons of God" here represent the more godly descendants of Adam (through his son Seth) who intermarried with those from the more sinful family line of Cain. Another possible understanding is that in Genesis 6 we see simply a poetic way of referring back to how mankind was first created. From the dust of the ground God formed Adam (a "son of God"), while God took a rib from the man to form Eve (a "daughter of man"). So in Genesis 6, when the "sons of God" marry the "daughters of men," it may simply mean that men are marrying women.

More Work Ahead

Angels exist for a reason, a purpose: God made them servants. They have work to do, and they always will. The fact that so many angels exist—and exist for all eternity—helps point us to the picture that our eternal heaven is a very busy place, a dynamic, energetic scene with lots of action, with God himself setting the pace.

When the writer of Hebrews points us toward eternity as if we were already there, he says, "You have come...to the heavenly Jerusalem, the city of the *living* God" (12:22). God is *alive* there—he's not a wax figure in a museum or an elderly grandfather wasting away in a rest home. He's going strong, and heaven is run *his* way, and the angels know it. That's why they stay so busy.

When we get there, I suppose we wouldn't even be able to keep up with angels if it weren't for the fact that we're getting new, spiritual bodies and capacities like theirs.

We have lots of exciting, fulfilling work waiting for us on the other side. So for now, let's learn all we can from the crew already on duty there—our faithful friends, the angels—and let's put it into practice right here.

Chapter Twelve

COMING TO CARRY ME
HOME

P EOPLE DIE. For thirty years now I've ministered to those who
were dying. I've been with them in the process, and I've been in
the room after death has occurred. I've watched their loved ones
mourn over their loss, trying to hold on to a body where there was
no longer any life.

But recently I've learned more about what actually happens in the
process between seeing these people holding on to life one minute, then
seeing them with no life at all the next.

I've come to believe from Scripture that angels take believers home to
heaven when we die. I have to tell you honestly that this is the first time I've
been really convinced of that. I had always wondered about it. But now I
realize there's strong justification for believing it.

Not long ago I preached the message of this chapter at the funeral of the
mother of someone on our ministry staff. Mrs. Huntsman was ninety-five
years old. Her husband is still living.

During the service I spoke about what happens when a believer dies,
and how the angels come to get that person.

After the service, I walked down to greet and comfort Mr. Huntsman,
and to tell him I would be praying for him. As I leaned over and spoke to
him, he answered so loudly you could hear him all over the chapel (apparently he had turned down his hearing aid). "Oh, Pastor Jeremiah," he said,

"it's the part about the angels I love. I just love that about the angels coming to get Gladys."

I was glad it was a comfort to him, and I wish I'd understood it earlier and been able to offer it to others. The loss of a friend or family member can be the deepest darkness known to God's people on earth. In pain the psalmist cried out to God, "You have taken my companions and loved ones from me; the darkness is my closest friend" (Psalm 88:18). But the Scriptures offer hope for us in those dark times.

Before we look closer at what the angels have to do with our death, let's look at death itself.

What Is Death?

The word *death* means "separation." In the New Testament it's the Greek word *thanatos*. Physical death is the separation of the spirit and soul from the body. We'll be more like the angels then, because we'll have lost the part of us that angels don't possess—our physical bodies. After death we no longer exist in both the physical and spiritual realms, but in the spiritual realm alone.

After a person dies his body is only a corpse—"the body without the spirit is dead" (James 2:26). The person's body will only decay, but his spirit and soul will go to be either forever with God or eternally apart from him.

God places great value on the death of the believer. "*Precious* in the sight of the Lord is the death of his saints" (Psalm 116:15). John in his vision heard heaven itself pronouncing this preciousness:

> Then I heard a voice from heaven say, "Write: *Blessed* are the dead who die in the Lord from now on."
>
> "Yes," says the Spirit, "they will rest from their labor, for their deeds will follow them." (Revelation 14:13)

"To die is *gain*," Paul said (Philippians 1:21).

Christians who grow in their relationship with God understand this blessedness of death. As a Dallas Seminary student I started my ministry career working as an intern chaplain at Baylor Hospital. I often went with the head chaplain to the family room to help someone deal with death. A few times I had to go by myself, when I was on duty alone. I got to the point where I could walk in the room where the family was and within two or three minutes know if I was dealing with Christians or non-Christians. It was uncanny. Death for a believer is difficult and challenging and nothing anybody wants to deal with. It's hard and scary and painful. But it's not despair. It isn't the end.

Not long ago a 34-year-old man in our church died of cancer, and I preached his funeral. I must confess it's been a lot harder for me to do that since I've had cancer myself.

The cancer had ravished his body in a short period of time. Before he died I visited him at his home. His wife was there, as well as his young son. We sat together in their living room. He talked about going to heaven just as if it he were going to the grocery store. It overwhelmed me. He was telling his little boy, "And when I get there, this is what it's going to be like. I know I'll miss you a lot, but just think what Daddy's going to get to do!"

I had never seen anything quite like it before. It was another indication to me that Christians die differently. There's no question about it. The way believers face death is one of the strongest evidences of the reality of our faith.

Angels for Our Final Journey

So where do angels enter in? Scripture gives us comforting precedence for their special service to us the time of our death.

Our Lord told a fascinating story in Luke 16 of two men who were as different as they could be. Jesus began their story in such a way as to make the most of the contrast:

There was a rich man who was dressed in purple and fine linen and lived in luxury every day.

At his gate was laid a beggar named Lazarus, covered with sores and longing to eat what fell from the rich man's table. Even the dogs came and licked his sores.

The time came when the beggar died and the angels carried him to Abraham's side.

The rich man also died and was buried. In hell...he was in torment....

Only a gate separated these two men. Lazarus begged on the outside, the rich man lived lavishly on the inside. But Lazarus knew God, and the rich man didn't.

Notice especially the contrast in what happened after their deaths. The rich man "died and was buried." Period. Next we see him in hell.

But when Lazarus died, *"the angels* carried him to Abraham's side." ("Abraham's side" was a picture in the Jewish mind of the feasting and joy we'll know in eternity.) In his lifetime the beggar had licking dogs as his companions, but at his death the angels were honored to convey him into heaven. And they weren't just *with* him; they *"carried* him."

Lazarus was regarded as one of the most inferior of persons in this life, but that didn't disqualify him from having an angel escort through eternity's doorway. Lowly Lazarus was awarded this privilege, and apparently so was the highest of men — the Son of Man himself.

Scripture hints that Jesus may have been carried by angels into heaven on the day of his ascension. In Mark 16:19 we read that "he was *taken up* into heaven." Luke writes that while Jesus was "blessing" his disciples, he left them and was *taken up* into heaven" (24:51). Based on a respected alternative rendering in the Greek text, the King James Version translates the sentence this way: "While he blessed them, he was parted from them, and *carried up* into heaven." In Acts 1:9 we read, "After he said this, he was *taken up* before their very eyes...." Angels may have had this privilege of taking or carrying Jesus up on his return trip home.

Why would angels come to provide this service to us at the time of our deaths?

One reason may be related to the fact that Satan is described as "the ruler of the kingdom of the air" (Ephesians 2:2). Perhaps we must cross this "kingdom of the air" in going from earth to heaven. Our temporary home here and our permanent home there may be separated by an immense stretch of enemy territory. It's a trip angels must take often, so it will be a great comfort to have them at our side as we traverse it ourselves.

In *Somewhere Angels,* Larry Libby gives children another reason:

> God wants you home so much he'll send his own angel to meet you.
> And don't be surprised if the angel is wearing a big smile.

Chapter Thirteen

HELL'S ANGELS

Y OU'VE DONE an opposites quiz before, haven't you? I say
"small," and if you're sound in mind (at least for the moment)
you're supposed to quickly answer "large." I say the word *dark-*
ness, you answer, *light*. I say *soft*, you respond with *hard*. I say
good, you say *bad*.

And what if I say... "God"?

If you answer "Satan," you're wrong (misinformed maybe, or perhaps a
little unsound of mind today).

Satan is not the opposite of God. Satan can't be God's opposite because
Satan himself was created by God. Nobody is God's counterpart. But isn't it
interesting how Satan has deceived us into believing he is God's equal in
power and significance?

We're going to do now what I promised you many pages back—we're
going to put our focus for a while on the fallen angels: Satan and the demons
who follow him.

When I preached a sermon series on angels in our church, the messages
on the devil and his fallen angels drew the biggest response. I never would
have dreamed that. I thought those would be sort of parentheses sermons,
dealing with necessary negative factors just to get them out of the way so we
could focus on positive things about angels. But there was more interest in
this than in anything else we covered.

So I know you're curious to learn more on this subject, for it's always good strategy to know your enemy. "We are not unaware of his schemes" (2 Corinthians 2:11), Paul says; therefore he was able to make plans "in order that Satan might not outwit us." We don't want to be unaware of his plots and maneuvers, though in this book we can only hit the highlights.

On the other hand, we want to avoid the preoccupation with the devil that seems to grip some people. Satan is not a center of attention in my life, and I don't think he should be for any Christian. Not that we should disregard him or take him for granted, but you can't focus on two things at the same time. If I'm always worried about Satan, I won't have time to worship God. As Amy Carmichael used to say, "I sing the doxology, and say goodbye to Satan."

I hope the richness of what we've already studied about angels will help you see this topic in perspective. Satan and the fallen angels who follow him were created to partake of the same splendid privileges we've seen the good angels enjoy. All that glorious existence should have been Satan's to delight in as well. How profoundly true is our judgment of his chosen course: "How you have fallen…!" (Isaiah 14:12).

Bible teachers point particularly to two Old Testament passages suggesting the story of Satan's downfall. In Ezekiel 28 we especially find indications of Satan's original state leading up to his fall, while Isaiah 14 seems to focus on Satan's inward rebellion that caused it.

Both of these passages have direct application to earthly rulers other than Satan: Ezekiel is writing "a lament concerning *the king of Tyre*" (28:12), while Isaiah introduces his words as a "taunt against *the king of Babylon.*" But the allusions to Satan in each one are strong, giving both passages a more profound bearing.

Here's a good way of looking at these passages: They point *both* to the earthly kings mentioned *and* to Satan, in the same way that some of the messianic passages point both to the Davidic kings of Israel and to Christ. They find their fulfillment on more than one level.

Satan Before

Before we look at the pictures these two prophets paint, let's begin with a key statement by Jesus. He told the Jews that Satan "was a murderer *from the beginning, not holding to the truth*" (John 8:44). Here we see that Satan's fallen state goes back at least before our known human history. This is echoed in 1 John 3:8, where we read that "the devil has been sinning *from the beginning.*"

But the phrase "not holding to the truth" in John 8:44 seems to imply that Satan *could* have held to the truth but didn't, or that he *once did*, but no longer does.

Now on to Ezekiel 28, a passage rich with mystery. In the opening verses of this chapter Ezekiel pronounces judgment against the king of Tyre. But after verse eleven, the prophet's descriptions are difficult if not impossible to ascribe to any human being. Instead he seems to move beyond the human ruler of Tyre and to speak about the true power behind the throne, the "king" who is none other than Satan.

Ezekiel is quoting a description given to him by "the Sovereign Lord" (28:12). He is not describing what he, the prophet, has seen, but what God himself has told him.

The passage is addressed directly to this "king of Tyre." The first several verses mirror his past to him. They go on to remind him that he was once "anointed as a *guardian cherub,*" God says, "for so I ordained you" (28:14).

This guardian cherub was perfect. "You were *the model of perfection,* full of wisdom and perfect in beauty" (28:12). He was perfect in intellect and perfect in form.

The guardian cherub had no light of his own, but from the start he was fully arrayed by his Creator to reflect God's glory:

> *Every precious stone* adorned you:
>> ruby, topaz and emerald,
>> chrysolite, onyx and jasper,

sapphire, turquoise and beryl.

Your settings and mountings were *made of gold;*

on the day you were created they were prepared. (28:13)

We also discover *where* God placed this guardian cherub:

You were in *Eden,*

the garden of God....

You were on the *holy mount of God;*

you walked among the fiery stones. (28:13-14)

Satan After

In the next verse we return to the theme of the cherub's perfection—and suddenly we watch that perfection come crashing down.

You were blameless in your ways

from the day you were created

till *wickedness was found in you.* (28:15)

The next verses spell out that wickedness, accusing the guardian cherub of violence and especially pride, leading to his expulsion from God's presence. Satan had everything, but he wanted more.

Through your widespread trade

you were filled with violence,

and you sinned.

So *I drove you in disgrace from the mount of God,*

and *I expelled you, O guardian cherub,*

from among the fiery stones.

Your heart became proud

on account of your beauty,

and you corrupted your wisdom

because of your splendor.

So *I threw you to the earth;*

I made a spectacle of you before kings.

By your many sins and dishonest trade

you have desecrated your sanctuaries. (28:16-18)

Perhaps the final lines in this prophecy against "the king of Tyre" look far into the future, to foretell Satan's end when he's thrown into the lake of fire (Revelation 20:10) and disappears forever from the sight of man or angel:

So *I made a fire come out from you,*

and it consumed you,

and *I reduced you to ashes* on the ground

in the sight of all who were watching.

All the nations who knew you

are appalled at you;

you have come to a horrible end

and will be no more. (28:18-19)

As a glimpse of Satan, which seems a likely interpretation, this passage is clear that he was not created evil. As John Calvin says, "everything damnable in him he brought upon himself, by his revolt and fall." All things in their original nature were created good, including Satan. But Satan chose to follow himself instead of following God, and so "corrupted" his "wisdom" (Ezekiel 28:17). Satan no longer speaks God's language, but has brought forth his own, as Jesus tells us: "When he lies, he speaks *his native language,* for he is a liar and the father of lies" (John 8:44).

Satan's Inner Rebellion

Isaiah 14 looks deeper into the nature of Satan's rebellion.

The passage opens this way: "O *morning star,* son of the dawn!" (14:12), or as the King James Version styles it, "O *Lucifer,* son of the morning"

("Lucifer" comes from a name meaning "light-bearer" that was used in Latin translations of this verse; we'll go ahead and use this traditional name here). This brilliant one being addressed here was the Satan "before."

But now this "taunt" (14:4) aimed at Lucifer begins,

> How *you have fallen from heaven...!*
> You have been cast down to the earth,
>   you who once laid low the nations! (14:12)

What follows is Lucifer's declaration of independence. Notice the five vows he speaks in his heart—five promises Lucifer makes to himself, each one beginning with the words "I will":

> You said in your heart,
>   "*I will* ascend to heaven;
> *I will* raise my throne
>   above the stars of God;
> *I will* sit enthroned on the mount of assembly,
>   on the utmost heights of the sacred mountain.
> *I will* ascend above the tops of the clouds;
>   *I will* make myself like the Most High." (14:13-14)

Lucifer first of all wanted God's *place.* He said, "I will ascend *to heaven,*" apparently referring to the highest and holiest heaven where God alone resides, a place even higher than where the angels dwell. (Remember that Paul speaks in 2 Corinthians 12:2 of three heavens.) Lucifer wanted to replace God at the pinnacle of everything. He wanted to be "enthroned... on the utmost heights of the sacred mountain," and to "ascend above the tops of the clouds." Both of these last phrases speak of the places of God's presence.

Second, Lucifer wanted God's *position* and *authority.* He said, "I will raise *my throne above the stars of God,*" and "I will sit *enthroned* on the mount of assembly." The "stars" and the "assembly" here are most likely references to the other angels. Lucifer wanted sole prominence and power over all of them.

Third, Lucifer was determined to take God's *likeness*. "I will make myself like the Most High." He wanted God's privileges, his independence, his worship.

How utterly unlike God he was in this! Just look at the stark contrast between Lucifer's words and the attitude of Christ:

> Who, being *in very nature God*,
>> did not consider equality with God something to be grasped,
> but *made himself nothing*,
>> taking the very nature of a servant,
>> being made in human likeness. (Philippians 2:6-7)

Lucifer's sin above all was pride. And pride goes before destruction, as Isaiah goes on to show:

> But you are brought down to the grave,
>> to the depths of the pit. (14:15)

Lucifer's pride turned an angel into a devil. His self-originated pride brought God's curse upon him. The devil became the sworn enemy of humility.

How could Satan's story have happened? How could such a plunge into ruin come about for someone who was "the model of perfection"?

We know the answer is pride. But when God created Lucifer, didn't he know that pride would captivate this angel's heart?

Yes, we must conclude, since God is all-knowing, he had to have known this.

But could God have prevented it?

Yes, God is all-powerful. He surely could have prevented Satan's fall.

Why didn't he then?

The answer seems to lie in the mystery that Lucifer was created with freedom to choose his course, just as we are. Lucifer used his gift against the Giver. And God "respected" his choice, just as he respects ours.

Lessons from Satan's Fall

What can we learn from Satan's fall?

First of all, recognize the power of pride. I don't believe any temptations face us more frequently or confront us more persistently or entice us more subtly than the temptation to pride. I heard it said this way: "The devil sleeps like an animal in the shadow of good works, waiting for us to conceive a secret admiration of ourselves."

How much are you secretly admiring yourself these days? You're surely more like Satan in those moments than while doing any other sin you could think of.

Satan's game plan is the strategy of pride. It's the approach he's used down through history and still uses today. I suppose he hasn't had a fresh idea since the day he started; he just keeps repackaging the old stuff over and over again. And men keep falling for it. His method *works*. We're as willing to be flattered by ourselves as by others.

But "God opposes the proud" (James 4:6, 1 Peter 5:5). If he so quickly and thoroughly opposed a perfect and glorious angel who became prideful, God can certainly put the brakes on any of the rest of us as well. How much of our spiritual ineffectiveness is related directly to pride?

Satanic activity in all its raw, deceptive form is at work even among God's people. He is the "enemy" who comes and sows weeds among the wheat (Matthew 13:24-30). The "I wills" of Satan still rear their heads today throughout our congregations. It's like a virus—little pockets of pride and discontent that become power pockets, growing like cancer.

Satan will get a church any way he can, and pride has proven the surest and quickest way.

Second, stay alert to Satan's purposes and plans. Having fallen himself, Satan went back to Eden to trigger the fall of mankind. Just as he brought unspeakable tragedy to Adam and Eve through his seductive skill, so he continues to carry out his deceitful program against angels and humanity. He wants to destroy us and render us useless to the kingdom of God. He's on an all-out mission to populate hell with non-Christians, including all your neighbors and friends and family members who have not yet received Christ. He wants to take with him into the fire as many "good" people as we'll let him have. He's delighted when those who still reject Christ as Savior are kept firmly in his grip by our failure to pray for them and witness to them.

Satan's legacy is everywhere. Every sinner and every sin is a mark to his credit. "He who does what is sinful is *of the devil*" (1 John 3:8). Jesus calls him not only "a liar" but also "the *father* of lies" (John 8:44), because every lie was ultimately born in his mouth.

That's why in the same verse Jesus told his unbelieving listeners, "You belong to *your father*, the devil." Sin is the image of Satan in those who have not been reborn as children of God. All of us are growing either in likeness to God or in likeness to the devil.

We can't afford to be asleep to Satan's strategy and tactics. Notice how Scripture's insights into his schemes and character make us instantly want to be on our guard. Notice precisely what these passages say that Satan *does:*

"Your enemy the devil *prowls around* like a roaring lion *looking for someone to devour*" (1 Peter 5:8).

He's "a strong man, fully armed," who "*guards* his own house" so that "his possessions are safe" (Luke 11:21).

He's "the ruler of the kingdom of the air, the spirit who is *now at work* in those who are disobedient" (Ephesians 2:2).

He's "the god of this age" who "has *blinded* the minds of unbelievers" (2 Corinthians 4:4).

"He was a *murderer* from the beginning, not holding to the truth, for there is no truth in him. When he *lies*, he speaks his native language, for he is *a liar* and the father of lies" (John 8:44).

He has this world in his grip. "We know … that the whole world is *under the control* of the evil one" (1 John 5:19).

And what's most galling of all is that this prowling, roaring, hungry, strong, greedy, active, blinding, murdering, controlling deceiver actually "masquerades as an angel of *light*" (2 Corinthians 11:14).

"The object of all these descriptions," writes Calvin,

> is to make us more cautious and vigilant, and more prepared for the contest.… Wherefore let this be the use to which we turn all these statements.

Even his names spell trouble. The word *Satan* means "accuser." *Devil* means "slanderer." He's called "the dragon, that ancient serpent" (Revelation 20:2), and "the tempter" (Matthew 4:3, 1 Thessalonians 3:5). His designations are "Beelzebub" (Matthew 10:25), meaning "lord of flies," and "Belial" (2 Corinthians 6:15), meaning "worthlessness" or "ruin."

Satan is not God's equal, but he is God's sworn enemy. His tactic with Eve in Eden was to discredit God, and this is still his procedure today. Do you care at all for the honor and glory of God? Do you have allegiance to God's kingdom? Then you must make God's enemy yours.

If the name *Christian* means anything to you, you have no choice but to resist the enemy of Christ, for "the reason the Son of God appeared was to destroy the devil's work" (1 John 3:8). Jesus calls him "the prince of this world" (John 12:31), but adds, "he has *no hold on me*" (14:30). "The prince of this world *now stands condemned*" (16:11). Through his own death and resurrection, Christ has already made Satan's defeat certain. The war is won. But all the battles have not yet been played out. Will you accept the privilege of being a soldier in these victories?

That leads to the third lesson: Remember the supremacy and preeminence of God. Satan did not get away with his pride. And he's not getting away with anything now. He is free on earth to do his damage only to the extent of the length of his chain, and God himself has chained him. The devil cannot go beyond God's permission. He cannot do anything against God's will and God's consent.

It's indeed a mystery. In one place Calvin comments this way on Satan's object and options:

> He eagerly and of set purpose opposes God, aiming at those things which he deems most contrary to the will of God. *But as God holds him bound and fettered by the curb of his power,* he executes those things only for which permission has been given him, and thus, however unwilling, obeys his Creator, being forced...to do Him service.

In Scripture we see this not only in the sweeping epic of Job, where Satan was able to batter the man only after God said, "He is in your hands" (1:12, 2:6), but also elsewhere. For example, an evil spirit tormented King Saul, but it is called "an evil spirit *from the Lord*" (1 Samuel 16:14, 19:9) because God allowed it.

Even Paul encountered this. A "messenger from Satan" came to torment him (2 Corinthians 12:7), but Paul deeply understood God's perspective. He didn't wrangle against Satan, but "pleaded with the Lord to take it away from me" (12:8), since he knew the Lord had sent it. Paul also discovered God's purpose in allowing the tormentor's visit: "to keep me from becoming conceited" (12:7).

It's true that Satan can be a controlling power even in the lives of believers who aren't depending on God. But even when Satan "has taken them captive to do his will," God still offers the hope and method for "escape from the trap of the devil" (2 Timothy 2:25). There's always "a way out" (1 Corinthians 10:13), especially for those who keep in mind the big picture and the final score: "The God of peace will soon crush Satan under your feet" (Romans 16:20).

For the time being, as part of Christ's body we feel the sting when Satan "strikes his heel"; but we'll also share in the retaliation when Christ "crushes his head" (Genesis 3:15).

Satan's Hosts

Satan is not alone in his spiritual attacks.

Jesus speaks of the eternal fire prepared "for the devil *and his angels*" (Matthew 25:41). Satan *"and his angels"* are referred to together in Revelation 12:9. In Matthew 12:24 he is called "Beelzebub, the prince *of demons."*

We have more than one enemy confronting us, and it's possible we may be attacked by more than one simultaneously. It was said of Mary Magdalene that Jesus drove "seven demons" out of her (Mark 16:9, Luke 8:2). One unfortunate man had been besieged by an entire *legion* of demons (Mark 5:9-15, Luke 8:30-33).

These spirits are rational beings, not diseases or ailments, or tricks of the imagination. They possess all the attributes of personality. They even believe in God, as James tells us: "You believe that there is one God. Good! Even *the demons believe* that — and shudder" (2:19). Demons think and believe and hear and speak.

Who are they, and where did they come from?

Satan himself could not have created them, because only God is the Creator. The best explanation is that they are fallen angels who at some point in time joined in Satan's rebellion.

Peter tells us:

> God did not spare *angels* when they sinned, but sent them to hell, putting them into gloomy dungeons to be held for judgment.... (2 Peter 2:4)

Jude speaks of "the *angels* who did not keep their positions of authority but abandoned their own home" (Jude 6).

One passage hints at the possibility that as many as a third of the angels in heaven fell when Satan did. In the book of Revelation, John saw "an enormous red dragon" whose tail "swept *a third of the stars* out of the sky and flung them to the earth" (12:3-4). The dragon is identified as Satan later in this chapter. And stars, as we've learned, frequently represent angels both in Revelation and elsewhere. The vision John saw here may well have been a playback of what happened in heaven before human history began.

Spiritual Warfare

Demons are Satan's servants, and are committed to his scheme to thwart the plan of God. Often in Scripture they are also called "evil spirits" or "unclean spirits." They are ruled by Satan himself, and they share in his dirty work.

With enemies like these, we need friends. God has provided them, and shows them to us in his Word.

Lock on to the fact that nothing demons do can be outside God's good purpose and designs. Never forget this: "Neither angels *nor demons... nor any powers...* nor anything else in all creation, will be able to separate us from the love of God that is in Christ Jesus our Lord" (Romans 8:38-39).

Calvin once more supplies a good picture. He shows us God "turning the unclean spirits hither and thither at his pleasure," all with the intention of "exercising believers." The demons are always "warring against them, assailing them with wiles, urging them with solicitations, pressing close upon them, disturbing, alarming, and occasionally wounding, but *never conquering or oppressing them.*"

Just as Satan and the demons share a common origin and a common passion and work, so they also must face a common fate. Paul assures us that Jesus "must reign until he has put *all his enemies* under his feet" (1 Corinthians 15:25). That includes the devil and every demon.

In every encounter between Jesus and demons in the Gospels, Jesus was the overcomer. His followers share in that power. When Christ's disciples returned "with joy" from a ministry trip, they reported to Jesus, "Lord, even *the demons submit to us* in your name" (Luke 10:17). And Jesus answered, "*I saw Satan fall* like lightning from heaven."

Jude says that God has kept the fallen angels "in darkness, *bound with everlasting chains* for judgment on the great Day" (Jude 6).

Meanwhile, until that great Day, we wrestle. We "*struggle* . . . against the powers of this dark world and against the spiritual forces of evil in the heavenly realms" (Ephesians 6:12).

In this struggle there is someone who shows us how to endure and how to win, someone whose life knew both spiritual warfare and the touch of angels more than anyone who ever walked the earth.

As you can feel with your fingers, the remaining pages in this book are few. Only a short while and a short space are left to devote to the topic of angels before our study here must come to an end. Together let's bring it to a close by spending that short while with this Someone whom angels have known so well.

Chapter Fourteen

THE ANGELS
AND JESUS

H E WAS "seen by angels," we're told in a short, sweet line of what sounds like a hymn Paul shares with us in 1 Timothy 3:16. Jesus left heaven, the home of spirits, and came to earth, the home of flesh.

And angels watched in wonder.

Oh, look: One of those angels who watched in wonder has just joined us. It's our old friend, the guide who took us earlier on all those fast trips through Scripture to watch the goings-on of angels.

We welcome him back, and thank him for the note he left us.

He asks if we'd like to travel back into the past again. We eagerly agree.

He says that this time we'll spend our entire journey within the span of one man's earthly lifetime. "This is one man's story," our guide tells us. "It's my *favorite* story," he adds. "And yours too."

We understand. And we're glad, because we're always finding something new in that story. What will we discover this time?

"Let's go," he says. And we're off.

At His Birth

Grassy hills, near a village, at night. We see shepherds cloaked in camel-hair coats, huddled around a campfire. We know where we are in terms of both geography and history: close to Bethlehem, two thousand years ago.

"By man's measure," says our guide, "it's been hundreds of years since we messengers appeared on earth with great openness. But a new day has arrived. Only months ago Gabriel came and spoke to Zechariah and then to Mary. Another of my brothers revealed himself to Joseph in a dream.

"Yes, in these days the world will see us more at work here. People will also notice more miracles of God. And our enemies the demons will be more exposed as well."

In the dark stillness on the hillside, we reflect on his words.

Suddenly the shepherds throw themselves to the ground, stricken in terror by a blinding light. We knew it was coming, but we're startled too.

The angel reassures the shaking shepherds, then speaks his news: "Today a Savior has been born *to you....*"

Our guide whispers. "Did you hear that? The Savior didn't come here for angels. He came for those shepherds, and for you, and for others like you."

Again he looks out across the hillside. We see the reflection of starlight and angel-light dancing in his eyes.

"And we're *glad* for you!" he shouts, just as the sky becomes jam-packed with countless angels. They all have that same look of ecstasy on their faces.

"GLORY TO GOD IN THE HIGHEST!" they exclaim. They're looking up.

Our guide happily explains. "They're exalting God, and telling all the rest of the angels they left behind to join in the praise as well. The sky here above this pasture could never hold all of us."

You and I can't get over the joy of all these messengers. The news they're announcing has nothing to do with them, really. But they're as happy about it as if they too had just been snatched from the clutches of hell. We decide it must be because they simply adore Jesus so much.

After all, up in heaven they've already been with him for ages and ages. They must know him so well, and love him so deeply. And since *he* was so glad to be coming here now, they can be glad with him.

At His Temptation

The volume fades on the angel chorus. So does the picture. Another scene fades in: brown, barren hills of the Judean wilderness. A man—the Son of Man—is on one hillside, but not alone. The dark form of the tempter is there too. Just a glimpse of him is all we can handle. We avert our eyes and wonder how Jesus can endure Satan's ugliness.

Again our guide explains: "In this encounter, the enemy need not clothe himself in light, as he does so often to deceive your kind. He knows that no disguise can veil his nature from the Son of God."

We keep our heads turned away, but we listen. Satan's words sound like garbled noise to us. But we can understand Jesus clearly. His strong voice keeps quoting Scripture, calmly and triumphantly. We fear and loathe this creature before him who dares to tempt him. Somehow, though, it makes us treasure every line Jesus speaks:

> It is written: "Man does not live on bread alone, but on every word that comes from the mouth of God."
> It is written: "Do not put the Lord your God to the test."
> It is written: "Worship the Lord your God, and serve him only."

We know that we, too, will be facing the tempter again. So we won't forget these counter-attack words from Jesus.

When we turn around, the tempter is gone. The battle is over.

Already angels are at Jesus' side and at his feet, to strengthen and nourish him.

"The Scriptures have told you," says our guide, "that the Son of Man for a little while was made lower than the angels. These years of his life on earth make up that 'little while.' During this window of time, my brothers and I can serve the Lord here in ways we never could in heaven.

"Long ago my fellow servants and I ministered to God's people Israel in the wilderness. Now Jesus is in the wilderness. We will minister to him as well."

In Gethsemane

We move to a different scene, but one where our guide has taken us before: an olive grove, with Jesus bent over in agony in Gethsemane.

A flicker of a memory enters our consciousness. Suddenly we remember the heart of Lucifer hammering away defiantly, *"I will... I will... I will... I will... I will...."* We shake off that distasteful thought, and focus our minds again on the praying Christ.

"Not my will," he cries with clean, pure earnestness, "but yours be done."

He pauses in his praying. Everything is so quiet. An angel appears at his side, wiping the sweat from his brow and temples.

With teary eyes our guide says, "None of us had ever done that before, until the 'little while' came. And now, the end approaches."

Before our eyes the scene rapidly advances. The disciples, who had been sleeping a stone's throw away, are awake and standing.

A mob of soldiers and others has entered the olive grove. They've come to arrest Jesus.

We look around. The angel is gone. But Jesus says to the tense crowd around him, "Do you think I cannot call on my Father, and he will at once put at my disposal more than twelve legions of angels?"

Our guide nods. "He's right," he tells us.

After His Resurrection

The night is over. Dawn is here—the beginning of a bright Jerusalem morning. We're in another garden in another section of the city.

We see soldiers, tired from a long, uneventful night, standing guard at a hillside tomb. You and I remember reading about this in the last chapter of Matthew.

Suddenly the ground is shaking. An angel appears out of nowhere, coming as fast as a lightning bolt and just as bright.

The soldiers are as good as dead. Trembling and pale, they flee.

The angel moves a massive stone that covers the mouth of the tomb. He rolls it aside effortlessly, then calmly sits down on top of it.

"My brother there—he's very strong," our guide tells us. "I know him well."

We step close enough to look inside the tomb. It's empty. Grave clothes are neatly folded on the low stone shelf where a corpse should be lying.

Now the sun is rising.

Two women walk hesitantly into the garden, staring from a distance at the tomb. The closer they get, the more worried they look.

The angel stays seated. We get the feeling that if he stood or made any move at all, those two women would be out of here faster than you could say Pontius Pilate.

We hear the angel clear his throat. He's about to say something.

Our guide leans over and tells us quietly, "He's so excited about this assignment he can hardly stand it. I know him well."

The angel's voice is calm and confident: "Do not be afraid," he says to the women. Instead of turning and running, they stand and listen.

He continues: "I know you seek *Jesus*, who was crucified. He is not here. He has risen!—*just as he said.*"

Our guide whispers to us again: "He relishes every word of this. I know him well."

The angel sweeps his arm wide toward the tomb's open door and says, "Come, see the place where he lay." The women cautiously peek in. Their faces look dazed. The truth is slowly sinking in.

"Go quickly!" the angel commands. His voice grows bolder with every phrase: "Tell his disciples: 'He has risen from the dead and is going ahead of you into Galilee. There you will see him.'"

A smile takes over his face, and he adds triumphantly:

"*Now* I have told you."

Our Conclusion

This last scene fades.

Our guide puts forth the same question he asked us in our earlier trip: "What have you learned?"

After a pause, you decide to answer for both of us:

"That angels truly love the Lord, and will always love to serve him…

and so will I."

SOURCE NOTES

Thomas Aquinas, *Summa Theologica* (1267-1273).

Joan Webster Anderson, *Where Angels Walk: True Stories of Heavenly Visitors* (Barton & Brett, Publishers, 1992)

John Calvin, *Institutes of the Christian Religion* (1536-1559; translated by Henry Beveridge, 1845-1846).

Lewis Sperry Chafer, *Major Bible Themes* (Durham Publishing, 1926).

Christianity Today: Timothy Jones, "Rumors of Angels" (April 5, 1993).

Douglas Connelly, *Angels Around Us* (Intervarsity Press, 1994).

W. A. Criswell, *Expository Sermons on Revelation* (Zondervan Publishing, 1962).

C. Fred Dickason, *Angels Elect and Evil* (Moody Press, 1975).

Millard J. Erickson, *Christian Theology* (Baker Book House, 1983-1985).

Expositors Bible Commentary (Zondervan Publishing, 1976-1992).

A. C. Gaebelein, *The Angels of God* (Baker Book House, 1969).

Billy Graham, *Angels: God's Secret Agents* (Word Publishing, 1975).

Matthew Henry, *Commentary on the Bible* (1704-1721).

John Phillips and Jerry Vines, *Exploring Daniel* (Loizeaux Brothers, 1990).

Hope Price, *Angels* (Macmillan Publishing [London], 1993).

Corrie ten Boom, *A Prisoner — And Yet* (Evangelical Publishers [Toronto], 1947).

Henry Clarence Thiessen, *Lectures in Systematic Theology* (Eerdmans Publishing, 1949).

Time: Nancy Gibbs, "Angels Among Us" (December 27, 1993).

A. W. Tozer, *The Pursuit of God* (Christian Publications, 1948); *The Divine Conquest* (Christian Publications, 1950); *The Knowledge of the Holy* (Harper Collins, 1961).

J. M. Wilson, "Angel," in *International Standard Bible Encyclopedia* (Eerdmans Publishing, 1915, 1979).

SCRIPTURE INDEX

SUBJECT INDEX

O Lord Almighty
(O Lord of Hosts,
O God of Heaven's Angelic Armies),
blessed is the man
who trusts in you.

Psalm 84:12